FOLK AROUND AND FIND OUT

GOOD FOLK: MODERN FOLKTALES BOOK #2

PENNY REID

WWW.PENNYREID.NINJA/NEWSLETTER/

FOLK AROUND AND FIND OUT
GOOD FOLK: MODERN FOLKTALES BOOK #2

PENNY REID

WWW.PENNYREID.NINJA/NEWSLETTER/

COPYRIGHT

This book is a work of fiction. Names, characters, places, rants, facts, contrivances, and incidents are either the product of the author's questionable imagination or are used factitiously. Any resemblance to actual persons, living or dead or undead, events, locales is entirely coincidental if not somewhat disturbing/concerning.

Copyright © 2022 by Cipher-Naught; All rights reserved.

No part of this book may be reproduced, scanned, photographed, instagrammed, tweeted, twittered, twatted, tumbled, or distributed in any printed or electronic form without explicit written permission from the author.

Made in the United States of America

Print ISBN: 978-1-942874-88-1

DEDICATION

For Ruth.

CHAPTER 1

HANK

"Why do people respect the package rather than the man?"

— MICHEL DE MONTAIGNE, *THE COMPLETE ESSAYS*

My day hadn't been great even before she walked in.

I'd just returned from the funeral of my longtime bookkeeper. He'd died from old age in his sleep surrounded by his five kids, loving wife, and eighteen grandchildren while leaving me with a reconciliation mess and this month's payroll to finish.

My newly trained bartender had sent a manifesto via text message, blaming his decision to quit on my unwillingness to build a dedicated meditation room and give him four paid half-hour breaks per shift to use it.

Three Diamond Whiskey bottles out of the six that had shipped from the distributor were broken in the crate. If you're keeping score, that's seven hundred dollars in Tennessee Whiskey and a crime against humanity.

On the plus side, the suit I'd worn to my parents' funerals fit and I still looked damn good in it.

Of course, I didn't know the newcomer was *her* at first. The door opened and closed, same sound as normal no matter who was coming or going. It was a Sunday mid-morning, still early yet for any of the dancers or bouncers and way too early for any customers.

But the moment she turned the corner and came into view, I gritted my teeth. *Here we go.* What could she want? *She better not be selling Bibles.*

"Charlotte." Standing behind the bar, I crossed my arms and sounded unfriendly. She'd caught me restocking paper products and the three surviving bottles of Diamond Whiskey. I was only half finished with my current task, but nowhere near half finished with my task list for the day. I did not have time for pious Charlotte Mitchell.

As a rule, I had time for two types of folks: people I paid, and people who paid me. A small number of exceptions to this rule existed: a few friends from college and in town, like Beau Winston or Patty Lee, and any woman I'd set my mind on seducing, but even then, I made sure the scales remained balanced—give and take, tit for tat, even-steven. Point is, Charlotte was obviously not the former exception, and there was no way she'd ever be interested in becoming the latter.

"Hank." She didn't look at me, but she did paste on an obligatory-looking smile that pulled her full lips tight and came nowhere close to her green eyes. Tracking Charlotte Mitchell's slow approach, I didn't miss how she took her time and peered around.

I wanted to snark, "Lost? I believe the wallpaper and sanctimony store is closer to downtown."

Instead, I ground out, "What do you want?"

I had no availability for charity cases, especially not this one. *That's* what Charlotte was: Green Valley's most infamously pitied citizen. A gorgeous—yet sadly, virtuous—teacher at the local elementary school and a bake sale-making, soccer mom SUV-driving, PTA-volunteering, hoity-toity, do-gooder single mother of four disease vectors (children) whose ass of a husband (now ex-husband, fella by the name of Kevin Buckley) had predictably run out on her a few years back with a nineteen-year-old exotic dancer.

One of mine, actually. I fought a grimace.

Carli Duvall—aka Bendy Bambi—had been a customer favorite, a talented dancer, a shrewd businessperson, and an asset to the club. Her regulars had complained for months after she disappeared, many taking their patronage to The G-Spot for a time and ultimately cutting into my bottom line. Less customers meant losing even more dancers. I'd almost lost the club and sheer stubbornness was the only reason I still operated it now. It had taken me over a year to recover from the mass exodus in the aftermath of her departure.

Don't get me wrong. Like everyone else, I'd initially felt sorry for Charlotte; I think anyone would. All things considered, she and her kids were probably better off without him. Given who he was and what his family was like, no one should've been surprised by her ex-husband's betrayal, but I did feel for the woman he'd duped and misused.

But then, while I'd been struggling to keep The Pink Pony afloat, people had blamed the club, and me by extension, for the dummy's infidelity. When the news broke, Patty Lee—who'd finally agreed to give me a chance—had called things off right before our third date. Sure, things hadn't been perfect, and our lack of chemistry left much to be desired. Still, after years of hoping, being dumped because Kevin Buckley left his wife had been incredibly frustrating.

It all sorta worked out. Patty and I were now relatively good friends; I sought her counsel whenever I needed a female perspective. And because she didn't pull her punches or ever worry about sparing feelings, unlike my best friend Beau, I found her advice incredibly helpful.

That said, I'd never cared much for or craved local goodwill, but folks had never been that blatantly hostile before. Going out to eat without the expectation of someone spitting in my food or keying my car were privileges I'd ceased taking for granted. The backlash had shocked me; I'd seen Buckley's infidelity coming a mile away. Why anyone who'd met the bastard felt surprised by his choices or thought I'd influenced them made no damn sense.

Point is, Kevin leaving Charlotte had been bad for my business and worse for my personal life, and I did not much care for his wife showing up here for reasons unknown.

While Charlotte continued her moseying, her head unhurriedly turning this way and that, I eyeballed her, catching glimpses of her perfect profile while simmering in my unease.

"I've never been in here," she said, her voice faraway, distracted. "It's nicer than I thought it would be."

I considered her words for a tick. The statements sounded benign, yet something about them made the skin at the back of my neck hot, which set my teeth on edge. Since Charlotte had returned to town a few years back—even before her husband had skipped out—she'd pointedly treated me like a leper from biblical times. Things were finally back on track with The Pony, and her presence here might derail my recent progress.

Making it to the bar, she stopped in front of a stool. Her pale green eyes were cool, surveying me like an afterthought. "May I order a drink yet?"

I studied her. Charlotte looked different than how she typically presented herself around town. She still had on that dainty gold cross around her neck, but gone were the pretty yet shapeless floral-print, button-up shirts and long, flowing skirts. Today, she'd put on dark makeup, taken time to fix her long hair into sleek waves, and the black tank top she wore highlighted her shoulders, arms, neck, and torso, making her generous tits look fantastic. *Pushup bra, a good one.*

"No," I said, flat and final.

"You're not open?"

"Not for you, no." Not for Charlotte and not for any of her kind.

Her face morphed into an expression of intense irritation and I smirked to cover an involuntary spike in temper. I didn't know Charlotte well—I didn't want to know Charlotte at all—but this was the version of her I knew best, the wordless, judgmental glare I encountered if we happened to cross paths at the grocery or hardware store. No amount of carefully applied makeup or fantastic tank-top twins could soften it.

This was *my* club. We hadn't accidentally stumbled across each other today. She'd come to me, sought me out, and she was still looking at me like I was trash? Faced with this familiar version of Charlotte in my territory, I tore my eyes from hers and scratched the heat climbing up my neck.

Our paths hadn't crossed in over a year. Perhaps she was here to fulfill her quota of self-righteous indignation. *How heavy is that halo, angel?*

One day I would ask. But not today.

Crouching behind the bar, I resumed stocking the whiskey. If I waited, she'd reveal her intentions. Then she'd leave. No need for me to pause work, especially when there was so much work to do.

"Do you have a rule against serving female customers?" she asked, and I knew without looking up that she'd leaned over the bar to scowl down at me.

"No. Mostly just you."

"Mostly just me," she parroted, then huffed a laugh; it also sounded irritated. "Okay, fine. Then may I have an application?"

My movements stilled and I stared at the bottle of whiskey in my hand, the one I hadn't yet set on the shelf.

May I have an application?

"Pardon me?" I looked up, and sure enough, Charlotte's long honey-colored hair was dangling over me from above, nearly touching my shoulder.

"I said, may I have an application? Please."

I had to blink before I could think. And I couldn't think while I was on my haunches, so I stood. She leaned back, sitting on the stool, watching me impassively like she expected me to jump and fulfill her request, like she'd asked for a driver's license application from the DMV and not an employment application from my club. The same place of business she and all the other small-minded folks condemned and hated.

Which was likely why I asked the stupid question, "What do you want an application for?"

Angling her chin, Charlotte Mitchell lifted one eyebrow, looking down her nose at me even though she was the one sitting, and said matter-of-factly with a smidge of southern tartness, "For a job, of course."

"Where?"

"Here."

I scratched my neck again, my eyes drifting to the right. This had to be a joke. *Perhaps Beau is somewhere, hiding with a camera?*

She snapped her fingers in front of my face. "Hey. Earth to Hank Weller. It's not a difficult request to fulfill. Either you have applications, or you don't."

"But . . ." I shook my head, unable to recall a moment in my life I'd been as confused. *This is a joke, this has to be—*

"Hank Weller, let me spell it out for you: I want you"—she pointed at me, using her loud, slow voice, the one I'd heard her employ with her children on the rare occasions they behaved like feral animals in public—"to give me"—she pointed to herself—"a job application"—now she mimed a piece of paper—"for The Pink Pony"—she gestured to my club—"so I can fill it out." She topped off her little show by pretending to write with an invisible pen.

"For what job?" What the heck did she think she was going to do? I needed a bartender, a bouncer, and now, as of this week, a bookkeeper. As far as I knew, she had no experience with any of—

"A stripper."

I choked. Before I could fully process this information, she tossed her thumb over her shoulder, indicating toward the way she came in, and said, "I saw the sign from the road, so I know you're hiring. Now . . ." Charlotte put her hand between us, palm up, and demanded in a voice that brooked no argument, "Hand it over. Please."

"You cannot be serious." An application? Dancers didn't fill out applications. Clearly, she had no idea how this worked. Like most clubs, none of my dancers were employees. They were independent contractors. Yes, they auditioned; yes, they completed payment forms and signed a work services agreement. But there was no application, no interview.

"I am serious. And I came prepared."

I counted to ten and searched my club for a camera again. Beau did not emerge from some hidden spot and declare this a prank. My eyes returned to Charlotte, flicked over her. *What the hell?*

Under my perusal she straightened her back, her breasts pushing higher and forward in a move that looked purposeful. "I'm in really good shape, exercising is my only hobby, and I know how to dance."

"You know how to dance . . ." I searched for Beau again. Nothing about this interaction made a lick of sense. Perhaps I was dreaming? *It's a possibility.*

"I do." Her chin lifted. "I've been taking classes and my instructor says I'm quite good. She even wrote me a reference." Charlotte turned and began digging in the little purse she brought.

"No—no. I don't need a reference." Debating whether or not to pinch myself, I ultimately decided against it. If this were a dream, I wanted to see where it would go.

I hoped Oscar the Grouch didn't show up and chase me around with that peanut butter sandwich again.

Ignoring my last statement, she placed the folded-up piece of paper on the bar and smoothed it out with her fingertips. "Here's the letter of recommendation. You can see here, I have excellent endurance and I can even play the trumpet while I'm on the pole—"

"Did you hit your head?" I made a face, leaning my hands against the bar top and scanning her forehead for an injury. Playing the trumpet while swinging on a pole? In what universe would that ever be sexy?

Her expression flattened.

"Blink twice if you're in danger."

Her eyes narrowed.

"Or is this a dissociative fugue? Which personality am I talking to? Let Charlotte come out for a minute."

"Hank," she seethed through clenched teeth. "Why are you giving me a hard time? Do you need more strippers or not?"

If this were a dream, she'd already have her top off. Thus, I decided I couldn't possibly be asleep. "I need more dancers, yes. But I do not need, nor do I want, *you*—or your emotional support trumpet—in my club."

She flinched. "Why not?"

Perhaps she was serious about dancing, but she couldn't possibly be serious about asking me why I'd never allow her in here, and I wasn't spelling it out for her. In fact, we were done talking. She'd taken up enough of my time. I turned away without another word, lifted the hatch, and left the bar. Walking past where she sat, I crossed toward the back. She could show herself out.

But then she called after me, "I need the money."

Her startling words and her imploring tone brought me up short. *She needs money?* That couldn't be right. Her ex-husband came from money, lots of it. The only thing Kevin had ever done right in his life was being born a Buckley. My father had been friends with the high society patriarch from North Carolina. I'd gone to boarding school with Kevin's older brother and the dude was as rich as he was insufferable. And he was staggeringly insufferable.

I glanced over my shoulder.

She hopped off the stool, her eyes wide with panicked pleading. That's when I comprehended the rest of her outfit, skimpy cutoff jean shorts paired with three-inch spiked heels. Her long, firm, pale legs went on and on, up to narrow hips and a narrower waist. The woman was tall and strong and had an exceptional body: perfect athletic proportions paired with a natural D-cup. I frowned.

Well, now, hold on. Wait a minute.

Trumpet or not, she'd be a sight to behold on the stage. I didn't have anyone on the roster near as tall as her with her kind of muscular shape. April was tall, long and lean, and platinum blond. I scratched my chin. If Charlotte could dance like she said, then—

NOPE! No. Absolutely not. Have you lost your mind?

I gave my head a rough shake. No way in hell was I bringing on Charlotte Mitchell. Looking like she did, and given her angelic reputation, I had no doubt she'd bring in new business. At first. It would be a coup for the club and all my dancers would benefit; new business was good for everyone.

But then what?

I could see her up on the stage, but dancers made most of their income from lap dances at tables and giving private dances in the champagne room. She wasn't a Carli or a Tina or even a Hannah. She was smart, but she wasn't shrewd or calculating enough to dance in my club. If she had been, her weak-minded husband never would've left. He would've been too afraid.

In this business, you were either the giver or the taker, and all my dancers were takers. I made sure of it.

Not to mention, folks would try to run me out of town. Again.

There'd be backlash for certain. Loads of it. And only recently had I *finally* been able to go to Daisy's Nuthouse for a cup of coffee and a snack without having to worry about dingles on my donut. Living my best life did not include dingly donuts.

I sighed. "Charlotte—"

"I need the money," she repeated, stalking closer and twisting her fingers. "And I'm not asking for special treatment. I'll audition, like anyone else. Treat me like I'm anyone else."

Well. That would certainly be a novelty for her, she who received differential martyrdom care wherever she went and expected nothing but the best from people. She'd get none of that here. She'd be chewed up and spit out. Successful dancers had hard limits, firm boundaries; they knew their worth and demanded the customers pay them their due. Most women weren't raised that way and—as far as I knew—Charlotte was exactly like most women.

But I couldn't say that. Her hackles would rise, and I'd already given her too much of my time and way too much of my attention.

Instead, I said, "If you're doing this for money, then this ain't a good fit. You wouldn't make much to start out, not for six months, at least. New dancers get the shitty shifts, afternoons during the week and mornings on the weekend, making yourself available to fill in for other dancers when they need to call out."

She bit her lip, chewing over my words before saying, "That's fine."

I lifted an incredulous eyebrow. "Oh really? You can dance in the afternoons? What about your teaching job?"

"School is out for summer."

"It's August. What happens when school is back in session?"
"Then I'll . . . figure it out."
"Not good enough."
"I'll—"
"No."
"Hank—"
"*No*," I said firmly, my patience at an end. "The answer is no. You're not worth the trouble."

It's possible that if she'd caught me on a different day, I would've had more tolerance, I might've been gentler and calmer. But I was tired of entitled morons dictating to me how to run my business. If I gave an inch, she'd probably demand that I add a dedicated meditation room to the club. And a chapel. And a sauna. And a tiki bar.

Besides, who the hell did she think she was? If she wanted charity, she'd come to the wrong place. Some of us lived in reality. This was my club. *Mine*. And even though it was often more trouble than it was worth, I had my people to think about: sixteen professional dancers, three bouncers, a bartender—all of whom relied on me and this club to put food on their tables. Unlike her, I never took or gave handouts.

Charlotte rocked backward, her eyes flashing and her hands coming to her hips. "What exactly is your problem with me?"

"You're still here," I gritted out, my temper ballooning. But given her past dirty looks, what her ex-husband had done to my business, and all the spit I'd been served in my food, was I surprised she'd pissed me off? No. No I was not.

Huffing, Charlotte's mouth formed a grim, angry smile. "Fine. Then I guess I'll leave."

Finally.

"You do that."

I turned and continued toward the back without waiting for the sound of her departure, determined to forget about her intrusion the moment she was gone. Down a bartender, bouncer, and a bookkeeper, the last thing my club needed—the absolute last thing—was renewed townie scrutiny courtesy of saintly Charlotte Mitchell.

CHAPTER 2

CHARLOTTE

"Men are always ready to respect anything that bores them."

— MARILYN MONROE, *MY STORY*

"What'd he say? Did you get the job? When do you start?" My aunt was on me the moment I slid into the passenger seat of her 1992 BMW M5.

"No." I closed my door with more force than necessary, then cringed. "Sorry," I said, apologizing for my thoughtlessness. Her car was falling apart. We'd had to remove the front bumper last week when the right side had fallen off and began dragging on the road.

The only excuse for my thoughtlessness was the bitter burn of humiliation that still stung my cheeks and blazed in my chest. It usually took a lot to embarrass me. Or, apparently, a mere ten minutes with Hank Weller. I did not feel like myself.

"What happened?" my aunt asked breathlessly, her tone thick with despair.

"He wouldn't give me a chance to audition." *Ugh!*

I sucked in a breath, telling myself to calm down.

"Oh thank goodness." A hand from the back seat settled on my shoulder, my mother's voice gentle. "Even though I don't understand why he wouldn't let you audition—you're ten times prettier than Hannah Townsend, or Tina Patterson, or any of those girls—I can't say I'm upset."

"Betty!" Aunt Maddie twisted in her seat. "Charlotte's plan is our best chance to find Heather. How can you say that?"

I let my aunt and my momma argue for a bit—they'd been bickering about my plan all week—while I simmered in my options. I did not agree with my mother's assertion that I was prettier than Hannah or Tina. I'd planned to interview as a stripper first, but then bring up the possibility of applying for his open bartender position if he didn't think I had the looks to be a dancer. Problem was, I had no experience being a bartender either.

Covering my momma's hand where it still rested on my shoulder, I patted her fingers while I turned to give her a tight smile, interrupting their argument. "Hey. We've talked this to death and we already agreed, my plan is the fastest way to find Heather. Can we stop fighting and just figure out what to do next?"

"We all didn't agree. I don't agree." My mother withdrew her fingers and crossed her arms. "Charlotte, you're like a bull in a china shop. You rush into things without thinking them through. How do you think Kevin and his family are going to react when they find out you're applying to be a stripper? They'll try to get custody of the kids and—"

"Momma." I sighed, rubbing my forehead. We'd already had this argument. I supposed we were having it again. "I think you're overreacting. I'll only be stripping for two weeks, then I'll quit. What are they going to tell the judge? That I'm unfit because I stripped for two weeks?"

"Yes!" My mother whisper-hissed.

"I disagree. But if that is the case, then I'll just tell the judge the truth," I said. "I'll tell them I was only stripping to find my cousin or news about her. Then I quit. Two weeks. What's so wrong about that? And on that note, what's so wrong about stripping? Lots of mothers are strippers. I can make that case, too."

"You are denser than dirt if you think a judge is going to care that lots of mothers are strippers, even if it's true." Momma sniffed, her eyes flashing. "And if the Buckleys file for custody, how are you going to pay for a lawyer this time, huh?"

I faced forward again, fighting a shiver of fear. "I'll sell the beach house in North Carolina." I made sure to firm my voice so she'd know I considered the matter closed.

Despite the twinge of anxiety caused by my mother's ridiculous statement, I truly believed no judge would take my kids away because I stripped for two weeks if the only reason I was doing it was to help find my cousin. I just did not believe it. If I'd thought my mother's doomsday predictions had any merit whatsoever, I never, ever, ever would've suggested my plan to my aunt and uncle.

Momma sputtered for a few seconds, then said, "You just got that cottage all pretty and set up as a rental, an extra income source, and now you're going to sell it? And how much money would you get from it in a sale? It's tiny."

"But it's beach waterfront. Someone could knock it down and build a McMansion on it. The land has value."

"Now, Betty," Aunt Maddie cut in, twisting around to face her sister. "Let Charlotte do this if she thinks it's best."

My mother made a low noise that sounded like a growl. "Now, Maddie, I know you're scared for Heather."

"This might be my only chance to find her, Betty. My only chance." Her voice wavered and she sniffled, turning back toward the windshield and pulling a tissue from the console at her right. "Charlotte's right. We all agreed. And I agree with Charlotte. If there were a custody case, I think a judge will be compassionate once they found out why she did this. And it's only two weeks."

I reached over and patted my aunt's leg, hating to see her so upset.

"Well. Fine," my mother said huffily. "I guess I'm overruled. What are we going to do now that Hank Weller won't give her an interview? Should I go in there and talk to him?"

I snorted at that. "I do not think having my mother talk to a strip club owner about why he refused to give your daughter an audition is a good idea. But thanks, Momma."

If memory served, my mother had wanted to do something similar when Hank Weller—the same Hank Weller I'd just begged for a job—had stood me up for my junior prom over a decade ago. "Should I talk to him? Should I call his mother?" she'd asked me at the time. Momma could not comprehend that her opinion didn't move mountains, whereas my daddy—who'd been dead set against my choice in date—had said, "I told you so."

My aunt whipped her head around and stared at both of us, her eyes rimmed with panic. "How are we going to find Heather now? What are we supposed to do?"

My cousin's friend had said Heather was stripping at a club on the outskirts of Green Valley. There were a few strip clubs along the parkway, but only two anywhere close to my hometown: The G-Spot and The Pink Pony.

"It's fine. I'll audition at The G-Spot."

"No!" my mother cried. "No you will not!"

Pressing my lips together, I said nothing. I'd wanted to audition there straightaway, but my momma had vetoed the idea, claiming The Pink Pony was the more genteel establishment, given the two options. She'd said, "If you're determined to do this stupid, reckless thing, then you should at least check The Pink Pony for Heather first."

Genteel. Like Hank's club was serving afternoon tea instead of local beauties in pasties and thongs. For all I knew, his club did serve afternoon tea. Regardless, after my momma had explained things, I understood her point.

According to my mother, where The G-Spot was rumored to cater to motorcycle gangs—and not the charitable, hobby, or friendly kind—The Pink Pony was where local folks went for bachelor and bachelorette parties. Our local firefighters held an annual women customers only all-male revue fundraiser there, and competition for tickets was always fierce. I'd never gone. When JT MacIntyre had wanted a space to host a community commission singles auction, he'd held it at The Pink Pony. For the record, I had not attended.

Meanwhile, also according to my mother (and don't ask me how or why she was such an expert on local strip clubs), The G-Spot kept the local sheriff's office plenty busy with drug busts, overdoses, and violent brawls. She'd said The G-Spot made The Pink Pony look like a country club. As far as I could figure, my mother didn't approve of The Pink Pony simply because it was a strip club. But she approved of The G-Spot even less and feared it plenty.

Aunt Maddie exhaled a shuddering sigh. "I don't know what to do." Her voice small, she covered her face with her hands. "I don't want you working at that place, Charlotte—even if it's for a little while. It's bad enough Heather—" Her voice caught and her shoulders shook with a sob.

I placed a comforting palm on my aunt's back. "It's fine. It's going to be fine," I soothed, forcing calm into my voice. "This is better, honestly. If Heather is working at The G-Spot, or if she ever worked there, I'll be able to find out right away."

"But Heather might be working at The Pink Pony," my mother protested. "We don't know which strip club she's working at, and if you're so darn determined, I don't see why you can't work at The Pink Pony first and—"

"Mother," I cut in. "Hank—Mr. Weller said no. He is not interested in me working at his club." I should have known better than to ask him for anything. For some reason, the man severely disliked me. Which was why I'd gone out of my way to avoid him at all costs since high school. Or he didn't dislike me in particular but was simply a mean person in general. "And besides, from the description Heather's friend gave Uncle Chuck, the club where she's supposed to be stripping sounds more like The G-Spot than The Pink Pony."

"That G-Spot club is dangerous," my mother said weakly, real fear entering her voice. "We—we could find someone who will track her down at a discount price."

"We've already been to seven different PI offices." My temples throbbed. No one was going to look for my cousin pro bono.

When my aunt had come to us last month, begging for help finding my cousin, I'd asked her why she didn't hire a private investigator. That was before I knew how much private investigators cost. That was also before my aunt and uncle confessed how my cousin had been slowly cleaning out their savings for the past two years to pay off drug debts and extensive legal fees.

None of us had twenty-thousand dollars lying around to put a private investigator on retainer. I'd debated whether or not to sell the beach cottage then, to pay for the PI, but I couldn't. I needed it. That place was my nest egg. It was my emergency investment in case one day Kevin suddenly agreed with his parents and wanted to fight me for custody.

He hadn't cared about custody when we divorced; it had been his family who'd made a fuss. Even so, I couldn't assume his disinterest would last forever. I'd specifically asked for the small cottage in the divorce because he hated how little it was. Of all his holdings, it was the one he cared about the least. If we ended up in court again, I didn't think he'd ever win, but even I realized how important it was to have money set aside just in case. As my momma had said, I knew I could be dense about certain things. But I wasn't denser than dirt.

"I'll be careful," I promised. "I'll get the dancers to trust me, and then they'll talk." The G-Spot was dangerous, but I felt certain I could handle it after I'd surreptitiously asked my friend Jackson James about the club last week.

As a sheriff's deputy who'd made plenty of arrests at The G-Spot, Jackson had given me an idea of what to expect. He'd said, unlike the tight ship and no-tolerance policy Hank had at The Pink Pony, some of the dancers at The G-Spot were strung out and had been arrested on drug and/or prostitution charges. But there hadn't been any arrests made in the last ten years that involved violence between a dancer and a customer.

"And I would only be there for two weeks at the most," I reminded my momma and my aunt. "Only long enough to talk to the staff, ask around."

My shoulders drooped, the earlier sting of embarrassment now mostly subsided, leaving me feeling spent. If I never saw Hank Weller again it would be too soon.

A long, long time ago, I had a giant crush on Hank. He was about three or four years older than me and had been in college at the time. Roscoe had been a good friend of mine in high school—I'd (platonically) loved how sweet, funny, and sincere he was—but I'd also shamelessly pushed to hang out at his house instead of mine in case Hank stopped by to see Roscoe's brother Beau. In retrospect, I'd been naïve, bordering on pathetic, in my pursuit of Hank Weller.

Fighting a yawn, I ran my hands up and down my arms, feeling a chill. I'd gone to bed too late last night and I'd woken up early this morning, wanting to finish my hair and makeup before the kids awoke. Then breakfast. Then dishes. Then a quick shopping trip with my aunt and Momma for some new clothes that made me look the part.

"No." Aunt Maddie shook her head abruptly, her hands dropping away. "We'll have to ask your friend again—what was her name? Hannah? Let's ask Hannah one more time."

I tried my best to disguise my frustration by pasting on another smile. "I already told you, Hannah is not going to talk to us. She won't tell us anything."

When we couldn't find an affordable private investigator, I'd reached out to my friendly acquaintance Hannah Townsend—currently a stripper at The Pink Pony—

and asked if she'd seen Heather or if she could help locate her. I've known Hannah my whole life. Unlike my male friendly acquaintances, I trusted her to hear me out and let me decide how to proceed.

In my experience, whenever I confided my troubles to a male friend or acquaintance, he always wanted to take over, dictate to and "fix things" for me, even if I'd been seeking nothing but advice. Which was why I didn't want to ask one of them to patronize The Pink Pony or The G-Spot and keep an eye out for Heather. I didn't trust them to follow my directions.

I took for granted that Hannah would confide in me, tell me honestly if my cousin worked with her, and be discreet. Not only did she not answer my questions, she'd turned to stone. She'd also advised me to stop asking around if—assuming Heather was stripping at a local club—I didn't want my cousin to cut and run.

Hannah had eventually explained that dancers, bouncers, and especially club owners never, never, never gave up information about each other. You never knew if a dancer was running from a bad situation, like trying to escape an abusive family. It was also how they kept the women safe from angry spouses and entitled customers, which was one of the reasons why all dancers had a stage name.

"You have four beautiful children who need you." My momma's voice cracked. "You have a good job. You're a respectable, Godly woman. I am asking you again to rethink this. What will people in town say? Think of your reputation. Your aunt and uncle cannot ask you to debase yourself in this way."

Gritting my teeth, I stared out the windshield. "I can still be respectable and help my family, Momma. No one is going to care if I spend two weeks this summer stripping in a local club. Why would they?"

"Charlotte." My mother shifted forward in her seat and spoke right next to my ear. "I know this might be hard for you to believe, but people do gossip in Green Valley." Her tone had turned patronizing, like it always did when she spoke to me about 'proper behavior.' "Your whole life, you've pretended like no one cares what you do. You never think or consider what people might say, how perception will impact your reputation. But you are gossiped about. Make no mistake. People have an opinion about you."

"Yes, Mother. I know gossip exists in this town, gossip exists everywhere," I seethed. "But I'm never going to care what other people say about me, nor am I going to pay attention to it."

"It would do you good to pay attention to what they say about you and what they say about other folks, too. I think you're the only person in this whole town who didn't know that Diane Donner ran away with that motorcycle man."

I huffed a dry laugh. "Are we seriously talking about Diane Donner right now? And that was like ten years ago, wasn't it?"

"It was four years ago, not ten," she said primly. "And this is exactly what I'm talking about, this is the problem with you. Folks are still talking about Diane and that man, and you don't even know when it happened."

"Who cares?! Why are we discussing this foolishness? What does Diane Donner have to do with anything?"

"You got nothing but cotton between your ears if you think folks in this town don't love to gossip and judge, and pretending they don't makes you the fool." She lifted her voice, now yelling at me. "Everybody knows the story except you! You bury your head in the sand and—"

"You think I have space in my brain for what other folks are doing or not doing?" I yelled back. "Two of my kids are picky eaters whose palate changes based on the weather. I can't keep up with who hates mustard and who hates mayonnaise, and you want me to give a crap about Diane Donner's boyfriend?"

"It was the scandal of the century!" she shrieked dramatically.

"Again, why would I care?!" I turned and faced her again, my eyes probably wild with frustration. But how the heck had we arrived here? My mother and I yelling at each other in the parking lot of Hank Weller's strip club about Diane Donner, former high society matron who'd disappeared ten—or, I guess, four—years ago? Who gave a flying flip about Diane Donner? We had bigger fish to fry.

"Listen." I tried to calm my temper, cool my tone. "I don't care about what other folks are doing or not doing unless they're my friend and need help. Now, can we please move on and focus on what I need to do to interview or audition at The G-Spot?"

Aunt Maddie, who'd started crying quietly during my shouting match with my mother, shook her head. "I don't know, Charlotte. I think I agree with your momma. I couldn't live with myself if you got hurt at that other club."

"Please, just trust me, okay? Finding Heather is the most important thing. Besides, you didn't ask, I offered." Dancing on stage in front of horny men couldn't be any worse or more challenging than holding twenty-seven parent–teacher conferences in three days, or cleaning up after kindergarteners five days a week, or solo balancing the needs of my own children 24-7.

"But taking your clothes off," my mother whined, no longer yelling. "Your modesty—"

I'd had enough. "Momma, I've had four children, my legs spread-eagle each time. Half the hospital has seen me more naked than I'll be at The G-Spot." *Assuming I get the job.* "And I've breastfed four babies. Everyone in this town has seen my boobs, *several* times. They are boobs, not a treasure chest full of pirate gold. And! I haven't gone to the bathroom alone since Kimmy was born. I poop in front of an audience every day. Modesty holds no meaning for me, and besides, what use am I getting out of this body? At least I'll get paid for showing it off."

My mother gasped and I forced myself to shut my mouth. I didn't want to upset my mother any more than was absolutely necessary. She'd always tried her best to love me, even when I didn't make things easy. But I didn't know how to be anyone other than myself. She'd always wanted a daughter as demure as she'd been: soft-spoken, decorous. Elegant. The poor woman had been given me instead.

God either had a wicked sense of humor or He was plain wicked.

"Sorry," I said, lifting my eyes to the ceiling of my aunt's car. The cloth above me was water-stained and sagging. "But it's true. I'm not worried about taking my clothes off in front of people. But I am worried about my cousin." I turned to my aunt again. "Let's go to The G-Spot. I'll see if they'll let me audition, and then we'll take things from there, okay?"

My aunt started the engine and nodded, visibly holding back more tears. I sent her a smile and buckled up.

I'd never been particularly close to my cousin—she was over ten years younger than me—but she was my family. Family came first. Always. I didn't have spare money to hire a PI, and I believed Hannah when she said no one would answer our questions. We couldn't go to the police since Heather was wanted in Florida for violating the terms of her parole.

I'd offered to infiltrate the clubs and pose as a stripper. What other option did we have? This was it. This was the way. And there was no use sitting in a parking lot, debating it for the hundredth time.

As much as I'd dreaded seeing and speaking to Hank again, I wasn't dreading the prospect of stripping—at The Pony or at The G-Spot. That said, I wasn't jumping for joy about it either, but I saw no reason to complain. It was something that needed to be done to locate my cousin while also not bringing her to the attention of law enforcement.

And doing what needed to be done without second-guessing myself or complaining about it was my superpower. When I died, my gravestone would probably read, "Charlotte Mitchell, she got shit done."

CHAPTER 3

HANK

"One should as a rule respect public opinion in so far as is necessary to avoid starvation and to keep out of prison, but anything that goes beyond this is voluntary submission to an unnecessary tyranny, and is likely to interfere with happiness in all kinds of ways."

— BERTRAND RUSSELL, *THE CONQUEST OF HAPPINESS*

In the same way Charlotte Mitchell's visit had contributed to a ruined Sunday, echoes of her pleading voice corrupted my double bartending shift on Monday. Likewise, thoughts of her long legs and frustrated expression had intruded on Tuesday while I worked after hours to catch up on payroll.

I wasn't obsessing, I was . . . curious. And wary. And suspicious.

Was she trying to sabotage The Pony? Did I need to watch my back? Did she hold a grudge because her ex had met Carli at my club?

Or, if she was telling the truth, why did she need money? Why didn't she have enough? If she was looking to dance at The Pony, then she must've been desperate. Had Kevin Buckley's family stopped paying child support? That seemed unlikely. I knew the judge who'd delivered the decision in her divorce proceedings. I could call and ask. I also knew the Buckleys. I could—

Wait a damn minute. Why do I care?

Glancing eastward over Bandit Lake, I dropped the cooler and tackle box I'd been carrying toward my boat, set my hands on my hips, and frowned at the orange and yellow gradient of the early August sky. I'd never been one to fret over the bad business decisions of other people. Charlotte had made a bad investment and now she was paying for it. She'd been an adult when she married Kevin. Her willful ignorance of human nature, lack of wisdom, and inability to read people wasn't my problem.

None of this was my business unless she targeted my club. Then I'd have to do something. Until then, living my best life did not include wondering about Charlotte Mitchell's financial solvency.

Decided, I bent to pick up my cooler and tackle box, then stepped on to the boat.

But to my eternal irritation, and likely due to my lack of sleep, I found myself unable to stop ruminating. When I was younger, she'd been a fixture at the Winston homestead during my school breaks. At least I was fairly certain the tall, sporty girl with messy blond hair, scraped knees, and a smart mouth was the same girl who'd grown up into the tall woman with honey-colored hair who'd made my life hellish for the last two years and then walked into my club on Sunday. If memory served, Beau's youngest brother, Roscoe, and Charlotte had been friendly in high school.

Yeah . . . I think that's her.

She'd been funnier then, and opinionated, talkative. She would ask me what book I was reading and then had a hundred follow-up questions when I told her the title. The one time we'd played Truth or Dare together, she'd always chosen dare. Nothing seemed to embarrass younger Charlotte, and I vaguely remembered admiring that about her.

Or that girl wasn't Charlotte? I'd have to ask Beau to be sure.

Lowering to my haunches, I flipped open the tackle box and withdrew a fly. Since she'd returned to the valley a few years back and Beau had made a point of introducing us at the Friday night jam session—this was months before her divorce from Kevin, but after he'd already started frequenting my club—I'd been immediately attracted to Charlotte's outside. Not sure there existed a straight man in Tennessee who wouldn't be.

She'd smiled politely at the time, shook my hand, said without feeling, "Nice to see you," and then dismissed me. I hadn't been surprised. I was the local strip club owner after all; I was used to folks pretending I didn't exist. Yet, for reasons unknown, Charlotte Mitchell was the only person on God's green earth who'd ever been able to piss me off with a single, contemptuous look.

I'd come to dislike her pious personality more than I liked looking at her exterior.

As I affixed the lure in place, I decided that if that girl during my school breaks had been Charlotte, she'd been completely different when we were young. She'd turned out exactly like everyone else, hadn't she? Like all the other boring, brainwashed, judgmental members of polite society.

Studying the early morning mist rising over the lake, I asked myself again, *Why do I care?*

I didn't. And I wouldn't. The end.

"Hey! Hank. You're never going to believe this."

At the sound of Beau's loud whisper, I stood from my tackle box and turned toward the dock, watching the redhead's approach. He appeared to be agitated and my stomach tightened.

"Shelly is pregnant," I said automatically, waiting for him to confirm my long-held fear at last.

His steps faltered and his eyebrows pulled together as he drew even with the boat. "What? No, dummy. Shelly isn't pregnant." He stepped on the vessel, placing his cooler next to mine and no longer whispering. "Why do you always think I'm going to say Shelly is pregnant?"

The tension in me eased and I turned back to the tackle box. "It was a joke. What's up?" It wasn't a joke. It was going to happen sooner or later. And when it did, I would be happy for him. I would. I'd be so . . . happy.

Beau Winston—my best friend since forever and the best person I knew—had been in a serious relationship for several years with the same woman. I hadn't been keeping track, but they'd been together more than five years but less than ten. Anyway, they weren't married, but they'd moved in together. Which meant it was only a matter of time before the two of them began populating the earth with their spawn.

Don't misunderstand, I got nothing against spawn (children), and my business partner's kids seemed all right. Someone has to pay into social security and keep Medicare afloat. But I can't employ children, nor are children—especially babies—likely to be customers of my club, or invest in my real-estate interests, or have extensive knowledge of the bond market. In short and in general, I had no use for kids.

But once Beau and Shelly had kids, the good times would be over. He'd be a dad. Since Beau was an exceptionally good man, he'd want to spend time with his spawn. That meant less fishing, no Saturday nights hanging out at Genie's, fewer camping trips, and no more Beau picking up bartending shifts at The Pink Pony. Something about gestating and birthing spawn made even the most fun-loving of women abhor clubs like mine. Shelly didn't even have kids and she wasn't especially fun nor loving.

So. Yeah. The writing was on the wall, and it was written in baby food.

"It's about Charlotte Mitchell," he said, tapping my tackle box with his shoe, the movement urgent. "And it's the nuttiest news since Diane Donner skipped town with Repo."

Oh no. My heart skipped a beat. *What has she done?* "What is it?"

Clearly, I'd been right to be suspicious. The woman was making her move. Was Charlotte spreading rumors around town? Was I doomed to live a life of dingly donuts? I was so damn tired of driving all the way to Knoxville for a decent cup of coffee.

"Charlotte," he said, pronouncing the T in her name with a crisp snap, "is stripping at The G-Spot."

"Uh . . ." I held perfectly still. "Come again?"

"That's right." He nodded with vigor, his forehead wrinkling. "You heard me right. She's stripping at The G-Spot. Hannah told me. I was checking out of the Piggly Wiggly late last night and she told me she was talking to Odell behind the register, who'd talked to Tina, and Tina had heard it from Catfish at the club, he was there when she asked for an audition."

"When? When did she audition?" I don't know why I asked the question. I already knew the answer.

"Sunday. But they didn't have her audition." Beau gave his head a disgusted shake. "Old Jasper took one look at her and hired her on the spot—no pun intended. Anyway, she starts this weekend."

I rubbed my forehead. *The G-Spot?* Jesus. If she'd be chewed up and spit out at my club, she'd be chewed up, spit out, doused in gasoline, and lit on fire at The G-Spot. Then they'd piss on her ashes.

"Hank—" Beau reached out and put a hand on my shoulder. "You have to step in."

My eyes widened and I reared back. "Me?"

"Yes, you." He gave me a small shake. "You should offer her a job at The Pony. Make her a bartender or a dishwasher or something—not a dancer."

I opened my mouth. Nothing came out.

"She can't dance at The G-Spot," he said with conviction. "We can't let that happen."

"Wha—why not?" I croaked.

"Why not? What do you mean why not?" Now he was looking at me like I'd lost my marbles. Or I was an idiot.

I glowered at the sky over his shoulder. The sun peeked over the edge of the tree line. If we didn't leave the dock soon, all the fish would go back to sleep.

Charlotte Michell had already ruined three days this week; I did not appreciate her flailing antics encroaching on my fishing time with Beau. The woman was determined to be a stripper? Fine. Last time I checked, she was an adult, responsible for her own choices. She had agency and free will. Good luck to her.

Beau's hand dropped and his blue eyes narrowed. "Those women over there are seasoned professionals, with fifteen years or more in the business. Or they're looking to dance someplace with lax rules. Jasper doesn't encourage it, but he doesn't step in either. This is Charlotte's first gig. You need to help her out. And if you're looking for a selfish reason to step in, then let me break it down for you: if you don't offer her an alternative, folks in town will pick up their pitchforks again and blame you when she gets hurt."

I hissed out a breath between clenched teeth and turned away. Well. This was fucking fantastic. Would I never be free of Charlotte Mitchell's stupidity?

"Come on, Hank. You owe her."

Rearing back, I spun around. "I owe her? *I* owe her? For what?"

"For Kevin."

I blinked at my friend's stern expression, atypical for his face, and I couldn't believe my ears. He'd watched the last two years unfold; he'd listened to me bitch and moan about how things were with the townies, all the hoops I'd jumped through to turn things around. How I'd hosted the damn firefighter fundraiser without charging a fee last year. How I'd grinned politely in the face of that blowhard JT MacIntyre and his demands for the community commission singles auction. Beau had never said a word other than to commiserate. I thought he was on my side.

And now he . . . what? Agreed with them?

"What are you talking about?" I asked, seething.

"Why didn't you step in with Kevin? Or with Carli? You knew what was going on."

"It was none of my—"

Beau snorted. "Yeah, no. That's not gonna fly. You've stepped in before and you've stepped in since. You've banned fellas from the club for giving too much attention to a particular dancer when they're married—I know you do, I've seen you do it, though you justify it with some other BS reason. Or if the guy is reasonable and going through a hard time, you take the time to have a talk and strongly advise him to take a break from the club. But with Kevin, you saw it and you let it happen."

Fucking Wednesday shot to hell.

"Hank." He lifted a finger between us, looking irritated. Beau never looked irritated. Beau always sounded affable. He forgave easily. He laughed often. He told jokes. But I knew nothing he said next would be funny. "You could've stepped in with Kevin, and you made the decision to stay out of it."

I was starting to resent the club. These days I netted more money in a month from my real-estate investments and rental properties than I made in a whole damn year at The Pony. Would the trouble and irritation it brought to my doorstep never cease? I swear, the only reason I kept it was to piss off the hoity-toity locals and because Jethro Winston was a silent partner. And, you know, I wanted to make sure my people were seen to, taken care of, kept safe, and—

"Hank. Answer me," Beau pushed, cutting into my thoughts.

Grunting, I threw my hands up. "Fine. I did."

"Why?"

"Why waste my time? Why step in when keeping quiet ultimately did everyone a favor? I know the Buckley family—I went to school with two of those kids at Belmont. They are pretentious, dishonorable bullies and no matter who Kevin had married, she was always going to be a first wife. Old man Buckley is on his seventh. I wouldn't be surprised if they were related to Henry the Eighth." I marched over to unwind the rope securing us to the dock and tugged. "If anyone owes anyone, Charlotte owes me. Where's my thank-you note? A fruit basket would've been nice."

"You've got to be kidding me. And what about Carli?"

I waved an impatient hand. "Carli knew what she was doing. Her eyes were wide open. She probably cleaned him out and is living her best life in the Bahamas." Unlike me, stuck here with scratches on my car and dirty looks whenever I went to the post office. With the boat unmoored, I stomped to the captain's chair. "It worked out for everyone but *me* and I do not owe anyone a damn thing."

"What about their kids?"

"I did them a favor, too. Who would want Kevin Buckley as a father? A crocodile would've been an improvement."

I heard Beau heave a sigh. "You are such a grumpy asshole sometimes."

"I never said I wasn't." I cut him a glance as he came to stand at my shoulder, leveling me with one of his *I'm disappointed in you* looks. I swallowed thickly, determined to remain unaffected. He would not talk me into this. I would not cave under Beau Winston's do-gooder pressure. Not this time.

"Hank."

I turned the engine. In my peripheral vision, I saw him cross his arms, and my throat worked again. Forget this. I should ask Patty to come fishing on Wednesdays instead of Beau. On the one hand, she didn't know how to fish. On the other hand, since we'd broken up and become friends, she never pushed me to do pointless shit out of some misplaced, do-gooder instinct.

"You got to do the right thing," he said, quiet and certain.

I scowled. "Why can't you let things alone?"

"I leave you alone plenty and you know it."

That was true. I'd known Beau for over twenty years and he rarely asked me for anything. I could count the number of times he'd asked me to do something altruistic on one hand, and he'd always been right to ask. The most recent example had been years ago when he asked me to give his brother Jethro a chance to do some carpentry work at the club, a simple favor that had turned out to be one of the best business decisions of my life.

"Besides," Beau continued, sounding irritatingly reasonable and wise, "this will not end well if you don't step in—not for Charlotte, not for her kids, and definitely not for you."

Well . . . *fuck.*

I guess The Pink Pony had a new employee.

CHAPTER 4

CHARLOTTE

"I have nothing but respect for you— and not much of that."

— GROUCHO MARX

"Oh! And we'll need robes." Sienna leaned over the kitchen island, picked up the pen she'd discarded a moment ago, and added something to the list on the piece of paper in the center of the counter. "Robes, wands, sorting hat . . . what are we missing?"

"They sell those chocolates, the ones from the movies. I think you can order them online." Finished with the last of the dishes, I leaned my hip against the counter and twisted my neck to scan the list she'd started before gazing past her to where the children were running around in the backyard. They were alive and all their screams were the good kind. "You could put together favor bags with the candy from the movie."

"That's a good idea." Sienna jotted down a few more lines to her list and I crossed my arms, trying to think.

A few weeks ago, while we'd been over for a playdate, Kimmy—my eldest—had gotten Sienna's son Ben and my son Joshua hooked on those stories about magic, and now Ben had asked his mother for a witch- and wizard-themed birthday party. Kimmy read the little kids a few excerpts from the first book, but it had been enough for them all to grab anything that looked like a broom and run around the backyard looking for something they called snitches. My three-and-a-half-year-old, Frankie, was using a dustpan.

I didn't care why they were outside running around, as long as they were outside running around.

"I could ask the Donner Bakery to make a cake that looks like a spell book." Sienna added this idea to her list. "Or one of the buildings. Or the castle."

"That'd be nice." Forget about the outside, I couldn't wait to taste what the bakery came up with for the inside. Our local bakery made *the best* cake and I rarely had occasion to sample it.

I didn't do big birthday parties for my kids. Prior to my recent divorce, always being pregnant and tired had been the main reason. But now, I didn't have the spare time or money to pull together something that required invites. But I did try my best to make the day special. We followed a schedule, always the same for each of my kids' birthdays.

I'd wake them up with kisses first thing in the morning while relating their birth story, cuddling and holding them close. They each had a wildly different birth story and I suspected it was their favorite part of the day. If their birthday fell on a school day, I let them stay home if they wanted and help me make their cake. If their birthday didn't fall on a school day, then they'd help me make their cake and the two of us would go for a walk while it baked, talking about whatever they wanted.

The afternoon was their own, but we all sat down for dinner together to whatever favorite meal they'd requested. My momma usually came over with a pile of small gifts. My ex-in-laws rarely visited, opting instead to send something extravagant in the mail.

My ex-mother-in-law tried to outdo my ex-father-in-law for the most expensive present of the year and that was fine. I'd never been great at gift-buying. They hardly saw the kids and wanted to spoil them a little? Whatever. That said, the kids didn't need a PlayStation 5 console for every room, and Kimmy wasn't responsible (or old enough) for the diamond earrings, bracelet, and necklace set her granddaddy had sent last year. Some items had to be held back or tucked someplace safe for later.

Anyway, after dinner there was the blowing out of candles, then cake and presents, then we'd watch a movie of the birthday kiddo's choosing, and then bedtime.

"I think a stack of books would be easier to cut and divvy up as a cake than a building," I pondered aloud, checking the time over the oven. I'd stopped by to pick up Joshua from a sleepover and we'd all stayed for pancakes. Getting to know and hanging out with Sienna Diaz and Raquel Ezra this summer had been the most fun I'd had since high school, but I didn't want to overstay my welcome.

"Hey, ladies. I got a text." Jethro, Sienna's husband, strolled into the kitchen and straight for his wife, giving her a kiss on the temple before sending me a friendly smile. "Beau is on his way over."

"Okay. Are you guys going out?" Sienna turned toward her husband. "We're going over ideas for Ben's birthday party."

"His birthday party?" Jethro looked nonplussed. "You mean for next spring?"

"I'm trying to get everything organized for the first few months of next year. I have that location shoot in Belize."

Jethro snagged a grape from the leftover breakfast fruit platter and looked at me. "Uh, no. Beau and I aren't going out. He's coming over here and he's bringing Hank with him."

My brain ground to a halt and every muscle in my body froze.

I'd been doing my utmost to forget about Sunday's humiliation-fest at The Pink Pony. The other club's owner, Mr. Jasper, had been considerably nicer. Skeevier, but nicer. He hadn't needed me to audition. I signed a work services agreement, filled out a 1099 so he could pay me, and that was it.

I didn't realize most strippers were independent contractors, but I supposed it made sense. It gave them freedom to perform at more than one club or leave for months at a time if they wanted. Jasper and one of the strippers who happened to be present—a woman who called herself Mason Dixon—also told me to save all my costume and props receipts as they'd be tax deductible.

"Funny thing, Beau was trying to get a hold of you"—Jethro lifted his chin toward his wife—"they were trying to track down Charlotte when they couldn't reach her phone. He asked that I make sure Charlotte stays put until they get here." Jethro popped the grape in his mouth and grabbed another.

Jethro and Sienna looked at me while I tried to breathe past the summersault in my stomach without squirming. What could Hank possibly want with me? He'd made it clear enough on Sunday that he found my existence offensive.

"How . . . interesting." Sienna tapped her bottom lip with the pen she still held. "To be clear, you're talking about our Hank? Strip club owner and Harvard dropout?"

"That's the one." Jethro nodded, still scrutinizing me. "I didn't think you and Hank got along, Charlotte."

I sputtered for a moment before managing, "We don't *not* get along." My voice was oddly pitched, the words arriving stunted and unsure, so I cleared my throat. "We barely know each other."

The side of his mouth tugged down. "He's not a bad guy, despite what the gossips in town like to spread around. He's—you know . . ."

"Pushy? Single-minded? Impatient? Thinks he knows better than everyone else?" Sienna filled in, smiling softly. She must've misread the turmoil shadowing my features, adding as though to explain, "I knew Hank in college. I didn't put up with his abruptness or grouchiness and I made him laugh, so he and I got along really well. But other people found him a bit much."

Huh. I didn't know Sienna and Hank had gone to college together . . . *did I?* It seemed like something I should've known. *Maybe I did know and I forgot.* Quite possible. My memory retention wasn't the best, thanks to the sleep deprivation associated with having kids.

"Did they say why they want to talk to Charlotte?" Sienna stole the grape from Jethro and quickly ate it, smiling at him while she chewed.

Giving her what looked like a mock-irritated glare, he grabbed a few more grapes and held them protectively against his chest. "Beau said Hank has an offer for Charlotte that she'll want to consider. That's all he said."

Once more, Sienna and Jethro turned their attention to me, and the pause that followed felt empty. Obviously, they wanted me to fill it. Mashing my lips together, I affixed my attention out the window again and silently begged one of my children to do something objectionable, like start crying for no reason or shove something into an orifice—theirs or someone else's.

Wouldn't you know it? The one time I wanted my kids to interrupt adult-time was the only harmonized, collectively well-behaved moment in their lives.

"Charlotte?" Sienna sing-songed, sounding playful. "What's going on? What kind of offer do you think Hank is going to make?"

"I suppose it's going to come out sooner or later," I muttered, lifting my eyes to the ceiling to avoid witnessing Sienna and Jethro's reactions. "I've decided to—to, uh, strip at The G-Spot."

Jethro made a choking noise, drawing my attention back to him. He looked visibly stunned.

Sienna glanced between us. "What? What's wrong?"

"Please tell me this is a joke," Jethro rasped, his eyes huge.

I gave him a steady stare. "It's not a joke and it'll be fine. I already talked to Jackson and he confirmed that violence against the dancers is extremely rare. No arrests have been made in over ten years."

"That doesn't mean it doesn't happen!" he exploded, making me flinch. "That means they don't report it because those bikers are mean fuckers and they don't want retaliation. Charlotte"—Jethro's eyes turned beseeching—"why are you doing this? Do you need money? We'll loan you money. Don't do this."

My chest seized and I caught my bottom lip between my teeth. I hadn't thought about underreporting being a possible explanation for no arrests.

Sienna turned her concerned attention to me. "I don't know anything about this —this—"

"Strip club. It's called The G-Spot and it's extremely dangerous," Jethro ground out.

"I don't know anything about this club, but I think what Jethro meant to say is, even though what you do and who you do it with is none of our business—and we won't interfere or meddle in your business if this is important to you—if the reason you're considering dancing at The G-Spot is because you need money and you don't feel like you have any options, please know that you can ask us."

"That is not what I meant," Jethro snapped, causing both Sienna and me to gape at him. I'd never heard Jethro speak that way to his wife or his kids. He was the most even-tempered person I knew. Cool, calm under pressure, self-assured.

But at present, a vein was pulsing in his forehead and he was giving me a fiery look that made the fine hairs on my forearms stand on end. "You cannot work there. You have four kids and you are not this stupid. I don't care what your reasons are, you will not. Do you hear me? And if I find out that you have, Beau, Cletus, and I will drive over there and extract you. I don't care if you're kicking and screaming. Hell, even Billy and Roscoe would fly out."

I felt heat pour from my face as I held his glare.

I didn't know Jethro Winston well. When I'd come over as a kid, Roscoe had been my friend and Jethro had been off stealing cars for the Iron Wraiths Motorcycle Club. He'd turned his life around since, but I knew the man had intimate familiarity with The G-Spot. It was The Wraith's favorite hangout besides the bar at the biker compound.

Sienna continued staring at her husband, apparently as shocked as me, and reached for his hand. "You can't tell Charlotte what to do—"

"Sienna, we'll discuss it later," he said darkly, firmly, and turned his hard look to her. Her mouth shut.

"Anyone home? Where are y'all?" Beau's affable voice interrupted the tense moment and I breathed out, feeling shaky and uncertain.

"We're in here, in the kitchen," Jethro said. Though his frown persisted, his gaze seemed to soften as it moved over my features. "Listen to me. I'm sorry I yelled. But please. This isn't about dancing or stripping. Your *safety* matters, and not only to your kids. You matter, Charlotte. And if Hank is here to give you an alternative, take it."

Before I could respond, or even think of what to say, footsteps tugged my attention over my shoulder and I watched as a smiling Beau Winston strolled into the kitchen followed by a sullen-looking Hank Weller. Beau wore cargo pants and a white T-shirt with the Winston Brothers auto repair shop logo in the upper-left corner over his chest. Hank wore faded jeans and a white undershirt. He'd put on a cotton, long-sleeved plaid overshirt but left it unbuttoned.

Standing side by side, the two men were approximately the same height, with Beau a mere inch or so shorter. But Hank was leaner and long-limbed, almost wiry in comparison to his friend, which made him appear much taller.

A flustered rush of nerves crashed over my head like a tidal wave and I quickly crossed my arms, exhaling spiky discomfort. I wasn't ready to face Hank Weller. I'd been given no time to prepare.

"Hey, everyone." Beau gave the room a wave, but his gaze settled on me. "Hey, Charlotte. How you been?"

I lifted my chin and pointedly ignored the narrowed scowl marring Hank's handsome face. "I am fine. How are you, Beau?" I'd always considered Hank unfairly handsome, even when he scowled.

"Can't complain. We—me and Hank—wondered if you might have a minute to review a—"

"Could y'all give Ms. Mitchell and me a few minutes, please?" Hank cut in, sounding flat and weary. He crossed to me and swept a hand toward the kitchen's exit. With mocking formality, he said, "Will you do me the honor of accompanying me to the front porch, Ms. Mitchell?"

I grinned meanly. "Sure thing, Mr. Weller. As always, and as you have proved time and time again, I am at your complete *disposal*."

Without waiting for his reaction to the words I shouldn't have said, I marched past him. Out the kitchen doorway, across the living room, through the screen door to the front porch. Feeling restless, I continued down the porch steps to the front yard. I'd always been a shouter, too loud for the cotillions and tea parties my momma favored. The only places I ever truly fit in were live sporting events and musical concerts.

If the ensuing minutes ended up in a shouting match between me and Hank, I didn't want Sienna to hear it. I liked her, and yelling on her front porch seemed rude.

"You cannot dance at The G-Spot," Hank said as soon as I was down the stairs.

I glanced over my shoulder long enough to say, "Pardon me?" but continued on until we drew even with his car.

"You can't strip there."

I turned and crossed my arms again, an incredulous expression on my face. "I'm sorry, but are you my daddy?"

"Do you want me to be your daddy?" he responded, the words sudden, his tone low. The question hit me right in the stomach.

I balked, stunned. A wicked kind of heat erupted outward from my abdomen and up my neck, making my thoughts scatter. I stared at him, stupefied. Had he . . . ?

I know he did not say what I think he said.

Hank's eyes widened infinitesimally, as though he also realized how the question sounded, and then his eyebrows slammed down. "Listen. That's not—never mind." Hank released a gruff sound. "What's important is that you can't work there. It's a dangerous place for someone who doesn't know how the business works. And even then, it's a dangerous place."

"Well. Okay, thanks for the information. I'll take it under advisement."

"You won't do it?"

A fissure of unease had me tensing.

Okay.

So.

I wasn't going to do it.

Stripping at The G-Spot had been one thing when I thought no arrests meant the place was safe; it was quite another thing entirely if the dancers were too afraid to report the customers, and violence was a common occurrence. After talking to Jethro and seeing his reaction, I couldn't dance at The G-Spot. My cousin's safety was important, my aunt and uncle's feelings were important, but my kids needed me. I was all they had. I wouldn't do anything to jeopardize their safety.

I was stubborn. I wasn't stupid.

But Hank didn't need to know that I'd already decided not to work at The G-Spot. I didn't care if he thought I was stupid, and what I did and where I worked was none of his business.

So I lied, and I wasn't quiet about it. "Oh no, I'm definitely going to be stripping at The G-Spot. They have been nothing but professional through the whole process, unlike some people."

My barb landed and he grimaced. "It is unsafe and you have four kids to worry about."

"Who? Me? I got four kids? Are you sure?" I made a big show of looking up at the sky and counting on my hands. "Kimmy, Joshua, Sonya . . ." I snapped my fingers. "Frankie. That's right. I always forget about Frankie. But he's the youngest, so he's used to it."

Hank's fists moved to his hips and his glare intensified.

This was so pointless. I didn't understand what we were doing out here. He didn't want me working at his club, so why the heck was he here? Was he . . . worried?

"Listen, Mr. Weller, you don't need to worry about me. I'll be fine."

"I'm not worried about you."

"Then why are you here?"

"I'm here because—according to Beau and apparently everyone else—if something happens to you at The G-Spot, then folks in this town are gonna make me out to be the bad guy."

"I'm sorry, what?" I tilted my head to the side as though to hear better. "What does my dancing at The G-Spot have to do with you?"

"Come on, Charlotte. You're not stupid."

"My goodness, you say the prettiest things." I pressed my hand to my chest in mock awe. "You should save that one for your wedding vows. 'Dearest Gertrude, I knew you were my soulmate "'cause you're not stupid.' With wordsmithing like that, it's a wonder Patty Lee ever cut you loose."

Hank's lips twitched even as his eyes narrowed, and if I didn't know any better, I'd think he was fighting a laugh. "Okay," he drawled, heaving a beleaguered sigh. "You win. What is it going to take for you to not work at The G-Spot? How much money do you need?"

"None of your damn business. I'm not looking for a handout and I don't need help from you." I turned away and marched toward the front porch, riding high on a wave of anger.

"Fine," he hollered after me. "You can be a bartender at The Pony. Happy?" It sounded like he'd said the words through gritted teeth.

I spun, my index finger lifted between us and ready for battle. "Okay, first of all, who do you think you are, showing up here at my friend's house while I'm trying to have a nice morning, arguing with me about where I can and cannot work?"

"As opposed to showing up at my workplace and arguing with me?"

"I was trying to apply for a job!" I yelled my frustration. "Where else did you want me to go? To your house? Do people track you down in restaurants when they want an interview? Swim out to your fishing boat on Bandit Lake dressed like mermaids? How do other dancers audition? Out the window of their automobile when they catch you at a red light? Besides, I can't be a bartender, I have no experience. I wanted to be a dancer, and I think I'd be damn good at it."

"No. You wouldn't. You don't understand even the most basic fundamentals of how this works," he yelled back. "Dancers are independent contractors, not employees. How much are you charging for lap dances? How about private ones? Do you have a time limit? What songs do you use? How about props and costumes? What's your budget? Do you own your own business? You have an S Corp? An LLC to receive the money? How are you planning on filing your taxes to account for the income?"

"I can do that. I can do all that. I've already put the wheels in motion so I can dance at The G-Spot. I know how to set up an S Corp, and an LLC, and an LLC structured like an S Corp. I know how to file new business paperwork, tax paperwork, all of it. That's not a problem, but thanks for giving me a heads-up."

He straightened, and something I'd said had clearly caught him off guard. "You know how to file the paperwork?"

"Yes. I'm figuring it out for Tennessee. I've only done it in Nevada. It can't be all that different."

Hank shuffled a few steps closer, no longer yelling. "How do you know?"

"I used to run the office and do bookkeeping for Kevin's father in Las Vegas, right after Kimmy was born. They were short-staffed, so I pitched in and then eventually took it over for a few years. So don't you worry that pretty head about little old me. The IRS and I are good friends."

"You're a bookkeeper?" He blinked, his voice no longer hostile.

"Yes. Well, I was."

"Why aren't you a bookkeeper now?"

"Is this an interview?"

"Charlotte."

"Fine." I heaved a sigh. "I needed a job that started when my kids went to school and ended when they got out. Being a teacher's aide made the most sense. It's not as much of a workload as a full teacher, I don't take work home usually, and I get the summers off."

"Kevin's alimony doesn't pay enough?"

Renewed irritation ignited in my chest and I ground out, "That is really none of your damn business."

"Okay. Fine." Hank held his hands up. "How about this? You need money, I need a bookkeeper. My bookkeeping position pays well and is a W-2, full-time position with benefits. It won't rely on tips, so you wouldn't have to build up to the income you need."

I wanted to spit in his face and tell him to shove his job offer up his ass 'til he could taste it. I swallowed the impulse.

I still needed to find my cousin. Working at The G-Spot was now firmly off the table, and that meant The Pink Pony was my only option for gaining access to and forging trust with the exotic dancer community in Green Valley. This was an opportunity and it would be stupid as raisins for me to pass it up because Hank Weller made me barmy.

He must've taken my silence for hesitation because he added, "You'll have a regular paycheck and wouldn't have to make initial investments in costumes, makeup, props, any of that. You can show up for work tomorrow and get started. What do you say?" He reached out his hand for me to shake.

I glanced at the offered fingers, frowning. I was going to say yes. If I wanted to help my cousin, this job was my only option.

Still . . .

I meandered forward and asked, "Why are you so set against me dancing at The Pony? What's wrong with me?"

He let his hand drop and openly inspected me for a tick, looking contemplative, then said, "How about this: in six months, if you're still interested in becoming a dancer, I will show you the ropes. I will train you and teach you everything you need to know. Deal?"

For some bonkers reason, my first instinct was to ask him if showing me the ropes meant I'd have to call him daddy, but I stopped myself before the bizarre statement exited my mouth. *Where had that come from?*

Squaring my shoulders, I said, "Fine. Deal," and accepted his handshake for a quick grasp.

It was a meaningless deal.

I wouldn't be working at The Pink Pony in six months. If all went well, I'd only be working there for two weeks at the most. And I couldn't wait for it to be over.

CHAPTER 5

CHARLOTTE

"You always get more respect when you don't have a happy ending."

— JULIA QUINN

*M*y momma and aunt exuberantly volunteered to watch the kids once I gave them the latest update about Hank's job offer. We also worked out a schedule for the next two weeks that would allow me to be present at The Pony as often as possible. The more I interacted with the dancers, the sooner I could earn their trust and ask about Heather.

Smoothing my hand along the front of my fitted, button-down dress shirt, I lifted my head high and walked the short distance from my car to the front door of The Pink Pony, mentally prepared to deflect and ignore any unpleasantness Hank Weller tossed my way.

I needed to keep my head down, ingratiate myself to the dancers, and determine whether Heather was one of them. If not, I'd try to arrange for one of The Pink Pony dancers to introduce me to a G-Spot dancer, crossing that bridge when I came to it.

Squaring my shoulders, I inhaled then exhaled quickly, tugged open the door, and came face-to-face with Dave.

"Dave!" I stumbled a step back, my brain confused by his presence.

Dave was one of Raquel Ezra's bodyguards. The famous Hollywood bombshell was dating my good friend Jackson James, the sheriff's deputy who I'd asked about the crime statistics at The G-Spot. Raquel—Rae to her friends—was also friendly with Sienna. They were thinking about opening up a production company together.

But what was Dave doing here instead of providing personal security to Rae?

"Charlotte." Dave's eyes were large as they moved over me. "What are you doing here?"

"I work here." I smiled. "Hank hired me yesterday. What are you doing here?"

Dave's expression didn't change, except his eyebrows snapped together. "Hired . . .?"

I glanced behind him, but I couldn't see into the club. It was too bright outside and too dark inside. "I'm the new bookkeeper."

His stunned features morphed into a relieved-looking smile. "Oh! Bookkeeper. Of course."

"What? Did you think I was a bouncer?" I managed to joke, feeling a little sore for some reason. Apparently, like Hank, Dave didn't think I'd be a good stripper either. Why did that make me feel so crummy?

He chuckled, his eyes twinkling with humor and something else. "Well, I hoped. I could use the help. And you're scary."

"You're a bouncer here?" I gave him a thoughtful frown. "Are you still working with Rae?"

"Yes. Still working with Rae, but she's out of town for a few months and I don't want to travel. Hank needed someone to fill in while he's looking for a new guy. Even when Rae is in town, she has Jackson now, doesn't need me and Miquel as often. In my downtime, I've been working here."

"Don't you work for a firm? Are they okay with you picking up shifts as a bouncer?"

"No, I don't work for the firm anymore. We're employed directly by Rae these days since we didn't want to be moved around anymore."

"You didn't?" This was news to me.

"Nah." The side of his mouth hooked upward and his gaze went from warm to warmer. "I'm finding a few good reasons to stay in Green Valley this time around." Dave winked. At me. While smoldering.

Oh my.

Surprised to silence, my mouth worked to no avail. I glanced down at my shoes, needing a minute to process his unexpected wink-smolder. Goodness, he was a handsome guy if you went for barrel-chested, blue-eyed Italians with lots of chest hair who were funny, reliable, sweet. Everything I knew about Dave, I really liked.

Even so . . .

I sighed.

Wearing a resigned smile I felt in my bones, I returned my attention to Dave and gave myself three seconds to enjoy how he was looking at me, his pretty eyes hot and full of interest. It was nice to be looked at that way. But ultimately pointless.

"Dave. Are you sweet on me?" I asked lightly, needing to draw my line in the sand but not wanting to injure any feelings. "If you are, you should know I'm nothing but sour."

"I find that hard to believe, Ms. Mitchell." He chuckled like he thought I was cute.

"It's true. I'm bitter and sour. I'm all salt and no sugar."

His gaze cooled and flicked over my face. "Nah, you're sugar. Perhaps not for me, but for someone," he said, his tone conciliatory and kind.

"No. I'm not." I shook my head adamantly. "Believe me, if I had sugar in me, I'd *definitely* have it for you."

His eyes crinkled. "Are you trying to let me down easy?"

"No. I'm being honest. I'm not capable of that anymore, no matter who. I'm too tired."

He frowned thoughtfully, looking hesitant. "At the risk of making things between us even more awkward—and I'm not arguing, I'm curious—what about Jackson? Weren't you two seeing each other for a few months?"

"You are not making things between us awkward. We're still friends, right?"

He nodded. "I hope so."

"Then I don't mind telling you, Jackson was my Hail Mary pass and doesn't count. Not even a little. Ultimately, it was like trying to date my brother." I laughed, and so did Dave. "I mean, we gave it a try, and it was good that we did. It made me realize I don't have the energy to try anymore. If I couldn't muster any extra energy for Jackson—who made it so easy, and who I've known my whole life—then . . ." I shrugged my shoulders. "Fact of the matter is, I have four servings of sugar in me daily and those go to Kimmy, Joshua, Sonya, and Frankie. That's all I have to give."

Dave's lips twisted to the side in a sorta smile and his chest expanded with a deep breath. "I'm sorry to hear that, Charlotte. Not so much for me, but for you. I think . . ." He lifted a hand and tucked an errant strand of hair behind my ear, his fingertips lingering at my jaw, his gaze unfocused. "I think, one day you'll meet someone with sugar to spare."

"What a nice thought," I said, my voice quiet. "But even if I did, I wouldn't take it. I don't think taking from others without giving my fair share is in my nature. It wouldn't feel right. The mere thought makes me even more salty, and sweaty, and . . . really sweaty."

He laughed again and his hand dropped back to his side. "Okay, okay. I don't need to be standing here all night, thinking about you being sweaty." He winked again, but this one was teasing and friendly. "You better get inside, I'm sure Hank is expecting you. Come on."

Giving him a wide smile, I stepped beyond him and into the dark interior of the club, needing to blink a few times for my eyes to acclimate. Once I was certain I wouldn't fall on my face, I gave Dave a goodbye wave, walked down the short hall to the main club entrance, turned the corner, and then stopped in my tracks.

If I'd been thinking or paying attention, I would've noticed the music prior to walking in. But I hadn't been paying attention, so I was surprised by the sight of the club three-fourths filled with customers and the image of . . . *Tina?* Yep, Tina Patterson spinning around the pole on the stage. Swallowing unnecessarily, I took in the rest of the activity.

Women were prancing around between tables, some in glittery outfits, some in skintight ones. Others left more to the imagination but were no less suggestive. I narrowed my eyes and studied them without meaning to, wanting to satisfy my curiosity as to why both Hank and Dave didn't think I'd make a good stripper.

The women were all shapes and sizes, colors, hair lengths, and facial features. I studied a dancer nearby. She was barely covered in a leopard-print dress; her face and body would likely be labeled as average by popular beauty culture. But watching her move made my neck hot and my pulse flutter. How she used her body, her confidence in herself . . . She was so sexy.

The man she was grinding on also seemed to think so. He had a hazy kind of look in his eye, like he was enjoying himself a little too much and he found keeping his hands still extremely . . . hard.

Yep. He's definitely finding it hard.

"What are you wearing?"

Startled, I whipped my head toward the question and discovered Hank Weller standing at the bottom of the stairs, looking up at me like I was grapefruit juice and he'd ordered orange soda.

"I—" I glanced down at my black pencil skirt, pale blue business shirt, and black heels. "What's wrong with what I'm wearing?"

He grumbled something I couldn't hear over the loud music and waved me forward impatiently. "Let me show you the office so we can go through the basics," Hank shouted. He took off without waiting for me to follow.

Shaking myself, I jogged over to catch up before he disappeared in the back. We power-walked down a long hallway that had a ton of framed photographs lining the walls and then turned a corner, the music fading the further we traveled. Unlike the main club area, the walls in the hall were white, not pink.

"There's a kitchen at the end there for everyone's use. It has a big fridge, a microwave, and a coffee maker. We don't keep our meals in the club's restaurant kitchen, so don't use those fridges. Serafina—that's the chef— gets testy about it. If you want coffee, use the one back here. If there's no coffee made, feel free to brew it. It's self-explanatory. Also, don't make popcorn or reheat fish in the microwave, it makes everything stink." He said all this without turning around and we pivoted around another corner. "Where did you park? You need to park in the back, in the employee lot. It's gated for safety. The front lot is for customers only. I have a key for you that opens the back door, and the code for the gate. It's electrified, so don't touch it."

"The gate is electrified?"

"It is." He glanced at me, giving me a quick inspection, then abruptly stopped and opened a door to our left. "Still, have one of the bouncers walk you out when you leave."

Goodness. Did they really need an electric fence? And how much did that cost to maintain? It seemed excessive, but maybe I didn't know enough to understand the necessity.

After my odd and unpleasant encounter with Hank yesterday, I'd stayed up way past my bedtime, educating myself on the basics of working as an exotic dancer and the typical business organization of strip clubs. In retrospect, it was something I should've done *before* asking Hank for a job.

But I hadn't looked up worst-case scenarios or horror stories of the business. Tonight I would.

Even though I wouldn't be dancing, the information I'd gathered yesterday provided me with some ideas on how to maximize the time I had at the club as well as how the payroll system might be organized. Thursdays, Fridays, and Saturdays would be the busiest days; more dancers were on the schedule, which meant I'd need to work on the weekends in order to meet as many of the dancers as possible.

I'd made a list of questions for Hank. Whether or not the dancers took a cut of their section's food and drink bill, what percentage, how much the house took from each lap dance, and so forth would dictate how much the dancers were paid every other week. This total would need to be calculated for each person and I'd need those details to run payroll.

"Here's your office." He stepped through the doorway and stood to one side so I could enter. "I put your position description on the desk, right there along with a statement of benefits, your salary information, and such. Assuming that all looks right, you can start right now. The laptop is new, has Office installed, and is already connected to the Wi-Fi."

Dismissing the position description and the salary information as irrelevant, I took in the space, surprised by how . . . normal it seemed. The furniture looked similar to my office back in Vegas for the Buckley company: graphite-colored desk, a rolling desk chair with lumbar support, white metal filing cabinets along one wall. The desk was free of knickknacks but someone had laid out an assortment of office supplies.

No art or photographs donned the walls, which were painted the same color as the hallway, but a half whiteboard, half corkboard combo had been affixed to the expanse above the desk. Last but definitely not least, a window looked over a view of the hills and valley, unobstructed by a parking lot, pavement, fence, or anything else. It felt like being perched on the top of a mountain.

"Goodness," I whispered under my breath, blinking out the window. "That's quite a view."

"I have the same view. The windows don't open for security reasons," he said in a way that sounded sharp, drawing my eyes to him. "My office is right next to yours, but it's bigger."

I fought a snort and an eye roll. *Of course it is* and of course he'd point out the difference. Reining in my salty impulses, I asked, "What about passwords?"

"I left the computer password on a sticky note—up there." Hank pointed to the corkboard. Before I could scrutinize the rest of the papers and information pinned to the board, he pulled out the office chair and motioned that I should sit. "Nothing else is password-protected and we use Google for email and for our calendar. Set up a new email account, one that you'll use exclusively for work, and let me know what it is. I'll add you to the calendar, which is how we assign and track the schedule." He leaned over me and tapped the papers on the desk next to the laptop. "And don't forget to look at the position description and employment benefits. If the salary isn't right, no need for you to settle in."

Since his eyes remained on me as he leaned back and he seemed so anxious about the subject, I picked up the position description and skimmed it. "This looks fine," I muttered, though I was a bit perplexed.

Everything seemed fairly standard for the most part. He'd added a few office-manager-type tasks—hiring and firing paperwork, ordering supplies, etc.—but nothing jumped out as odd or beyond the scope of what I knew to be typical for a small business office. That said, the workload seemed extremely light. I couldn't imagine the duties described taking more than twenty or twenty-five hours a week, given the size of his business—unless I was missing something.

You're probably missing something.

Keeping these questions and suspicions to myself, I reached for the benefits information, and my eyebrows soared as soon as I spotted the salary figure, grateful Hank didn't have a full view of my face. *Good Lord.* This job paid triple what my teacher's aide position paid and had a full month of paid time off. The health benefits weren't too shabby either.

Finding my voice required several stunned moments and I finally managed, "I'd say this is more than fair."

He grunted, a sound of both acknowledgement and impatience. "Fine. Moving on."

A tad flustered by the generosity of the position's compensation and Hank's rushing me through everything, I cleared my throat of nerves and opened the laptop. Reading the password on the sticky note, I logged in with exceeding carefulness and breathed a silent sigh of relief when the machine unlocked on my first try. It's surprisingly difficult to type a random series of letters, numbers, and symbols when someone is watching over your shoulder, especially if that person is radiating antagonism and looks like a Barbie doll's (or Ken doll's) beautiful but dissolute older brother.

I methodically clicked around the desktop, opening the Wi-Fi window to ensure I was connected, then I opened a browser and navigated to Google. "Good. Well. That all seems in order. What about FastFinance?"

When he didn't answer, I glanced up at him. His wide mouth wasn't curved in a frown anymore and his intelligent eyes held mine with sharp candor.

"What about FastFinance?" he asked.

"Uh, there's a password for FastFinance. How do I—or, wait. Do you use something else for payroll and reconciliation? A different system? QuickBooks? Mint?"

Hank tilted his head to the side and his stare turned calculating, as though I'd said something interesting. Or I was something interesting instead of something to be merely tolerated. "We use spreadsheets for all that."

My mouth dropped open and I forgot to be nervous. He had to be joking. "I—you —what?"

"We use spreadsheets. They're saved on the desktop and the naming should be self-explanatory."

"Spreadsheets?" I croaked. *This is a joke.* "What about reconciliation between your bank accounts, credit cards, and your expenditures? How do you categorize for taxes?"

Hank's perusal suddenly felt shifty and he scratched his jaw. "I download the bank and credit card statements and you copy/paste them into the spreadsheet." At my continued horrified expression, he added, "The spreadsheets are all backed up on the cloud. Why? Should we use FastFinance?"

Not thinking before responding—what the heck did I care if he used spreadsheets or stone tablets, I wasn't staying more than two weeks—I said, "Yes! Definitely. I would. FastFinance and systems like it automate so much. Creates invoices, paychecks, tax forms. You can run profit/loss statements whenever you want, check expenditures every month for trends. Hank, I know you said this was a full-time position, but you might not need someone full-time if you used FastFinance. Adding categories is a snap and makes reconciliation so much faster. Payroll might be able to be automated if you link it to the club's payment system."

The side of his mouth ticked up and he studied me intently, a seasoning of censure in his tone as he said, "You've been here five minutes and you're already trying to make yourself redundant."

"No," I said with mock sweetness, folding my hands over my lap and crossing my legs. His eyes darted to my bare knees, then away. "I'm not trying to make myself redundant. I'm trying to bring you into the twenty-first century. How old was your last bookkeeper? One hundred?"

"He was ninety-five."

When I saw that Hank wasn't joking, I barked a laugh. "You're serious. Your last bookkeeper was ninety-five?"

"Yes. And his stage name was Father Christmas."

"What? He had a stage name? Why?"

Hank leaned his shoulder against the doorjamb, settling in for story time. "We used him in all the holiday shows. He'd dress up like Santa and tell customers whether they were naughty or nice."

Unbelievable . . . and hilarious. "And if they were nice?"

"They'd get a front-facing lap dance on the house in the main room."

Unable to stem the impulse, I smiled. "And if they were naughty?"

"They paid double the price and got a back-facing lap dance in the champagne room."

Entranced and oddly thrilled, I asked, "Which is better?"

Something like a grin spread over Hank's typically stoic features, his hazel eyes sparkling like topaz as his eyelids lowered by half. "It depends on whether they like it naughty or nice."

Staring up at him, I could hear myself breathing and feel the beat of my heart and nothing else. His words were liquid fire in my veins. I'd forgotten how devastating his smiles were, how sinister-looking, and how they made me instantly *feel*.

Suddenly, I was sixteen again, gazing starstruck at Hank Weller's sinfully addictive face as he gave someone—never me—a tempting, mischievous grin. Whenever I thought of the Hank from my youth, the word *tempting* always came to mind, something I wanted but I knew would ultimately be bad for me, and I'd try not to faint from swooning.

Hank's grin waned as our gazes held and tangled. At least to me it felt like they were tangling.

Abruptly, he dropped his attention to the floor, then someplace in the vicinity of my knees, and then he cleared his throat. "Listen, you can't wear that kind of stuff in here." He flicked his hand toward my clothes, all his earlier charismatic mischievousness evaporated as though it had never been.

Grateful for the reprieve from his attention—but also flustered. *What the hell, Charlotte? Hank Weller is as sour as you. And he can't stand you! You don't need more bitterness, you're tart enough already*—I again inspected my outfit. "What's so wrong with what I'm wearing?"

"Folks will think it's part of an act, naughty librarian or secretary," he said matter-of-factly, looking and sounding grumpy about it. "Something like that."

"You want me to wear baggy clothes?" I had a bunch of loose blouses and long skirts for school. They were comfortable and the length of the skirt allowed me to wipe off sticky or paint-covered kindergartener hands when there were no paper towels within reach. Plus, the floral print hid stains.

"It would be better if you dressed like me, T-shirts and jeans. All the kitchen staff, the bouncers, all non-talent positions dress like this. It separates us from the show."

I nodded, considering. "Could I wear jean shorts? Yoga pants?"

"That's fine." He shrugged, pushing away from the wall and backing out of the office. "I suppose I don't care what you wear on your bottom half, as long as you're wearing a loose T-shirt on your top half."

"Okay. Good to know."

Hank frowned. Maybe he'd just remembered that I was odious.

He moved like he was going to leave, and so I stood abruptly. "Wait a minute. Could I—um—is it okay if I introduce myself to everyone?"

"Sure," he said, bored of my questions and existence, his attention now pointed down the hallway.

Praise Jesus! Hank obviously didn't know it, but he was doing me a big favor. Therefore, since I felt kindly toward him at the moment, I offered, "And is it okay if I set you up with FastFinance?"

He looked at me then, his expression less bored, more contemplative. "How about a trial? Do they have free trials?"

"They do. I think it lasts a month."

"Do that. If I like it, we'll keep it."

"Okay, but you're definitely going to like it." I sat back down and grinned to myself. I was about to rock his world. With automation.

Hank made a scoffing sound. "You think you know what I'll like?"

I smirked a knowing smirk up at him even though his question sounded supremely unfriendly. "I think you're a business owner, and business owners can't resist a succinct profit and loss statement and reduced overhead costs. That sort of stuff gets y'all hot."

Some of his hostility burned off and the smirk he shot me in return felt challenging rather than mean. "You're right. It does get me hot. If this program works as well as you say, I'll pay you full-time even if you cut your hours back. How about that, angel?"

Ignoring how he'd made *angel* sound like a dirty word, I wagged a finger like he was a naughty boy, because clearly I must've been out of my mind. "Ah, see—that sort of talk gets *me* hot."

Hank's smirk grew into another of his heart-stopping, sinfully seductive grins, his stare intensifying its focus. He leaned into the room, parted his lips, and then—

He promptly snapped his mouth shut and blinked.

"I—" Hank's frown turned severe and he blinked several more times, looking confounded. He then gave his head a firm shake. "I have to go."

Before I could say another word, he darted away, back toward the club's main room, and left me staring at the spot he'd vacated, wondering what the heck was wrong with me. Had I . . .?

Noooooo.

Maybe.

Yes.

Oh no.

I'd flirted with Hank Weller. And he was technically now my boss.

I never flirted with anyone anymore. Those days of impracticality, letting my feelings be swept up in the lie of a flirtation, were far behind me. The only interactions that got me hot and bothered these days were the fictional, period drama ones I watched on TV after the kids went to bed. Rolling my eyes at myself, I chalked this odd behavior up to nerves and made myself a promise to never flirt with his surly butt again, which shouldn't be difficult.

After all, I would only be here for one week. Two tops.

CHAPTER 6

CHARLOTTE

"In youth, it was a way I had,
   To do my best to please.
   And change, with every passing lad
   To suit his theories.

But now I know the things I know
   And do the things I do,
   And if you do not like me so,
   To hell, my love, with you."

— DOROTHY PARKER, *THE COMPLETE POEMS OF DOROTHY PARKER*

"*H*ow are things going at the club?" Sienna nudged my shoulder with hers. Her tone was friendly, but also tinged with forced nonchalance, making me suspect my friend was worried about me but didn't want me to know how worried.

"Oh, fine." I sent her an unconcerned smile, not exactly lying, but not being precisely truthful either.

Today was the Tuesday after my full weekend working at The Pink Pony and one of my self-determined days off. Sienna and I stood next to each other behind the swing sets in her big backyard. Jethro had custom-built an impressive playground for his three boys, complete with a pirate ship, lookout, a swinging bridge, several slides leading down from the ship, a whole playhouse inside the ship, and several more swings jutting from either side.

When Melanie Ball had cornered me in the Piggly Wiggly last month, telling me, and I quote, "I'm so jealous that you're invited over to the Winston's house, how'd you manage that?" I'd assumed the basis of her jealousy was Jethro's playground. But then she'd straightened me out.

It was Sienna.

Melanie Ball was jealous that Sienna and I were becoming friends. According to Melanie, all the parents at school were green with envy, and she wanted me to know. This didn't make me feel good, or bad, or anything other than bewildered as to why Melanie had chased me down between the onions and potatoes to communicate her feelings on the subject. What did she expect me to do with this information? Apologize? Gloat? Write a song about it? And she'd been blocking the Yukon Gold while she went on and on. Mashed potatoes don't taste right if you use only russets. It took me twenty minutes—and Frankie screaming—for her to move.

Anyway.

Presently, Sienna pushed her youngest kiddo on the impressive swing set, and I pushed mine. They kept trying to grab on to each other's hands and then laughing like this was the funniest thing ever. It was cute.

Baby and toddler giggles usually put me in a good mood, but not today. Today, I couldn't quite decide how I felt. On the one hand, I was frustrated with Hank Weller. The phrase *self-explanatory* had ended up being a theme with him. Everything, it seemed, was self-explanatory.

I'd sent him my list of questions once my new email account completed setup on Thursday, and he'd responded via email that the payouts and percentages should be self-explanatory once I looked at the previous few month's payrolls.

I'd asked him what he'd like my preferred days and hours to be, and he messaged back that I should base my schedule on what made the most sense for any given day and that it was—you guessed it—self-explanatory.

"You don't sound so sure," Sienna said, inspecting me. "Hank isn't giving you grief, is he?"

"No. Not at all," I replied lightly. Hank wasn't giving me grief; he wasn't giving me anything at all.

I should've been thrilled with his hands-off approach. My real goal in working at the club was to locate and contact my cousin, not overhaul and fix Hank's tangled web of financials. He'd avoided me this weekend, allowing me freedom to meander around The Pony, and I'd already found my cousin.

More precisely, I'd found a photograph of her in a bra and panty set, huddled with a bunch of other dancers. She was in one of the many, many, many framed photographs lining the back hallway. I had no idea when it was taken or if it meant she currently worked at The Pony, used to work at The Pony, or had visited The Pony the night the photo was taken.

So the more independence he gave me to continue my snooping, the better, right? Right?!

Sigh.

I peered over Frankie's bobbing head to where Joshua and Ben stood together beyond the border of the playground, seemingly in deep conversation. My heart pinged. Joshua kept trying to get Ben to play this vintage board game we'd found at the thrift store called *Stock Market*, and Ben had no interest. Kimmy and I played *Stock Market* with Joshua a few times, but she only participated when I'd bribed her with an extra scoop of ice cream after dinner.

Poor kid, he couldn't seem to find anyone who shared his interests. He seemed so lonely.

"Is he being nice?" Sienna asked, drawing my attention away from the two boys in the distance.

"I'm sorry. What are we talking about?"

"Hank. Is Hank being nice?" She worried her lip.

"Hank is not being mean. He's given me plenty of autonomy and that's . . . good." I wasn't sure if I was trying to convince Sienna or me.

"What does that mean?"

I shrugged, distracted. "We haven't spoken except the first day."

"First day?" Her tone hardened. "You mean last Thursday?"

"That's right." I hadn't seen Hank except in passing, didn't talk to him in person at all, and had stopped sending him emails when every question or clarification had been met with, *It's self-explanatory.*

I realized it was silly for me to care about the club's ancient reporting system, but I did. Don't get me wrong, I cared about finding my cousin. My aunt and uncle were counting on me and I wouldn't let them down. But those archaic spreadsheets? For tracking *payroll*? His antiquated system was a crime against modern bookkeeping best practices.

"You're brand new to the job, and Hank—your boss—hasn't spoken to you in five days?"

"It's no big deal." I made sure to infuse my words with confidence and worked to ignore the nagging guilt. "I like all the freedom."

It didn't matter if Hank trained me for the job. Practically, I knew it was probably best if he didn't give me any more of his time or attention. I'd be leaving in another week . . . *or I'll stay?*

Pushing the persistent thought aside, I listened as Sienna inhaled through her nose and said something in Spanish. Based on her tone, I assumed it was a curse and it ripped at something inside me that had already frayed.

I felt torn.

Hank didn't want me working at The Pony. Fact. His determination to make everything difficult made me want to piss him off by sticking around for years. That impulse was plain silly. Teenager Charlotte would've done that kind of thing, but adult Charlotte knew not to cut off my nose to spite my face.

Regardless of Hank's unhelpfulness, I'd worked until midnight on Thursday, Friday, Saturday, and Sunday, losing myself in the spreadsheets and enjoying every single second of it.

"I see a lot of Dave, though." I tried to mollify Sienna's spike in temper. "And that's been nice."

She smiled back, the curve of her mouth stiff. "That is nice. Tell him I say hi."

"I will."

Years before Dave had worked as Rae's personal bodyguard or Hank's bouncer, he'd been a guard for Sienna and they were still friendly.

Dave had been the one to walk me to my car every night after I'd spent my time in the office going through old payroll, credit card statements, receipts, and expenditures, studying the flow of the business and getting an idea of how the club functioned. Fred—the previous bookkeeper—had maintained folders on the desktop labeled clearly with their contents.

Tax forms were in a folder named *Tax Forms*, and other folders within were organized by year, then employee last name. You better believe I scanned the folders and searched for my cousin. None of the names matched, but that didn't mean much. Heather could have been using a fake identity.

None of the payroll records clearly detailed house percentages and portions for the dancers, rates for the lap dances, etc., which was frustrating. I found conflicting information from one spreadsheet to the next, from one dancer to the next, one week to the next, and all the contradictory data gave me a headache even as it energized me to solve the puzzle.

"Dave's the best," Sienna said, returning her focus to Pedro in the swing, chuckling at his antics as he made a grab for Frankie. Glancing at me again, she opened her mouth, maybe to comment on the two rascals. Instead, her scrutiny became an inspection. "Seriously, if you need Hank to be more supportive and helpful, let me know. I'll talk to him."

"Please do not talk to Hank." It was better if he left me alone. Then I would be free to question the dancers and kitchen staff about Heather. "Everything is fine."

"I feel like you two would like each other better if you got to know each other outside of work."

I offered a small smile, too tired and careworn to manage more than that.

What I needed was to ask one of the dancers about the photo of Heather without raising suspicion, which meant I needed to start interacting with them more than the quick introductions I'd made on Thursday and Friday nights.

So far I'd met nine of the dancers. I already knew Hannah Townsend and had an acquaintance with Tina Patterson, but the rest had been unknown to me. Each of the new faces had been friendly and excited to have a replacement bookkeeper.

Yet Hannah greeted me with a pleasant smile but eyed me with suspicion. She'd always been smart, and I had no doubt she knew why I'd taken a job at The Pony. I only hoped she'd keep the information to herself and not ruin my chances of finding Heather.

The ladies' unified kindness on Saturday night settled my nerves, giving me hope that Hannah hadn't revealed my true motive for taking the bookkeeping job, and I figured I'd be able to ask one of them about Heather and the photo sometime soon. I considered bringing in cupcakes or muffins this weekend as a thank-you for their warm welcome, and then using the opportunity to request information about the photos in the hallway.

My primary objective seemed to be progressing well, but every night when I drove home after Dave walked me to my car, I'd felt that twinge of guilt.

I was lying to these women about my objectives, and that didn't feel right no matter how important and well-meaning my intentions. Would they forgive me for deceiving them after I quit?

Maybe I could . . . stay for a bit longer than two weeks?

Righting Frankie's swing and giving him a soft push, I finally allowed myself to consider the invasive idea that had taken root in the back of my mind since last Thursday after work. I needed to find my cousin, but I hadn't expected to like the job this much. Except Hank, everyone else had been gracious. I missed working with numbers. And adults. And it paid *really* well.

The kids' school was starting up again soon, but I wished staying at The Pony was a possibility. Especially if setting up FastFinance for the club saved as much time as I thought it would. I could lay the kids down at night and then work remotely for a few hours, driving to the club two times a week on the weekends in case someone needed to meet about a payroll issue or if Hank had questions about the canned reports.

The part of me that had wanted to immediately dismiss the idea finally silenced as I realized the truth: a big part of me liked the notion too much to set it aside. I enjoyed working in an office environment, seeing people in the breakroom, and chatting between their shifts.

At the kids' school, I suspected conversations in the breakroom stalled whenever I arrived because I wasn't only a teacher's aide, I was a parent. Compounding complicated matters, Kimmy—my oldest—had been a tricky child to teach and to parent. She challenged authority constantly and I suspected this contributed to me feeling like an outsider in the teachers' lounge.

But not at The Pony. I'd immediately felt like part of the team. Sure, excluding the kitchen staff and bouncers, my coworkers were all mostly naked and covered in glitter, but that didn't bother me any. I worked with kindergartners nine months out of the year. They also liked to take off their clothes and paint their bodies with glitter.

Maybe Hank will let me get cakes for birthdays and help arrange staff parties.

I smiled at the thought, and then I frowned.

The main issue—other than Hank being a surly butt—was time. After my kiddos went to bed was the only time to clean my house uninterrupted, follow up on and arrange for doctor and dentist visits, fix leaky faucets, do laundry, make appointments, sew torn clothes, prepare meals for the next day, patch and paint holes in the wall, mow the lawn, weed the garden, and so forth. As much as I enjoyed bookkeeping and accounting, I only had twenty-four hours in a day.

"You look tired," Sienna said, yanking me out of my musings. "And I've never seen you look tired before. You're the most spirited, energetic person I know and I don't like seeing you so low energy."

I shrugged again, giving her a half smile. "I think I need to adjust to the change in my schedule. I'm sure all will resolve itself in a week or so." That twinge of guilt returned. I breathed through it.

Don't feel guilty, Charlotte. You want to stay after Heather is located, but you don't have the time. You're not an octopus, you can't do everything.

"Stay for dinner." Sienna lifted her chin toward the house. "Jethro is making ribs. I think Beau and Shelly will be here, too. And Cletus and Jenn are bringing over their dog. The kids will love him."

I studied my lengthening shadow. I should get the kids home and to bed on time. My mother and aunt had been too indulgent while I'd been doing reconnaissance at the club, letting them stay up too late. "I don't know—"

"Jenn is bringing three desserts."

"Okay, fine. Twist my arm." I had things to do at home, but I always had things to do at home. Jennifer Winston was the best pastry chef in Tennessee—if not the whole world—and I'd be off my rocker to turn down sampling one of her desserts, let alone three.

Sienna laughed, pushing her shiny curtain of long dark hair over a shoulder and giving me a heart-stopping grin. Really, the woman was too gorgeous for words. And she always looked so fashionable. Today she had on a pink tank-top tunic and brown leggings with beaded brown sandals to match. Her toenails and fingernails were painted the same color as her top and she wore pink quartz earrings.

I glanced down at myself in my yoga pants, sneakers, and tie-dye T-shirt from my volleyball days in high school. It was faded, and other than being a little tight around the chest, it still fit okay. It also happened to be the only clean item in my closet since my mother and aunt had neglected to do any laundry over the weekend. My hair was currently in a bun of doubtful stability using two pencils and a paperclip. I rarely chose waking up early to do my hair. Sleep was precious.

Note to self: order some more hair ties. I used to have hair ties, but then my oldest daughter was born and now I had no hair ties or hairbrushes or scissors or tape. And as much as I admired Sienna's earrings, it had been so long since I'd worn a pair, I wasn't sure I knew where any of my earrings were. Likewise, I reckoned the last time I'd had my nails painted was on the day I'd signed my divorce papers.

"Yay! I'm glad you're staying." Sienna nudged my shoulder again, her eyes sparkling. "I think it'll be fun. And productive."

Her tone and odd word choice had me studying her. "Productive? What do you mean?"

"What's wrong with productive?" She avoided my gaze.

Wait a minute. She sounded suspicious. "Why do you sound like that?"

Her smile stretched. "Like what?"

"Like you're tricking me somehow."

Sienna gasped, but the lingering smile ruined her attempt at acting offended. "I would never."

"Hmm." I peered at her, not liking something about her expression.

Before I could question her further, Kimmy materialized next to me, asking me to help her and Sonya keep a frog alive. They'd caught it and sealed it in a jar, and I forgot what I was supposed to be suspicious about. I was too busy trying to rescue a frog from the suffocation of my daughters' love.

* * *

I have good instincts about the ripeness of fruit, when to check on the kids if they're too quiet, whether or not I'm going to enjoy a movie by looking at the poster, and now—apparently—about having cause to be suspicious of Sienna Diaz.

Hank walked into the Winston homestead right behind Beau and Shelly. He wore jeans, a dark gray T-shirt, and a neutral expression. In one hand he held a basket of fresh biscuits; in the other was a twelve-pack of beer. He greeted all the Winstons and their significant others with mild friendliness, their children with tepid tolerance, and then he caught sight of me. His expression immediately frosted, and not the sugary, delicious kind of frosted.

Great.

Making no attempt to wipe his features of displeasure, Hank handed over his biscuits to Jethro, shook Drew Runous's hand, grabbed an appetizer off the tray on the sideboard, and accepted a cold beer from Beau. Jaw working, he then made a beeline for me.

"What are you doing here?" he demanded quietly, standing at my shoulder.

Sigh. Why must he be so ornery with me all the time? I was already exhausted and feeling angsty about my kids' well-being, and my aunt and uncle's well-being, and Heather's well-being, and my lack of clean laundry, and pining for a job I didn't know how to juggle, given all my other commitments, without his attitude heaping a wet blanket on top of my rained-out parade.

Plastering on a smile, I faced his chiseled profile and said, "I'm with the caterer," with intense mock cheerfulness. "Do you need your drink refreshed? More salt for your canapé?"

Without turning his head, Hank's gaze shifted to the side and narrowed. "Why aren't you at *work*?"

"I have Mondays and Tuesdays off."

"Do you?" he drawled. "Does your boss know?"

"He said my hours were self-explanatory," I responded tartly. "Thus, I explained them to myself. Do let me know if you need more salt, I got plenty." I turned, intent on leaving Mr. Surly-Butt to his beer, but was forced to halt abruptly.

Joshua blocked my path, his arms crossed, a thundercloud behind his eyes. Inclining his head once toward Hank, he muttered, "Excuse me, sir." Then his gaze shifted to mine and he said, "Mother."

My heart pinged again. *Poor little pumpkin.* I could guess the issue, but I asked anyway, "What's wrong?"

"They're watching cartoons," he said, like the watching of cartoons by other children explained his foul mood. And since I knew my kids, it did.

Kimmy loved stories about witches and fairies, fighting about whether the sky was blue just to be contradictory, and swimming whenever she got the chance. Sonya loved drawing, painting, and making everything she touched into art. She also enjoyed snuggling and leaving love letters for us around the house, which were just folded up pieces of paper that mainly consisted of hearts and her name. Frankie loved big construction trucks, all sports, wearing costumes, and singing along to Broadway musicals.

And Joshua loved news magazines, listening to podcasts about ancient civilizations and the current status of financial markets, and studying maps. The older the map, the better.

"Why don't you read a book?" I lifted my hand toward the two big bookshelves in the family room. "I'm sure they have an atlas."

Joshua's glower intensified. "Can I get *The Economist* out of the car?"

I peeked quickly over my shoulder, hoping Hank had moved on. No such luck. He stood behind me, his eyes on Joshua, an inscrutable expression on his face.

Squatting down, I placed a hand on my son's shoulder. "You've already read that issue a few times. I'm sure they have a book here you can read. Or some puzzles?"

The seven-year-old gave me a disdainful look. "You mean children's books. No, thank you."

I tried not to laugh. "Honey, I hate to break it to you, but you are a child."

His lip curled faintly. "I guess I'll see if they have an atlas," he said, great suffering permeating his tone. Dragging his feet, he scuffed over to the bookshelf and lowered to his knees in front of it, his little hand skimming over the spines.

As I stood, the ping in my heart intensified into an ache. Joshua had trouble making friends. No one his age wanted to discuss the things that interested him and he was too stubborn to feign interest in anything he wasn't passionate about. I needed to find him a group of like-minded kids, but I honestly didn't know where to start.

When I get home tonight, I'll stay up and do a search for kid investment groups. Something like that.

"Did I hear that right?"

Startled, I blinked the speaker of the question into focus, having forgotten Hank still hovered by my arm. "Pardon? Which part?"

To my surprise, Hank's antagonistic expression had mellowed and he lifted his beer bottle toward Joshua. "Does that child read *The Economist*? The news magazine?"

I debated whether or not to answer, unsure of Hank Weller's purpose in asking the question.

I'd experienced the full range of reactions to Joshua's peculiarities, everything from *Wow! He must be so smart. You should be doing so much more to challenge him*, to *How could you allow your young child to be exposed to such things? Don't you want him to have a normal childhood?*

If I had a dollar for every kid-related unsolicited opinion I'd been forced to endure from strangers, I would have enough money to hire a PI firm to find my cousin *and* pay off my home's new air conditioner.

Eventually, I admitted, "He does read *The Economist*, the news magazine," and braced myself for whatever judgy statement would follow.

"Which issue is in your car?" Hank asked, looking thoughtful.

"Uh, the one from three weeks ago, I think. We get them free from the dentist's office. They hold old issues for us." A subscription was beyond our means. I couldn't justify the cost and I hadn't been able to convince any of the grandparents to pay for an annual subscription. It wasn't flashy enough for Kevin's parents, and my momma didn't understand why anyone would want to read a news magazine.

He tilted his head toward the front door. "I have last week's issue in my car. Do you want me to get it?"

"You do?" I faced him fully.

"I do. And I already read it. Your kid can have it if he wants."

"Um . . ." I hesitated.

Hank had proven that he wasn't a helpful person. Getting him to give me the most basic of information about the job he paid me for had been like pulling up dandelion roots. I'd felt like a burden from the first moment I'd walked into his club and he'd done nothing to dispel that impression. In fact, he'd leaned into it fiercely, making sure I felt every inch like a tedious obligation. I hated feeling like an obligation. Hated it.

Therefore, Hank freely offering help now gave me pause. Could I trust it? Or would he use the offer as ammunition later to make me feel like crap?

My attention darted to Joshua curled up in a ball in front of the bookshelf, apparently having abandoned his search for an atlas in favor of looking resolutely forlorn. Nothing is more dramatic or pathetic than a child who is determined to be bored.

"Sure." I surrendered to his offer of help, bracing myself for whatever put-upon expression Hank would wear once I accepted. "Yes, please. That'd be great. Thank you. I really would appreciate it."

But Hank surprised me, nodding once and saying, "'Kay. Be right back." He handed me his beer and the napkin holding his appetizer, dusting his hands on his pants. He then turned and walked out of the house.

I stood frozen, watching his retreating back.

That was . . . strange.

Hank Weller acting helpful for no reason? *Nah.* I didn't buy it. He must've had a hidden motive.

CHAPTER 7

HANK

"The small hopes and plans and pleasures of children should be tenderly respected by grown-up people, and never rudely thwarted or ridiculed."

— LOUISA MAY ALCOTT, *LITTLE MEN*

"Is he reading the newspaper?" Ashley, née Winston, Runous—the only Winston sister—looked toward Charlotte's spawn where he sat on the floor, her tone a whisper.

"It appears so." I studied the miniature human as his eyes moved over the page he read. I'd given him *The Economist*, *The Washington Post*, and today's *Wall Street Journal*. The kid's upper lip had a grey smudge along the left side where he'd inadvertently left a trace of newsprint ink while picking his nose. *Disease vectors. Every single one of them.*

I'd been watching this weirdo kid since I'd handed him my latest copy of *The Economist* as well as today's paper, convinced he'd flip it open and search for comics. He didn't. He'd skimmed over the world news and then focused on the financial section.

I was . . . entranced. Against my will. *Do most kids read stock market reports? Is that a thing now?*

"Huh." Ashley set her hands on her hips, looking as perplexed as I felt. Giving her head a quick shake, she glanced at me. "You didn't bring Patty this time?"

"Nah. She has softball practice. Hey." I lifted my chin toward her. "You have a kid, right?"

This question earned me a wary once-over. "Yes. I have a kid. In fact, I have two."

"Do either of yours read the newspaper?"

"No, Hank." She sounded both exasperated and amused. "Our youngest is a newborn and Bethany is four. Most infants and four-year-olds don't read the financial section of *The Wall Street Journal*."

I gestured toward Charlotte's child. "How old is that one?"

"*That one*? You mean Joshua? You can't tell how old he is?"

"I have no idea. All children look the same to me."

A laugh burst out of her. "Hank."

I held my hands up. "I'm never exposed to children. He could be anywhere between three and seventeen."

Ashley continued laughing, rolling her eyes to the ceiling before turning her attention back to the child on the floor still reading the newspaper. "'Exposed to children.' You talk about them like they're a contagion."

I stopped myself before saying, *Well, aren't they?* Instead, I scrutinized the little boy. He'd picked his nose again, smearing more ink on his face.

"Bless his heart," Ashley said with a chuckle, pulling a pack of tissues from somewhere and starting over to him.

I caught her arm. "Wait. Where are you going?"

"I'm going to wipe his face and nose before he gives himself a full mustache."

Letting her go, I glanced between the tissue pack and her eyes, allowing my curiosity to make a rash decision for me. "Here, I'll do it. Give those over."

This kid made no sense. Kids weren't supposed to be interested in interesting things. They were supposed to be interested in pointless things, making too much noise, spreading disease, and telling stupidly long stories that had no ending and made no sense. I wanted—no, I *needed*—to figure out what this child was up to.

With obvious reluctance, Beau's sister placed the pack of tissues in my hand.

"These are heavy." I tested the weight of the tissues. "Why are these heavy? And they feel squishy."

"They're wet wipes." She gave me an appraising look. "He's picking his nose because it's running. Joshua has allergies and his nose runs in the summer, my daughter Bethany is the same. Joshua needs his face and fingers cleaned, and then he needs to blow his nose into the wipe. Do you think you can handle that?"

I grimaced and handed her back the tissues. "No. I don't think I can."

Ashley laughed again, making no secret that she was laughing *at* me. "Oh my goodness, don't you know how to blow your own nose? It's exactly the same. Don't be such a baby."

"How about I watch and learn this time?" I ground out, unamused. But I did follow her, my curiosity about this kid still a problem I needed to solve.

Ashley—without greeting the child or warning him—walked over and whipped out a wipe. Then she held it up to his nose and said, "Blow."

Joshua didn't look up from the paper, but he did blow his nose right into the wet tissue on command. Ashley then proceeded to wipe off Joshua's face with a new wipe. His hands were cleaned last.

"There," she said. "Good as new. I'm keeping the wet wipes, but I'll go grab you a box of tissues. When I bring them, you need to use the tissues, Joshua."

"Thank you, Miss Ashley," the one she called Joshua said, sparing her a small smile before his gaze skipped over to me.

I stiffened as he inspected me. His eyes were the same as Charlotte's—same shape, same color—and held the same sort of dismissive quality when looking me over. I couldn't decide if I liked it or if it made me nervous before he finished with his quick examination. The boy promptly returned his attention to the paper.

Standing, Ashley tussled his hair and left, taking her packet of clean wet wipes and the dirty ones with her. Meanwhile, I cocked my head to read the title of the article that supposedly held little Joshua's interest. *The Fed to Increase Interest Rates.*

"Do you understand what that means?" I asked, pointing at the headline and feeling a little silly as his amber eyes lifted up, up, up to where I stood hovering over him, demanding he demonstrate his knowledge of the Fed. Without allowing myself to consider the impulse, I sat on the floor next to him and pointed to the headline again. "Do you know what the Fed is? Or what interest rates are?"

"Yes," he said, but then his gaze sparked to life and he sat up straighter. "Do you want me to explain it to you?"

I felt my mouth curve as my eyes moved between his. The kid wasn't asking in a rude way, like I was a dummy; rather, I got the sense that explaining how the Federal Reserve worked was a topic he'd really enjoy.

Still skeptical, obviously, I said, "Sure. Tell me everything you know."

At once, he folded the paper and set it aside. "Okay, first thing you got to know is why it was created. Lots of people think it's always been around since Hamilton, but that's not true. It was created in 1913 after the Federal Reserve Act passed."

Leaning my shoulders against the bookcase behind us, I stretched my legs out, crossed them at the ankle, and spent the next several minutes being schooled about the creation and function of the Federal Reserve. By a kid. Who picked his nose.

Well, shit.

One of Charlotte's other kids wandered over at some point. A girl, probably younger than Joshua, given her height. She began drawing on the newspaper Joshua had discarded using blue and pink markers that smelled faintly of fruit. Ignoring the impulse to stop her vandalism of the newspaper—I'd already read it, after all—I gave my attention back to the boy.

And you know what? Hell, if I didn't learn a lot.

And you know what else? About five minutes into the conversation, which mostly consisted of me asking Joshua questions and him giving me damn fine answers, filling in the blanks of my knowledge gaps, I forgot I was speaking to a kid.

Until he picked his nose again.

". . . and the United Kingdom has the Bank of England, which does the same sort of thing." He said this while he shoved his index finger into the right hole and twisted it, slathering it up real good, then sniffling as he withdrew the wet tip.

Grimacing, I caught his wrist before he could wipe his finger on his pants. "Hold on. Don't wipe that shit on your clothes." Twisting my neck, I looked for a napkin or something. I discovered a box of tissues next to me. Ashley must've dropped it off while the kid and I were discussing international monetary policy.

Holding the diseased digit up and away, I wiped it with a tissue like I'd watched Ashley do earlier.

"Did you also like to read the news when you were my age?" Joshua asked, sniffling again, not seeming to mind I was wiping off his finger without asking.

"No." I inspected his nose. It was running. Clear liquid oozed out. Kids are impressively gross. Worse, they do this gross stuff like we as adults should be proud, and most parents act like it's the greatest thing ever.

For example, Jethro's oldest—Ben, I think . . . or Bryce? *Do they have one named Bryce?*—went poop in the toilet when he was two or three, dragging his diaper out into the living room after him, bottom covered in his own number two. And do you know what Jethro did? He clapped.

And not a slow, sarcastic clap either, which is what I would've done. But actual applause, smiling, saying, "Great job!" and "You did so great!" A 'normal' thing parents do when their kids go poop in the toilet. Think about the insanity for a second.

Why would anyone willingly sign up for that? I liked that kid, but I didn't want any part of *that*.

"What did you like doing?" Joshua sniffled again. "When you were my age, what did you like to do?"

"You know, the usual." I pressed the tissue against his nose and the kid blew out without me saying anything, like he was a Pavlovian dog. "I liked video games, riding my bike to the junkyard, fucking shit up and . . . uh . . ." I grimaced. I didn't know much about kids, but I did know it wasn't seemly to curse in front of them. Yet another reason to avoid children. "Sorry."

"It's okay. You probably don't know any better words."

Before I could react to that surprising declaration, Charlotte's small girl-child walked over and tapped me on the shoulder, thrusting her chin out. She, too, had a runny nose. Scowling at her cherub face—which, I noted, didn't scare her at all—I held a tissue up and she blew into it. Then she took one from the box and wiped at her lip, saying, "Thank you, Mr. Hank."

"You're welcome," I said automatically then paused, studying her. "Wait a minute, how'd you know my name?"

The girl pointed across the room and I followed the line created by her finger. Beau stood with Jennifer Winston and they were smiling at each other, two of Green Valley's most beloved citizens, basking in each other's mutual appreciation. *Gag.*

"Miss Jennifer told me," the child confirmed. Then she added, "I like your face, Mr. Hank. I like looking at it."

Turning incredulous eyes to the little girl, a shocked laugh escaped my lips. "You are quite forward."

She smiled, all charisma and baby teeth, mesmerizing and leaving me with an odd, warm feeling in my chest. Then she walked back to the picture she was drawing on my old newspaper.

Discomfited by my involuntary reaction to the little charmer, I kept one cautious eye on her and turned the remainder of my attention back to Joshua. "It's not okay and I do know better words. I shouldn't have used that word in front of you and your baby sister. I apologize."

"I've heard the F-word plenty of times." His shoulders lifted. "My grandma uses it a lot, but she says it's because she doesn't know any better words."

I placed the used snot rags on the corner of the coffee table then handed him the box of tissues. "But your momma doesn't use it?"

Joshua frowned thoughtfully, considering my question.

My eyes automatically searched the family room for Charlotte and I didn't find her or her yoga pants. *Yoga pants.* I shook my head, irritated with myself for being talked into hiring Charlotte. *And now I'm stuck being just her boss.*

I lowered my eyebrows at the wrongness of the thought. What I really meant was that I was stuck with her. At the club. I didn't want her at the club. Or anywhere. Even if I wasn't her boss, I wouldn't want her—

I shook my head. Whatever. I knew what I meant, and for better or worse, I was her boss. Despite what folks in town thought about me, I had strict professional standards for myself and for my team. Customers pushing and rallying against personal boundaries—weekly, daily, hourly—was central to the nature of my business. Maintaining a safe environment at all times was no small task.

The next time she and I spoke, I'd inform her that yoga pants weren't allowed as part of her work attire. Despite looking sleep-deprived when I'd walked in—her hair pulled in a lopsided bun, her eyes tired and shadowed—the woman was still stunning. The club didn't need the fineness of her ass and long legs and generous tits on display in a businessy dress shirt and tight skirt, nor did the club need her too-snug T-shirts and curve-enhancing yoga pants. She was a disaster waiting to happen.

Someone would see her and assume she was a dancer, chaos would ensue, and my club would be on the hook again.

Even angry, the woman was beautiful. She hadn't seemed happy to see me earlier. And speaking of, that rankled. Here I was helping her, wasn't I? I'd given her a job, I'd saved her from stripping at The G-Spot, I'd gone above and beyond, and she'd been downright salty to me when I'd walked in.

My lips curved of their own accord at the memory. *With the caterer. Did I want more salt for my canapé.* Why I smiled now while recalling her words then, I had no idea. That woman had giant balls and tits of steel and a spine of solid titanium. No wonder her kids were so . . . so . . .

Impressive.

"No. Momma says, 'Oh crumbs!'" Joshua said finally, cutting through my musings. "Or sometimes, 'Frankenstein and beans.'" He lifted his arm as though to wipe his nose on his shirt sleeve.

Again, I caught his wrist, huffing my impatience.

"For Christ's sake, blow your own nose, kid. You got working fingers, use them." I released his wrist and tapped the box full of clean tissues. "You don't cuss either? Never said the F-word?"

He set the box on his lap and plucked at the opening, curling back the lip of cardboard. "I have no reason to use that word." His eyes cut to mine, held, then he added, "Yet." Pulling out a tissue, he finally wiped his own nose.

Something about the way he said *yet* made me smile. "The day is coming, though?" I tapped his elbow with mine, whispering conspiratorially.

Joshua seemed to give my question some thought, answering solemnly, "Eventually."

My mouth curved again. Damn, I was having fun. This kid was fun. He didn't talk like I'd expected kids to talk. When was the last time I'd been surprised by anyone?

Uh, about a week and a half ago when their momma walked into your club offering to strip. That's when.

Fine. When was the last time I'd been surprised in a good way by anyone? I couldn't think of it. Despite the oozing liquid, despite his inability or willingness to blow his own nose when necessary, and despite his short stature and slightly creepy child-voice, this miniature human wasn't half bad.

Actually, he was more than half good. Joshua was awesome.

I can admit when I'm wrong. The last thirty minutes constituted the most enjoyable and interesting conversation I'd had with another person—not counting Beau—in months. As I reflected on this fact, I caught his baby sister staring at my face. Her marker hovered above the paper and she was eating the end of her long hair, chewing on a few strands and making them wet. She smiled at me, the hair leaking out of her mouth.

It should've been disgusting. Perhaps I was coming down with something, but I didn't think she was disgusting. She was aggressively adorable.

"You are not what I expected." I leaned back to get a better look at Joshua and his sister, no longer bothered by those cautious amber eyes he shared with his momma anymore. I could appreciate how discerning they made both him and Charlotte look.

He stared at me but said nothing, and I liked that, too. I liked that he didn't talk in order to say something or hear himself. How many adults did that? Not many.

"You've got layers, kid. I thought all kids your age were kind of—you know."

"Plebeian?"

My eyebrows ticked up. "Did you say 'plebeian'?" I couldn't have been more tickled.

"Yes."

"How do you even know that word?" What would this kid say next? I had no idea.

His gaze seemed to turn even more cagey and he whispered, "Do you know who Mike Duncan is?"

I searched my memory. "No," I whispered back. "Who is he?"

"That's how I know." Joshua nodded once, the movement intensely serious. "You should listen to him. He changed my life."

Before I could question who this Mike Duncan fella was who required us to whisper his name with reverence, someone kicked my shoe.

"This looks like some deep conversation." Beau moseyed up, grinning at the kid, then at me. "What are y'all talking about over here?"

"The Federal Reserve and Roman society during the days of Caesar Augustus," came Joshua's response.

"Uh . . ." Beau's attention bounced between us. "Okay, then. Food is ready when you are." He gestured to the little girl. "Sonya, you want to come eat? Your momma has a plate ready for you."

"No. I want to stay with Mr. Hank." She turned her blue-gray eyes to me, a hint of pleading there, and a pleasant sense of something I couldn't label had me sitting straighter with delighted surprise.

No one—and I mean absolutely no person on this whole green earth—has ever preferred my company to Beau Winston's. No. One. Not once.

Until now.

I couldn't help it. I grinned at Sonya. Then I winked.

She grinned back, blinking both her eyes then squinting like she was trying to wink but couldn't manage, and that made me toss my head back and laugh. Man, I loved this kid and I didn't even care she ate her hair, that's how adorable she was. Illegal levels of endearing.

"What's your middle name, Sonya?" I asked her.

"Marie," Joshua answered for his little sister. "Sonya Marie Mitchell."

I lifted a quick eyebrow at the fact that these kids apparently had their momma's last name instead of their daddy's, and addressed Sonya. "You are the cutest human being on the face of the earth, Sonya Marie. And that is a fact."

"You're cute, too," she said, and she didn't sound at all shy about it.

"Hank," Beau scolded, bringing my attention back to him. He'd donned a lopsided smile. "She's only four and she needs to eat."

"I'm almost five!" the cutie in question piped in.

"See? She's almost five." I hadn't known her age, but I'd figured she was less than seven. "Bring her plate over here. She can eat here, can't she?" I tugged the leg of the coffee table over. "We used to eat out here all the time."

He opened his mouth to argue, but Joshua cut in, "Can I eat with Mr. Hank too, please? I'm not finished."

Beau gave me a quelling look, though he still smiled, and turned back toward the kitchen. "I'll ask their momma. Be right back."

Joshua waited until Beau had taken three steps before angling his shoulders toward me. "France's central bank is called the Banque de France and it was founded waaaay before ours. Way back in the 1800s, even though they've had lots of different governments since then. They have a new government every fifty years, seems like."

"Don't you think it's good that they have that kind of flexibility?" I scratched my short beard.

"What do you mean?"

"Folks in this country seem to think the world would end if our current form of government changed. I'm not saying I want the government to collapse, but it definitely seems broken and needs some changing."

He lifted a hand between us, his palm facing me. "Don't get me started on the two-party system in this country. It makes no sense. And how we vote for the primaries is a travesty."

"Agreed." Man, this kid really got it. "Nothing is getting done—and possibly it's too broken to fix, and that's okay. I like the recent French model where they come together peacefully to throw it out if it's not working rather than treating documents written by old dudes from two hundred years ago like they're the fu—uh, friggin' Ten Commandments."

He nodded vigorously. "I agree. Why do people think the government is the same thing as the country? They're two different things. If the majority isn't represented, then I think the government is invalid. How can we call ourselves a republic?" Joshua's hand movements became frenzied and he jumped up like he couldn't hold still with all the excitement of our discussion. "Like when Julius Caesar took the power away from the senate!"

"Then they ceased being a republic." I nodded at his logic. "In France, the country remains, but—wait. What's she doing?" I lifted my arms up and away from my sides, looking to Joshua for help as Sonya plopped herself down on my lap. "What—what are you doing? What is she doing?"

"She's sitting on your lap," he offered unhelpfully.

"Yes, Joshua. I know she's sitting on my lap, but *why* is she sitting on my lap?"

Joshua started bouncing on the balls of his feet and swinging his arms back and forth. "She likes to snuggle and you got a grown-up lap."

"Hmm." My arms were still held up in an *I surrender* pose. Meanwhile, Sonya had wrapped her small ones around my chest.

"I'll help. Put your arms around her." Without waiting for me to comply, Joshua grabbed my wrists and positioned my arms around his baby sister. "There. Like that. That's what you do."

The little muffin tucked her head under my chin, her ear pressed against my heart. I caught a whiff of playdough, scented blue marker ink, and sweet-smelling soap. It was like holding a warm pillow, or a big, semi-clean puppy. I liked puppies.

A moment later, while I was still processing how I'd found myself in this lovely mess, one of her little hands reached for mine and pressed a folded-up piece of newspaper in my palm. She then immediately tucked her hands under her chin and lay limply against my chest.

I turned the small rectangle of paper around, inspecting it. "What's this?"

Joshua gave me a sidelong look, his arms pausing mid-swing. "If you want to know, open it." He spoke with a measured cadence, like I required information to be fed to me slowly.

I paused, thinking, but then opened the rectangle and studied the drawing it revealed. "It's a . . . it's a few letters. And lots of hearts."

"It's a love note. I get them from her all the time. See? That's her name and those hearts mean love." Joshua pointed to the letters that had been written in blue marker. They weren't written in a straight line but sorta in a cloud shape. All the right ones to spell *Sonya* were there, just not in the right order.

"Why would she write me a love note?"

Joshua heaved an exasperated-sounding sigh and started swinging his arms again for no discernable reason. "If you want to know, ask her." Once more, he used that measured cadence. He must've suspected I had difficulty keeping up with a seven- and a four-year-old, which was true.

Giving Sonya a little squeeze, I asked, "Honey, why'd you give me this note?"

Her aggressively adorable wee little-kid voice responded, "Because I love you."

Aghast, I said, "You don't even know me. You shouldn't love folks you don't know."

My words were met with a giggle. "You're silly, Mr. Hank. You should love everyone. That's what Jesus says. And I love you. And your face a lot."

I opened my mouth to contradict, to explain that she should never love a book based on its cover or a man based on his face, that loving everyone would ultimately break her heart over and over, and then she wouldn't be able to love anyone. I wanted to tell her that loving yourself and only those few folks that mattered and treated her right—and even then, loving with balance, ensuring the scales were always even, making sure to keep score—was the only way to avoid getting hurt or used, and that she should always demand proof of someone's love before she offered hers in return.

But then she tilted her head back, her little fingers reached up, and she stroked my beard like she was tenderly caressing a beloved pet.

"You got to love everybody because everybody needs love," she said. "And if we don't love them, who will?"

CHAPTER 8

CHARLOTTE

"... the love, respect, and confidence of my children was the sweetest reward I could receive for my efforts to be the woman I would have them copy."

— LOUISA MAY ALCOTT, *LITTLE WOMEN*

J'm not sure anything could have prepared me for the sight of Joshua dancing around and talking animatedly to Hank Weller while Hank cradled Sonya in his arms and nodded along, equally as animated, to whatever Joshua was saying.

While I stood at the entrance to the family room in shock, I watched as this man —the same Hank Weller who made sure, every chance he got, I knew how much my mere presence irritated him—brushed an absentminded kiss against the top of Sonya's head and grinned at Joshua.

My heart cracked, and I lost my breath with the spike of pain.

Any ideas I'd had about continuing on with my bookkeeper role at The Pony evaporated. I did not have the time, not when Joshua and Sonya were obviously so starved for adult interaction that they'd gravitated toward *Hank Weller* of all people.

What I did have were little people who needed me and who were obviously not receiving enough of my attention at home.

Frankenstein and beans! Get yourself together, Charlotte.

Making a firm mental note in all capital letters, I resolved to give Sonya more hugs and to find more time to listen to Joshua talk about topics that mattered to him. I would also figure out how to get Kimmy more time at the pool, and I'd enroll

Frankie in that preschool community theater camp as soon as I finished paying off the new water heater and AC system installed at the beginning of the summer.

I would help my cousin and I would do my best to sort out Hank's jumbled mess of a financial system during the next week, but then I had to give him my two weeks' notice. I needed to do better. I needed to be more present. I did *not* need more demands on my time and attention. Squaring my shoulders, I sucked in a bracing breath and crossed to Sonya and Joshua with measured steps.

Hank caught sight of me first, his eyes doing a double take at my approach. I didn't allow myself to guess as to why. My days of trying to read the male mind were at an end, so I avoided Hank's gaze, focusing instead on my children and the lingering lead weight in my chest.

"Hey, y'all," I interrupted as Joshua paused to take a breath. "Time for dinner."

Sonya turned her head and reached her hand out toward me. "Can't we eat in here, Momma?"

"No, baby. We're going to eat real fast and then go." I caught sight of a pile of used tissues on the corner of the coffee table and grabbed them. "Say thank you to Mr. Weller and then come on with me."

Joshua grumbled something I didn't hear and then turned back to Hank. "It was really nice talking with you. If you have any more questions about international banks or central monetary policy, let my mom know."

"Thanks, Joshua. I will." Hank helped Sonya climb off his lap and gave both kids a smile I'd never seen on his face before. It looked gentle and warm and it made my throat catch and my eyes sting.

This involuntary physical reaction always occurred when someone took the time to be kind to one of my kids or went out of their way to make one of them feel special. Being a single parent was often lonely and difficult and overwhelming and draining, but what frustrated me the most was the sense that I was the *only* person in the world who understood and appreciated how special these four humans were. Except for the odd occasion of an overworked teacher really taking the time, or another parent noticing and offering praise, it was solely up to me to make them feel and understand their immense value.

I'd never expected any such thing, any such kindness, from Hank Weller.

While I was distracted by confusion and my emotions, Sonya reached out and cupped Hank's face, her hand stroking his cheek. "Goodbye," she said, and I wasn't certain if she was talking to him or his beard.

"Goodbye, Sonya Marie." He captured her hand and kissed the back of it. "You take good care of your momma."

I almost choked at that.

But then Joshua said, "You should come over and play sometime. I have a lot of maps," and my brain snapped out of its stupor.

Hank's sharp eyes jumped to mine and I jolted, both of us talking over each other.

He said, "Well, now, perhaps if your mom is—"

And I said, "Mr. Weller is exceedingly busy and barely has any time to play."

Joshua looked between the two of us, his eyebrows furrowed, and Sonya gasped.

"Oh no! No time to play?" She looked over at Hank with sympathy, her bottom lip protruding. "That's so sad."

Reaching down, I picked her up before she tried to sit on his lap again and comfort him. Sonya was forever trying to comfort everybody. "That's what happens when you're an adult. Less time to play. It's the way it is."

"Unless you have kids," Sonya said, cupping my face with the same hand she'd pressed to Hank's jaw and sliding her nose against mine. She was such a lover. "You get to play with us all the time, Momma."

"That's right. Unless you have kids, and Hank has no kids, so . . ." I cleared my throat, unsure where I was going with that train of thought, especially since it wasn't true and it didn't matter. Plenty of adults without kids played all the time. Before more nonsense left my mouth, I said firmly, "Now, let's go. Thank you and goodbye, Mr. Weller."

With a hurried smile but without quite meeting Hank's eyes, I grabbed Joshua's hand and marched us into the kitchen, heat climbing up the back of my neck as I went. But I refused to surrender to embarrassment. I would do more, be a better mother so that Sonya didn't feel the need to cuddle up on the first open lap she spotted and Joshua didn't feel so starved for engaging conversation that he bent the first random ear he found. That's what needed to be done and so I would do it.

And under no circumstances would Hank Weller ever be invited over to *play,* nor would I be continuing at The Pony.

Talk about a wake-up call.

* * *

Since I'd been allowed to unilaterally define my self-explanatory shift hours, I decided to arrive at The Pony between 2:00 PM and 3:00 PM Wednesday through Sunday and leave between 10:00 PM and 11:00 PM for the remainder of my time working at the club. One full work week should allow me to accomplish everything necessary, including locating my cousin, the set up of FastFinance, the import and categorization of last year's numbers, and the automation of payroll such that I wouldn't be leaving Hank or anyone else in a lurch.

And I promised myself that if he had questions after I quit, I wouldn't respond with, "Figure it out, it's self-explanatory." I would make myself available to help.

Whether he knew it or not, he was helping me find my cousin. And that's what decent people do.

But I would have to corner him about the discrepancies before quitting. I needed my questions about income percentages and payouts answered so that I could fully set up the automations. I couldn't do it if he wasn't willing to help me help him.

On Wednesday, I arrived at The Pony slightly after 2:30 PM and almost plowed right into Hank.

"Oh!" I stepped backward, my bottom hitting the door and making it swing open again.

Hank turned and glanced at me, his expression morphing from surprised to something else to neutral in the blink of an eye. "What are you doing here so early?"

I thought about making some prickly rejoinder reminiscent of yesterday when I'd told him that since my hours were self-explanatory, I'd explained them to myself. Instead, because my time here was limited and I still felt a little tender toward him for being so kind to my kids, I said, "To set up FastFinance, I need you to log into your bank accounts, restaurant system, and credit cards to grant the program access. I'll then import the data and begin categorizing it so we can automate payroll by next week."

He seemed to lose his air of indifference as I spoke, and he nodded eagerly when I'd finished. "Okay. When? Is now good?"

"Now is fine." I walked past him and toward my office. "Let me log in and we can get started."

I sensed him trail after me, and my back straightened, a little shiver running down my spine. I hadn't expected to see him so soon, nor had I expected him to be eager to upgrade to FastFinance. I'd planned to track him down later inside the club and had mentally prepared myself for an argument.

Since that wouldn't be the case, I'd have to do something with all this excess fighting-energy. Maybe I'd do some pushups in my office after we'd finished.

I walked into the office and opened the laptop, quickly signing into the device and then running the FastFinance app, signing in there as well. I also pulled out the stack of payroll spreadsheets I'd printed on Sunday, a paper trail of contradictory payouts and percentages. Hopefully, I could leverage Hank's interest in FastFinance to force some answers out of him. Once he did, I would thank him for his time and then turn the whole of my attention toward finding my cousin.

Hopefully by the end of the evening, I'd know where Heather was and how to contact her.

Hank wheeled an office chair through the door and sat next to me, angling his long legs to one side as I clicked through the screens necessary to link his other accounts. Hank filled in all the required fields to grant access, typed in the one-time password code when prompted, and that's when I pounced.

Clearing my throat while we waited for the accounting systems to sync, I said, "I was thinking of going back through the last three years and assigning expenditures based on the categories defined in the spreadsheets."

He glanced at me, looking genuinely curious. "Why?"

"Then you could compare year over year costs, see if what made money three years ago is still working for you. Or, conversely, see if something you've been buying for years is suddenly eating into your bottom line. It would help you maximize profits."

"Makes sense." Perking up, he nodded enthusiastically. "Actually, yeah. Good idea, that would really help. And you'll still have payroll ready? Next week?"

"About that . . ." I cleared my throat again, hesitating.

"What? What is it?"

"I'm sorry to be the one to tell you this, but it appears Fred mishandled the payroll."

Hank reared back. "What do you mean? He was skimming money?"

"No. I don't think so. It looks like he was overpaying some of your contractors while underpaying others."

"Are you serious?"

"Unfortunately."

His eyes narrowed with plain suspicion. "How do you figure that?"

I explained to Hank how the percentages given to each dancer changed from week to week. I'd decided to approach the issue this way rather than ask him again for the breakdown. It seemed like Hank didn't like to be asked for anything. He wanted me to figure it out.

My son Joshua was the same way. He never volunteered anything about his feelings. I had to make an assumption in order for him to confirm or deny it, but he never answered direct questions.

"I went back three months and they're all over the place, and inconsistent. For example"—I picked up the last six payroll summaries and showed him my findings—"one week Tina is making twenty percent of her food bill and the next week she made five. It's like he pulled the numbers out of thin air."

"Jesus." Hank's eyes were rimmed with surprise as he picked up the sheets I'd printed.

I gave him a few minutes to study the documents before adding, "Unless this was purposeful, I can go back and straighten it out, but that means you might have to pay people for their lost income. And that might be—"

"Expensive." Hank dropped the papers and leaned forward, setting his elbows on his knees and covering his face. "Goddamn it."

I grimaced at his taking of the Lord's name in vain, studying the top of his head and curtailing the instinct to sift my hands though his hair to soothe him, and not because I was worried about messing up his hair. He always had messy hair, *always*. Even in my earliest memories of Hank Weller, his hair had been an adorable disgrace, sticking out all over the place. He probably showered at night and never brushed it during the day.

But you know what? It looked like sex hair and it suited him. Hank seemed so distant and emotionless, controlled and exacting all the time, the messiness of his hair was a reminder that Hank was indeed human, a handsome, sexy, alluring human who was also prone to being a surly butthead.

"Doesn't matter. I'll figure out how to pay for it. It's not their fault Fred fucked up their pay. Ultimately, it's my responsibility." He sat up abruptly, turning a stark expression my way. "Please do it. And go back as far as you can."

A small, admiring smile pulled at my mouth. Hank might've been a surly butthead around me, but he was a decent person. At least he was decent to his employees and staff, and that counted for a lot in my book.

"I can only go as far back as the restaurant system will allow, which is ten years."

"That's fine. I took this place over nine years ago, so use that as your starting point." Hank's stark eyes moved over me.

I allowed my smile to linger, trying to infuse my features with a dose of sympathy, hoping he'd see I was on his side as I asked, "Can you please send me the right percentages? I can't refer back to historical records for the information, so it's not *self-explanatory*. If you want me to fix this, then I need the real numbers."

The side of his mouth ticked up, a slight spark brightening the hazel of his eyes and turning them gold. "Yes, Ms. Mitchell," he said, his tone somewhere between amused and conciliatory. "And I apologize. I should have sent you the house cuts right from the start."

"Yes, you should have." I lifted my chin and spoke my thoughts before I could catch myself. "You know, I'm not your enemy, even though you seem to think I am."

Hank surprised me by asking, "Aren't you?" and the question sounded real.

Straightening in my seat, I peered at him. "Of course I'm not." I had no idea whether he was being silly or serious. The question had been silly, but he looked entirely serious. So I asked, "What have I ever done to you?"

His pointed stare felt apprehensive. "Are you messing with me?"

"No. Why? What did I do?" Now I was on the edge of my seat and wracking my brain and beyond frustrated. Could this supposed slight explain his rudeness when I'd tried to audition? Why he always made a bracing face when he saw me around town? What could I have possibly done? Prior to last week, I hadn't spoken to him in years.

"You honestly have no idea." His forehead cleared of wrinkles and he tapped his fingers on his knee.

I crossed my arms. "No idea about what? Please, enlighten me."

"Your ex-husband ran off with one of my dancers."

My expression immediately narrowed into a glare. "And that's my fault how?"

"No, Charlotte. That's not your fault. But"—he leaned closer—"people in town blame me for Buckley leaving. They blame my club, and I'd assumed you did—and do—as well."

He was speaking nonsense and I allowed my expression to tell him so. "I'm sorry, I think I need more coffee, but I don't . . . Wait." I blinked. "Are you saying—hold on." I leaned back to get the full measure of him. "Are you saying folks around here" —I spun a finger in the air—"are trying to punish you and The Pony for Kevin leaving town? And you think I've been holding a grudge about it all this time? Are you serious?"

"As spit in soup."

"That's hooky."

The corner of Hank's lips tugged upward. "Hooky?"

"Yes. Hooky. Kevin didn't abandon me." I pressed the fingertips of both hands against my chest. "I'd asked for a divorce the month before he left town. I didn't know he'd run off with that Bambi woman until a week after it happened." I'd felt so much guilt about asking him to leave at first, wondering if I was being selfish and putting my needs above the possibility that he would eventually be a good dad one day. Was I depriving my children of a relationship with their father? Assuming he ever decided to wake up and be one?

I got over that fear real quick once he was gone.

Hank's eyebrows arched high on his forehead. "You left him? Before Carli?"

"Was her name Carli? If so, correct. Kev wasn't living with us. He didn't visit the kids that month after moving out, never asked to." The kids hadn't asked for him either, but I wouldn't share that detail. "He got an apartment in Knoxville, and at that point we only spoke through our lawyers. If folks are blaming you, that's like shaving a hairless cat." At his persistent confusion, I added, "It makes no sense."

Hank studied me, his features frozen, then eventually sucked in a deep breath. "That information isn't widely known, Charlotte. I certainly had no idea you'd asked Kevin for a divorce or kicked him out months prior."

"What did you want me to do? Take out an advertisement?"

"No," he drawled, his jaw working. "But if people had known, then it would've saved me a bunch of trouble."

I blinked at him, stunned, unable to believe my ears, and surrendered to my sarcastic impulses before I could hold my tongue. "Oh. I'm sorry, Hank. My marriage had fallen apart and my baby had colic, so I wasn't sleeping, and I didn't know how or if I'd have money to pay the mortgage or pay for food. But you're right, I should've been thinking about your good standing in the community."

He held his hand up, rolling his eyes. "All right, all right—"

I wasn't finished. "I know how much your spotless reputation means to you, how you never do or say anything to shock the locals, like using your parents' house on Bandit Lake to throw raging parties in middle and high school and charging for entry *and* mandatory valet parking."

"Okay. That was—"

"Or stealing your daddy's Mercedes and running away to Mexico for a summer."

His jaw worked. "Now, wait a minute."

"Or dropping out of college during your senior year to buy and reopen a rundown strip club in your hometown. How blind and selfish of me." I pressed my fingertips to my chest once again; his attention flickered there. "Please, forgive me for my oversight, Mr. Weller."

Hank's lips formed a firm line, his eyes narrowing even as they shone bright with humor. Maybe he didn't like it, but he definitely thought my sass was funny.

"Fine, Charlotte. Your points are good ones." Despite his best efforts, a smile finally claimed his lips, and his eyes slid over me, lingering on my hand still resting on my chest, in a way that made my stomach feel fluttery. "In retrospect, I reckon I understand why some people—without being aware you'd already left Kevin—decided I had culpability. I run this club and I thought you two were still together. I could've stepped in and discouraged the acquaintance. I didn't."

"That shouldn't be your job." On impulse, I started to reach out for his hand and then stopped, yanking mine back and curling it into a fist on my knee. His fingers stopped their tapping. "If I see a quadruple bypass patient with uncontrolled high blood pressure eating a bag of potato chips, no one expects me to step in and take the bag away. People in this country have the freedom to screw up their lives however they wish and would throw a fit if they couldn't, but folks in town expect you to be the cock-blocking big brother of Eastern Tennessee?"

Hank barked a laugh at *cock-blocking big brother*. "I'm not your brother."

"Exactly. Kevin is responsible for Kevin—that's how adulthood works. Go on and tell me." I made a *gimme* motion with my hands. "What have folks been doing that has your boxers twisted so tight? It must've been harsh, given the dirty looks you've been sending my way."

Full-on grinning now, Hank leaned an inch closer. "You really had no idea?"

"I really had no idea and I've never blamed you for what happened with Kevin. I've been kinda busy, in case you hadn't noticed. And no one gossips to me about my own divorce. They give me lots of *Bless your heart*s, tuna casseroles, and pity. Which, whatever. I like tuna, even if it's pity-tuna."

He chuckled and I joined him while we swapped stares, his pretty eyes absent their earlier prickly and butt-hurt quality. They almost looked . . . warm.

Hope swelled, confusing me. I didn't know what I was hoping for, and propelling me to fill the silence. "Did people make your life difficult?"

Hank leaned his elbow on the desk, filling my vision. "Nothing some TV dinners and a good paint job didn't fix."

I didn't understand what TV dinners had to do with this situation, but I let it go. Since Hank seemed to be in a mood to clear things up, I now had a follow-up question. "You knew what was going on with Kevin and Bambi?"

His expression sobered and he nodded.

"How long?"

"About six months, or a little less."

Absorbing this news, I allowed my unfocused attention to drift beyond Hank, feeling the now-familiar void where my love for Kevin used to be, as well as an odd sense of relief. We'd moved back to Green Valley six months prior to me asking for a divorce. He'd probably started cheating with Bambi the same month we returned to my hometown.

If second-guessing in the face of irrefutable evidence were an Olympic sport, I'd be a gold medalist. The old fear constantly crept in, worrying I'd made the wrong decision asking Kevin to move out. But learning that he'd been cheating on me as soon as we moved helped ease my irrational fears.

What kind of example did I want to set for my sons and daughters? How could I teach my sons it was perfectly fine to step out on their spouses? Break their promises? How could I tell my daughters to accept less than what they deserved? I wanted to lead by example, not only with my words.

But even now, even knowing how long he'd been carrying on with Bambi, and as ridiculous as it sounded, part of me still hoped Kevin would return one day a changed man, someone worthy of being a father, willing to be the fun-loving man I'd married, and want to have a relationship with our kids.

Movement had me refocusing my attention on Hank.

"I knew for a few months they were messing around and I did nothing." His smile gone, he leaned back slowly, removing his elbow from the desk and looking contrite, not an expression I'd ever expected to see on his face. And his tone was softer than I'd ever heard it. I half expected him to follow the admission with another apology. He did not.

I nodded mutely as I had no further follow-up questions. For the record, I didn't believe marrying Kevin had been a mistake. I was glad we'd married. I now had four amazing children. My mistake had been hoping for the best for too long when all evidence pointed to the worst.

"Your kids are great," he blurted, surprising me. His gaze dropped to the desk for a moment then returned to mine. "I enjoyed talking to them, to Joshua and Sonya, on Tuesday. They're . . . really great."

"They're the nice ones." I smirked. "Kimmy and Frankie are my hellraisers. If you see them coming, run—don't walk—in the other direction."

He chuckled, but I didn't. I was serious.

For a protracted moment, Hank and I simply looked each other. He wore a new expression, one I'd never seen before and didn't know how to read. And you know what? I didn't want to. I was done trying to decipher looks that didn't belong to my children. I surrendered to my Hank Weller illiteracy.

I only have four servings of sugar. I need to stop trying to scrape the bottom of the bag for another half cup.

"I'm sorry if I overstepped," he said, still wearing that new expression I refused to interpret.

"Overstepped?"

"You seemed upset when you came over to get Joshua and Sonya from me." Hank waved a hand through the air in a vague movement. "Like you didn't want them talking to me."

"What? No. I have no problem with you talking to my kids. Why would you think that?" I wrinkled my nose. "You must really think I'm a snob."

"I don't," he said a little too quickly.

I raised an eyebrow in challenge.

He ducked his head a smidge. "All right, fine. I suppose I did think you were a tad snobby prior to this conversation."

I lifted my hands a little way above my legs and then let them fall. "Well, I'm not. What you see is what you get with me. Feel free to engage my kids in conversation any time you like, but don't say I didn't warn you about Kimmy and Frankie. If you see us coming, you're not going to hurt my feelings if you duck behind a dumpster."

"Glad we cleared that up," he said, an enigmatic, subtle curve to his lips.

I sensed myself wanting to parse through and interpret his expression, so I glanced at my laptop. "I better get back to work. My boss is a real butthead."

He laughed and it quickly tapered into a version of that grin again. The one I used to be addicted to as a teenager. The one he'd never pointed at me until recently, and always while giving me the sense he wielded this grin without understanding the true nature of its power or lure. To Hank, he was probably simply smiling, not meaning anything by it. And I definitely wouldn't read anything into it.

Yet, in an alternate, hypothetical, fantasy universe, one where Hank *did* mean to tempt and suggest with that smile, I still had no spare energy to give. Not to Hank, not to Dave, not to anyone.

I closed my mind to the temptation of his features, a temptation he wasn't actually offering, and one which—even in that alternate, fantasy universe—I could never accept. Affixing a polite, business-appropriate smile in place, I said nothing and waited for him to leave. He was in my office, after all. And it wasn't like I could say, *Hey. Stop grinning at me so I can get back to work.*

Drawing in a deep breath, Hank stood and stepped around his chair. "Hey. Thank you for asking and pushing the issue. And I'm sorry I've made things hard for you. It's important to me that we have a professional environment here and I'll . . ." His chest expanded again. He frowned. I suspected his dissatisfied expression wasn't pointed at me but toward himself. "I haven't been fulfilling my obligations as your employer. I'll make myself more available for questions so you won't have to push at all."

His apology rocked my world more than his grin of temptation and I struggled for a moment to arrange my thoughts. Goodness. Was there anything sexier than a man who admits when he's wrong? *A man who's giving you a foot rub while admitting he's wrong.*

Wait.

No, no, no.

These thoughts were not allowed. Hank was my boss, he wasn't allowed to be this sexy. And I still planned to quit in one week. He'd probably start avoiding me again after. If I hadn't forced him to employ me, he wouldn't be speaking to me now. I would not permit the resurrection of my disastrous crush, not at my age. Not now, not ever.

He stood over me. It was my turn to speak, and the lull in conversation was on the edge of becoming noticeable.

I filled the silence with the first clumsy thing that came to mind. "Well, you know me." I pointed to myself with my thumbs, managing to croak, "Pushy is my middle name."

"Actually, Charlotte—" He breathed a light laugh, those pretty eyes scrutinizing and considering. "I don't think I know you well at all."

CHAPTER 9

CHARLOTTE

"I got no respect for a man who won't hit back. You kill my dog, you better hide your cat."

— MUHAMMAD ALI, *THE GREATEST: MY OWN STORY*

Since I now had the information needed to untangle the club's finances and set it on the right path moving forward, I needed to turn my attention back to the actual reason I worked at The Pony: befriending the dancers and finding Heather.

Not wanting to ask Hank for insight—the less we interacted moving forward the better, lest my crush reassert itself—I asked Dave for advice Wednesday night as he walked me to my car. Or rather, I suppose it was super early Thursday morning.

"If I wanted to bring in some food tomorrow for the dancers and staff, a special treat to thank them for their warm welcome, what should I bring? Muffins from the Donner Bakery at the Lodge? Or cream puffs? Or what?"

"Eh." He tilted his head back and forth. "I wouldn't bring in baked goods. Serafina, the chef, gets weird about that kind of stuff. And some of the ladies—the dancers—are always talking about their bodies and dieting. But what about a big fancy fruit tray?"

"Oh! I can do that myself." We reached my car and I pulled out my key fob to unlock the door.

"With, like, a healthy dip and less healthy dip." Dave reached around me and opened my door. "Do sugar-free peanut butter on one side and Nutella on the other. That way your bases are covered."

"Hmm. What if one of them has a nut allergy?" Peanut butter was contraband at the kids' school, and for good reason. "I'll bring in the nut dips and keep them covered and put out an allergy-safe dip, then ask if anyone has an allergy, and if not, put out the other dips. And I'll hold back the strawberries, too. Thanks, Dave." I smiled at the bouncer.

He returned my smile, hesitated for a moment, then said, "You have the most beautiful smile, Charlotte. I hope it's okay for me to say so."

I pressed my lips together but was unable to hide the pleasure his words gave me. Dave hadn't asked me out again. He'd been nothing but professional and friendly since my first day. I didn't mistake this sweet talk now for a renewal of his interest. It was clear that Dave was simply a good person paying me a kind compliment.

"It is perfectly fine for you to say, but thanks for checking. And I think you've got a beautiful smile, too. Thanks for giving it to me so often."

His smile widened and he stepped back. "Anytime. Drive safe."

Now I hesitated, a sudden question nagging at me. "Dave, may I ask—and please let me know if this is overstepping—why haven't you asked out one of the dancers? They all seem so lovely and sweet."

"Oh, they are, for the most part. But Hank has a strict no-fraternization policy with all the dancers. None of the staff can date them, and they can't date each other. Tina told me two dancers kissed backstage a few years ago after flirting for a few weeks and Hank ended their work agreements"—Dave snapped his fingers—"just like that."

I crossed my arms. "For kissing? That's harsh."

"I don't know. Hank, he . . . well, he knows the business." Dave's eyes moved between mine, calculating. "Hey. Did you know he's one of them?"

I blinked, about to ask *One of who?* but then a jolt of understanding hit me like a lightning strike. "Hank was a stripper? I mean, a dancer? Hank was an exotic dancer?"

"Was and is." Dave appeared delighted by my reaction. "We get both bachelorette parties and bachelor parties that want an all-male show, or a mix of both. Tina says it's mostly in the fall, but there's a few sprinkled throughout the rest of the year. I've only seen two so far. But Hank's got this—this team of five dudes plus him for those events."

I don't know why, but I felt like laughing. I was *floored*.

"You look surprised." He said this with a twinkle in his eye. "And a little disturbed."

"I am surprised." Without looking, I let my purse fall to the seat behind me and then propped my hand on the open door. "Can I ask, did he start stripping when he bought the club? Or . . .?"

"Tina said he stripped in college as soon as he turned eighteen. Some sort of super ritzy, exclusive gentlemen's club or high-class strip joint up in Boston. They supposedly catered to all tastes, kinks, and spectrums of sexuality."

"Well, okay then." My heart spasmed and the air in my lungs turned hot. My brain didn't know how to process this information, and the resultant emotions were an incoherent mixture of sad, curious, alarmed, and . . . *enchanted?* Why the heck was I enchanted?

"Yeah. Anyway. I only tell you because the man has walked the walk, and—"

"And swung on the pole?" The quip emerged before I could stop it.

Dave laughed. Then he rolled his lips between his teeth. "Sorry. I shouldn't have laughed at that."

"No. I shouldn't have said it. Sorry. I'm shocked." I continued pondering Hank and the club and everything I knew about both, and a new question occurred to me. "Hey, if there's sometimes male dancers here, do they all use the same dressing room?"

The process for accessing the dressing room had been explained to me last weekend. It was always locked from the inside and weighted to close automatically unless you put something on the floor to prop it open—which was forbidden. To enter, you had to ring the tiny doorbell and wait for someone to let you in. Unless you were a dancer. If you were a dancer, you knocked to announce yourself and then used your key.

I hadn't asked where the dancers kept their keys while working, but I burned with curiosity.

"No, guest dancers don't use that area." Dave paused, studying me, then asked, "Have you been inside the dressing room?"

I shook my head.

"It's not one big room like you might think. There is a shared area where house costumes are kept, a couple of big mirrors, emergency sewing and makeup supplies, that sort of stuff. But that's not half of it. The whole space is as big as the kitchens, bigger probably. Past the shared area, each of the regular dancers has their own changing room with a door that also locks."

"Wow." That seemed like a lot of privacy for people who were mostly naked in a professional capacity.

"For any dancer who isn't regularly on the schedule, Hank repurposes his office and the office you're using. He doesn't want his core dancers to be made uncomfortable by the presence of new people and there's only so many private rooms with locks back there."

"Does Hank have his own dressing room?"

"I don't think so." Dave scratched his chin thoughtfully. "I don't know, actually. Ask Tina. She's been here the longest. The offices don't have the bell system like the main dressing area does, but they have keys, so they're kept locked during those events that require guest dancers. It's a whole system and he gets really tense about it." Dave laughed lightly, giving me the sense he found Hank being tense amusing.

"He's so exacting about everything," I commiserated, but I didn't find Hank being tense amusing. It stressed me out.

"I don't know." Dave shrugged. "It makes sense once you get to know how he runs things. He's strict with the dancers and everyone else. The rules are spelled out, and he never bends them, no matter who asks. At first, I thought it was because he got off on controlling everyone. But once I found out about his history, I think he's so harsh because he understands the nature of the business? These people who come in here, they'd take advantage of the dancers if they thought they could get away with it. With Hank in charge, they know they can't, so they don't even try."

I cocked my head to the side, studying the barrel-chested bouncer. "You sound like you approve."

"I do. Makes my job easy, doesn't it?" Dave walked a few steps backward toward his own car. "This isn't the first strip club I've worked at, but it is by far the safest."

* * *

Tina, Hannah, Hope, Fiona, Jiff, Piper, Everly, Laney, Susannah, April, Kilby, Jenny, Sita, Mary, Brooke, and . . . Emma? Darn it. I couldn't remember the last one's name. It was either Emma or Ella and I didn't want to ask.

Repeating the dancers' names in my head over and over, I strolled down the hallway mid-afternoon on Thursday and paused at the door leading to the dressing rooms.

I'd taken for granted that Hank possessed a key since he was the owner of the club. But as I hesitated outside the door, my finger hovering above the button that would ring the bell, I questioned whether he had a key at all. I'd never seen him entering the dressing room or hovering anywhere near it.

Then again, according to Dave, Hank was one of the dancers and possibly had his own dressing room inside.

Hmm.

Shaking myself from the irrelevant thought detour, I rang the bell. Then I folded my hands, stepped back, and waited.

"Who is it?" came a voice from beyond the door.

"It's Charlotte. I—I brought—"

I didn't get to finish my sentence before the door was pulled open, revealing a tall, lean, tan, platinum blond, white woman with a bold, square jaw and lovely blue-green eyes. "Well, hello! Come on in," April said, waving me forward with a smile.

When I met April last week, she told me how she was originally from northern California. She'd spent some time in the film industry out there but ultimately preferred a career where she dictated how and when people touched her, and she loved working for herself.

"About that—I brought a fruit tray and it's in the breakroom. I wanted to say thanks to y'all for the warm welcome and to give you ladies a heads-up that it's in there."

"Stay right there," she told me. So I did. April had this aura about her. Maybe it was her height—three inches taller than my five-foot-ten-inches—or maybe it was the forthright cadence of her voice or the direct way she looked everyone straight in the eye, but when April told you to do something, you did it.

"Hey! Lovelies!" she shouted, turning her head slightly. "Charlotte brought food and it's in the breakroom. Come and get it!"

A chorus of *Awww* and *Thank you, Charlotte!* and *Yay!* and *Food?! I love food!* greeted our ears, making April and me laugh.

"Can she bring it back here?" Everly poked her head around the corner and pushed her glasses higher on her nose. Giving me a small wave, she whispered, "I skipped lunch and I'm starving. But I'm trying on new outfits and my shift starts in an hour." The curvaceous dancer widened her eyes with mock panic. "Do you mind, Charlotte?"

"Not at all. Let me go grab it." I tossed a thumb over my shoulder.

"Thank you. You're such a sweetie." Her sandy-blond head disappeared and I blinked at the spot where she'd been. I'd only ever seen Everly in brightly colored wigs before now.

"How can I help?" April asked. "Do you want me to move the food? Or should I stay here by the door?"

"I can get the fruit. But, uh, do you know if anyone is allergic to nuts? Or strawberries? I have a few different dips, but I don't want to break out the peanut butter if it's going to send someone into anaphylactic shock."

"No. No nut allergies and no strawberry allergies. Hope and I can't have wheat, Fiona is lactose intolerant, and I think Piper can't eat apples and pears. But I made dairy-free, wheat-free peanut butter cookies for the cookie exchange two years ago. Everyone partook. But thanks for checking, gorgeous." April winked at me, letting the door start to close. "I'll be right here when you ring the bell."

With one last smile, I strolled to the breakroom with a spring in my step. I really liked April, and Everly, and Hope, and Piper, and all the ladies. Not for the first time, I worried what would happen when I left. I hoped Hank would keep FastFinance and be open to learning the program and running payroll himself. I didn't want him hiring another out-of-touch bookkeeper and mucking everything up again. I'd been working day and night to fix the mess Fred made, and those ladies deserved someone looking out for them.

Distracted by the weight of these thoughts, I stepped into the breakroom without paying attention to the conversation coming from the table by the corner until the voices abruptly ceased.

Hannah and Hank.

I halted, taking in the scene. They hadn't been in here a few minutes ago when I'd dropped off the tray, but whatever they were currently discussing looked serious. A knot of worry twisted in my stomach. I hoped she hadn't said anything to Hank, not yet. Not until I found Heather and finished convincing him to adopt FastFinance.

Some of my fears were eased as Hannah sent me a small, watery smile. She looked miserable, and that made me worry for completely different reasons. Hank, meanwhile, didn't look up as I entered but instead stared at Hannah like she was an unsolvable problem, or she had an unsolvable problem.

"Everything okay?" I asked, hesitating by the doorway. "Should I come back?"

"It's fine." This response came from Hannah. She sniffled. Hank said nothing and continued staring at Hannah, scraping his teeth against his bottom lip, his leg bouncing with restless energy.

"I'm going to grab this tray and take it to the ladies," I said, narrating my movements. "I'll be out of y'all's hair in a sec."

"Actually, wait." Hank finally glanced my way while kicking a third chair out with his booted foot. "You might be able to help us."

"Okay." I sidestepped around the table where I'd placed the fruit, but I didn't sit in the chair he'd offered, instead placing my hands on the back of it. I didn't want to leave April waiting for me by the door to the dressing rooms. "How can I help?"

"Go ahead." Hank nodded to Hannah. "Tell her what you told me."

Hannah sighed and glanced down at her hands. I noted she held a crushed, used tissue. "I've been applying for some office jobs."

My gaze darted between Hank's fierce glare and Hannah's wobbly chin. "Is that a problem? I don't—I think—I mean, if you want to work in an office, then . . . what's the problem?"

"She got a job. A good one. But then one of the guys she'd be working with turned out to be a regular here. He recognized her and they let her go after a week."

Hannah's face crumpled and she dabbed at her eyes with the tissue. "I'll keep applying, I guess."

I knew Hannah had graduated with her associate degree two years ago and was almost finished with her four-year degree, set to graduate at the end of the fall semester with a bachelor's in business administration. She'd been working toward this for a long time, and my heart broke for her.

I swallowed around a swell of emotion and sat in the chair, hesitating a second before reaching over and holding Hannah's hand. "That sucks. You earned that job."

"It's okay." She sucked in an unsteady breath. "I guess I'm glad I didn't stop picking up my shifts here. Lesson learned."

Hank made an impatient sound and folded his arms, hunching and looking like the world's handsomest troll.

"It's not okay." I squeezed her hand. "And this might sound hollow, but it's their loss. Truly. Years from now, when you look back, you might even be thankful they let you go. Who wants to work for a place where they treat people like that? They might've saved you a bunch of heartache in the end, if you'd invested your time only to find out later how awful they are."

"I know." She closed her eyes. "I know."

I released her hand and sat back. "This is something I used to tell all my new hires when I was in charge of staffing at the Buckley company back in Vegas. When you apply for a job, it's not simply them interviewing you. You should be interviewing that company, too. You might be the best candidate for a particular position, but if their culture and priorities don't align with yours, then they aren't a good fit for *you*. Clearly, they aren't a good fit for you and are undeserving of your talents. Good riddance."

Hannah chuckled, peering at me and shaking her head. "Okay, Momma."

We were more or less the same age, but Hannah calling me *Momma* didn't bother me. I took being maternal as a compliment in all situations and contexts. "Now, come help me carry this big fancy fruit platter into the dressing room. I have strawberries and three kinds of dip in the fridge, and one is Nutella. There's nothing wrong that can't be made better with a little strawberry and Nutella magic."

Smiling finally, Hannah stood. "That does sound good. I'll grab the tray, you get the strawberries and Nutella."

Hank and I also stood, but he stopped me from following after Hannah with a hand around my wrist, drawing my attention to his. The man's grumpy expression had disappeared and his eyes gazed at me, their weight feeling warm and friendly. "Go on, Hannah. Charlotte will be there in a minute."

"This looks amazing, Charlotte," Hannah called over her shoulder as she left, her shoulders no longer hunched.

Hank waited until the sound of Hannah's steps had faded before speaking. "I want to thank you for your cool-headed approach just now." He lifted his chin toward the door to the hall. "My solution for Hannah had included taking out an ad in the newspaper and publishing John Wilson's pink pony along with a photo I have of him that he'd not want his mother to see. So, thank you. I appreciate you lending us all your expertise."

"You're welcome." I couldn't help but feel both proud and self-conscious in the face of his show of gratitude and kind praise, nor could I ignore the admiration I felt for him in the moment and how protective he was of Hannah, how much consideration he gave his employees and contractors.

Warmth rushed through me as we stared at each other before I realized a few seconds had ticked by and we were still staring at each other.

Crossing my arms abruptly, I worked to rearrange my expression from one of moony admiration to hopefully something resembling simple curiosity. "Uh, John Wilson? Who is that?"

"The regular who got Hannah fired." He released my wrist. "Still might put the photo in the newspaper, though. Or make him pay me not to."

I laughed at his rhetorical threat. But then, when he didn't crack a smile, I reared back. "You're serious?"

"Why not? He shames Hannah out of a job she earned, he should get a taste of his own medicine."

I gaped at him, my mouth moving but with no sound coming out.

"Think of me as the fairness fairy." He smirked; it looked mean with intent, anticipation of deeds not yet done. "People always get what's coming to them, sooner or later. And I've never minded being the person who delivers it."

CHAPTER 10

HANK

"Respect was invented to cover the empty place where love should be."

— LEO TOLSTOY, *ANNA KARENINA*

Upon leaving the Winston homestead last Tuesday after dinner, I'd immediately texted my lawyer to find and send me Charlotte's divorce settlement. I also wanted any depositions and all related court filings in public record.

Those two kids of hers had figuratively charmed my pants off. But when Charlotte had appeared and unceremoniously took them away, I'd felt oddly bereft and embarrassed, a modicum uncomfortable, and a bit more than a tad concerned about Charlotte's money problems. If she needed money, then the money was likely for her kids, which meant her ex's family wasn't contributing their fair share to Joshua and Sonya (and Kimmy and Frankie). The unfairness infuriated me. Someone needed to do something.

Friday morning, the day after Charlotte brought in that fruit tray and improved Hannah's outlook on life, I received the whole packet via email. After printing out the hefty load of documents, I headed over to Genie's Country Western Bar for a sandwich and beer, wanting to avoid being interrupted by club business or have Charlotte stumble across me reading through her divorce settlement. She might've considered it an invasion of privacy.

I did not.

The documents were public record. If she didn't want folks reading them, she should've asked they be sealed. I needed to understand why this woman—who clearly should've been heading up her own company or working as a CFO for a giant corporation—wanted to strip at The Pony for money. Something didn't add up.

Despite Kevin's extensive real-estate portfolio, Charlotte only got their big house in Green Valley and a three-bedroom, 1700-square-foot vacation beach cottage on the coast in North Carolina. Both properties were fully paid off. She'd also received a relatively modest—given who the Buckleys were and how much money Kevin made, according to his tax returns—amount of child support for each kid that paid until they were eighteen and increased at the same rate as inflation year over year. No matter if she got married or won the lottery, the child support was guaranteed.

Additionally, Kevin (meaning, Kevin's daddy) had agreed to set up a trust fund for each of the kids to help fund college, or to give them a start in life if they didn't go to college, or whatever. Charlotte didn't have any access to those accounts; they were controlled by Buckley Sr. until the child came of age, but a minimum amount had been guaranteed. The Buckleys also paid into a health savings account for each of the kids. But not for Charlotte.

According to the records, the only thing Charlotte had been adamant about was that Kevin and his family be denied unsupervised access to her kids or be allowed to dictate where they went to school. The Buckleys had wanted all the kids to go to Belmont and had noted the preference in the final settlement, going so far as to offer to pay for tuition and give Charlotte a stipend for every kid who graduated from the school. It was the same boarding school I'd been forced to attend.

If memory served, her kids currently attended the same school where Charlotte worked as a teacher's aide, a medium-sized charter school that had preschool through eighth grade. It was possible that the kids could go to Belmont for high school, but based on my reading of the settlement, it didn't seem likely Charlotte would go in that direction.

Obviously, Charlotte wanted total control over day-to-day decisions. It appeared that she'd traded both the stipend and the offer of a generous, irrevocable, lifelong monthly alimony payment for this one demand.

I'd told her once that she wasn't stupid. I'd been wrong. She was an idiot.

That said, if she was an idiot, then so was I. This payroll mistake Charlotte had found made me question all over again why I kept The Pink Pony. It wasn't my main or even tertiary source of income, and now it looked like it would be costing me more than it earned this fiscal year.

You should sell it.

Batting away that thought, I turned my attention back to marinating in Charlotte's poor business decisions rather than mine. Not only had Kevin's family been in a rush to get the divorce settled, the alimony payment would've guaranteed a life of leisure for her. She could've delayed signing the settlement for years until she got everything. But she'd traded the money for immediate control over her kids' visits with their dad, dad's family, and schooling choice? That made no sense.

My lawyer had also preemptively requested access to the visitation documents. Kevin had been given two weekends of court supervised visitation each month that he'd never used—not once. He hadn't seen his kids since skipping town, at least not according to the court records. But his mother had.

The former Mrs. William Anton Buckley III—the first wife—visited with her grandkids once a month. Each of those visits had been supervised and took place at a park in downtown Green Valley near Charlotte's house. I vaguely remembered the woman from my days at Belmont. She seemed exactly like every other society matron I'd ever encountered, which is to say similar to my mother. Also, all her kids were assholes.

"Hey, Hank. Do you want another beer?"

I glanced up. Patty Lee stood at the edge of my booth, frowning at the spread of papers in front of me. I immediately started stacking them, not wanting her to see Charlotte's name. I still didn't believe I was doing anything untoward looking through Charlotte's court filings, but my definition of untoward often didn't align with that of the rest of society. Better to be safe than sorry. Patty and I were good friends, but so were she and Charlotte.

Charlotte and Patty are good friends.

I rubbed my bottom lip, turning this interesting fact over in my mind. "No more beer. I have work later."

She leaned her hip against the side of the booth. "Okay. Can I get you anything else?"

Yes. Information.

Something about Patty I sincerely appreciated was, unlike Beau, she never worried about being *nice*. She was kind but never focused on niceties. Like me, she spoke the truth and expected other folks to be adult enough to handle it. I could trust what she said. Plus, she was book-smart. If I ever joined a trivia team, I'd want Patty on my side.

Therefore, Patty being smart, and honest, and knowing both me and Charlotte real well meant her insight and advice would be especially valuable at present.

I surveyed the bar; it was the post-lunch lull; I was one of three customers in the big place. "Can I talk to you about something?"

"Sure." She also glanced around the bar. "Do you mind if I sit? I pulled a double yesterday and my feet are tired."

"Fine by me." I gestured to the bench across from me, then tucked the papers back into the large folder, out of sight.

Patty scooched into the bench and tucked her short, black hair behind her ears. Her chest rose and fell with a tired breath. "What's up?"

While studying this woman I'd spent years trying to figure out, wanting her to give me a chance but not wanting to be pushy about it, I wondered why it had taken me a mere two days to get over her. I'd been sore about the reason we broke up but hadn't felt particularly upset that it had ended. She'd called things off after our third date and we hung out as friends a week later.

Patty had always been beautiful. But I considered lots of women beautiful and knew lots of beautiful women. It had never been the physical with Patty that captured my attention. She had an intangible grace and confidence. She was cool under pressure. She knew she was smart but never felt like she was finished learning. And she was exceptionally talented at reading people.

My leg began to bounce. I forced it to stop. "Tell me, how long have you and Charlotte Mitchell been friends?"

"Why are you asking about Charlotte Mitchell?" Her expression didn't change, but her tone sounded suspicious.

I debated how best to answer without misdirection and settled on, "She works for me."

"I know." Patty gave me a once-over. "I admit, I was surprised when I heard. But she's always been good with numbers, and you needed a bookkeeper."

"Patty . . ." I sighed, tired of this discontent in the center of my chest. It had been growing steadily since Charlotte and I had shouted at each other outside the Winston house and I'd offered her the bookkeeping job. I didn't like the feeling, I didn't want it, and I thought I finally understood the source.

"What is it?" Patty's voice gentled. "You look upset."

"If I talked to you about something, asked your advice, will you promise to keep it between us?"

She leaned forward. "Is there—did something happen with Charlotte? At The Pony? Is she okay?"

"Promise me."

"Hank—"

Lowering my voice even though we were alone, I inclined my head forward. "Charlotte's fine, but I need to talk a particular situation over with you as a friend, something that's troubling me. I need to know you're not going to repeat what I say to anyone, especially Charlotte."

She blew out a long breath, her cheeks puffing out. "Fine. I promise I won't say anything to anyone."

"Especially Charlotte."

"Especially Charlotte—as long as keeping what you're about to say a secret from Charlotte doesn't ultimately hurt her, or her kids."

I thought about that, then nodded. "It won't."

"Then shoot."

Picking up my beer for a swallow, I decided not to second-guess my instincts. I needed perspective and I trusted Patty. I'd always admired her straightforward, honest approach to every person and situation, and I still did. I trusted her to be logical and well-reasoned even when her feelings were involved. The woman had an exceptional talent of separating her emotions and biases from a problem, never pulling her punches to spare feelings.

Which was ultimately why I confessed, "I think I'm attracted to her."

Her chin dipped, her eyes blowing wide. "Say what?"

"It's distracting. And unprofessional."

"Unprofessional?" Her voice cracked with the question.

"Yes. Thinking about her as much as I do, in the ways I've been thinking, is unprofessional."

"I see . . ." Her forehead wrinkled with a confused-looking frown, making me think she didn't actually see.

"See here, I don't want to lose her as a bookkeeper. I'm her boss. I shouldn't be thinking about or noticing her this way. I've never had this problem before and I don't know what to do about it. And if I could stop, I would've done so already."

"She's only been working with you for a week."

"Nine days, if you include today." I rubbed my forehead. "I know this is a *me* problem. I know this isn't her fault, she's done nothing to encourage me, nothing at all. But . . ." I grunted, not knowing how to explain how frustrated my own brain was making me. I peeked at Patty.

She still gaped at me. "I—I honestly don't know what to say. Why would you hire her if you were attracted to her?"

"Wait. Let me back up a bit." I squirmed in my seat. "Charlotte asked for a job at The Pony."

"I know."

"No." I chewed on my lip as I argued with myself whether or not to tell Patty the whole story. I decided it wasn't gossip, it was context. "She . . . she wanted to be a dancer."

Her jaw swung open. "Are you serious?"

"Yes. She showed up in a nothing tank top and short shorts, her lace bra showing, which I wouldn't remark upon except you know how she usually dresses. It was a surprise. I thought I was dreaming."

Patty made a choking sound, her eyes bulging wider.

"I told her no, obviously," I rushed to add. "But I'd be lying if I said I hadn't been tempted to watch her audition." I didn't volunteer that I'd been attracted to the way Charlotte looked for a while, but I'd disliked her personality—or my perception of her personality—more than I'd liked her exterior.

"Thank goodness you didn't." Patty leaned back in the booth, still looking stunned. "Why did she want to dance at The Pony? Didn't she worry about how people would react?"

"You should ask her that."

Patty frowned, her gaze falling to the table. "She's always been kinda clueless about that sort of thing. People gossip and it's like she doesn't even hear it or think it matters. It matters. Her kids would've suffered in the court of public opinion. She can be so brainless."

I didn't like Patty calling Charlotte brainless, even though I agreed with her in this specific instance, so I redirected the conversation. "Anyway, she then tried The G-Spot and they offered her a place on their schedule. That's when Beau inserted himself." I proceeded to tell Patty the rest of the story, about Beau dragging me over to rescue Charlotte and offer her a job—any job, as long as it wasn't as a dancer—but once I realized she could replace my bookkeeper, I offered her that position instead.

"Last week, she started. And she's doing a real bang-up job. She has us moving over to a new financial system and she already showed me some reports, fixing some terrible messes Fred left. She's also real good with the human resources stuff. I think she'll be able to help some of the dancers with their résumés, the ones who are ready to move elsewhere, into different careers. I'm impressed."

"And that's why you're attracted to her," Patty filled in, crossing her arms and, if I was reading her right, looking mildly irritated. "You think she's impressive."

I considered Patty for a tick, her posture, the turn of her lips. "Why would you assume that?"

She huffed a laugh devoid of humor. "That's why you wanted to date me."

Rearing back an inch, I studied my friend. *What put a bee in her bonnet?* "Is it so wrong to be thought of as impressive?"

"Hank, you make surface-level judgments about people and define them based on one thing. Then you put them in buckets without actually knowing who they are. You were never attracted to me, we had no chemistry, and you're probably not attracted to Charlotte either. We're in your impressive bucket, and so we're someone you'd like to date. I mean, Charlotte is an odd choice for this bucket, but that must be what you've done. It's what you always do to women you claim to be attracted to."

I shook my head, ready to deny her claim. Admittedly, I'd felt no chemistry with Patty during our dates, so the theory held water in Patty's case. But that wasn't the case with Charlotte. *Definitely not the case with Charlotte.*

"You did the same thing to Sienna Diaz in college. She told me how you two dated," Patty went on, picking up my half-empty beer and placing it on a coaster. She then produced a towel and wiped off the water ring left behind. "You thought she was impressive, and so she became someone you wanted to date. Same thing with

Genevieve Taylor. She graduated from the right school, is the best defense lawyer in all of Tennessee, will likely run for office next year, and so she is date-worthy."

I mulled over Patty's words. Patty was impressive. Odd but impressive. She had several advanced degrees—two PhDs and a master's, all from Baylor—that she had no intention of ever using. She was a perpetual student, she loved learning. She'd turned her momma's business around when she was seventeen years old, and now they were thinking about franchising. She was a hard worker, great at softball, and a talented painter. Patty was definitely impressive.

"I still don't see the problem with admiring an impressive woman." I picked up my beer for a gulp, careful to put it back on the coaster.

"There's nothing wrong with it. But don't mistake it for attraction. A woman wants to be wanted for more than her accomplishments!"

I snorted. When I thought of Charlotte, when I'd caught myself daydreaming about Charlotte more and more since she'd strolled into my club, wearing her tiny gold cross and black tank top, the fantasies had nothing to do with her accomplishments.

"Go on." Patty hit the table. "Tell me what else you find impressive about Charlotte. I know there is a list."

"She's . . ."

"Yes?"

I scratched the side of my jaw. "She's a good mom." *And her kids—the middle two, at least—are amazing.*

Patty blinked once, frowning. "And?"

"She's really strong. I mean, she can lift a crate of whiskey, no problem. I caught her bringing in liquor crates with our bartender on Wednesday." It was sexy as fuck.

"So can lots of people." Patty's gaze narrowed.

"No, listen. We had to move tables around the main room last weekend, and she pitched in like a trooper, lifting loads like Dave, Henry, and me. And she's funny—so damn funny. Sweet. Too sweet. And witty." My eyes moved to a spot over Patty's head. "She doesn't seem to get embarrassed no matter what, and I love that. And Christ, her body. I can't stop thinking about her legs. She's got this freckle on her knee, right above the kneecap, and I keep looking for it when she wears shorts or skirts. Isn't that stupid?" I chuckled, grinning at Patty. "I love that she can laugh at herself and makes me laugh at myself and . . . What?" I stopped talking.

Patty's eyes were enormous and her mouth had fallen open.

"Hank!" She reached over and smacked my hand. "You *like* Charlotte."

"That's what I've been saying."

"No. You said that you were attracted to her. But you *like* her, too. You like her as a person. She's not doing anything, she's simply existing, and you're falling for her.

And I'm sorry, but these things you're listing don't sound 'impressive.'" Patty put finger quotes around the word *impressive*.

I scoffed, offended on Charlotte's behalf. "Excuse you?"

"No, no. Don't misunderstand. Me, Genevieve, Sienna, we're all impressive on *paper*. We could be garbage-fire humans with the depth and personality of a Japanese land snail, but our résumés look amazing. However, Charlotte, what has she done? What has she 'accomplished'? Hauling liquor crates? Having freckly knees?" Patty turned her head to the side, smiling at me.

"She's accomplished plenty," I ground out, shifting in my seat. Perhaps it was a bad idea to discuss this with Patty.

"How many degrees does she have? How many movie deals? Does she have an Oscar? Or did she graduate top of her class from Princeton law school?"

Letting my head rest against the back of the booth, I scowled at Patty, not liking what she was implying. It sounded like she was saying Charlotte was less-than because she didn't have fancy degrees or awards, and I took extreme issue with that.

"Let me put it this way instead." She drummed her fingers on the wood surface, making tapping sounds with her short nails. "Would Genevieve and I laugh at ourselves? Are we self-deprecating? Do we have any freckles on our knees?"

"I don't know. Why does it matter? You both broke up with me."

"You seem to like those things. And are we sweet? Are we too sweet? Are we witty? Do we get embarrassed often?"

"I have no idea."

She hit the table again. "And yet, you dated both of us. Tell me Hank, why did you like me for so long?"

My gaze lost focus and drifted over Patty again, not wanting to answer because the first thing that popped into my head was *you're impressive*.

Licking my lips, I said, "You're pretty. And honest. Hardworking—you have a solid work ethic. And . . ."

A small, superior-sounding chuckle left her. Giving her back my attention, I found her shaking her head.

"Face it. You *like* Charlotte. You like who she is as a person. You're attracted to her personality as much as you're attracted to her body and beauty. You're used to making judgments about worth based on shallow factors, based on what you think you *should* like rather than what you *actually* like, and that's why you feel conflicted."

"That's bullshit. You make it sound like you and Genevieve and Sienna are shallow. You're not."

Ignoring me, she added, "Your parents and that stupid boarding school you went to brainwashed you to only notice people based on how good they look on paper.

Yeah, you fought against it tooth and nail, but it seeped in. Deep down, you're not like that, not really. If you were, why would Beau Winston still be your best friend?"

"Are you kidding me?" I curled my lip. "Everybody likes Beau. He's awesome."

"Yes. In Green Valley, everyone loves Beau. But if you were to take Beau to a dinner party with your old boarding school chums, he's a local auto mechanic and that would make him the butt of every snobby joke. If you were to take Charlotte, she's a divorced single mom of four kids, college dropout, and teacher's aide. That's who she is on paper. She'd hardly fare better than Beau—or you. You're a strip club owner from BFE Tennessee. You'd both be sneered at, whereas you take me with my PhDs from Baylor, or Genevieve with her degree from Princeton and impressive court record, or Sienna and her Oscar, and everyone would immediately agree we belong there."

"Wait a minute. You—" I had trouble drawing in a full breath. Patty's true meaning finally permeated, leaving me feeling shitty. "You're not like that."

"I'm not. Nor is Genevieve or Sienna. Which was ultimately why we all broke up with you. None of us wanted to be a trophy."

My lips parted along with the clouds in my mind, the mysteries of my previous failures revealed. "You thought I was using you?" My voice turned dusty. "I was using you for your impressiveness?"

That was my parents' modus operandi and I'd done everything in my power to never be anything like either of them. This revelation felt like being sucker-punched.

"No, and yes. You weren't using me on purpose. But if you're honest with yourself, you would admit that you weren't really attracted to me either."

I swallowed, looking beyond her. "I was—"

"You weren't."

Her declaration had me focusing on her again.

She smiled at me like was I cute. "You thought I was pretty, and I am pretty, but my knee freckles never drove you to distraction. You never waxed poetic about my legs and sweetness while in a bar sitting across from your ex-girlfriend."

"Fine. You have me there." I released a tremendous breath, the simmering discomfort in my chest intensifying. "What do I do about Charlotte?"

"Oh, honey." Patty made a soft, sad clicking noise with her tongue. "There's nothing to do other than try to see her as a friend, try to curtail your attraction, and end those feelings before they grow too big. It's only been about a week. Who knows?" She shrugged. "It could go away on its own."

I took another swig of my beer. *That seems unlikely.* How was I supposed to stop being attracted to someone I didn't want to be attracted to in the first place?

"Hank, you know nothing can ever happen between you two, right?" Patty tilted her head, inspecting me from a new angle.

"I know." Using my thumbnail, I picked at the corner of the damp label at the back of my beer bottle. "I'm her boss, and unless she quit—"

"No. That's not what I mean."

This earned her a raised eyebrow. "I'm not asking out my employee, Patty. That would be highly unprofessional."

She lifted her hands up, showing me her palms. "Sure. But even if she weren't your employee, or you didn't have high standards in the workplace, the main issue is her kids."

"What's wrong with her kids? Her having kids doesn't bother me."

Patty glared at me like I was a dummy. "Nothing is wrong with her kids, but they are part of a package deal. Charlotte can't ever be in a relationship with you for the same reason she can't be a stripper."

I blinked, confused, and then I flinched. Patty's meaning finally dawned on my thick-as-molasses brain.

Well, fuckity fuck fuck fuck. A hot breath vacated my lungs, and my mouth curved with a bitter twist. I felt raw.

Of course.

Charlotte couldn't be with me. Not ever. She was 100% saint and I was 100% sinner, an undesirable in this town. I'd made certain to earn the title with every methodically subversive choice I'd made since turning twelve. And hell, I'd gleefully worn my badge of dishonor, prideful of my place as a thorn in the sides of polite society and decent folk while succeeding in a business they hated but couldn't do anything about.

I was part of the Chamber of Commerce. Members of the city council frequented my place of business. My club didn't contribute to crime, didn't decrease property values, and provided gainful employment for a staff of nine citizens in our small town. That didn't count the independent contractors (i.e., dancers). My club served as a venue for charity auctions and community events. They loved the novelty of visiting a hedonistic hub for a single night and then going to church the next day.

"You know what people would say, how they'd react." Patty's tone adopted an academic quality, coolly logical. "This town is small and Charlotte's kids would be shunned. Not by everyone, but those sweet children would suffer if you publicly dated their mother. Her mom church group would question her morals, she'd be stared at and whispered about for cavorting with a strip club owner. Parents wouldn't want their children playing with her children. Her job at the charter school might be an issue, too."

There was no denying what Patty said was likely true, and she'd know. Going on three dates with me had cost her some acquaintances, gotten her kicked off a charity committee, and made her the subject of extreme gossip. She hadn't seemed to care, but she was a single woman and her own boss.

The thought of Joshua or Sonya being shunned? Charlotte losing her teaching job? I found I couldn't swallow.

"And don't forget about the Buckleys. I don't know how much you know about her divorce, about what she gave up and how hard she fought, but her ex's family would definitely start sniffing around again and try to take custody."

Like hell.

An unexpected spike of anxiety hit me square in the stomach, immediately followed by a fierce, hot wave of protectiveness, strong enough to catch me off guard and make my tongue feel too thick to form words. I had to force my hand to loosen its grip on the beer bottle.

"Sorry, Hank." Smiling, but now with a generous slathering of sympathy, Patty scooched toward the end of the booth's bench seat. "I like you, and I really like Charlotte, and I know for a fact that if she were attracted to you, if she reciprocated your feelings, it wouldn't occur to her to care what other people thought. Like I said, she can be brainless that way."

"But I would know, and her kids would pay the price," I muttered, more miserable than I had a right to be.

My choices had always been my own, impacting only me, and I'd preferred it that way. It had never occurred to me I might one day want something—or someone—and my decisions would or could negatively affect them, making their life difficult.

Patty sighed and said, "Maybe . . ."

I searched her unfocused, introspective features, my chest squeezing. "What? What is it?"

If she had a solution, I was all ears.

"Never mind." She grimaced, her gaze apologetic. "It was a ridiculous idea."

"Tell me."

Bracingly, she said, "I know you've never touched your trust fund or your parents' investments. They've got to be enormous by now."

"I do dip into my parents' investments from time to time, usually when I want to give money away to people they hated."

She made a face. "You know what I mean. You could easily live on it or use it to buy a new business."

Rubbing my chin, I considered her statement. Clearly, she had no idea about my other income sources, and that was fine. But I wanted to be certain I understood her point. "You mean run an additional business that makes me look less offensive to the Bible-thumping folks?"

"No." Her expression turned bleak. "What I mean is, if you really wanted to pursue Charlotte, if you were serious about it, you could sell the club and do something completely different. Not run two businesses. You can't keep The Pony if you want to pursue Charlotte."

I stared at her, absorbing this bit of wisdom. Given how hypocritical and judgmental "decent" folks in this town were, I didn't doubt she was right.

"See? Not a good idea." She waved her hand between us like she was shooing the suggestion away. "Never mind."

It wasn't as ridiculous as she thought. *I could reach out to that agent fella in Louisiana and—*

Wait. No.

Why was I entertaining this idea? If I sold the club, Charlotte would be at the mercy of some unknown person. I couldn't do that. Charlotte worked for me. I was her *boss*. She needed this job. And here I was, contemplating the sale of my business, exposing Charlotte and my entire staff to some hypothetical new owner, hinging on the possibility she'd one day want to give things a try with me? Had I lost my mind?

"I guess, I don't know, pray she quits? That's the best you can hope for. Pray she quits and you won't have to see her all the time." Patty stuffed the towel she'd used to wipe off the table into her apron. "Otherwise, you'll need to figure out how to remain professional with someone you're in serious danger of falling for. And it's only going to get worse. Charlotte is amazing, and beautiful, and impressive in every way that actually matters."

"I'm starting to figure that out, unfortunately." I rubbed my bottom lip again, working to ignore the discontent in my chest. Over the course of this conversation, it had morphed from a simmer to a boil.

"Take it from me." Patty stood, stepped over to my side, and placed a gentle hand on my shoulder. "Unrequited love in close proximity is like breaking your own heart. Every day." She gave me a squeeze. "I don't recommend it."

CHAPTER 11

CHARLOTTE

"I can be hurt," she said, "only by people I respect."

— MARY BALOGH, *THEN COMES SEDUCTION*

Friday afternoon, Hannah knocked on the doorframe to my office approximately five minutes after I sat down and opened my laptop.

"We need to talk," she said, her blue eyes reflecting the seriousness of her tone.

"Sure." I glanced around the space for a second seat, belatedly remembering there was only one in the room. "Let me grab the chair from Hank's office."

"Don't fuss over it." She stepped inside and closed the door. "This might be quick."

Even so, I stood. I didn't like people hovering over me. Kevin's father used to do this—insist everyone sit while he stood and hovered—and it drove me bananas. The man loved mind games.

"Listen," she started as soon as the door closed. "I know what you're doing here. I know you're only working here to find Heather, and I want you to reconsider."

Shoot. I'd been worried about this. "Are you going to tell them?"

I was so close. After leaving Hank in the breakroom yesterday, I'd spent an hour in the dressing area, chatting up the ladies. I didn't like tricking folks, and my guilt had ballooned along with the certainty that I'd be able to discover Heather's whereabouts soon, likely before Sunday.

"As of right now, no. But I don't like you charming everyone, making them like you so much, when I know you're only here to find your cousin. That said"—

Hannah drew herself up, her shoulders square—"no, I will not tell them or Hank that you're looking for Glitterati. Not yet."

"Glitter—wait, Heather? Heather's stage name is Glitterati?"

"Her stage name was Glitterati when she worked here, yes."

"But she doesn't work here anymore?"

Hannah leveled me with a stony stare that communicated both impatience and disappointment.

"I'm sorry." I leaned my hip against the desk. "I know you said you wouldn't tell me anything about Heather, and I'm not trying to push you. You don't want to tell me, fine. But my aunt and uncle are beside themselves with worry. All I want is for you to let me ask the other dancers about my cousin. Please don't make things more difficult for me to find her."

"I know you, Charlotte. I know you don't like deceiving folks. And I can tell you're genuinely enjoying yourself here—you fit right in. Are you planning to stay? Once you find Heather, will you stay?"

I slouched, her question deflating me. "I wish I could. Truly, I wish I could, but I can't. I don't have the time to spare away from the kids. My momma and aunt have been watching them, but they're acting like candy is a food group and letting them stay up too late. I have a mountain of laundry that hasn't been done yet, and—"

"Okay. Fine. I understand, you can't stay." She looked disappointed. Not disappointed with me this time but with the situation. "When will you leave? As soon as you find Heather?"

"No. I'm trying to bring The Pony's finances into the twenty-first century." I exhaled a dry laugh. "Fred may have made a great Santa Claus, but he left a mess of Hank's payroll. I'm almost finished going back nine years and fixing those issues, and I've imported all the spreadsheets at the same time—not only expenditures but income from the restaurant receipts as well. Once that's done, I need to categorize, program some canned reports, the annual profit/loss analysis, and write up a 'how to' for monthly reconciliations. Then—"

Hannah lifted a hand to stop me listing my litany of tasks, a genuine smile on her face. "You are ridiculous, you know that? You're a saint."

"I'm not a saint." I rolled my eyes.

"No. You are. You're the only person who takes a job under false pretenses, then sticks around to solve as many problems as possible before fading back into your heavenly ether. You *are* ridiculous. I bet you're even planning to give two weeks' notice."

"Giving two weeks' notice is standard." A twinge of defensiveness had me standing straighter. "I might be here under false pretenses, but I'm not a thief, nor am I incompetent. Hank is paying me to do a job. I'm going to do it to the best of my ability, and then I'm giving two weeks' notice like a professional."

"Fine, fine. I figured as much when you kept staying late, working past midnight at your desk." Still wearing her friendly smile, Hannah placed a hand on her hip. "This is what I will do. I will give you all the information I have on your cousin—"

"You will?" I clasped my palms together, hope leaping like a glorious stag in my chest.

"Yes. But you have to promise that you will speak to her first before telling your aunt and uncle that you found her. And if she doesn't want to speak to her parents, you have to promise you'll never hand over her contact information or anything else about her. You can't even tell them that you found her. Can you do that?"

"I . . ." I shifted on my feet, my heart sinking. "What if she's in danger?"

"I know you. I do not know your aunt and uncle. I trust you. I do not trust them. Even if Glitterati is in danger, even if you offer to help and she turns you down, then you have to let her be the best judge of how to live her own life and back off."

My face had twisted into a grimace, but I couldn't help it. Nor could I lie. Hannah was right, I didn't like deceiving folks. "I'm sorry, Hannah. I don't know if I can do that. If she were one of my kids and she were in danger, I couldn't—"

"Then I'm not telling you anything." She lifted her chin. "Furthermore, I'm going straight to Hank when he gets in and telling him why you wanted to work here. And then you'll be fired and you'll never find her. Nor will you be able to finish bringing The Pony's financials into the twenty-first century."

Ugh. When had she gotten so tough? Hannah from my childhood was sweet and shy. When she performed as her stage name—Goldie—her persona was also sweet and shy but to an exaggerated degree. Who knew she had gumption beneath her soft-spoken exterior? Not me.

"Fine." I lifted a helpless hand, then let it drop to my thigh. "I promise, I will talk to her first. If she doesn't want her parents to know where she is, I will not tell them I found her."

"That means you'll have to lie to your family and say you couldn't find her. Are you going to be able to lie to them?"

I worried my lip, unwilling to pacify her with half-truths. "How about if you arrange for a call? Then, if she doesn't want our help, I can tell them the truth. I'll say I was able to speak with her through an intermediary, but I don't know how to contact her or where she is."

Hannah opened her mouth, presumably to contradict something about my suggestion.

I could guess which part and quickly added, "An intermediary who would prefer to remain anonymous. I will not let anyone know who arranged the call."

She nodded thoughtfully. "Fine. That's acceptable. We have a deal."

We shook on it, but she continued to nod thoughtfully, her eyes moving over me, considering.

"What is it?" I asked. "You look like there's something more you want to say."

"I suppose there is." Hannah gave me one more wary once-over. "But before I get to that, I want to drop some wisdom on you."

I barely concealed the instinct to roll my eyes again. What kind of wisdom did Hannah Townsend possess that I did not possess? I had four kids, she still lived with her mother. I'd moved across the country and then back again; I didn't think she'd traveled beyond the southeast USA. I'd lived through a hellacious divorce, but I'd never seen or heard about her dating anyone. And if she had, believe me—folks would have talked loud enough that even I would've heard. Hannah Townsend and her momma were the subject of so much gossip in town, the local newspaper should've started a weekly column years ago.

Point was, like me, she had limited life experience and had grown up sheltered until she suddenly wasn't. What could she possibly tell me that I didn't already know?

Despite my doubts, I leaned my hip back against the desk and waved my hand between us. "Okay. Go for it. Drop your wisdom."

"I've been doing this a long time. I've been dancing here for a long time. And in my experience, there's a couple of different reasons why people turn to this profession. Few folks are here as a Plan A. There are some exceptions. But for the most part, exotic dancing is a Plan B or C or D or E. For me, it was a Plan C."

Hannah pushed her fingers into her blond hair and paced across my office. She turned when she reached the window and leaned back against the sill, folding her arms. "People think, since dancing is rarely a Plan A, that we're all exploited. But what they don't seem to grasp is that no matter what your profession, if you're desperate, you're more likely to be taken advantage of. If you're a janitor and you don't feel like you have any other option, or if you're a computer programmer or a doctor or a lawyer or a waitress or a stay-at-home parent—whatever it is—if you're doing a job because you don't feel like you have any other options, you're probably being exploited."

Struggling to swallow past the sudden thickness in my throat, I absorbed her wise words and I felt dually humbled. First, I'd been so wrong about Hannah. She had wisdom to impart, loads of it, and I was a close-minded raisins for brains for assuming she didn't.

Second, what she'd said resonated soul deep. When I was with Kevin in Vegas, when I'd been desperate, I'd been exploited. I'd never admitted it to myself, but being desperate meant that I'd been easy to manipulate. Standing up for myself had been impossible. My desperation meant he'd had all the power.

"Did you know your cousin was an addict?" Hannah asked.

"I did." I nodded, watching my friend carefully. "She got in with a bad crowd and has been using since she was fourteen."

"Hank doesn't allow any drugs here. If he finds out, then you're gone and you're never allowed back. Heather hid it well, but being an addict meant she was desperate. I think he could sense her desperation, though he didn't know the real reason for it. Hank is the one who trained me, taught me how to do this job. He taught me how to exploit rather than be exploited. That's how you stay safe and keep your sisters safe, too."

"Heather didn't do that?"

"Heather bent the rules for customers, gave longer lap dances, let folks touch her where she shouldn't, and that made things dangerous for the rest of us. The thing about Hank is that, even if you're really good, even if you bring in lots of good business, if you're burning out or you hate the work, or you're starting to—you know—lose yourself in it, he will make sure you have a different place to go. He doesn't want anybody to feel like this is their only option. And he did that with her."

I felt like I might fall off the desk. "He . . . he found her another job?"

"He did. She works in a factory now. I think he was worried she might turn to drugs, to keep her attitude sunny and her energy up. He didn't know she was already using."

"But you did," I guessed.

"I did. My mother, she . . ." Hannah heaved a heavy sigh and rubbed her forehead. "You know her history, how my daddy left us, how she hit that car while under the influence and shattered her leg, how I became a stripper at The Pink Pony and a hostess at The Front Porch to pay the bills." Her lips curved into a subversive twist and she glanced at the ceiling. "Poor little Hannah Townsend, the stripper with a heart of gold."

Everyone knew this version of events. Just like, according to Hank, everyone knew Kevin left me heartbroken, abandoning his kids for a stripper. *False.* Just like everyone knew Hank was a dissolute, unethical, ne'er-do-well. *Also false.*

"*Please.* Like I couldn't work at Payton Mills or a hundred other places," she went on. "But those were my Plan D, E, and F. This job is difficult, it's tough if you're not mentally prepared, but I've never felt desperate. Stripping has never felt like my only option."

"Because of Hank? You know he'll help you leave if you burned out?"

"That's right. But Heather? When she got here, she felt like she had no choice." Hannah refocused her gaze on me. "I know about addiction. I've lived with it most of my life until my mother got clean. But even now, even years sober, it's always there. Always a threat. Sometimes the only thing you can do for an addict is let the person know that when they're ready to change, when they've hit rock bottom or the bottom of a water barrel, when they're ready to work on it for *themselves*, you'll be there. You'll be waiting."

"If Heather is sober—"

"She is. Now. But sobriety is the first step. You—her parents—can't fight this battle for her. Believe me, I tried with my mother. I tried to be *everything* she needed, almost killing myself in the process, and it only made things worse. This isn't their battle to fight, and it isn't yours."

My heart hurt, and not caring whether Hannah would be hovering over me or not, I flopped into the chair.

Placing my elbows on my knees, I buried my face in my hands. "How do I tell her parents this? As a mother, my instinct is always going to be to rush in and help my babies. I understand helping; I don't understand letting my baby fall."

"There's a reason adults are too heavy to carry, Charlotte. They need to learn how to carry themselves. Obviously, there are some exceptions. But take my momma as an example. My mother was sober for years. She didn't actually start living again until she met Jed and he insisted none of us put up with her helpless, self-pitying BS."

A short laugh erupted from my chest and I peeked at Hannah from between my fingers.

Her smile looked hazy, as though lost in a memory. "He challenged her and forced her to want better for herself. I don't think she ever would have changed if not for him coming into our lives. My way of dealing with things—which was to give and give and ruin myself and always feel guilty for not giving enough—did nothing but teach her how to take and take and be helpless. If I'd stopped giving earlier, if I'd forced her to stand on her own, she would've. And I think the same thing is true with your cousin."

"You are not responsible for your mother being an alcoholic or for her busted leg, Hannah. You were a child. She should've been protecting you."

"I know that." She glanced at her fingers. "Or I try my best to know that, but it's hard. I understand what your aunt and uncle are going through, in a way. It's so hard to watch someone you love struggle and not want to rescue them. But I also need to accept that my mother—like Heather—has to be in control of her successes and failures. They're not mine, they're hers."

"Heather has to decide to do it for herself. Not because her parents are panicked, not because they love her," I said, connecting the dots Hannah had spelled out.

"Correct. I guess that's why she and I got kind of close and still keep in touch. She'd act helpless and I told her to own her shit, reminding her that she's the one who is deciding to be helpless. I don't put up with her garbage, the garbage is a symptom of the disease. I don't loan her money—ever—and I don't let her lie to me. I think she's doing okay right now. She's not using, at least." Hannah's solemn expression made her appear a lot older than her twenty-eight years. "But I don't know if she's ready to see her parents. There's so much guilt there. She's a little too fragile. If they really want her to succeed, then they need to give her the room to do it on her own terms."

Absorbing this, I leaned back in the chair and pondered out loud, "Maybe I shouldn't call her."

"Maybe you shouldn't," Hannah agreed, inspecting me.

I inspected her right back. "What if . . . What if we do this: you keep in contact with Heather. If she's in danger, you let us know so we can help. And when you feel like she's ready, like she can handle it, you let her know I want to reach out." I pressed my palms together. "I know it's a lot to ask. You're not her keeper and you have enough going on, but if you could—"

"I'll do it," she said softly, giving me a half smile. "I talk to her every week anyway. I'll let you know when I think she's ready or if she truly needs a rescue."

"Thank you, Hannah." My eyes stung and I blinked away the sensation, but I did need to clear my throat of emotion before speaking. "Given your history with Heather, and your mother, I trust you."

"Good. Like I said, I trust you, Charlotte. I wouldn't let just any old person come in here under false pretenses." She winked at me and I laughed.

We were companionably silent for a stretch while reality settled on my shoulders. With respect to my aunt and uncle, my job here was done. Hannah would be my intermediary, should the need arise. Yet, for the time being, I'd let Heather be. Aunt Maddie wouldn't like how the situation had resolved—which is to say, it wasn't resolved; like so many things in life, it was ongoing—but my aunt and uncle would have to trust my judgment.

"You know how on airplanes they always say you should put on your own mask before helping anyone else?" Hannah asked philosophically, breaking the quiet moment.

I nodded.

"That's an allegory for life, I think. If your own mask isn't on, you can't breathe, and then you can't help anybody, right? I spent so much time trying to force my momma to put on her mask without putting on mine, I forgot to breathe and I suffocated both of us in the process."

My lips twisted to one side. "You are awfully wise, Hannah Townsend."

"Thank you, Charlotte Mitchell." She returned my grin, though hers looked faintly brittle. "But you know, sometimes, I wish I didn't need to be."

CHAPTER 12

CHARLOTTE

"Sounds naïve, respecting someone who doesn't give a shit about you."

— TOBA BETA, *MASTER OF STUPIDITY*

My office door remained propped open after Hannah left. Wide open. I needed to explain myself to Hank, tell him the real reason I'd wanted to audition as a dancer almost two weeks ago, and I wanted to do it as soon as he arrived at The Pony.

It's not that I'd chicken out if I didn't talk to him as soon as possible. Bravery rarely failed me, and I wasn't generally a *chickening out* kind of person—oftentimes to my detriment. Once I decided to do a thing, I felt restless until that thing was done. This restless energy cut into my productivity with the FastFinance migration. It had me tensing and lifting my head every time someone walked down the hall past my door.

But I'd be lying if my anxiousness didn't also have at least a little bit to do with the re-emergence of my crush on Hank Weller. Our recent interactions plus watching him with my kids at the Winston gathering meant I was dwelling on his finer attributes more than was wise.

I hoped, once I explained my reasons for lying, he'd be open to a friendship. I wanted to know him, to continue being friendly with him. Or, at the very least, we wouldn't avoid each other if we crossed paths in town. It would be great if we smiled and waved. *That would be nice.*

April sauntered back and forth twice, winking at me both times. Hope and Dave strolled by, their heads together, laughing. They both gave me a wave. One of the line cooks. One of the bartenders. Hank.

HANK!

I jumped from my seat and darted after him. "Hank! Do you have a minute to—"

"Nope. Busy." He didn't pause, his long legs carrying him hurriedly down the hall.

Not one to be deterred, I jogged to catch him. "This is really important. And it shouldn't take too long."

His steps slowed and I saw his shoulders rise and fall. He paused. Then, setting his hands on his hips, he turned and faced me, his expression frosty. "What?"

I flinched.

My reaction made his eyes turn colder. "What is it? What do you want? I have things to do."

Considering he'd apologized to me yesterday and promised he'd stop treating me like a nuisance, I tried not to feel the pinpricks of hurt at his clipped tone and blatant impatience. But I did feel hurt and—and *oh well*. I still had a bit of a crush on him, maybe I always would—big surprise, I had terrible taste in men—but obviously he was still the same alluring yet coldhearted meanie who'd stood me up for junior prom. I couldn't count on him to show up or be consistent when it mattered.

But I didn't need him to like me and we didn't need to be friends. I simply needed him to listen. And the sooner I told him, the sooner it would be over and the sooner I'd be out of his adorably askew sex hair for good.

Forcing my flailing emotions down, down, down to where he could not affect them, I crossed my arms tightly over my chest. "I've been—I've misled you."

Clearly, this was not what he'd expected me to say. Some of his frigid aloofness melted into confusion. "What are you—"

"I never wanted to strip here or anywhere else," I plowed ahead, seeing no reason to gentle the information or employ a softer approach, given how impatient he seemed to be. Heck, he'd probably be overjoyed by the news of my departure. "I never wanted to be a dancer, I never needed the money. I lied to you. I came here because my cousin has been missing for over a year, and her parents—my aunt and uncle—got a tip that she was stripping in Green Valley. I volunteered to pose as a dancer for a few weeks to gain the trust of the ladies so I could find my cousin, who, it turns out, is one of your dancers. Well, she *was* one of your dancers. So, there you go."

He gaped at me and I mentally shrugged off the bewilderment behind his expression. He could think whatever he wanted. He clearly couldn't stand me. So be it.

I soldiered on, matter-of-fact. "I thought you should know the truth. This is me giving you my two weeks' notice. I'll train whoever you want me to train. And, well, that's it. Bye."

Turning on my heel, I marched back down the hall the way I came, feeling like crying for the second time today. I breathed in, I breathed out, and must've been so focused on not crying, I didn't hear Hank's steps follow.

"Wait," he said, entering the room after me and shutting the door quickly. "Wait a minute." He'd lifted a hand, his eyes searching.

I raised my chin and let him look while not allowing myself to study his features too intently. Maybe this news made him only mildly happy, maybe he was ecstatic. Whatever. I didn't want to know. He wanted me gone, I would be gone. I was certain there would be much rejoicing. The end.

Finally, after a long moment of staring at me, he shifted his weight to his back foot, cleared his throat, and said, "Why don't you start at the beginning. Please."

"Fine," I said evenly and turned. Walking to the far side of the space, I claimed the spot by the window Hannah had occupied earlier. "I have a cousin. She's almost twenty. She went missing a year ago. My aunt and uncle were worried. They got a tip she was dancing at a club on the outskirts of Green Valley."

While I told him about my aunt and uncle being scared out of their minds for their daughter, about how they'd wanted to borrow money from me and my mother to hire a PI, about how I'd offered to pose as a dancer instead, I carefully distanced myself from whatever reaction my revelations elicited, a survival skill I'd mastered while married to Kevin.

I did not tell him that Heather was using drugs while working at The Pony or that she was an addict prior to running off, but I did tell him how I'd approached Hannah first, and how she'd made me realize that to find Heather, I would have to lie. I'd have to go undercover at one of the strip clubs.

"You never needed the money?" Hank interrupted, sounding curious rather than ranting about betrayal. Ranting about betrayal had been the response I'd expected.

"Correct," I said, bracing for him to scream at me any minute.

Any minute.

Any minute now . . .

"And Hannah knew what you were up to?" he asked, his confusion plain, like he found this particular part suspect.

I tensed. "Don't blame Hannah. She came to me with an ultimatum and told me to tell you the truth. The circumstances with my cousin . . . her issues are complicated, and Hannah is trying to do the right thing. I'm the one who put Hannah in an impossible situation, and I guess I still am. But that's neither here nor there. Point is, Hannah cares about you. You can trust her."

"And that's why you're telling me now?" Again, he sounded like he sincerely wished to understand but wasn't angry—yet. "Hannah forced your hand and you want to keep looking for this cousin?"

"No. I know how to reach my cousin now, and I could've quit without telling you everything. I'm telling you the truth now because I wanted you to know that you did nothing wrong. This is my fault. No matter what job I'd been hired for, the plan was always for me to stay two weeks to find Heather and then quit."

His eyes flickered, a quick series of emotions arresting his features, an enigmatic parade of thoughts and feelings. "Only two weeks?" he asked, his voice scratchy. "That's—"

"Yes. Almost up. But I'm changing the plan. I want to give you a full two weeks' notice, longer if you need me. I'm invested in seeing the transition to FastFinance through to the end and helping train the new person."

Despite telling myself to block out his reaction, some compulsion had me attempting to interpret it. Hank looked off-kilter and torn and mighty confused. He did not look angry, though. His mouth opened, then closed, then he frowned at the floor, and then his eyes drifted shut.

"Charlotte—"

I stepped away from the window. "Listen, I've worked *really hard* to modernize your bookkeeping." The same compulsion that had demanded I attempt to decipher his reactions urged me to explain myself.

Meanwhile, all my other instincts told me to let it go. He didn't want me here; he'd *never* wanted me here.

Why I kept on talking, I had no idea. "You do not need a full-time person. You don't even really need a person at all if you let me train you. It will take you an hour once every two weeks to run payroll, three or so hours a month to reconcile your charges, and a few hours a year to generate your 1099s, W-2s, and pull together your profit and loss statements for the IRS."

Hank's eyes opened while I spoke and met mine, a subtle curve tugging his lips. "I don't want to be spending *any* hours doing that," he said, his voice sounding oddly gentle and amused. "I already have too much to do, too many irons in the fire, which is why I hired you."

His mellow attitude, as well as the warm softness in his handsome gaze, threw me for a loop, and my heart flip-flopped. This man was giving me whiplash with his mercurial mood swings.

I found I needed to swallow before I could speak. "Okay. Fair enough." I held my hands up. "I thought you might say that, so I have a suggestion, assuming you're willing to hear me out."

He stared at me, the small curve to his mouth eventually becoming a small smile. "Go ahead. What's your suggestion?"

"What if you offered Hannah the job?"

Hank's attention drifted out the window behind me and he rubbed his chin. "Hannah." He said her name like he was trying it on.

"She's graduating with her bachelor's degree in business administration soon and she's obviously told you she's ready to move on, do something else. But it's also clear she's worried about her work history and ability to get a job in an office, given what happened at the last place."

"That's . . . true."

I could see his mind debating these facts.

"She knows as much as you do about how to audition dancers, when to schedule each dancer, which bouncers prefer which shifts, what events to book, how to settle ruffled feathers."

His eyes found mine again and he frowned. It was thoughtful, not upset. "You've been paying attention."

I took this as a good sign and continued. "Hire her as a business manager. She's more than capable of taking on most of the staffing and booking responsibilities—the auditioning, hiring, firing, talent search, job postings, scheduling, and whatnot that takes up so much of your time."

"That would free up a lot of my time."

"With me gone, you have the money for her salary, so it's not going to impact your overhead costs either. She can take over the tasks you're tired of managing while also doing what was once my job, like ordering supplies and checking timesheets since the bookkeeping is now all automated. Put it all together and it's a great full-time position for Hannah."

Hank's head bobbed faintly. "Okay," he said, his tone still disarmingly mild. "And you'll stay? You'll stick around for two weeks to train her on FastFinance and how to run the reports? Reconciliation and payroll?"

"I will." I crossed my arms when my heart flip-flopped again. "And if she has questions after those two weeks, you both know how to reach me. I'll make myself available."

"You must feel pretty guilty about lying." His statement sounded teasing.

"No . . ." I scratched my neck, took a deep breath, tugged on the hem of my shorts, and tried not to squirm in place while he watched. But then I finally admitted, "And yes. Yes, I do feel guilty, but guilt is not why I'm giving two weeks or offering to be a resource moving forward."

"Oh yeah?" His gaze seemed to sharpen and he took two steps further into the room, two steps closer to me. "Then why? What do you get out of it? Why would you want to help me when I've been nothing but intolerable toward you?"

Seeing you for two more weeks would be nice.

I couldn't say that. I couldn't even admit the thought to myself. I didn't understand my reaction to this man, nor did I wish to. It was what it was, and I didn't have the energy or time to figure it out.

Thus, I settled on, "It's called being a decent person."

He snorted. "You mean being able to live with yourself, which is the same thing as avoidance of guilt. Let me do you a favor and assuage that guilt right now. Lying in order to find your cousin because you're worried about her and want to help her and there's no other way to track her down isn't something to feel guilty about, Charlotte."

I gave him a jerky nod, but—*dammit*. He was being so great about all this. Why did he have to be so great when I was about to leave?

"What you did and why you did it were completely justified." Hank's eyes moved over me, a quick down-up sweep. "You shouldn't feel any guilt."

I sent him a glare of mock annoyance. "Don't tell me what to feel."

He cracked a smile, drawling, "I'm not telling you what to feel, angel. I'm telling you what *not* to feel."

Determined to ignore how confoundedly endearing he'd made that sound, I waved my hand through the air in a dismissive gesture. "*Anyway.* I will stay for two weeks, and then I'll be available to Hannah for questions."

"Thank you," he said, watching me closely. "That's awfully *decent* of you."

"You're welcome." I strolled to the desk and pulled out my chair. Sitting, I opened the laptop, and some odd, self-destructive impulse compelled me to mutter, "There you go. Looks like your prayers have been answered."

This statement was met with silence, so I glanced at him. His eyebrows were pulled together and his stare was fastened to my face, like I'd said something odd.

"I'm leaving," I spelled out, trying to infuse my words with teasing levity like he had. "You didn't want me here to begin with. What I meant was, it looks like you got your wish."

Hank surprised me by not immediately agreeing. Instead, he swallowed thickly, his gaze dimming by degrees, his hand reaching for the doorknob behind him. "Oh yeah, right," he said, turning, pausing for a tick, staring at the doorknob like he'd never seen one before, taking a deep breath, and then finally opening the door. "Lucky me."

CHAPTER 13

HANK

> "... before I can live with other folks I've got to live with myself. The one thing that doesn't abide by majority rule is a person's conscience."
>
> — HARPER LEE, *TO KILL A MOCKINGBIRD*

Chest tight and concentration impossible, I bungled my third drink order of the night. Halfway through making an Old Fashioned instead of a Manhattan, I cursed under my breath, realizing the error after I'd already poured the top-shelf bourbon. Dumping the contents, I started over, my earlier conversation with Charlotte on repeat in my head. I cursed again.

I needed to apologize.

For no less than the hundredth time, my attention drifted to the hallway leading to the offices. Likely, she was still there, still working, still believing I wanted her gone, and still thinking I was the world's biggest bucket of turds. Turns out, the only experience more frustrating than being attracted to Charlotte and believing I'd be seeing her at work five days a week was being attracted to Charlotte and knowing there existed no excuse to see her again after the next fourteen days.

"You all right, boss?"

I blinked, my eyes finding Tina standing on the other side of the bar, a tray in her hands, a wrinkle between her eyebrows.

"Fine." Squinting, I poured the Manhattan into a waiting glass. The music tonight gave me a headache. "Sorry about messing up your drink order earlier."

"That's okay." She waved away my apology. "Are you sure you're all right?"

I nodded. "Just fine." Stamping on a tight smile, I leaned to the side to peer around her. "Better get back to it." The patrons at her cluster of tables were looking at us, not the stage.

Tina's expression of concern hardened into the mask she typically wore while working the floor. She flipped the long black hair of her wig and cocked her hip to the side. As she sauntered off, I forced my eyes to the top-shelf rye—which was running low—rather than allowing them to stray again. I needed to concentrate on work and forget about the woman in the office down the hall who thought of me as a villain. Usually, I wouldn't care what anyone thought.

But with this woman . . . I needed to apologize.

Charlotte had caught me at a bad moment earlier, my discussion with Patty still fresh in my mind. Working together long-term despite the preposterous intensity of my attraction had held me hostage with dread and I'd been frantic to build a wall between us, establish boundaries, create distance. As such, I'd snapped at her. My intentions hadn't been disrespect or meanness but to avoid Charlotte until I had more intellect available and my guard raised.

That's what I focused on for the rest of the night: avoiding Charlotte and raising my guard.

Avoiding her turned out to be easy. She didn't look for me; she stayed in her office, and according to Dave when we finally closed, she'd left around midnight.

Fortifying my defenses turned out to be less easy. Making drinks, locking up, driving home, brushing my teeth, dropping into bed—all done while my brain reminded the rest of me over and over: Charlotte would be gone for good in less than fourteen days and there wasn't a damn thing I could do about it.

* * *

I took Saturday off to get my head on straight.

Sleep eluded me. After spending a few hours tossing and turning, I decided to work on the boat before the afternoon heat. Starting today, this next week was set to be a scorcher.

After, perhaps I'd take a leisurely hike on the shady slopes of Cooper Road Trail, catch up on paperwork and emails relating to my rental properties and the management company, look into my parents' estate and earnings. Then I'd take a nap before meeting Beau for drinks at Genie's, as was our custom on the weekends. I wanted to prove to myself that, given a little time, distance, and immersion in tedious tasks, my preoccupation with the woman would fade as quickly as it had materialized.

This plan did not work.

Tending to my boat made me wonder if she liked fishing, or swimming, or boating; I bet Charlotte and her kids would love my boat, and Sonya seemed like an intuitive sort of person; she'd make an excellent fisherwoman. But they'd need gear—I'd have to get some child-sized poles. Did her kids know how to swim? What kind of bathing suit did Charlotte own? Pretty soon, I was thinking about Charlotte in a bikini, and me taking off the bikini, and I dropped the wrench I'd been holding into the water, feeling more frustrated than I had a right to be about the loss of a $1.20 wrench.

The families camping and picnicking at the head of Cooper Road Trail reminded me of Charlotte and her kids and had me automatically wondering whether they camped, or liked to, or would be open to it. Joshua seemed like he'd enjoy camping as long as we incorporated a historical component or made trail maps, which wouldn't be a problem. I knew how to map trails and I could teach him. For camping, would Charlotte prefer an RV or a tent? It made sense to have the kids sleep in a tent while she and I slept in the RV. Or—

Spitting out several curses, I ran the trail instead of hiking it. *Okay, psycho. Cool your jets, this ain't your family.*

Upon returning home, I marched to the bathroom and took a cold shower. It was hot outside. I was not still thinking about RV alone time with Charlotte. I was hot and needed to cool off. Because it was hot. Outside.

More focused after my shower, I sorted through emails and paperwork from my parents' estate. This went fine for about a half hour before my trust fund statement had me contemplating Charlotte's unfair divorce settlement. I made a mental note to ask my lawyer specifically who—which investment firm—had control over her kids' trusts, as I doubted Buckley Sr. directed the day-to-day investments, and whether I might be able to—

Shoving away from the desk, disgusted with the direction of my thoughts, and knowing I'd never be able to nap, I left my house and texted Beau.

Hank: -(￣▽)_🍺~~ ...?
Beau: Is that cake or beer?

Smirking, I navigated to my saved text emojis, looking for a different one along the same vein. Thing is, I was a late and reluctant adopter of cell phones. Yeah, I know my generation grew up with them, it *should* feel natural, blah blah blah. Whatever. I've always hated them. My phone is often dead and I use text emojis whenever possible to communicate. They amused me.

If I can't say everything that needs to be said with a text emoji, I call. I don't like calling either, so usually I won't, letting the silence speak for itself. But if you're getting a text message with words, it's 'cause I like you enough to make the effort.

Sometimes Beau received text messages with words, sometimes I sent cat memes, but mostly I used text emojis.

Hank: (/^-^)o日 日o(^0^|)
Beau: Now? It's not even 4
Hank: (●´△`●)
Hank: (ﾉ'-`)ﾉ
Hank: ヽ('ー`)ノ
Hank: (ノ˛ᴍ)
Beau: Fine I'll be there in 30mins. Need to stop at the store first

Pleased, I headed straight to Genie's. Nothing but alone time with my thoughts was likely the crux of the problem. If anyone could distract me, it would be my good-natured best friend and whatever funny story or joke he'd been saving up for Saturday night drinks.

Despite my dissatisfaction at the notion of not seeing Charlotte once her two weeks were over, I told myself as I walked through the door to the bar that distance between us would ultimately be a good thing. Separation should make this discontent fade.

It's not like we ran in the same circles. I was hardly the church-going type and she had no reason to visit the club after her last day. Avoiding her would be easy.

Ordering a beer and claiming a stool, I reckoned what I needed starting now was to steer clear of her, all thoughts of her and all mentions of her, for the next two weeks. Then I'd get my head on straight for good, reach out to a few former female acquaintances who were always up for a good time, and push this particular female from my mind.

Unhelpfully, the first words out of Beau's mouth upon tapping me on the shoulder were, "Did Charlotte quit?"

Turning on my barstool, I spat, "Yes. She quit yesterday. How are you?"

"Is—what happened?" He gave me his wide-eyed concerned look.

Deflated and exhausted, I gestured to the empty stool on my right. "Take a seat. I'll buy you a beer."

He moved slowly to claim the seat. "Is this a beer story? Or a whiskey story?"

"It's a beer story," I lied, not wanting to admit out loud how twisted up and turned around I'd been all day. And yesterday. And the day before that.

I snagged Genie's attention, pointed to my beer, to Beau, and then held up two fingers. She nodded once and turned toward the row of pint glasses.

"Thank goodness, you had me worried." Beau leaned rather than sat on the stool next to mine. "Tina told Maisy at Utterly Ice Cream, Maisy told Belle Cooper, and I saw Belle at the Piggly Wiggly just now."

Before he could further illuminate the various branches of his gossip tree, I proceeded to quickly summarize what happened with Charlotte yesterday afternoon, revealing her real reasons for wanting to work at The Pony, how she'd upgraded the finance systems, and how I was thinking of offering Hannah the job of business manager. Genie delivered Beau's beer halfway through my recitation and he'd nearly finished his bottle by the time I concluded my story.

"Charlotte's suggestion to offer Hannah the job is smart, makes a lot of sense. Hannah is graduating in the fall and it'll be a good fit," I said, my voice monotone as I used my thumb to wipe off condensation from my bottle. "And if Charlotte's new financial reporting system works as well as she thinks it does, Hannah'll take over some of my work. That'll be . . . nice."

"That *will* be nice." Beau now fully sat on his stool. "Instead of being short-staffed and overworked, you might have more free time and flexibility."

"Ideally, yes."

He nodded faintly. "Seems like everything worked out for the best."

"Seems like." I took a gulp of my beer rather than try to sip and swallow around the rocks in my throat, sensing his eyes on my profile.

"Then what's got you down?"

Angling my shoulders, I faced him. "Pardon?"

"You look and sound irritated." Beau inspected me. "Is it 'cause Charlotte lied? About why she wanted the job?"

"No." I reached for a pretzel. We hadn't ordered food, but I wasn't hungry. "I'm not irritated with her."

"You're not?"

"No," I said, and that was the truth. I wasn't irritated with Charlotte. I was irritated with myself for liking everything about her to the point of not being able to concentrate. I was also irritated at how suddenly all this had occurred. How could everything be hunky-dory last week and now I was a fucking mess?

Beau leaned an elbow on the bar and rubbed his chin, surprising me by asking, "Did you ever find out why she doesn't like you? Was it due to Kevin and Carli?"

"Uh, no. We talked about Kevin. She's not upset with me about that. Turns out Charlotte left him weeks before he ran off. They weren't even living together at the time."

"Huh. Then why was she always avoiding you?" He hit my shoulder lightly. "You should ask her before her last day."

"What? Why? What's the point? It's not like I'll be seeing her again." I kept my voice painstakingly disinterested.

"Yeah, you will."

I frowned. "I will?"

"Charlotte and her kids are coming over more often to the homestead, sticking around for family dinners. She and Sienna seem to be hitting it off, and their kids are about the same age. You'll be seeing her a lot."

Well, shiiiiiit . . . ?

I couldn't decide whether I loved this news or hated it. Probably both. My pragmatic side, the logical part focused on self-preservation and maintaining sanity, hated it. Every other part of me, especially my subversive and masochistic impulses, loved it.

When my complicated silence persisted, Beau continued, "When she's over at the house, y'all are going to need to get along."

"We get along," I hedged, rubbing the back of my neck and once more recalling how much of an asshole I'd been to her last night. "We mostly get along," I amended.

"No, y'all don't. Before she worked at The Pony, she'd cross the street whenever she saw you in town. I've watched her do it for years, even before Kevin left. And if everything is working out for the best, you're not upset about her lying to you, and you two get along as you say, why do you still look and sound so irritated now? You should clear the air with her, once and for all."

"I'm not irritated," I insisted again. "I'm—I'm tired." And confused. And preoccupied by thoughts of a woman who is so entirely out of my reach, she might as well be the secret to time travel.

Or . . . you could sell that damn club and become respectable. I grimaced, only 50% hating the idea. But selling the club wouldn't solve the other problem. Even if I was respectable, Charlotte couldn't stand me, and I deserved her ire.

"You're tired?" His eyes swept over me.

"Yeah. And, you know, dreading this week." I rubbed my forehead, my brain groggy from lack of sleep and two beers. I would ask Beau to drive me home.

"Why? What's happening this week?"

"I'm training the new bartender—he starts tomorrow, early. Then I'm offering the job to Hannah, which means I'll need to fill her spot on the schedule. Auditioning new dancers, making sure the one selected is a good fit with the rest of the team, orientation—it always takes forever."

"Hannah can audition her own replacement, though. And Charlotte can train Hannah before her two weeks is up, right?"

"That's true." I swallowed the remainder of my beer, wincing at the reminder of Charlotte's impending departure from the club. How was I supposed to manage this already cumbersome preoccupation if I'd be seeing her for family dinners at the Winstons'? "Also, I got two hen parties," I went on. "One on Monday and one on Tuesday."

Beau let out a low whistle. "That's a lot of chickens, back-to-back. And before the fall?"

"The weddings are in the fall, but all those spots were booked. These two decided to hold their bachelorette parties early rather than go somewhere else."

Beau's face scrunched up. It was his thinking face. "Fred passing away, Charlotte starting as your new bookkeeper and then quitting less than two weeks later, interviewing for and hiring a new bartender, Hannah moving from contractor to employee, training the new bartender, training Hannah, the new finance system to learn, and two bachelorette parties before the season starts. Hank"—he gave me a commiserating once-over—"that's a lot of changes for you all at once."

"What do you mean?"

"Seeing as how you don't do well with change, it seems like a lot all at once. I'm guessing that's why you look so irritated."

I reared back a smidge. "What do you mean I 'don't do well with change'? I do fine with change."

He chuckled. "Come on, Hank. You know you don't like disruption, even the good kind. You hate surprises. You like your schedules, you thrive on knowing what to expect."

"You make me sound like an old fuddy-duddy."

Beau's smile widened and his eyes did that stupid sparkly thing. This usually meant I'd accidentally said something funny and he was laughing at me. I gritted my teeth.

"Well, first of all," he drawled, "you just said 'fuddy-duddy' non-ironically, which I'm pretty sure proves my point. And so, I rest my case."

"Fuck off. I'm barely thirty. I'm adventurous and I'm fun, goddamn it," I snapped, gesturing for Genie to bring me another beer. "And take my keys. You're driving me home."

"I didn't say you weren't fun, but you're only fun and adventurous when it's scheduled or you're given a heads-up beforehand. God help anyone who surprises you."

"That's not—"

Beau cut me off with raised eyebrows and a smirk, but he wasn't finished. "Which was—*is*—why I figured you'd be mad at Charlotte for lying about her reasons for wanting to work at The Pony."

"Because it was a surprise," I filled in.

"Correct. And based on what I know about Charlotte," he said reasonably, "it's probably not the last of her surprises."

"You think she's still lying about something?" I trusted his judgment, and if he thought there was something else, I wanted to know.

"No. But you know, she's always doing and saying the last thing people expect." He was back to rubbing his chin. "Some folks find that fun. Sienna loves it, so does Jet. But you . . ." His eyes lost focus, giving me the sense he was pondering weighty matters. Without looking at me, he continued, "It's good she's leaving. I'm not so sure her brand of unexpected would agree with you or your management style"—his eyes cut to mine—"in the long-term."

I returned my scowl to my empty beer, nodding as I considered Beau's words, layering them over Patty's statements from yesterday.

In every way that mattered—lifestyle, choices, temperament, values—Charlotte and I were incompatible. This assertion wasn't a surprise, but acceptance settled like clay in my stomach and grit on my tongue.

It was going to be a long two weeks.

* * *

Last night, we left Genie's around 10:00 PM and I fell asleep on the way home. I didn't remember Beau rousing me to walk inside, but I did wake up Sunday morning in my own bed with a Post-it note stuck to my forehead.

Clear the air with Charlotte before her last day so family dinners aren't more awkward than Cletus's constant sausage references make them. Everybody except you likes her. Make it right.

I wasn't hung over—not at all—so when I chuckled at his note, at the metric ton of irony contained on one small slip of paper, my head didn't hurt. Beau thought I didn't like Charlotte? I should've been an actor.

Telling Beau, confessing my attraction for the woman, this—this . . . *thing*, this troubling fixation for and on Charlotte Mitchell, would've been pointless. Patty had been right: I was a reprobate, I'd always be a reprobate, and Charlotte was a saint, an angel. Even if by some miracle she reciprocated my interest, nothing could ever come of it. No use bringing up a wish that was doomed from the start.

However . . .

Crumpling his note and tossing it in the trash, I decided that if my ability to concentrate didn't improve, I'd have to consult Beau and ask for his help. He didn't need to know Charlotte was the source of my fascination, but he had experience regarding hopeless attraction. If anyone knew how to move past a woman, it was Beau.

My dead cell phone couldn't tell me the time, and based on the light filtering through the blinds, I reckoned it couldn't be any later than seven or eight. But when I moseyed to the kitchen for coffee and glanced at the clock on the microwave, it announced that I'd overslept. By a lot.

"Shit!"

Coffee forgotten, I plugged my cell into the wall socket and jumped in the shower, not bothering to trim my beard as I quickly towel-dried off. Running back to the phone, I powered it on and hurriedly dressed, cursing the whole time.

First thing I needed to do was call Louis, the new bartender starting today, and apologize for being so late. I'd tell him—

Several texts made my phone buzz. With dread clawing up my throat, I picked it up to read them.

865-555-9090: This is Charlotte. What's your ETA? The new bartender is here about a half hour early. I let him in and gave him the new hire paperwork to fill out. When he's done, do you want me to give him a tour?
865-555-9090: I'm giving him a tour
865-555-9090: I can't seem to get the AC to come on. It's real hot. Do you want me to call Beau?
865-555-9090: I'm calling Beau. This thing is broken and Serafina is baking bread ????
865-555-9090: Sorry for all the messages but are you okay? You're really late and you are never late

I finished reading her last text and a new one came through.

865-555-9090: Beau is on his way over to you, but if you don't text me back in the next 5 mins, I'm calling Jackson to drive over and check on you in official capacity. Better hide the bongs and thongs

Rolling my eyes, even as I breathed a laugh of both humor and relief, I messaged her back.

Hank: Phone was dead. On my way in. Thanks for taking care of Louis

As soon as I hit send, I realized what I'd just done. It hadn't occurred to me to use a text emoji instead of words to respond. Typing out words had felt natural, normal, and not at all irritating, and that made absolutely no sense.

"Huh."

Before I could marvel too much at this anomaly in my behavior, I heard the sound of someone at the front, unlocking the door. Only one person had keys to my house.

"Beau?" Leaving the cell on my side table to charge, I walked out of my bedroom just as he opened the door.

"What the hell, Hank?" Beau shifted his weight from one foot to the other, his eyes round. "I get a call from Charlotte that the club's AC is broken, your new bartender is waiting, she can't reach you, and you're two hours late for work. And you're not answering your phone."

"Sorry," I winced, pushing a hand through my still-wet hair. "My phone was dead and I just woke up."

He straightened, taking full measure of me. "You slept fourteen hours?"

"I suppose so." Glancing behind him out the open door, I turned back to my bedroom. "I have to go. The club should've opened twenty minutes ago, and I—"

"Charlotte took care of that," Beau said, following me down the hall to my room and hovering at the door.

I spun around. "I'm sorry, what? Charlotte took care of what?"

He gave me a patient, slightly aggrieved look. "Don't be mad at her. She called me when she couldn't reach you. Dave and Hector called in sick and customers started showing up. She—"

"There's no bouncers?" My voice pitched high. "What the—"

"Just listen for a sec. The AC is broke. No one can enter the club, it's not safe."

The AC broke?

Great. Just fucking great. How much was that going to cost? We'd had problems with the unit earlier in the summer, but it had been working fine for over a month. Instead of The Pink Pony, it should've been named The Debt Horse.

I sighed. It's not that I didn't have the money to buy a new AC; I could use funds from one of my real-estate accounts without making a debt on the principal. It's that I hated investments where I put in more than I got out.

Working to keep my frustration buried, I said, "We've been through this before. Open all the doors and it'll be a wet T-shirt contest kind of day. That's what we did back in June when the AC broke last time. The dancers and the customers didn't mind the heat so much as long as everyone stayed wet."

"Come on, Hank. That was just four hours in June, not all damn day in August. And water on the ground is a slipping hazard, a lawsuit waiting to happen. It's too hot inside to serve alcohol—someone would pass out from dehydration—and your license doesn't cover outside. Plus, the bartender is brand new. He shouldn't be serving by himself on his first day."

"Is that so?" I drew myself up to my full height and set my hands on my hips, indignation hardening my words. Beau's statements didn't sound like they originated from Beau's brain, and I only needed one guess to figure out who'd made these proclamations. "What did Charlotte do, huh? No bouncers, no alcohol, nobody allowed inside. How did she 'open' The Pony?"

"Oh, you'll see." Beau sought to hide his grin by glancing at his shoes, but the movement was too late. I saw it and heard it clear as a bell as he said, "I know you don't like surprises, but try to go with the flow just this once."

CHAPTER 14

HANK

"When you are content to be simply yourself and don't compare or compete, everyone will respect you."

— LAO TZU, *TAO TE CHING*

"Un-fucking-believable," I muttered to no one, absorbing the scene in the parking lot of The Pony as I slowed my Jaguar.

A car wash.

That's what she did. By the looks of it, she'd called in every available dancer, and every single one of them were wearing string bikinis while washing patrons' cars. And trucks. And—

Is that a tractor?

Yep. That was a tractor. A bright green John Deere tractor, looking shiny and new.

I sighed, frustration swelling in my chest. A car wash? What did the dancers think? Were they okay with this? Giving free shows to anyone driving by? How were they getting paid? Were they getting paid? Or did Charlotte expect them to give their labor away for free?

What a fucking travesty. It's not like my team could give lap dances outside in the parking lot; we'd have the whole town after us for public indecency, and that's all I needed. *This fucking place. I should just sell it and be done with it.* If it weren't for the people who relied on me, I probably would've, and didn't that make me the dummy? Keeping a bad investment because I cared about the people.

I bit back a growl.

Movement beyond the passenger window caught my attention and I did a double take. Kilby and Piper were strolling over, big ol' grins on their faces, sunglasses hiding their eyes. As they approached, Kilby made a *roll down your window* motion with her hand.

Despite their smiles, I braced myself for an earful. "Kilby, Piper. I hope—"

"Hey, boss," Piper chirped, bending to lean into the car. "Do you want a wash?"

I stiffened. "Uh—"

"Come on, pull up." Kilby also leaned down, lowering her sunglasses so she could give me a wink. "This thing is filthy. When's the last time it saw some water?"

I scratched the back of my neck, studying them, looking for signs of discontent and finding none. "Are you—Kilby, hold on a sec. Get in the car, will ya?"

"Sure thing. I'll show you where to park. Charlotte's got a system." She opened the door, hesitating when she spotted the leather seat. Her bikini was soaked.

"It's fine. They got that coating on them, water won't hurt."

Piper stepped back and waved with both hands, then turned and jogged back to where most of the action took place. Eight automobiles were parked side-by-side, all being worked on by one of the dancers. I saw some of the chairs and tables from inside the club had been lined up near each car, and a few fellas were sitting at them, watching each of the ladies soap up and spray down, Solo cups on the surface of the tables.

Despite the short distance between where we were and where she pointed, Kilby buckled up. "Just there, behind Grady's truck. That's the end of the line."

I shifted in my seat and frowned at her. "You said Charlotte has a system?"

"That's right." She turned a cheerful grin my way. "Each person in line can either drive up to the next available dancer's spot or they can wait until their preferred girl is ready. See Hannah's line?" Kilby pointed to a row of about three cars behind where Hannah, wearing a gold bikini, was currently working on detailing a motorcycle.

"But . . . how are y'all getting paid?" I scowled at the smiling faces of the dancers and the folks getting their cars washed as I pulled up behind Grady's truck.

"Charlotte is using her phone to accept credit card payments through an online payment system. I guess the club has an account? Anyway, customers pay her direct. The cost of three minutes of car washing equals one minute of a lap dance, and the guys are tipping us in cash."

"She—" I choked on my words, then laughed. "She's charging one-third the rate of a lap dance per car?"

"No. It takes me thirty minutes to wash a car, so it's the same rate as a ten-minute lap dance—which, if you're doing the math, is a lot of money. We've been busy since we opened. Charlotte told everyone to call their friends to come by now since we'll be closed tonight. Can't wash cars in the dark."

Holy shit. "This is . . . brilliant."

"Right? And I've already made my quota in tips for a Sunday." Kilby unclicked her seatbelt as I stopped the car, her hand already on the door handle. "Anyone in particular you want washing your car? I have two guys in my lane, but—"

"No. No one needs to wash my car. I can wash my own car."

She shrugged, chuckling as she opened the door. "Okay, boss. Suit yourself. But go see Charlotte if you change your mind. She can give you an idea of how long the wait will be."

"Wait—Kilby."

"Yep?" She turned and bent to peer in the car again.

"What's in the Solo cups?" Lifting my hand, I pointed to the two guys in her area, sipping from their red cups.

"Oh. That's lemonade. Charlotte had her momma bring over her kids and they set up a lemonade stand." Kilby gestured to somewhere behind me and she laughed, shaking her head. "Hank, you should seriously think about hiring some kids as bouncers. Just them being here, nearby, is enough to keep all these guys in line. I'm hearing more *please*s and *thank-you*s from customers than I ever have before."

Confusion was soon followed by a spike of trepidation, worry making my heart beat double. *Charlotte brought her kids? Here?*

Kilby shut the door, leaving me to process, and strolled over to the two men sipping their lemonade at her table.

Cutting the engine, I took a moment to stare out my windshield, trying to think through all the ways this creative approach might backfire on my business. We could, technically, host a car wash if we wanted. We weren't serving alcohol outside, so no problems there. All the ladies were dressed in bathing suits, no lap dances, no one could complain about public indecency or nudity. Apparently, all the dancers were making bank, getting paid for their time, and all the customers looked pleased.

And the presence of four little kids was keeping everyone in line . . . ?

Four little kids. I appreciated her bringing her kids by to keep my patrons from getting handsy, but was that wise? What would the Buckleys say?

My attention shifted to the rearview mirror and I inspected the lemonade stand behind me. A folding table with a red-and-white-checked tablecloth, three pitchers of yellowish liquid set to one side and a stack of red Solo cups on the other, and a sign announcing lemonade for sale in two sizes—large and extra-large. Ice, apparently, was extra.

Joshua and Sonya stood in front of the table, smiling up at Grady as he said something. A woman I suspected was Charlotte's momma held a little boy on her lap where she sat behind the table, and an older girl—older than Joshua, in any case—

lifted one of the pitchers to pour liquid into a waiting cup. This one looked like a Buckley rather than like Charlotte. Same curly blond hair, same fair skin, same wide face shape and wee little nose. She must've been Charlotte's oldest.

A knock against my window had me glancing to my left. Beau smiled down at me through the glass for a tick, then reached for and opened my door.

"How you holdin' up, buddy?" My best friend looked like he wanted to laugh.

Beau had driven separate and must've beaten me here by several minutes as he already held a red cup in his hand, the sound of ice hitting the side of the cup audible as he jostled it.

I stood from the car, my hands lifting and falling to my thighs. "I honestly don't know what to say."

"It's a lot. But you got to admit, Charlotte did wonders with no notice and a shit situation. Don't be mad at her."

Shaking my head, I glanced at the sky. "I'm not mad. I'm . . ."

"What?"

"Impressed."

Beau grinned, clapping me on the shoulder. "Good. That's good."

"But Beau"—I tilted my head toward the lemonade stand—"do you think that's okay?"

"What? The kids? They're having a great time."

"No, I mean, do you think Charlotte will get in trouble?" I lowered my voice. "Bringing them around here?" When his forehead wrinkled, I added, "Her ex's family, the in-laws, they're not what I would call scrupulous people. Do you think if word got back to them that her kids were here, she'd find herself in front of a judge, fighting for custody again?"

Beau scratched his jaw, peering at me like I wasn't someone he recognized. "Hank, given everything that's gone wrong today, this is what you're worried about right now? Whether or not Charlotte might get in trouble with her ex's family for having her kids here?"

I nodded, seeing no reason to deflect. "I went to school with the Buckleys. They're a bunch of stuffy assholes. And—don't ask me how I know this—Charlotte had to give up a lot to keep full custody of the kids. I don't want her to, you know, do anything to jeopardize custody."

"Evidently, she thinks it's okay, otherwise she wouldn't have brought them."

"But what do *you* think?" I wanted Beau's opinion. He was better at gauging polite society stuff than I was. Based on Patty's assessment on Friday, Beau was probably better at gauging polite society stuff than Charlotte, too.

After a time of simply staring at me, he sighed. "I don't rightly know, but you make a good point." Biting his bottom lip, he glanced toward the lemonade stand. "I can, uh, ask Cletus and Jet to swing by, Drew, too. They can act as bouncers so Charlotte can send the kids home. You can donate some of today's proceeds to charity? Like reading literacy or something similar. That would look good in front of a judge."

"Yeah. I can do that."

"I'll also talk Jackson and some of the deputies into stopping by, having their cars washed. Jedediah Lawson won't mind bringing over a firetruck or two. If the Buckleys do make a stink, we can say it was for charity and the city had some vehicles washed. That should keep them off Charlotte's back."

"Good plan." I gathered a deep breath, taking another look around the parking lot now that I could see past my worry for Charlotte. "Hey, speaking of, where is Charlotte?"

"She's over there with your new bartender." Beau pointed toward the front of The Pink Pony.

My eyes followed and I immediately straightened, devouring the sight of Charlotte's exposed midriff, black sports bra with a zipper down the front, T-shirt draped over one shoulder, and her long, tight, black leggings. She also wore sunglasses, looking like a boss and telling everyone what to do while wearing a dazzling smile.

While I gaped, Beau said something about Shelly stopping by, or that he would be heading inside to work on the AC, or that aliens had just landed. Whatever. I wasn't listening.

My feet carried me over to Charlotte as all my previous worries and fleeting indignation fled my brain, eclipsed by a corporeal response to the magnetic vision before me. Jesus F. Christ, this woman. Calling the shots, bossing everyone around, turning the day's lemons into lemonade and inviting her kids over to sell it.

My breath hot in my lungs, I drew closer, gazing at her gorgeous, brilliant, determined features. Did she ever stop making the best out of every shitty situation? I wouldn't be surprised if she could spin gold from straw. What would it take to halt the hurricane of optimism, hard work, and competence that was Charlotte Mitchell?

And why was this version of her so fucking sexy?

"There you are," she said suddenly, her face pointed in my direction. Handing a phone and clipboard over to Louis and leaving him with a line of waiting patrons, she marched over to me.

As soon as she made it within arm's reach, but before I could say a word, she grabbed my elbow and tugged me to a small copse of trees just off the parking lot. Once we were under the shade, she took off my sunglasses, hooked them into my shirt, and whipped out a bottle of sunscreen from someplace unknown. She flipped open the top and proceeded to squeeze out a quantity of white liquid. Without asking, she smeared it on my face.

Any residual questions I'd wanted to ask dissipated as her hands moved over my skin.

"Did you bring a swimsuit? I told Beau to make sure you brought one." Her capable, strong palms slid to my neck. "Shelly said she'd grab one of hers for me. I should've just had my momma bring one when she brought the kids."

I sucked in air, my lips parting as I stared down at her lovely upturned face, her cheeks flushed red from the heat, her intelligent eyes barely visible behind her glasses. She focused solely on the progress of lotion being slathered over my features.

"Don't worry, I have plenty of sunscreen and bug spray," she said. Her fingers lowered inside the collar of my T-shirt and I squeezed my eyes shut to keep from groaning as something hotter than a Tennessee summer raced to the base of my spine.

She stepped to the side and behind me, rubbing the whole time and working me into a lather. The way she kneaded my shoulders felt like a massage. Clearly, it had been way too long since I'd been touched by a woman.

Then again, I'd never experienced a reaction like this from something so benign as applying sunscreen lotion. *It's the woman.* This *woman.*

"But the liquor delivery will be here in the next half hour. They were also late," she said, the statements making no sense to me in my present state.

Withdrawing her hands, Charlotte was apparently finished applying my sunscreen. I missed her touch immediately, and some unhinged instinct tempted me to take off my shirt and ask her to do my back. And front.

Stepping around to face me once more—but not standing quite as close now that I'd been painted in sunscreen—she wiped at the side of her face with the shirt laying on her shoulder.

"What do you want to do?" she asked, peering up at me. "Do you want me to wait for the delivery? Louis can help, but someone needs to take payment for the car wash."

"Delivery . . ." I parroted, dazed, my attention not knowing where to settle. Everywhere was equally good. Her hair was up in a ponytail. Sweat beaded and collected on her upper lip, dripped down her neck, and rolled between the swell of her absolutely fucking fantastic, perfection-personified breasts. At one point, she must've been sprayed with a hose. She was damp, and that made me want—

"Delivery!" The meaning of her monologue finally dawned on me and I brought both my hands up, balling them into fists. "Shit. The delivery."

"Yep. That's why I was here so early this morning." She placed her hands on her hips, surveying me. "Dave and Hector weren't feeling well last night—some sort of stomach bug. I told them to take the morning off and I'd help bring in the crates. I hope that was okay?"

I nodded, speechless, trying and failing not to be distracted by how she dabbed at her chest and neck with the cotton shirt. She had another freckle, a beauty mark, on her shoulder. If I licked it now, I'd taste salt.

Put your tongue back in your mouth, son. There will be no licking.

I snapped my mouth shut again, almost biting my tongue.

She gave me a searching stare, then glanced down at herself. "Oh. Sorry. I know you said baggy T-shirts only, and to be fair, I was wearing the shirt when I arrived, but it is hotter than Satan's laundromat in that club. You're lucky I'm not in my underwear."

"Yeah. *Lucky.*" I forced a smile and plucked my sunglasses from my shirt, sliding them back into place so I could hide my eyes and look my fill of the woman.

That's right, I wanted to look my fill. There'd be no licking, but it wasn't as though Charlotte would be working for me anymore. She'd given her notice. She'd never needed the money. We were no longer in an unequal power dynamic. We were equals, and there was nothing unprofessional about me checking her out. Nothing at all.

She's got to work out. I'd never seen biceps like that on a woman. And she had a six-pack.

Despite her brilliance and creativity this morning, the presence of her kids and mother, and the general organized chaos happening mere feet away, it was on the tip of my tongue to ask her about her workout routine when she asked me, "Can I change?"

"Pardon?"

"Is it okay if I change into a swimsuit?" She plucked at her pants, looking uncertain. "All the girls are in theirs already, and so is Serafina. She was making bread this morning and the ovens warmed everything up."

"I . . ." My mouth remained open even though no additional sound emerged. *Is today my birthday?*

"As soon as the AC is fixed, I'll put my clothes back on, I promise. But my body is producing inappropriate sweat marks in these pants. I keep having to hose off." She shuffled a step forward, gesturing to the white cotton on her shoulder. "I promise I'll put this baggy T-shirt over my swimsuit, but it's just so—"

"Hot."

"Right." A half smile pulled her mouth to one side. "When Shelly gets here, can I change?"

I pretended to consider her request. If Charlotte Mitchell wanted to put on a bathing suit and let me have that memory, who was I to tell her no?

"I'll leave it up to you," I finally said. "It's not like I'm your boss anymore. If, uh, putting on a bathing suit makes you more comfortable, then you should do what you think is best." A sudden thought occurred to me and I frowned, adding, "But no washing anyone's car."

Her lips parted, perhaps to protest, so I added, "Except mine. You can wash mine, if you want. But only behind the club. You're not being paid to put on a show for these fellas and you've already done enough outside of your job description. I know it's hot, but keep that T-shirt on."

She laughed lightly, taking off her sunglasses, and I greedily gazed into her gorgeous green eyes. They were warm today, emerald, still assessing, and her small smile looked grateful. "Thank you. Hannah and April both said they thought it would be no big deal if I wore a swimsuit, but I wanted to triple-check with you first."

I lifted an eyebrow at that. "No big deal?"

"Yeah. I believe Hannah's words were, 'What's one more mostly naked lady?'" Charlotte chuckled and stepped back.

I gave her a noncommittal smile. Charlotte being mostly naked was not in the same ballpark, world, or universe as a dancer being mostly naked while working.

Much of my adult life had been spent around folks who made their living being naked, and there was one thing I knew for certain: when dancers were working, being naked was no big deal. Just like when a model walked down a catwalk in underwear, they were simply wearing a uniform to do a job.

But when dancers were naked for any other reason besides work? It was a big fucking deal. Just like it was a big deal for most folks, except nudists and Germans.

"I better get back." She tossed her thumb over her shoulder. "Louis has been a real trooper, but I don't want to leave him alone for too long if I don't have to."

"Sure thing." I'd planned to apologize to her about my shitty behavior on Friday as soon as I arrived. But I reckoned it could wait until things settled.

"You're going to seriously regret wearing those jeans today." She gestured to my pants. "Or did you bring a swimsuit?"

I glanced at my jeans, then back at her. "I have swim trunks in my office. I'll change after we unload the delivery—*we*, meaning me and Louis. Unloading the truck isn't in your job description."

"Make sure you put sunscreen on yourself if you change into a suit. And okay, fine, about unloading the truck," she grumbled. "But may I just say, I don't mind helping at all. And it'll go faster if it's you and me unloading it. I already know where everything goes. And with the club hotter than Satan's—"

"Laundromat?" I smirked.

"I was going to say, *hotter than Satan's dim sum food truck* this time, but yes." She also smiled, wiping at her upper lip. "It's just, the faster we work getting everything done inside the club, the better. I swear, it's got to be over a hundred degrees in there already. I hope Beau and Shelly work fast."

"You're not paid to—"

"I know. But like I said, I don't mind. If it bothers you so much that unloading trucks isn't in my job description, then just give me a bonus. Organizing car washes isn't in my job description either."

I made a low, considering sound in the back of my throat, finally relenting. "Fine. Louis can take the payment for the car wash. You and I will unload the truck and I'll make sure your last paycheck has a bonus. Happy?"

"Blissfully." Batting her eyelashes, she returned her sunglasses to her nose. Then she turned from me, giving me an excellent view of her magnificent backside, and marched back over to poor Louis, who was presently swarmed with customers wanting their cars washed.

CHAPTER 15

HANK

"To get back my youth I would do anything in the world, except take exercise, get up early, or be respectable."

— OSCAR WILDE, *THE PICTURE OF DORIAN GRAY*

I'd never cared much about or ascribed to rules of social engagement. Stuffy folks and their arbitrary ideas about societal norms could stick those rules up their lily-white asses. That said, I had no idea what to do about Joshua and Sonya.

So . . .

Did I just . . .

Walk over?

Joshua and I made eye contact again across the parking lot, this made eye contact number six. I smiled tentatively and so did he. He also lifted his hand in a wave. Shifting on my feet, I returned his wave, not sure what to do, my attention relocating to his grandma, Mrs. Mitchell.

Charlotte's momma looked like she'd rather be anywhere else but here, her nose up in the air as though the trees around my club stank of bad reputation and new money. The woman didn't know me, but I suspected she didn't like me much; that didn't make her strange in this town; but it did make me wary of approaching the kids with her playing morality-police.

Redirecting her attention to the boy firecracker on her lap, who presently appeared determined to knock down every lemonade cup on the table, her face pulled into a frustrated glower. *Hmm.* I doubted she'd react well if I approached.

However, the urge to exchange a few words with Joshua and Sonya was strong. What were the rules about a strip club owner approaching little kids he sorta knew, had enjoyed spending time with, and had thought about from time to time over the past week? Was I—the strip club owner—allowed to talk to them? I suspected decent people didn't want their kids or grandkids talking to strip club owners.

Or perhaps I could buy a lemonade, and if Joshua spoke to me first, it would be okay for me to ask how he was doing. That wouldn't be untoward, right? I mean, they were selling lemonade. And buying lemonade would be a perfectly acceptable reason to approach.

Yeah. That's what I'd do. Then I could say hi to Joshua and Sonya and—

"Thirsty?" Hannah asked, suddenly at my elbow.

I glanced to the side. She held out a red Solo cup full of lemonade. Frowning, I accepted it with a grumbled "Thanks."

Well, there went that plan.

"You're welcome, boss." She winked at me. "I like these swim trunks on you."

I mumbled another thanks as I took a sip of the ice-cold drink. Feeling resigned, I sighed and scanned the lot for Charlotte. After she and I had finished bringing in the liquor delivery, I'd changed into my swim trunks and taken over the handling of credit cards. Meanwhile, she'd changed into the bathing suit Shelly had brought for her: a black string bikini that was too small.

Per her promise, and to my infinite regret, she'd covered up her delectable body with the big white T-shirt right after giving me a glorious and torturous eyeful, not that I was complaining. I didn't want any of the customers mistaking Charlotte for a dancer. I'd meant what I said. She wasn't being paid to put on a show; it wasn't in her job description. If anyone said or did anything to the contrary, like trying to talk her into washing their car or giving her a tip, I'd send her home straightaway.

When we left the hot confines of the club, she set about directing the queue of vehicles. Her baggy shirt left just her legs exposed from mid-thigh down. I hoped that'd be enough to discourage the customers.

The day wore on. Every so often, I'd glance up from processing payments to make sure all was well, but also because each time I lifted my gaze, her T-shirt was just a little bit wetter, and I'd find myself staring at her just a little bit longer until she sensed my stare. She'd smile her happy smile, one that made my stomach tense and my chest inexplicably hot, and then give me a friendly wave. Meanwhile, I'd endeavor to swallow around my heart as it climbed further up my throat.

Presently, she stood next to Jackson James—who she used to date not so long ago—and directed three new sheriff's deputy cars as they rolled into the lot. Jackson and Charlotte smiled at each other, he laughed at something she said, and she hit him on the shoulder. I told myself to stop grinding my teeth.

"Have you been working out, boss?" Hannah asked, reminding me she was still hovering at my elbow.

I'd forgotten she was there.

"I'm always working out, Hannah. Every day." If I wanted to drink beer and eat burgers, daily workouts were compulsory to stay in dancing-shape.

Female dancers could have curves and softness or be all lean lines and lankiness; they came in a variety of different shapes and sizes. Male dancers could not. The only things that varied between me and the other guys who did the hen parties were the color of our skin, how many inches we were over five-foot-ten-inches or under six-foot-three-inches, and the bulkiness of our build. No softness allowed.

"It's just that you're looking really great and I hoped you could give me some tips—"

"What do you really want?" I didn't mind the compliments, but I knew when someone was greasing me up to ask for a favor. Hannah might as well have been holding two sticks of butter.

She chuckled, then sighed. "All right. Um, I heard a rumor that Charlotte is leaving."

"That's right. She turned in her notice." I glanced back at the lemonade stand. Perhaps if I finished this serving of lemonade real quick, I could stroll over and ask for another. I took a big gulp from the red cup.

"Do you have someone in mind to replace her? if not, I'd like to apply."

Great minds think alike. "Why didn't you apply when Fred died?"

"He died on a Tuesday and Charlotte was hired the next Wednesday. You didn't even post the job." She crossed her arms. Then she waved at somebody.

I followed her line of sight. The recipient of her wave had been Jackson. He waved back. I grimaced.

"That's fair," I said, crossing my arms and not waving at Jackson. What did he want with Charlotte? He'd left her for that bombshell movie star earlier in the summer, Raquel Ezra, one of Sienna Diaz's actress friends. Why the hell was he chatting up his ex now?

The morning heat had only yielded a hotter afternoon, and I'd felt a smidge guilty about standing in the shade while Charlotte corralled customers. That said, the guilt hadn't outweighed my enjoyment of watching her dart from one car to the next, barking orders to the dancers and the guys sitting at their tables, and getting caught in the crosshairs of an errant stream of water. But I did not enjoy watching her talk to her ex-boyfriend.

When I didn't return Jackson's greeting, he dropped his hand and stopped waving.

I felt Hannah's eyes on me, so I faced her.

"I thought," she went on, "before you post the position, I should let you know I'm interested."

"You're hired."

Her lips parted. "What?"

"It's yours if you want it. But I have to warn you, Charlotte is updating the position description. It won't be the same job she or Fred had—there will be more responsibilities." As though pulled, I glanced at where Charlotte had been standing, relaxing when I spotted that she and Jackson were now separated.

"What kind of responsibilities?"

Returning my attention to Hannah, I used the next few minutes and the lull in processing car wash requests to describe the new position, including the tasks she'd be taking over from me, wanting her to be fully prepared for the range of responsibilities.

"But before you're hired—assuming you still want the job—the position description will be finalized and documented, signed off by both of us. We can revisit and update it in six months if you feel like there's some scope creep and you're doing additional work. I don't want you doing work you're not being—"

"*Paid for*, I know. It's your personal mantra." She chuckled, happy—excited, even. "Gosh, Hank. I can't thank you enough. I—I can't—"

"Don't thank me. You do the work and you'll get paid for the work you do. No thanks required."

She looked like she wanted to give me a hug, so I flatted my lips, kept my arms crossed, and shifted away. She'd get mostly shoulder and arm if she decided to go for it. I had a strict no-touching policy with my dancers and employees. Handshakes were okay, nothing else. They needed to know that I saw them as professionals. Touching was a two-way street and not something I welcomed.

In a business full of blurred lines, paramount importance should be placed on clearly defined and enforced boundaries. Firsthand, I'd witnessed the ramifications when the people in charge of keeping dancers safe allowed lines to be crossed. That behavior and those consequences would never be okay with me.

Hannah bounced on the balls of her feet and hopped back a distance, still smiling, still looking pleased, but thankfully taking the hint. "Well, okay then. I guess—do you—when do I start?"

"Go talk to Charlotte when you get a moment. The two of you can work on the schedule and I'll finalize the PD, benefits, and salary with her on Wednesday. Then we'll see what we see. Sound good?"

"Sounds great!"

"What sounds great?"

We both turned and made room for Beau as he strolled up, smiling his charming smile at Hannah, then me.

Hannah looked at me as though for permission to tell him. I nodded once.

"I'm retiring, Beau. I'm hanging up my pasties for a desk job."

"If that's what you want, then that's great, Hannah." Beau wrapped her in a hug of congratulations.

"Thanks," she said shyly, accepting his embrace with enthusiasm.

Hannah's stage name was Goldie, on account of her gold hair, and had been ever since she'd started with me years ago. Right now, she was glowing. That was great to see.

"It was all Charlotte's idea," I announced as they detached. Beau already knew this, of course. I'd told him last night, but I wanted Hannah to be aware, to give credit where credit was due. "She suggested you for the job when she turned in her notice. She's the one who suggested I increase the responsibilities."

"Are you serious?" Hannah squealed, spinning around, presumably to find Charlotte.

"Yep."

"Well, let me go say thank you, then!"

"Who's stopping you?" I grumped back, pleased for Hannah, of course, but irritated at the reminder that Charlotte would be replaced. By anyone.

Hannah snorted at my tone, rolling her eyes at me, but said nothing. She turned away and jogged toward Charlotte.

Beau moved to stand at my shoulder as Hannah departed. "Shelly got your AC working again. She's still inside, testing a few things out, but the unit should last for a good while now. When I fixed it in June, I forgot to—"

"Fine. Thanks. How long before we can go back inside?"

Beau gathered a deep breath before responding. "You'll have to wait until tomorrow. It'll need at least eighteen hours to cool down the inside."

"Great."

"Give everyone the night off. They've done enough today."

"I will."

"Go out, all together. Have a few beers. Relax with your staff. Seems like an opportunity."

I nodded, liking this idea, but said nothing. I'd ask Charlotte what she thought.

"Hank. You're still irritated. I would've thought you'd be happy with how the day went, all things considered. Looks like most of your regulars came out for this little event."

Grunting, my attention snagged on the lemonade stand, and my vision narrowed as disappointment thrummed in my chest. It looked like Charlotte's momma was abandoning the post. The kids were already in their car, their grandma sliding into the driver's seat. Beau's brothers had taken over, with Jethro taking the money and Cletus pouring the lemonade.

I'd missed my chance.

Well, that's just fucking great.

Mouth sour from more than just lemonade, I tossed the remainder of my drink to the ground and turned a frown on Beau. "Hey, let me ask you something." I reckoned he would know whether or not it'd be okay for me to be seen saying hi to Joshua and Sonya without causing trouble for Charlotte. If presented with a future opportunity while in public, I didn't want to miss out on talking to them again.

"What's up?" Beau wiped his hands off on a rag, paying close attention to his cuticles.

"Let's say I sorta know two kids in a family of four and think they're awesome. Just really awesome people." I gestured to Charlotte's momma's car, currently pulling out of the lot.

"You mean Charlotte's kids?"

"Yeah. Joshua and Sonya, specifically. I don't know the other two." I lifted my eyes beyond him and continued in an academic tone. "What I want to know is, on a scale from one to ten, how socially—socially—" My brain stopped because it was officially my birthday. And New Year's and Cinco de Mayo and Rama Navami, and Shelly Sullivan was now my most favorite person in the entire world.

"Hey," Beau said from someplace to my right, nudging me. "Hank."

I didn't acknowledge him; I was too busy watching Charlotte.

Correction: I was too busy staring at Charlotte.

"Hank," Beau grit out again, then whispered harshly, "did you hear me?"

Ignoring him, I pulled off my sunglasses to get a better look. Approximately one moment ago, she'd been walking around in her mostly dry tent of a T-shirt, but now Charlotte was soaking wet, engaging in a water fight, her and April against Hope and Hannah. All the women were laughing, and most of the guys were watching, open-mouthed, enjoying the show. Me included.

This, the vision before me, was literally what wet dreams were made of. I did not hesitate taking mental snapshots of Charlotte Mitchell, wet and flushed and hot and laughing her great laugh, looking carefree and like she was having the time of her life.

Thank you, Universe. Tomorrow, I was buying Shelly Sullivan a car. Or a boat. Or a house. Whatever she wanted.

Beau snapped his fingers in front of my face. I frowned at his interruption.

"What? What do you want?" Didn't he realize this was a once in a lifetime event? Couldn't he give me five damn minutes?

"What is the matter with you?" he asked, sounding more amused than irritated. "The heat addled your brain or something?"

"Can't you see I'm busy?"

Beau lifted an eyebrow—he did this a lot recently—and glanced pointedly toward the water fight and Charlotte. "I can see you checking out your *employee*, Hank," he accused, though he wore a confused smile, his tone disbelieving. "Is something going on I should know about?"

"She's not my employee anymore. She quit." Giving my complete attention back to the women spraying each other with water, I chewed on my bottom lip and pulled in a deep breath, holding it in my lungs, my brain close to catching on fire.

"She's your employee for nearly two more weeks," he said, but I wasn't listening.

If there was a god, clearly it loved me and had plotted to give me this moment to make me happy. But it also hated me a little because Charlotte had just picked up a soapy sponge and tossed it at Hannah, which made Hannah toss a soapy sponge right back at her.

And now she was covered in soap and I was close to suffocating in lust.

Before I could catch the impulse, a muttered half groan of "Jesus" fell out of me and I lowered the clipboard I'd been holding to cover my groin.

Beau made an unhappy sound. "You cannot be serious right now." He hit my shoulder, his tone turning urgent. "Please tell me you're not—"

"Shh."

"Don't *shh* me, I'm trying to—"

I reached to the side and, without looking, endeavored to cover his mouth with my hand. "Shut up, Beau. Just let me have this."

Laughing like something was unbelievable, he caught my wrist and yanked it away. "I am so confused. I mean, you spend day in and day out surrounded by gorgeous, naked women and have never looked at any of them twice. And now you're staring at Charlotte like she's a wish fulfillment. You couldn't stand her three weeks ago."

April and Hope were holding up their hands, calling a truce, and I frowned, aggravated at the potential cease-fire. *No. Don't stop. Fight fight fight.*

"I'm not going to date a dancer who works for my club, dummy." Making a face, I answered his non-question, craning my neck. Charlotte had dropped out of sight behind a car.

"Why not?"

"I'm their—you know—I'm their mentor, their boss. They need to be able to trust me, and it would be incredibly unprofessional, not to mention unethical. Besides, I don't think of them like that. They're family, like having a bunch of sisters and brothers."

He made a sound as though to argue.

I added, "Unlike some folks, I have morals and don't date my subordinates." I said this last part to tease him, but also hoping it would shut him up.

Before he and Shelly started dating, he'd been her boss at the Winston Brothers auto repair shop. Actually, technically, he was still her boss and they'd been together for years.

"Ha ha. You know it wasn't like that with Shelly. She and—never mind," he grumbled, huffed, then hit my shoulder again. "Are you—are you planning on asking Charlotte out? Now that she's not working for you?"

Charlotte reappeared. The hose she held no longer sprayed water, and the water fight seemed to be at an end, but that didn't matter. The big, baggy white T-shirt she'd been wearing was now—finally—completely soaked, clinging to every heavenly curve, molded over her luscious skin, and highlighting the fact that the bikini Shelly brought was definitely two sizes too small.

Wet dreams, indeed. Thank you, unknown deity, whoever you are.

"Hank?"

"What?"

"Are you planning on asking her out?" I registered a hint of uncertainty in Beau's voice and it struck a nerve in me, the same one Patty had plucked on Friday.

"Of course not," I snapped.

"Why 'of course not'?" His tone had mellowed, sounded curious. "Obviously, you like her. Or the way she looks, at least."

"But nothing could ever happen between us, could it? I'm a sleezy strip club owner and she's a church-going single mother of four." Too distracted to modulate my tone, unintentional bitterness crept into the words, bitterness that surprised me.

He sighed loudly. "You're not sleezy."

"I'm a reprobate and a stain on—on . . ." Sidetracked, I frowned as Charlotte pulled the fabric away from her front, apparently just realizing how transparent the wet T-shirt had become.

The other ladies circled around her. Emma handed her a limp towel, and Everly wagged a finger at one of the firefighters who was holding out cash toward Charlotte, saying something about Charlotte not being a dancer.

Oh. Shit.

A spike of freezing sobriety and shame had me shoving my clipboard at Beau, grabbing one of the dry towels nearby and jogging over, leaving without another word. Hadn't I said not more than three hours ago that Charlotte wasn't being paid to put on a show? Hadn't I preached to her about her job description? And what had I done? I was such a fucking hypocrite.

Reprimanding myself for not stepping in earlier, I held up the dry towel and wrapped it around her shoulders as soon as I reached her, tucking her under my arm.

"Hey, you okay?" I asked, sending the firefighter who'd tried to give Charlotte cash a pointed look. *Back off, asshole.*

"I'm perfectly fine, Hank. How are you?" she said, sounding fine, if not a little perplexed.

"Sorry, Charlotte." Hope was suddenly in our path, her contrite gaze darting to mine, then away. "I wasn't thinking."

"What? Honey, you have nothing to be sorry about." Charlotte, wearing a wide, unconcerned-looking smile, grabbed Hope's hand and gave it a squeeze. "I haven't laughed like that in ages. So much fun."

Hope took a step back, her lips forming a tight smile. "I better get to work."

"I'll return just as soon as I find a dry shirt," Charlotte said on a laugh, wringing out her shirt.

No, she won't. I'm sending her home.

Mentally cursing myself with each step we took toward the club, I led her away, unable to fathom my reckless selfishness. I should've put a stop to the water fight as soon as Hope sprayed Charlotte with the hose, not stood around like a brainless fuck, holding my dick and gathering spank-bank material.

Charlotte had quit on Friday. But for today and the next twelve days, she was still technically on the clock. My job and responsibilities remained unchanged until the very last hour of her very last shift. She would not be exploited—not by me, not by anyone.

* * *

Hanging back, I hovered by the bar, not sure whether to stay or go.

"Can I borrow the shirt you were wearing earlier? I don't want to wear those leggings again," she grumbled, draping her towel on the back of a chair, which left the wet tee clinging to her body again.

"Uh, sure thing." Wanting to bite my knuckle, I gritted my teeth instead.

Charlotte's gaze flickered to mine. "I don't have to if you—"

"No, no. It's fine. My clothes are right there, on the table." Since my assurances didn't sound at all convincing, I cleared my throat and added, "Thanks for your help today. I appreciate you arranging everything so quickly. And so, uh, well."

"No problem," she said, turning and giving me an even better view of her ass than before, and what a glorious ass it—

Nope. Think of . . . think city council meetings. JT MacIntyre. And babies crying on airplanes.

I backed up another step, but then stopped, hesitating. Leaving her alone inside the suffocating club wasn't a good idea. Shelly may have fixed the AC, but it was still, as Charlotte had said, hotter than Satan's laundromat in here, hotter than outside, even, with the main room cooler than the offices and changing rooms in the back, since we couldn't open the windows and there were no blinds. Passing out due to heat exposure didn't seem outside of the realm of possibility. I should've hosed down, too.

Admittedly, some strange instinct also had me feeling protective of her after everything that I'd let happen in the parking lot. Best we stick together, she hurry up, and I send her home as soon as possible.

But I hesitated where usually I'd make a decision, take action, and stick to it. I asked, "Do you—do you want me to . . .?" I pointed behind me with my thumb.

"Nah." Charlotte pulled her shirt over her head and I immediately dropped my attention to my flip-flops, my neck and face flushing hot, a pulse of something that felt a lot like need or longing pressing outward against every inch of my skin. I heard her shirt fall to the floor with a wet splat. "It's not like I got anything you haven't seen already."

Mouth twisting with a sardonic smile, I clenched my jaw to keep a tortured laugh inside my lungs, but thoughtless words had my mouth running. "What you don't know or seem to understand about men is a lot."

"Oh really?" She sounded amused and a little closer, likely picking through my clothes on the table nearby.

Which meant, in a moment, she'd be wearing my shirt.

I closed my eyes and managed a strangled, "Yes."

"What is it that I don't know? Enlighten me."

"I'd rather not."

She chuckled. There was a brief silence. Then she chuckled again. "Do you really have your eyes closed? Afraid I'll shock your delicate sensibilities with my stretch marks?"

"No," I rasped, ignoring the impulse to show her my stretch marks if she showed me hers.

"Oh. Before I forget . . ." I heard a chair scrape against the floor, the rustle of fabric before she continued the thought. "I meant to tell you when we were unloading the boxes earlier, I put the rye behind the bar. Louis said we were running short. Is it okay for the liquor to be exposed to such high heat?"

Finally, a safe subject. "The hard stuff should be fine for the short term, and the wine is all in the fridge. But Louis? Our new bartender? How would Louis know what we're running low on?"

"This morning, when you didn't arrive after I gave him the tour, I told him to do an inventory of the stock up here." Charlotte sounded like she stood directly in front of me and I fought the temptation to sneak a peek. "He made a list of what was low and I put the list on your desk after I looked it over."

I grinned at her thoughtfulness and cleverness. "Thank you, Charlotte. That's very, *very* helpful."

"You're welcome, Hank. But you know—" She paused again and I waited, the beat of my heart urging me to open my eyes. Anticipation caused a little death of my self-control every time I inhaled the smothering atmosphere. "If you really wanted to thank me," she finally said, her tone teasing, "you'd tell me if you plan to offer that job to Hannah. And if you *really* wanted to thank me, you'd offer her the job today. You can open your eyes now."

Blinking, I found her wearing my cotton button-down shirt and—as I'd suspected—standing directly in front of me. My chest tightened. She hadn't buttoned it fully. Compelled by the sight, I shuffled forward, officially jealous of my shirt. Charlotte had crossed her arms. This drew my attention to the swell of her breasts, the too-small triangles of her black bikini just visible in the open collar.

I felt my grin stretch. Hannah must not have told or thanked Charlotte earlier before their water fight. *Interesting.*

"Hmm. How else can I express my gratitude?" I asked, wanting to tease her back.

"Hurry the hell up and make up your pretty little mind about Hannah so I can get someone trained."

My feet carried me an inch closer, my attention affixed to her mouth. She had a great mouth. "*Little* mind?"

"No. *Pretty* little mind. Don't forget the pretty. It's so pretty."

I noted how several strands of her hair had sprung free from her long ponytail and pasted themselves to her neck.

"That a compliment or an insult?" I asked, taking a long look at her bare legs.

"Why can't it be both?" Smiling, she leaned closer, intercepting my gaze and filling my vision, so close.

Fire in my lungs, I spoke nonsense, not considering my words. "You wound me, Charlotte. And here I thought you respected me."

"I do. Mostly," she said on a laugh. God, she was so beautiful, especially when she laughed. And I loved her laugh, how easily she laughed, how funny she was, kind, sweet. Not two feet separated us now. She was the only thing I saw.

"Mostly?" I said, just above a whisper.

Charlotte's always-assessing eyes seemed to darken, dance, her voice mimicking mine: low, intimate. "When you offer Hannah the job, you'll have my full respect."

"And what, precisely, does your full respect get me?" I truly wanted to know.

She cocked her head to the side, her gaze sliding to my lips. My heart kicked up.

"Well," she whispered. "What do you want?"

I bit my tongue to keep from answering, the words on the tip of my tongue too honest. Halting the momentum of our effortless but dangerous banter felt like walking into a wall, and looking down at her wearing my shirt, at the hazy look in her eyes, the urge to close the distance between us was almost unbearable.

Did she feel it, too? She had to, right? This thing—this distraction and preoccupation, this pull—it couldn't be one-sided, could it?

"Charlotte—" I licked my lips.

Her eyes remained fastened to my mouth as she breathed out, "Yes?"

I struggled to swallow. I hated this. I wasn't used to it, this indecision, the second-guessing.

What were we? I wasn't her boss, not really. She could leave whenever she wanted. By her own admission, she only gave me two weeks' notice because she wanted to stay and help, not because she needed to. She wasn't my employee. We weren't colleagues. We were barely friends. Acquaintances, certainly. An acquaintance I admired, and respected, and desired, but what did that—

"Fuck it." I grabbed her arms and tugged her close, silencing her startled gasp with a kiss.

CHAPTER 16

HANK

"So she thoroughly taught him that one cannot take pleasure without giving pleasure, and that every gesture, every caress, every touch, every glance, every last bit of the body has its secret, which brings happiness to the person who knows how to wake it."

— HERMANN HESSE, *SIDDHARTHA*

Her surprise yielded, quickly becoming unconditional surrender, and she sighed against my mouth, her body melting. But her hands were grasping, greedy, her nails digging aggressively into my sides. I rewarded her fervor by grabbing two handfuls of her backside and giving the generous globes an enthusiastic, lascivious squeeze.

Who the hell am I kidding? It was a reward for me, and she felt fantastic.

Charlotte overwhelmed me, dragged me under the tide of a fantasy becoming reality. I wanted my hands to always be full of her, her mouth always on mine, and her response to my touch always this restless and anxious. Certainty that kissing her had been the right choice—the only choice—swept through me, a satisfaction close to painful swelling in my chest, leaving my brain buzzing while an urgent thought surfaced.

She's mine. Mine. MINE.

Yes.

Parting my lips to breathe, I licked at the seam of hers, my body rocking rhythmically, instinctively, searching, my hands sliding up her back, wrapping her in a tighter hold. Her lips parted and our tongues met, stroked, mated, electric shocks and expanding rightness arresting my lungs. She moaned, pressing closer. The sound reverberated to the base of my spine, and my hips snapped forward on instinct.

Her breath hitched, an excited sound, and her arms twined around my neck, molding to me beautifully, her curves impatient beneath my hands. We didn't click together like hard edges of a puzzle but with fingers linking, giving and taking, reforming, accommodating, our bodies moving in perfect unison. As our tongues tangled, I swear, part of my soul left my body, an offering of both gratitude and an appeal that this moment last forever. She tasted of hunger. Heaven. Heat.

Gasping for air, Charlotte lifted her chin and I immediately fastened my mouth to her jaw, then neck, kisses wet and biting as I pulled the side of the shirt—my shirt—to the side. I needed to taste that freckle I'd spotted earlier. *Warmth and salt. Perfect.*

Charlotte moaned again, then panted, the sounds harsh and uneven and eager. Her palms roamed lower, down my back, then slid around to my front to massage and grab at my chest and abdomen.

"You are so sexy," she said on a trembling breath. "I need—I need—" she whimpered as my hands pushed up her shirtfront, massaging her generous tits through the flimsy fabric triangles of the too-small bikini.

"Jesus fucking fuck," I growled, every coherent thought obscured by clouds of disorienting desire. *This is new.* I'd never been beyond the reach of my reason before. It was like jumping with no parachute and no mind for my own safety, and I didn't care. I loved it. I wanted it. Needed it.

In my defense, her breasts were the most erotic gratification, made for my hands, the perfect weight. And her responsiveness, how she sucked in a tight breath and pushed her chest forward, the soft keening sound slipping past her lips—also perfect.

How had I survived without touching her before now? And why weren't her breasts in my mouth? I needed to taste more of her skin. I needed her nipple growing hard under my tongue and fingers. I needed to tease her, I needed—I needed *her*, more of her filling my hands, more friction, more of her sounds, more of her surrounding me, and less potential for space between us.

Clumsily backing her up, we halted when her thighs met a table. I lifted her in one mindless, fluid motion, unbuttoning the shirt she wore with frantic, shaking hands.

"Ah, God. Hank. Wait, wait, wait." Her fingers spasmed on my sides, then moved to my shoulders, pushing at me with gentle pressure. "Do you—do you have a condom?"

"I—" I blinked. *Condom?* No. No, no. I wasn't fucking her in my bar. This wasn't—

"I'm not having sex without a condom," she said hurriedly, her nails already digging back into my skin, indulging in a nipping kiss and catching my bottom lip.

Giving my head a quick shake to form words, I focused on undoing the buttons of the shirt, saying, "I do have a condom, but—"

"I have an implanted IUD since Frankie was born, but I stopped having sex without condoms way before that. I know they're not infallible—which is why Frankie is here—but through some miracle, the only STD I got from Kevin was chlamydia—all cleared up, by the way—and there's no way I'll ever—"

"Charlotte." Regretfully abandoning the shirt, I pressed my thumb against her lips, loving the softness, knowing they'd feel like heaven wrapped around my cock and grimacing with the effort to shove that addictive image aside. "We're not having sex."

"We're not?" she whispered, flinching a millimeter away, her mouth moving against my finger. "Then what are we doing?"

I couldn't pull enough air into my lungs; my head was fuzzy. All the blood had rushed south.

What are we doing?

"Hank?"

As I stared into her wide eyes, I wavered. Rational Hank wanted a chance with her, wanted her to be a part of my life in some real way—at *least*—and far more than this desperate groping. And I wanted to be part of hers.

But irrational Hank wanted to fuck her. Hard and fast. Right now. On this table. With her ankles on my shoulders, and my thumb on her slippery clit, and her breast in my mouth, and her nails scratching up my neck as she screamed my name and came around my cock, over and over.

Decisions, decisions.

We could do both?

While I wavered, Charlotte dropped her hands from my body. I blinked, startled to find the haze in her expression had seemed to clear, leaving her eyes stark and her mouth open. "I'm sorry," she choked out. "I—I don't know what I'm—oh my God, I'm so sorry."

"No, no. Don't apologize." I stole a kiss, gathering her hands in both of mine, wanting them back on me. I kissed her again. "You're so addictive," I muttered unthinkingly between kisses, still undecided—to fuck or not to fuck, that was the question.

Obviously, she wanted me. Good. But making love in my club wasn't an option. I wanted something . . . something else for our first time. Perhaps . . . I'd make her orgasm now, then explain how things would be moving forward. We'd cement this thing between us, and everything would be settled.

Which left only one question: fingers or mouth?

Decisions, decisions.

We could do both?

Something that sounded like a strangled groan tumbled from her lips while I mentally debated and she bowed away, taking her mouth from mine. I blinked her into focus again. The red of her cheeks flushed a deeper shade, and she leaned back.

Frustrated, I watched as she curled her shoulders and withdrew her fingers from mine to clutch her forehead. "No. God. I am sorry. I don't—we have to stop." She released a harsh breath. "What the hell was I thinking? Of course we're not about to have—have—"

I caught her cheeks between my palms and lifted her chin, kissing her. I needed to, but also to shut her up. I didn't know what was going on in her head, but apparently, I needed to think of the right words and quick. She was withdrawing.

Charlotte kissed me back, but not with her earlier surrender. A new tension in her body kept her shoulders pulled forward. She still tasted like heaven, but also like hesitation.

Unwilling to let her go far, I leaned my forehead against hers and separated our mouths, my breathing labored. "Charlotte—"

"Hank—"

"Let me say something." Lifting my chin, I ensnared her eyes and narrowed mine to show I meant business.

"Wait. I—I shouldn't have—"

I stepped more completely between her legs. "Angel, please. Let me speak."

At my use of the endearment, or it was the *please,* her gaze softened and some of her tension visibly eased. Charlotte swallowed, nodded, and her hands rose to my wrists. I felt unease there too, like she didn't know whether to hold on or remove my palms from her face.

Tucking a honeyed strand of hair behind her ear, I let my fingertips trail softly against her earlobe down to the silky skin of her neck, a spike of pleasurable warmth shooting down my spine as she shivered. "If you let me," I whispered, "I will make you come on this table, right now. I will kneel and eat your pussy until you see stars. And I will fuck and make love to you literally anywhere else, as many times as you want, in whatever positions you prefer. But not here, not in my club. And not 'til we settle a few things between us."

Her lashes fluttered. "What kinds of things?"

"You and me and the future kind of things." I smoothed my hand from her shoulder to her forearm, twisting my wrist to lace our fingers together. Perhaps it was temporary madness, but I added, "Specifically, what I need to do in order to make this happen for us, to make things right for you. Just so you know, nothing is off the table. I'll do anything." And I meant every word.

Despite the omnipresent heat of the club, her cheeks lost some of their color. "I . . . see."

"Do you?" I tugged her closer, nipping at her lips, unable to help myself. Jesus, fuck. She was so delicious. I couldn't wait to put my mouth on her cunt. My mouth watered at the thought. "Then name a time and place so I can get started."

A new sort of laugh burst out of her, a nervous-sounding one, and it chilled the satisfied buzzing in my brain. I was the one who pulled away this time, needing to see her eyes. They were assessing, as always, but also cagey. Her lovely mouth pressed into a grim-looking line and she seemed to swallow with some trouble.

"Hank." She said my name softly, gently, and with a quiet kind of desperation that sounded like the wrong kind of pleading.

I said nothing, but my hands tightened of their own accord, my heart beating louder between my ears. We stared at each other, and the riddle of her features—this look she was giving me—had me standing straighter.

Her chin wobbled. She firmed it and cleared her throat. "I honestly can't believe I'm doing this, and my teenage self would never forgive me," she said, words tumbling out of her, her voice scratchy, "but—uh—I think—I think we just, um—" She took a deep breath, her eyebrows pulling together in a pacifying kind of entreaty. "It's just that I got carried away. I made a mistake. I shouldn't have and I can't do this. And I'm sorry."

The chill slid down the back of my neck and twisted around my chest. "Carried away," I repeated, a cold heaviness landing in my stomach.

Charlotte shook her head. "I can't do this." Abruptly, she leaned away, extracting herself, removing her hands from mine. "This isn't—I'm not—"

"Whoa. Slow down."

I made to take her hand again and she balled it into a fist, twisting to the side. Flinching, I automatically stepped back, wanting to give her space if she needed it while also hating the increased distance between us. Which might've been why words vacated my mouth unchecked.

Desperate words.

Stream of consciousness, total fucking lunacy.

"I don't have to eat you out if you don't want. We'll do whatever you want. I just need to make you feel good. Whatever that means for you. I want us to be—to be together, however I fit in your life. Tell me what you want me to do and I'll do it. We could—"

"I find you attractive!" she hollered as she jumped off the table, her hands stiff and fluttering around her head like she was batting away mosquitos. The way she spoke gave me the sense the statement was an accusation, but she was the guilty party.

"Ditto," I croaked, taking another step back. I watched her button the shirt—my shirt—starting with the very top button while my rambling statements from seconds prior caught up with me.

We'll do whatever you want.

I just need to make you feel good.
Whatever that means for you.
Tell me what you want me to do and I'll do it.
Christ. Had I just . . . begged?

"No. I find you *very* attractive," she ground out, continuing as though this was unfortunate news. The worst news. "I like you *a lot*. I'd very much like for you to be in my life. I want to be with you. But that's impossible."

My stomach did this swooping thing at her tone, lifting then diving, making me slightly nauseous. *It's the club.* If I sold the club, if I made myself respectable, would that make things possible between us?

The urge to offer her whatever she wanted, to be whatever she wanted, still hadn't fully subsided and I didn't recognize or particularly like this desire in myself, this desperation. I said nothing, not trusting myself to speak.

"It's impossible and it doesn't matter. I'm not in a place right now—and will never be again—where I can name a time to meet someone for—for—for *positions*. Or a future." Her chin was tucked to her chest, her eyes on the placket of the shirt, her fingers fumbling on the buttons. "In fact, I don't want to, not really. I mean, I do. But I also don't. It wouldn't be fair to you, or good for me. Not with anyone."

When her meaning finally landed, I flinched as I absorbed it. "Not with anyone."

She nodded jerkily. "That's right. I've officially retired from having a sex and/or love life. Not with a butcher, not a baker, not a candlestick maker. Or a bouncer at a club either. Or the club's exceptionally stubborn, sexy, smart, sweet, and surprising owner. No matter how much I . . ." She seemed to be gulping in air again, her eyes closing.

Once more, her chin wobbled. Once more, she firmed it. "I'm so sorry."

I winced. "Stop apologizing."

She gave her head a stiff shake. "I never should have kissed you back," she whispered, the words slow and measured, even as emotion strained each syllable. "It was a mistake and I regret it. An incredibly irresponsible and reckless mistake. I have no excuse other than I really, really wanted to kiss you, and I still really, really want to. And I shouldn't. I can't. It's selfish. And I *am* sorry, but mostly for myself."

Before I could unravel this last part, Charlotte grabbed the towel I'd wrapped her in earlier and sprinted out of the club, leaving me in Satan's laundromat, buried under a mountain of confusion. Despair—*she thinks kissing me was a mistake, she doesn't want to be with anyone*—and hope—*but she still wants me*—warred with each other while I stood perfectly still, my ears ringing, my stomach at my feet.

However, try as I might, I felt no regret.

Not for kissing her. Not for turning down sex when she offered. Not even for begging.

CHAPTER 17

HANK

"For it is in your power to retire into yourself whenever you choose."

— MARCUS AURELIUS, *MEDITATIONS*

"*Y*ou're in a bad mood."

I shot Beau a glare. It was Wednesday morning. I didn't need my best friend telling me I was in a bad mood. I knew I was in a bad mood. We were fishing, or trying to. I couldn't concentrate and had lost two of my best lures because—*Charlotte.*

"Are you trying to scare all the fish away with your loud talking?" I snapped.

"No." He gave me a good-natured side-eye. "But I think you are with that thundercloud on your face. What's wrong? Did something happen yesterday at the hen party? Your G-string too tight or something?"

Grunting, I made no effort to adjust my scowl, a virtually permanent expression since Charlotte left the club on Sunday after telling me she was 'retired.'

Neither of the bachelorette parties had been especially rowdy this week. The matron of honor last night had seemed pleased and had tipped generously both before and after our live performances. But I hadn't been in the right frame of mind to entertain for either of them. I'd forced it, using a trick I'd been taught during my first few months as a dancer in Boston.

Most of us dancers, in order to get through any particular shift, pictured someone else's face and body in place of whichever customer stuffed bills in our underwear or sat still for a lap dance. This was standard. A simple coping mechanism. I'd done it loads of times. Every dancer I knew did.

But for the last two nights, for the first time in my life, instead of some random celebrity or actress, and despite repeatedly telling my brain to stop, the woman I found myself imagining was a real person. My chest tightened just thinking about it.

Every woman who'd touched me had been Charlotte.

Every woman who'd watched me with a hazy expression had been Charlotte.

Every woman I'd winked at and made laugh and blush had been Charlotte.

The Pony provided a service within specified boundaries spelled out and agreed upon ahead of time between consenting adults, all parties fully aware of the rules and requirements, with special attention paid to fairness, equitability of pay, and safety. We followed clearly defined procedures. Nothing untoward occurred in my club, nothing wrong or illegal or risky.

Rules meant I hadn't felt discontent after a show in a long, long time. But I did this week. And I did now.

"Come on, Hank. What happened?" Beau sounded concerned. "And don't tell me nothing. Something is obviously on your mind."

"I don't want to talk about it." I turned my face away, swallowing around the gravel in my throat.

How did I explain to Beau that I'd used Charlotte Mitchell as my mental stand-in for all of the women last night? That I'd found myself imagining her long, athletic body, golden hair, sunny smile, and dismissive, assessing eyes in place of every person who'd touched me with their gaze and fingertips? That I'd barely slept due to the baffling, relentless, pointless ache of longing?

For the first time in my whole damn life, a situation of my own making, a circumstance built from my choices, left me unsatisfied and restless. I wanted Charlotte, to be with her, and I knew she wanted me, too. She'd said as much. I needed to figure out how to arrange things such that whatever obstacle made her hesitate was removed.

Whatever she wanted, I'd do it if she'd give us a chance. It was possible my promises had been influenced by heat-of-the-moment lunacy at the time, but I still meant them two days later. *She's not giving anyone a chance.* Chewing on my lip, I pondered this quandary for no less than the thousandth time in fifty-six hours.

Okay, backing up. This was where we stood:

Fact 1: Charlotte had admitted she wanted me.

Fact 2: I wanted her.

Fact 3: She didn't want to be with anyone.

Fact 4: Women spoke in riddles.

A grumbly sound vibrated in my chest, and my face pulled into a scowl. I rubbed my bottom lip with my index finger, remembering our kiss, the perfection of her touch, taste, her laugh and smile and gorgeous eyes. She didn't want to meet anyone for positions? *Clearly she hasn't tried the right positions . . . or the right partner.*

Not for the first time in my life, my lip curled into a sneer as I thought of Kevin Buckley. I swore to the deity who'd put Charlotte in the wet T-shirt and too-small bikini, if I ever saw that dick-sandwich again, I'd—

Well, I'd—

Hmm.

Now, let's see. Those assholes cared about one thing: money. I'd figure out a way to collapse his business deals, short his stocks, and undercut his real-estate holdings. *Yeah . . .* Then I'd ruin his credit. I made a mental note to talk to Cletus Winston. He'd have some good ideas. Plus, I liked that he was a tit-for-tat kinda guy, always kept the scales balanced. Yet, at the same time, I never knew what he would want in return whenever I asked a favor. Usually, it was information.

Anything would be worth it to make sure Kevin Buckley gets what he deserves.

Beau heaved a sigh. "Fine. If you don't wish to discuss it, I'm not going to force you. When you're ready, you know where I live."

"I do. And I'll let you know," I said, reeling in my bait. I set my rod aside. "We should head back. I got a—a busy day."

Charlotte hadn't worked Monday or Tuesday, but today she'd be back in the office. I covered my face with my hands and rubbed. She'd said she didn't want to plan a future with anyone, which possibly meant she didn't want to feel pressured. There had to be a way for us to be together without her feeling pressured by it.

But I didn't want to pressure her. She was amazingly generous, giving, and kind. Clever and funny. Sweet. She'd stayed at The Pony and fixed my whole damn finance system when she didn't need to, when most folks would've just left after obtaining the information they were after.

If anyone deserved to be made happy, it was Charlotte. I wanted to make her happy, make her feel good. Make her feel great. Make her come. Give her orgasms—lots of them. It only seemed fair. How did I get her to agree?

"Oh. That's right," Beau's cheerful voice said. "Today is Charlotte's party?"

Grinding my teeth and letting my hands drop, I nodded.

The party. The going-away party for Charlotte. I'd been informed by Hannah and the dancers on Monday evening after my set that they were planning to give her a big send-off and it was my job to bring a gift.

"Huh." Beau laughed lightly. "Charlotte worked at The Pony less than two weeks before she gave her notice and y'all are throwing her a going-away party. She must've made a big impression."

He had no idea. Three weeks ago, my biggest worry was whether my funeral suit would fit. Now I was a disaster. Because of a woman. A generous, sweet, sexy, smart, stunning, capable woman. *How do I fix this? How do I arrange things to make her happy?*

"Hank?"

Giving my head a shake, I muttered, "It was Hannah's idea." I stood and busied myself with the anchor.

"When's her last day?"

"Uh, she's got eight days left, which she'll use to, you know, come in as needed to help Hannah acclimate." Hannah had told me as much last night. Apparently, the two women had talked and settled everything without me.

"Why're y'all throwing her party now instead of on her last day?" Beau also stood, wrapping his line so it wouldn't tangle.

I shrugged, scratching my neck. "A few reasons. Wednesdays generally aren't busy. Charlotte's kids are back at school in two weeks and her regular job starts again next week—on Monday. Everyone wanted to accommodate her schedule." They liked her. A lot.

Beau's eyes were on me; I felt them. Turning over my shoulder, I glanced his way. He clearly had something to say. He was doing that thing with his mouth where his bottom teeth jutted out and tapped against his top teeth.

"What?"

"It's—and don't get me wrong, I'm glad it all worked out—is it strange that I'm a bit irritated with Charlotte on your behalf?"

I felt my mouth hook to the side.

He went on, "She lied to you about why she wanted a job at The Pony, made everyone freak out when she accepted that job at The G-Spot. Feels manipulative."

He'd always been this way, predisposed to think well of me despite evidence to the contrary, or be upset on my behalf when I didn't seem upset enough.

My smile stretched with appreciation for my friend. "No. It wasn't like that. She really was going to take that job at The G-Spot. It wasn't a manipulation."

"If you say so." He didn't look convinced. "Did she say something to you?"

I straightened. "How do you mean?"

Beau stood, reeling in his line, and shrugged. "It's just, on Sunday at the car wash, you called yourself sleezy. Did she call you sleezy or something? Is that why she never—you know—why she avoided you in town for so long?"

"No." I didn't know precisely why she'd always avoided me, but I felt certain that wasn't it. Crossing the small deck to stand next to him, I caught his line as it emerged from the water, careful to keep my fingers free of the hook. "She'd never. Charlotte wouldn't say that—she's not like that."

He relinquished his fishing pole to my grip. Using his newly freed hands, Beau hit my shoulder. "Then where'd that shit come from? Why're you calling yourself sleezy all of a sudden?"

I turned away and shrugged, speaking facts, "It's not all of a sudden. Folks in town have been calling me sleezy for years."

"They're full of shit, and you've never called yourself sleezy."

"What's the big deal?" My back to him, I tucked his pole next to mine, making sure the hook was secure.

"You're not."

I snorted but said nothing, not in a mind to argue.

"If Charlotte is the one making you think of yourself this way, I'm glad she's leaving. Good riddance."

Sighing, I turned to face him and stopped short of rolling my eyes. "It's not Charlotte, and don't be mad at her. I don't care if folks think I'm sleezy, you know that. Why would I care? What difference does it make to me? And Charlotte really helped the club, making a huge difference in the short and long run."

Beau's clear blue eyes inspected me, his features scowling and suspicious. "But you being 'sleezy,' or people thinking you are, that might one day interfere with you doing something you want? Or getting something you want?"

Swallowing around more gravel, I looked away, his guess too close to the mark. "Doesn't matter. You were right on Saturday when we were at Genie's."

"Oh yeah? How's that?"

I forced myself to say, "It's good she worked for the club, and it's also good she's leaving. Everything is working out for the best."

I wondered how many times I'd have to say the words before I believed them.

CHAPTER 18

HANK

"I've always rejected being understood. To be understood is to prostitute oneself."

— FERNANDO PESSOA, *THE BOOK OF DISQUIET*

Back in the good old days, Beau and I would finish fishing sometime around mid-morning, then go back to my place to play video games and eat pizza all afternoon. Today we parted ways at the dock. Neither of us had much time for sitting around on couches these days, and I couldn't remember the last time I ate pizza.

Driving into town, I reflected on the dearth of pizza in my life. Unlike a burger, pizzas were typically shared, and I supposed that explained it. Other than Beau, and Patty on an odd occasion, who would split a pizza with me?

Frowning as I parked, I thought about how much I liked pizza. I'd always liked pizza. So why had I been denying myself pizza? Because I didn't have a pizza-eating partner? I couldn't put my consumption of pizzas on hold while I waited for someone to magically appear and want to eat a pizza with me. What if that never happened?

Or, what if they wanted to eat pizza with me, but they'd given up cheese and bread and tomato sauce for life? What then? Was I supposed to waste my entire life wishing things were different and go pizza-less forever?

"I'm going to order a damn pizza tonight," I grumbled to no one, slamming the door of my truck.

Dinner decided, I marched toward the main strip of shops, my destination the jewelry store on Walnut Street. The staff always assigned me the gift for going-away parties while they handled the event particulars. As was my habit whenever one of our longtime staff members or dancers left, and even though Charlotte hadn't worked at The Pony for very long, the plan was to buy a random, ridiculously expensive piece of jewelry. Ideally, it would be returnable for store credit only, then the recipient would be forced to obtain something they really wanted, or a few things depending on how they spent the credit.

Charitable donations and ostentatious gifts for folks they would never approve of were the only occasions upon which I withdrew funds from the sizable inheritance left to me by my parents. Not much in life gave me as much pleasure as buying exotic dancers flashy diamond broaches, and then signing the card, 'From Dr. and Dr. Weller.'

My parents would've hated their snooty savings being spent as such. But I couldn't think of anything better to spend their money on than causes, people, and things they abhorred. *Actually, they might've approved of Charlotte.*

I grimaced at the thought, shoving it aside, and pulled off my sunglasses as I crossed Walnut Street. Typically, like for the gold Rolex I'd bought Beau many years ago, I went to Knoxville for an expensive purchase such as this. But Ferdinand's Fine Jewelry in our small downtown made more sense in Charlotte's case. When she returned the item, I didn't want her to have the hassle of driving all the way into Knoxville. Between work and four kids, I reckoned the woman was busy. I understood that and I—

Wait.

"Wait a damn minute," I muttered to no one. *That's the issue.*

My feet stalled a few doors down from Ferdinand's and I tucked my sunglasses into my chest pocket, feeling certain I was on to something. Charlotte—being a single mom, working, and managing a home by herself—had decided to stop sharing pizza because she simply had no time to eat pizza.

I snapped my fingers. That had to be it. She was overextended, had too much to do, and no help to do it. She didn't want a relationship with anyone, they'd be another time-suck. However, that seemed unfair to Charlotte. Why should she have to give up all the good things about having a partner? The woman clearly had unmet needs, and I could be just the good things.

Wanting to weigh this theory against her statements on Sunday, I endeavored to recall precisely what she'd said. But before I could, I stiffened because I heard her. Here. Now.

Holding very still, I strained my ears.

Not so far away, a voice that sounded exactly like Charlotte's said, "I know you don't want to see her, but this isn't something I can control."

My chest tightened. Compelled, I rounded the side of the building and crept toward the alley. Her voice was louder and clearer with each careful footstep.

"The court has given your paternal grandmother the right to visit with y'all twice a month if she wants, and she wants. Honey, you know I have tried and tried to excuse all y'all from these. If I could get you out of it, I would. But I'm there to shield you from her nasty comments, you know I will. I always do."

"Why don't I get a say?" a kid's voice grumbled back. "If I don't want to go, why should I have to? It's not fair."

I came to a stop at the edge of the alley, needing to swallow twice at the sight of Charlotte in profile, wearing one of her long, floral skirts. Today she'd paired it with a brown tank top. She'd crouched down in front of the kid, who I recognized from the lemonade stand on Sunday—Kimmy, the tallest and oldest of the four Mitchell children, the one that looked just like her daddy and all the rest of the Buckley brood.

Charlotte's shoulders rose and fell like she carried the weight of the world on them. I couldn't help but think she, of all people, deserved more, better, easier. She deserved everything.

Her chin tipping up, she said, "Fine. You know what, fine. You're preaching to the choir here. Let's walk over together and we'll say you aren't feeling good and need to miss this time. Once I have my phone, I'll call Aunt Maddie and she'll pick you up from the park."

"No." Kimmy crossed her arms and seethed through clenched teeth, "I said I'm not going at all. I'm not going back to the park."

"I can't leave you here by yourself."

"Call Nanna now. Or Aunt Maddie. Or what about Jackson? Have one of them meet me here."

Involuntarily, I grimaced at Jackson's name but continued to eavesdrop.

"I don't have my phone or my purse. You ran off and I ran after you. I have to get back to the park for your brothers and sister before your grandmother reports both of us missing or complains to the court-appointed supervisor, or she turns her nastiness on Joshua. You know she will with me not there, especially since she supposedly has some 'big news to share,' whatever that means. Kimmy"—Charlotte placed her hands on the girl's hips—"I'm begging here. Will you please come with me? You don't have to stay, but I do need you to come with me. I don't want to leave your brothers and sister with her either, not if I'm not there."

Kimmy pressed her lips together, shining eyes lifting to the sky. Her chin wobbled in a way reminiscent of Charlotte's unsteady chin on Sunday, and for some reason this had my breath catching in my chest.

"Please don't make me, Momma," she begged brokenly. "I don't want to see her. Please. She's so mean to me. All she does is pick on me and tell me how ugly I am, how mannerless and stupid. I hate her."

Shit. I knew *exactly* what that was like.

"I won't let her, I promise. That's why I petitioned the court to let me come, too.

Thank you for telling me what she's been doing. Now that I know, now that I'm allowed to be there, I won't let her speak to you that way anymore. She won't be telling you lies about yourself. But we have to go back. I can't leave Joshua and Sonya and Frankie there either, and I really, *really* can't give her any reason to take us back to court for custody. Please. Please come with me."

Charlotte also sounded broken. Obviously, I didn't know or understand all the particulars of the situation, but her tone made me slightly nauseous and feeling galvanized to *do something*.

On pure instinct, I darted forward without any real plan. Furthermore, I spoke before I could think on the intelligence of speaking while having no plan. "Hey, Charlotte."

Charlotte's head whipped toward me, eyes bugging out. "H-Hank," she said on a breath. Her mouth dropped open, her jaw moving up and down with no additional sound. I'd startled her.

Ignoring how beautiful she looked while startled, I tossed my thumb over my shoulder. "Can I help? Utterly Ice Cream is just there."

"I—ice cream? What?" Standing and facing me, she placed one hand on her daughter's shoulder and spoke as though winded.

"I can sit with Kimmy for a bit at the ice cream shop, if you need someone to do it." My gaze shifted to Kimmy. She looked caught between the distrust of a stranger and the promise of ice cream. Or possibly it was the allure of missing out on her nasty grandmother. I didn't want to make the girl uncomfortable, so I withdrew my phone from my back pocket. "Or you—I have my cell. You could text or call your momma. We could meet her there."

Charlotte's gaze darted between me and the phone in my hand. She seemed to be having trouble parsing through the suddenness of my presence and my words.

"Please, Momma?" Kimmy's voice pulled both my attention and Charlotte's to her. "Can I go to the shop and wait for Nanna?"

Charlotte shoulders drooped, her body appearing to deflate. "Yes, honey. That's fine. But you'll have to wait with Ha—Mr. Weller. Is that okay?" Her hand came to her forehead.

The little girl shifted her gaze to mine, wariness plain as the nose on her face. Surprising me, she said, "That's fine."

This kid must really hate her paternal grandmother. *I can relate.*

Unlocking my phone, I gave Kimmy a small incline of my head, then approached Charlotte to hand her the cell. "Here you go."

Charlotte let her hand fall away from her forehead and accepted the cell with a tight smile. Mouthing, *Thank you*, her eyes didn't quite meet mine.

That was fine. I was too busy being eyeballed by her oldest child. We stood in silence, regarding each other as Charlotte sent her text. The kid really did look like a

Buckley. It was odd seeing the same features on her small face that I'd despised as a youth. But I didn't despise this kid; I didn't even know her. Plus, with Charlotte being who she was, and Joshua and Sonya being who they were, there had to be something worth knowing about Kimmy.

"Nanna will meet you at Utterly Ice Cream in about twenty minutes," Charlotte finally said, addressing Kimmy. "But I don't have any cash on me, so you'll have to wait until she gets there if you want a cone."

"Why can't he buy it for me?" Kimmy tilted her chin toward me.

Charlotte's eyes immediately narrowed and she clenched her jaw. "Kimberly Dawn Mitchell, that was incredibly rude. You are not entitled to ice cream. Mr. Weller is doing us a kindness and does not owe you an ice cream cone or anything else. In fact, now Nanna won't be buying you one either. Apologize, now."

Kimmy's eyes flashed with something that looked like resentment, but instead of snarking back—which I suspected was her habit, given the fierceness in her expression—she turned to me and said, "I am sorry for being rude."

I worked to hide an inexplicable smile. This kid reminded me of myself at her age, so much. Except, this child apparently knew when to pick her battles. I never apologized. Ever. Even when I knew I was being a shit. I'd take a whooping and no dinner and four hours in a dark closet and whatever else over admitting to any wrongdoing.

Charlotte turned to me, her gaze meeting mine this time, and I didn't miss the faint blush creeping up her cheeks. I didn't miss it partially because I was hungry for the sight of her, but also because it suited her, made her lovely eyes bright. Greedily, I memorized this version of Charlotte. She didn't embarrass easily; I knew that and admired her for it. And it's not that I wanted her embarrassed, but that wouldn't keep me from appreciating the aftermath.

"Thank you," she said, looking uncertain. "And I'm sorry."

"Don't be sorry and don't worry about it," I said, hoping my expression communicated more than my admiration for her blushing cheeks and bright eyes. "It's no problem. I'm happy to help."

She gave me a relieved and grateful smile. It made my chest swell and a certainty rose to the surface. I could do this. I could be just the good things for Charlotte and none of the time-suck, energy-vampire things.

For the first time in my life with someone other than Beau, I wanted to be a help, and I wasn't expecting anything in return.

* * *

"What kind of ice cream would you get if you could?"

"Dunno," Kimmy said, flat and disinterested and glaring, again reminding me so much of me as a kid that this time I did smile. But just a small one.

"Hmm." Leaning back in my chair, I crossed my arms. We were sitting at a table under the awning of the ice cream parlor and I was doing my best to ignore the disapproving glares sent our way by busybodies coming out of the shop and by folks meandering past. Admittedly, this was the first time I'd experienced discomfort at being the recipient of such stares rather than reveling in the disdain.

Anyway.

Since I wasn't allowed to purchase Kimmy ice cream, I'd purchased us both a bottle of water. The kid had been quiet the entire walk to the shop, while I'd purchased the waters, and when we'd selected a table. Quiet and surly and contemptuous.

Sonya was loving. Joshua was knowledgeable. Kimmy was bullheaded and unpleasant, and I didn't mind one whit. It was like hanging out with a younger version of me, which meant I had a fair idea of how to talk to her without pissing her off even more.

Scratching my jaw, I maintained a conversational tone as I said, "Now, usually I'd try to make small talk, ask you about yourself, as that is what most folks expect. But you have the look of a person who was expecting to eat Italian leftovers for lunch, only to discover someone else beat you to it. I'm wondering if you'd prefer we just sit in silence. If so, you don't even have to speak. Just nod."

Her narrowed eyes widened slightly. "You'd sit in silence? If I wanted?"

"Absolutely. I like silence. Sometimes—actually, most times and with most people—it's preferable."

She cocked an eyebrow, her head tilting at the same time, openly inspecting me like she found my statement surprising. "How do you know my mother?"

Debating only for a split second, I settled on, "I was her boss for a bit."

"Where? In Vegas?"

"No. Here."

"You work at my school?" Kimmy asked with evident distaste.

"Nope. I own a—a—" I blinked. Suddenly, I felt like swallowing my tongue. The last thing I wanted to do was explain to a little girl what a strip club was, or what people did there, or why they did it.

Huh.

I'd never experienced shame or discomfort about my job or the nature of my business before right this minute. The discontent that had plagued me after my sets for the last two hen parties reared its ugly, irritating head. *How disconcerting.*

"You own a what?" she asked, leaning closer.

"I'm a business owner. Your momma did some bookkeeping for me." There. That about covered it without revealing too much.

"What kind of business?" she pushed, clearly smelling blood in the water.

I couldn't stop my stretching smile. "How about I tell you all about it when you're older?"

Her intelligent eyes flickered between mine. "How old?"

"Thirty."

Surprising me, she grinned, her earlier surliness forgotten. "Is it really bad?"

"No," I hedged, scratching my neck. "It's complicated."

"If it's not bad, why can't you tell me?"

More conflicted than I'd ever remembered feeling, I asked, "How old are you?"

"Nine." She shrugged. "But most folks think I'm older, like eleven or twelve. I skipped first grade and I'm tall."

I studied her for a long moment, frowning. I had also skipped first grade. *Interesting.*

Finally, I said, "If it's okay with your momma, I'll tell you. But you should know, it's something that might chip away at your childhood, make you grow up too fast, before you're ready. I'd be taking something from you if I told you now rather than wait 'til you're older. Do you want a shorter childhood? Or a longer one?"

She frowned at me thoughtfully. We stared at each other for a good while. I was impressed with how seriously she seemed to consider my words.

When I was a kid, I couldn't wait to no longer be one, no longer helpless and controlled by my parents' whims, ignored until I wasn't. But if Kimmy had to take a minute and think about what she'd be losing if her childhood ended prematurely, then clearly her childhood had been much better than mine.

"A longer one," she finally said, her gaze clearing.

I nodded once. "Then I'll tell you when you're older."

Kimmy lifted her chin higher. "It probably has to do with war, right? My brother Joshua is always talking about that shit—sorry, that *stuff*—and I hate it. Gives me nightmares."

Thinking about the comparison, I admitted, "It's similar. It's something adults do that doesn't and shouldn't make any sense to kids."

"But you do it?"

"I do."

"Why?" She sounded honestly curious.

"I want to ensure it's done as safely and fairly as possible," I said, which was the truth now, but hadn't always been the only reason.

Pissing off and embarrassing my parents, getting under the skin of polite society, cementing my place as a social outcast—those were the main reasons I'd bought The Pony at the ripe age of twenty-one. But I didn't think Charlotte would appreciate me detailing the nuances of the situation with her rebellious nine-year-old.

Kimmy's face scrunched up. "You do something bad so it hurts as few people as possible? So it's fair?"

"It's not bad. But it's not necessarily good either. Like I said, it's complicated."

Her lips twisted to the side. "It sounds bad."

Despite myself, I laughed. "Well, I guess some folks think it's bad, but I don't. I wouldn't do it if I thought it was."

"Goodness gracious. There you are." Mrs. Mitchell appeared out of thin air and rounded on Kimmy. She gave her shoulder a squeeze, not seeing or noticing me yet. "I'm so glad you got out of seeing that awful woman. You're a treasure, and bless her heart, Mrs. Buckley is a miserable, vicious bitch. Don't tell your momma I said that, though. She wouldn't like me calling people names, even if they're true."

"My lips are sealed, Nanna. Thanks for coming." Kimmy stood and gave her grandmother a hug.

I also stood, feeling oddly inspired to display some basic manners. "Mrs. Mitchell," I said, extending a hand.

The woman stiffened as her gaze shot to mine and her eyebrows pulled together. "Oh. Uh, Hank Weller. Didn't see you—but of course Charlotte said you were . . ." She frowned, not finishing her thought, and stood straighter. The woman did not accept my handshake.

I let my arm fall back to my side, not surprised. I was a touch bothered by her frosty reception. But, whatever. I was the town sleazeball. I'd practically put it on my business cards. Of course she couldn't be seen shaking my hand.

Taking a protective stance behind Kimmy, Mrs. Mitchell glanced between us with clear agitation. "What were y'all talking about? Before I got here?"

"Mr. Weller was telling me about his job," Kimmy said, looking up to eye her grandmother slyly.

Mrs. Mitchell gaped at Kimmy, then her giant eyes swung to me. I tried not to take pleasure in the older woman's panicked expression, but old habits die hard.

Clearing my features of amusement, I nodded once. "That's right. It's been a very enlightening conversation. Hasn't it, Kimmy?"

Kimmy stood up straighter, grinning like a shark, greedy for her nanna's reaction. "Do you think Momma would let Mr. Weller come to career day at school?"

Mrs. Mitchell turned white as a sheet and seemed to be choking on air. I couldn't help it, I barked a laugh and swapped an amused stare with Kimmy, who was giggling.

Unthinkingly, I lightly tapped the back of my fingers against Kimmy's shoulder. "Okay, okay. We've had our fun. Don't give her a heart attack."

Kimmy sent me a big old smile, saying, "Sorry, Nanna. That was a joke. Mr. Weller won't tell me what he does 'cause he said knowing about it will shorten my childhood. So I figured it was something you wouldn't want me knowing."

Mrs. Mitchell's gaze swung to mine. "So you . . . didn't tell her?"

"No, ma'am." I tried to sound contrite and mostly succeeded.

"Thank God." The woman's hand came to her chest and she took a moment to breathe her relief before a disapproving look hardened her features, flinty eyes settling on me. "Mr. Weller. Now, I know we were present at your car wash this last weekend, but you should not take that as a sign that we approve of you or your establishment. We don't. Though, it is nice that you helped out the firefighters with their fundraiser last year."

"It was no big—"

She lifted her hand and kept on going, "Quite frankly, just being in your parking lot—and on a Sunday of all days—was mortifying. I attended only because Charlotte begged me to bring the kids. And as you know, the only reason Charlotte applied to work at your establishment was to find her cousin."

"Yes. I know." I glanced at Kimmy and found her watching me with a curious expression.

"You own that club we were at? The horse one?" Kimmy asked, looking between me and her grandma. "What's wrong with owning a club?"

"Hush, Kimmy. Adults are talking." Mrs. Mitchell lifted her chin high so she could look down her nose at me. "I want you to know this: I felt obligated to be helpful, seeing as how you had a part to play in locating my sister's daughter. But our debt is now settled, do you understand? I do not feel obligated to you any further. And I think it would be best for Charlotte if you had no contact with—"

"Oh good. You're all here." Charlotte, sounding breathless, appeared suddenly at her momma's shoulder, cutting off whatever unpleasantness the woman was about to administer and saving me from saying something I might regret.

I wasn't angry. Her words didn't make me mad. They fatigued me. Where in my youth I might've felt amusement, at almost thirty I just felt tired. Tired of the assumptions, tired of the clutched pearls, tired of the ruffled feathers.

Grateful for her interruption, I watched as Charlotte hefted a little boy into her mother's arms. "Could you walk these beauties home for me? I made lunch and I made dinner, both are in the fridge. I'm running late for work"—she turned to me—"and training Hannah. That starts today and I want to make sure we have plenty of time."

"Honestly, Charlotte. I don't see why you're still working at that place. We have what we needed," Mrs. Mitchell ground out, accepting the little boy with a huffing, impatient sound.

"I'm not explaining this again, Mother." Charlotte bent to give the boy a kiss and brushed his hair out of his eyes, her tone unusually tight. "You be a good boy for Kimmy, okay? No biting."

While Charlotte's mother launched another protest about her continuing at The

Pony, I felt little fingers tug at mine and I glanced down to find Joshua gazing up at me, an uncertain-looking smile on his face. "Hi, Mr. Hank."

I tightened my fingers on his hand and felt my mouth curve into an immediate grin. "Hi, Mr. Joshua." Lowering to my haunches so I could look at him in the eye, I asked, "Read any good articles recently? What's the Fed up to?"

His uncertainty vanished and his eyes grew round. "Not much since their last interest rate hike, but earnings reports are due at the end of next month and we'll know more about inflation then."

"Keep me posted," I said before I could think better of it as my attention had snagged on adorable Sonya, who was holding out a leaf to me with a shy smile. "Hey, Miss Sonya, what's this?"

"It's for you. It's a flower."

"It's not a flower," Joshua said with a sigh. "It's a leaf."

"Well, I prefer leaves over flowers. Thank you." I grinned at Sonya and accepted the leaf with reverence, her little-kid voice 100% cute this time and 0% creepy.

"Can you play today?" Sonya asked.

Joshua faced me, his expectant expression mirroring his sister's. "Can you? If you come over, you can see my map collection. I can play Mike Duncan's podcast for you."

"I—uh . . ." Oh geez. Maps? Was it strange I really wanted to say yes?

But I couldn't, could I? Even if their momma agreed, I couldn't dismiss the plethora of judgmental looks Kimmy and I had received just sitting together in front of the ice cream shop, or the way Mrs. Mitchell had been ready to chew me out. If I wasn't fit for their nanna to shake hands with, I certainly wasn't fit for a playdate. Me inviting myself over just to hang out with and enjoy her kids wouldn't be much of a help to Charlotte. That'd be selfish.

"I'll talk to your momma," I finally said, my voice scratchy for some reason, and I gave them both a smile I hoped reached my eyes. "I have work this week, but we'll see if we can't make something happen eventually."

Joshua's gaze turned somber, distant, and he nodded, backing up a step. The change in him sent my heart plummeting to the sidewalk. *Crap.* Who knew disappointing a kid felt like being sucker-punched?

Uncertain what to do and feeling awkward, I stood and tried to turn my attention back to the heated discussion between Charlotte and her momma. Judging by the unhappy, squinty look Mrs. Mitchell sent me as I straightened, their argument appeared to be at its end and neither of them were happy.

"You don't mind driving me, do you?" Charlotte asked, drawing my attention to her.

"Happy to," I said automatically, and wondered at the immediate suffusion of pride and pleasure in my chest.

"It's settled. I'll be home before bedtime, okay?" Charlotte quickly bent and gave Sonya, Joshua, Frankie, and Kimmy hugs and kisses, her fingers lingering in Kimmy's curly blond hair. "Make good choices, please. And be kind."

"Mr. Weller was just telling me about his job before Nanna walked up." Kimmy glanced at me, but this statement was clearly for the benefit of her mother. "I think I'd like to give his job a try."

I sent the little girl a flat look, unimpressed with her attempt at riling up her momma. Couldn't she see the woman had plenty on her plate and was stretched too thin? Bracing for a stern look and word from Charlotte, I squared my shoulders, ready to contradict the little troublemaker.

But it turned out I didn't need to.

In response to her daughter's baiting, Charlotte shocked the hell out of me by asking mildly, "Do you, now?" She glanced at her watch, not seeming at all concerned by her eldest's revelation. "That's nice, honey. He could do a presentation for career day at the school. Are you done with your water? Did you thank Mr. Weller? We really do need to go."

CHAPTER 19

CHARLOTTE

"The true measure of a man is how he treats you when others are not looking."

— ALESSANDRA TORRE

*H*ank's good manners made me nervous, distracting me from the 'big news' my ex-mother-in-law had dropped in my lap with her characteristic dramatic flourish.

I recognized Mrs. Buckley's vague statements at the start of the visit for what they were, intended to provoke my temper and tease my curiosity. I knew the games she played, and so I'd ignored her upon returning to the park, only speaking directly to the woman—a sharp reprimand—when she commented on Joshua's weight.

But as soon as I'd gathered the kids to leave, she'd said, "Oh. Before you hear it from anyone else, you should know that Kevin has returned to his father's house. He's back with the company in Asheville and we're all so thrilled."

The sinister light behind her eyes had dimmed considerably when I gave her nothing but a blank look in response. What did Kevin's return to North Carolina and into the bosom of his psycho family have to do with me?

It wasn't until I'd herded Joshua, Sonya, and Frankie almost to Walnut Street that a slight shiver of fear traveled down my spine accompanied by the irrational thought, *What if he wants to see the kids? What if he wants more visitation? What if he wants custody?*

Fear was soon eclipsed by good sense and reality. *He doesn't and won't. He never did. He doesn't care.*

Even so, try as I might, I couldn't completely shake the absurd notions—they clung to my consciousness like toilet paper to a shoe. Which was likely why Hank's atypical display of manners made me so nervous.

As soon as we relinquished the kids to my momma, Hank placed a hand on the small of my back, encouraging me to walk a little in front of him unless someone else blocked our side of the sidewalk, in which case he stepped carefully and closely to my side and held his free hand out, which ultimately diverted the other person out of our way. Really, out of *my* way. It was like walking with a bodyguard and it made me feel strange, like I was someone important. Plus, you know, his hand on my back had me feeling other things.

I wasn't entertaining those things. I'm retired from having a sex life.

And if his handling of me on the sidewalk wasn't enough, he opened the passenger door of the truck for me and offered a hand to help me up, saying, "Watch your step," and "I'll have the AC on in a tick," before shutting the door carefully once I settled and buckled.

And then, as soon as he started the car, he turned on the AC and adjusted all the vents to point at me, even though it was hot as baked potatoes outside, asking, "Comfortable?"

I nodded, watching him out of the corner of my eyes. "I'm just fine, thank you. How are you?"

He buckled up and checked his rearview mirror. Instead of answering my question, he said, "For the record, I did *not* talk to Kimmy about my job or the club."

Oh. That's why he's being so mannerly, treating me like glass. He didn't want me to holler at him. Ha!

I felt my shoulders relax. "I know that. I can tell when she's trying to ruffle my feathers. And I trust you. No worries on that front."

He pulled out of the parking lot, casting a quick look my way. "You trust me?"

"Uh . . ." I hadn't necessarily meant to vocalize it, but it was the truth. Obviously. "I wouldn't have left Kimmy with you if I didn't trust you, Hank," I said softly, making sure my smile was just as soft.

His gaze strayed to my lips and his parted, giving me the sense a critical thought rested on the tip of his tongue. But then he frowned and pointed his glare out the windshield. I released the breath I held, my chest tight.

I'd been dreading this moment. Ever since I left The Pink Pony on Sunday, I'd been dreading seeing him again, and being alone with him, and it being awkward. But I'd done this to myself; I'd asked him to drive me into work specifically so I could rip off the Band-Aid and get this conversation over with.

The tick, tick, tick of his blinker and the whoosh of cool air leaving the vents was the only sound in his truck for what felt like an hour, but it couldn't have been more than ten seconds. We were paused at a stop sign, waiting for pedestrians to cross in front of us. My brain was so full of contradictory thoughts and wants, irrational anxieties and unrealistic notions, I didn't note who the pedestrians were or what they looked like.

"Charlotte."

I closed my eyes briefly, then forced them open. "Yes?"

He pressed on the gas. "May we please discuss what happened on Sunday?"

Here we go.

Shoving all thoughts of Kevin's return and his despicable momma to the side—I'd think about those trash fires later—I twisted my fingers in the fabric of my long skirt and stared forward. "What is there to say?"

I had no idea what he'd say next or if he'd say anything at all. And I had no idea what I wanted him to say if he did speak. See? Contradictory thoughts.

"You said it was a mistake." His hands moved on the steering wheel. "Why was it a mistake?"

Forcing myself to release the skirt, I smoothed it over my knees. At least his question was an easy one. "I'm—like I said, I'm retired from doing that kind of thing. With anyone."

"This is what I want to talk about, you being 'retired from having a love and sex life.' Why are you retired?"

Another easy question. "I realized a while ago that I can't have everything I want. I've prioritized what I think is most important, and I'm content with my priorities. Compromise isn't always a bad thing, especially when it's good for the people you love."

The truck slowed then halted at another stop sign. More pedestrians were crossing, and he took the opportunity to face me. To my surprise, he wore a smile that felt both amused and disbelieving. "That answer sounded rehearsed, Ms. Mitchell."

"Well, you know . . ." I tilted my head back and forth, growing warm around the neck at his pointed attention. "Sometimes I say it to myself in front of the mirror for morning affirmations when I get—" I snapped my mouth shut, realizing what I was about to say.

He lifted an eyebrow. "When you get what?"

I persisted in pressing my lips together. I couldn't say, *When I get horny.* I might've been a brazen loudmouth at times, but even I knew that statement was inappropriate.

"Charlotte?"

Crossing my arms, I held myself stiffly. "Why do you want to know? Why do you care? I said it was a mistake. I apologize if I sent you mixed signals by kissing you back, but to be perfectly candid, you caught me off guard. I'm not sure what you think you want from me. I responded the best I could, given the circumstances."

"You were surprised," Hank said on a sigh. "I surprised you."

"Of course I was. You didn't want me working at The Pony in the first place, you barely suffer through my presence, you can't be bothered to answer any of my questions, and—"

"Wait, wait, wait. That is not true." He lifted a hand and waved it in the air, batting away facts.

"That is so true." I shivered, the blasting air now too cold, and reached forward to lower the AC fan. I also made sure to redirect several of the vents in his direction.

"I apologized for being a dismissive asshole. Last week, I apologized. The day before you quit."

"And then, when I tried to talk to you to turn in my notice, to explain, you were right back to being a dismissive stinker."

"That's—I—" Hank sucked in a breath, and then snapped his mouth shut. He glowered out the windshield, his eyebrows pulled low.

"You?" I smirked at his grumpy demeanor.

Hank flipped on his blinker and veered off the road. "I couldn't be with someone who works for me and I was grumpy about it. It's unprofessional, and this—you—were the first time I chafed under my own rules."

I flinched. "I—wha—excuse me?"

All remaining thoughts of Kevin and Mrs. Buckley fled my brain. Hank had my complete and full attention now.

Hank's eyes sliced to mine, then back out the windshield. "Allow me to apologize for being rude on Friday before you turned in your notice. It . . ." He shook his head, his voice mellowing. "It blindsided me in the moment, but ultimately I was relieved." He brought the truck to a stop.

"Relieved because you never wanted me to work there in the first place," I supplied, too busy staring at his profile to take note of which tree-shaded, out-of-the-way spot he'd parked us.

"No." He engaged the brake but didn't cut the engine. Facing me, Hank wore an expression I couldn't read, not in a million years. But his tone was low and quiet. "Relieved because, if you don't work for me, I'd be able to ask you out."

I flinched again, my lips parting, a wave of hot, stunned awareness hitting me square in the chest.

The side of his mouth tugged a millimeter upward. "Did I surprise you again?"

Unable to speak, I nodded.

I needed a minute.

Or a whole damn day.

Don't get me wrong, I knew he must've been attracted to me on some level; he'd made that abundantly clear on Sunday when he'd kissed me like the world was ending. We'd made out, it had been hot, I'd been completely mindless, and there was no denying his equal enthusiasm *in the moment*.

But then he'd said things after that didn't make sense—about giving me whatever I wanted, doing whatever I wanted, being whatever I wanted—which later I'd chalked up to him being caught up in the moment.

Yet, for the last few days I tripped on the fact that, when I'd assumed we'd be hooking up for a simple quickie, he'd turned me down. He'd said no, not in the bar, but that he'd meet me later for anytime, anyplace. And that had made no damn sense.

What with getting the kids ready for school in less than two weeks, starting my real job next week, and preparing for the court-mandated visit with the Wicked Witch of the Buckley family today, I didn't have a ton of time or mental energy to spare. I'd stopped wondering about Hank and his motives and the kiss. There were only so many hours in a day and I was tired of my circular thoughts.

Plus, this was Hank Weller. Hank Weller had been a hellraiser almost since birth. Hank Weller owned a strip club and loved to ruffle feathers. Hank Weller eschewed all conventions of polite society and took delight in flouting their rules. Hank Weller made hearts race and cheeks blush every time he walked in a room, but he didn't *date* people . . . did he?

The subtle curve of his mouth grew into a scandalously adorable smirk, his smoldering eyes moving over me. "But we don't have to date if you don't have time for me. We can focus on you, and just the good stuff."

I felt my body come alive under his gaze, heat rising and pressing against my skin. Faced with his lethal look and feeling like an overwhelmed, bashful teenager, I lowered my attention to the seat between us, unable to maintain eye contact without spontaneously combusting. I closed my eyes.

"Hank—"

"Charlotte."

My heart rate went from sixty to approximately two thousand in zero-point-zero seconds. Goodness. The way he said my name, like it gave him both pleasure and pain, like the idea of me tortured him. How did he do that?

I heard the click of my belt being unfastened, the band of it losing tension against my chest. In the next moment, his hand plucked mine from my lap and my eyes flew open, locking with his. He'd scooched closer, enough to make his threading of our fingers together an easy movement. And the way he was looking at me made all the oxygen in the truck's cab evaporate.

Had anyone ever looked at me like this? And now *Hank Weller*, of all people. It was a fantastical, long-buried desire come true. *Am I dreaming?*

I didn't want to wake up.

"I know you have a lot on your plate," he said, his voice hypnotic. "I heard you when you said you're not in a place right now to think about a future with anyone. You're short on time, and energy, and attention, I get it. But"—his tongue darted out to lick his lips, his other hand dropping to my knee—"I meant what I said on Sunday."

"Which part?" He'd come closer while he spoke, his hand sliding higher on my leg. I tilted my head back to maintain eye contact.

"I'll do—" His head descended; he placed a light kiss on my neck; my breath caught. "Whatever you want—" Another kiss, this one with a scrape of teeth that had me shivering. "Whenever you want—" His hand on my leg slid my skirt upward. "However you want."

He raised his head then, spearing me with a heavy-lidded stare. "Will you let me?" Holding my eyes, he brushed his lips against mine, teasing me. "Will you let me be the one who takes care of you? The one who makes you feel good? You're all keyed up, frustrated. It's not fair, you being neglected like this. I'd be happy to help if you wanted."

He was right. I'd been feeling needy and frustrated for a long, long time. But like fantasies of him, I'd buried it all. Better to forget about silly wishes and dreams.

This wasn't a dream. This was happening.

Panting now, ensnared by his offer, hypnotized by it, I nodded and whispered, "Yes."

Lost in his sudden seduction and the promise of him, wanting it, starving for it, how could I say no? He'd found precisely the right words to unlock every single one of my inhibitions, and when his hand finally lifted the hem of my skirt to my waist, I widened my legs to accommodate him.

I felt his smile against my neck and the heat of a whispered, "That's my angel," as he tugged down the side of my cotton undies. I helped him, lifting my hips until he exposed me, parting me with a gliding stroke.

Hank leaned back, his eyes sharpening on my spread legs. "So wet. And so fucking pretty."

Sucking in a trembling breath, both at the vocalization of his praise and the feel of his skillful caress, I gripped his shoulder with the hand he didn't hold captive. My stomach twisted, my body ached, strained where he gave me the lightest touch, making me senseless with wanting more, wanting everything.

"I could do this all day," he mused, sounding distracted, his stare ravenous as it roved over my body.

Overwhelmed, my head fell back as he fondled me, teased me. He released the hand he'd held and moved lower, cupping my breast over my camisole, his fingers covetous, greedy. Shifting to the side, he gently tugged the strap down to bare my skin for his gaze and hot mouth.

I felt drugged, heavy, dizzy and beyond confusion, pulled beneath the undertow of where need meets scarcity and depravation. Prior to our frantic fumbling at his bar, it had been so long. So long since I'd been touched, longer still since I'd been touched with the intent to arouse, to please, to satisfy. I couldn't think, couldn't remember it ever feeling this good, this intentional and focused, and Hank had barely rounded second base.

"More," I said on a broken moan, his teasing making me wild. "Harder. And—" *I need to hear his voice.* "And keep talking."

Hank's movements stalled. But before I could overthink or second-guess my blurted requests, he shifted his body and pushed a long finger inside me. I gasped.

"You like that." The words were a rough command, not a question.

I bit my lip and nodded, a little whine escaping my throat. I gripped both his shoulders now, needing to anchor myself to something solid as he added another finger and quickened the pace of his invasion, the base of his palm pressing and rubbing against me with each thrust.

"Are you going to come?" he asked darkly between the wet, full-mouth kisses he lavished on my neck, chest, and breasts, the sounds of his fingers working my entrance a sloppy, erotic accompaniment. "Are you going to come for me, angel?"

His tongue swirled around my nipple, then he trailed his lips lower to nip at the side of my breast, sucking it into his mouth. The pleasure-pain of his assault made my hips lift, tilt, and rock against his hand. A pleased sound rumbled out of him, the vibrations echoing through my ribs.

"Fuck. You're so fucking gorgeous," he whispered roughly, his words sounding dazed. "I can't wait to fuck you. I can't wait to fill you with my cock. You'd like that, wouldn't you?"

The image he conjured—a suppressed, secret fantasy becoming reality—sent me spiraling. My whole body heated with a brilliant, flashing pulse and tensed at his filthy words. I cursed, my hands sliding to his arms, my abdomen twisting, coiling with vicious, spikey heaviness. I fought and surrendered in a single breath, unable to draw another, lost to my body's bliss. Coming apart, holding on to him, I stifled the cry of ecstasy before it could rip from my lungs.

But, holy effing fracking fricking Frankenstein, it felt fantastic. So good and raw and necessary and monumental and gratifying and *finally*.

"So good," he said somewhere near my ear, echoing my thoughts as I slowly re-emerged with the present, his mouth and tongue laving my skin between statements of admiration, his arms wrapping around my body to hold me. "So beautiful."

Drawing me close, pulling me almost on top of his lap, he tucked me under his chin. My fingers had been twisted in his shirtsleeves and I released the fabric when he repositioned me, leaving me at a loss as to where to place my hands.

Before I could feel too awkward about it, he gently plucked one from my lap and threaded our fingers together, just like he'd done before. But this time, he lifted my knuckles to his lips and kissed them.

"Thank you," he said. Then he laughed lightly, a supremely pleased, sexy, rumble of a sound. "I think I really needed that."

I also laughed, but mine was bewildered. "You're welcome?" Reality had begun to set in. If I'd been confused and unsettled before, I was downright discombobulated now.

The truck was still running, the air was still on, and this was not good for the environment. Being a responsible global citizen, I latched on to this irresponsible use of fossil fuels.

"We should, uh—" I had to swallow around the dryness in my throat. "We should get going. To work. The exhaust isn't good for the glaciers and I have Hannah to train and . . . uh, yeah."

It was rare for me to be at a loss for words. I felt verbally bankrupt at the moment.

His arms squeezed my shoulders. Placing one more kiss on the back of my hand, then forehead, he gracefully set me back in my seat. Realizing my skirt was still up, my camisole still askew, and my underwear around one ankle, I yanked down the hem of the floral fabric while yanking up my shirt straps, putting myself back together after our—our—

Our whatever that was.

My body hadn't quite recovered. It felt loose and happy and lazy and wonderful, and I blamed it for my fumbling attempt to pull up my underwear. Meanwhile, Hank had buckled his seatbelt with self-assured movements and was now looking mighty satisfied with himself.

I glared at his profile as he backed out from under the trees where we'd parked, some sort of utility road with a pull-off.

"Did you just win a bet?" I asked, working to keep my tone light. I pushed my hair behind my shoulders and tucked it behind my ears so I'd have something to do with my hands.

"No. Why?" He smiled at me, his eyes vivid and attentive, like he thought I was cute, or delightful, or something like that.

I folded my arms over my stomach, not knowing how to cope with this strange turn of events and how easily I'd been seduced by Hank Weller. I wasn't embarrassed; I didn't know what I was. "You look . . ."

"What?"

"Sorta smug, I guess."

We'd reached the main road and Hank stopped the truck before pulling into traffic, even though there was no traffic. Turning toward me, his smile softened and he sighed. It sounded content.

What the heck was going on? What man ever looked *that* pleased after giving an orgasm but not receiving one?

"I suppose I'm just relieved we got everything settled." Still grinning, his eyebrows pulled together as they moved over me. "Buckle up."

"I'm afraid I'm going to need some help here. What, precisely, did we get settled?" I reached for the belt, my fingers clumsy.

Hank's look told me he thought the question was strange. "You know."

"Humor me. What is it that you think we settled?"

"You'll come to me"—his attention returned to the windshield—"when you need me. I'll take care of you."

"I'll come to you when I need you?" What was he talking about?

"Yeah." His smile slipped, just a tad. "Like I said, I know you have a lot going on, no time for thinking about a future with anyone, no room in your life for another commitment."

My mind working frantically, I could do nothing but stare at him, certain I had to be misunderstanding what he was offering.

But then he continued, his tone easy and light. "There's no pressure here, no bad stuff, no inconvenience to you, nothing that will require you to spend any time on me. Whenever you want me to step in and see to your needs, say the word and I will."

CHAPTER 20

CHARLOTTE

"We must respect the other fellow's religion, but only in the sense and to the extent that we respect his theory that his wife is beautiful and his children smart."

— H.L. MENCKEN, *MINORITY REPORT*

"Hank, you had one job. One. Job." April shook her head as she served herself some fruit, disappointment prominent on her features.

"I'll get her gift before next week, I promise," he said. Seemingly unfazed by the tall blonde's admonishment, he smirked at me. "Charlotte can even pick it out in person if she has the time. And only if she wants to."

I dropped my eyes to the plate of cake sitting on my lap. Cheeks burning and stomach rolling ever since the interlude with Hank in his truck earlier, I hadn't been prepared to eat cake. But upon arriving at The Pony, the entire staff and all the dancers had been gathered in the breakroom, waiting for me, primed with excited smiles on their faces and a going-away cake with my name on it baked by Serafina. They'd even purchased balloons.

"We missed you on Sunday, Charlotte," Everly said, taking the seat next to mine.

Fighting a spike of alarm, I affixed a smile to my face while I chewed on the big piece of cake I'd just shoveled in my mouth. Swallowing hastily, I asked, "Sunday? What? Why? What happened on Sunday?"

"After the car wash." Jiff took the seat next to Everly and pushed a streak of purple hair off her forehead. "We went out to Genie's, went dancing." Jiff studied my face for a minute. "Wait, did no one tell you?"

"She left a bit suddenly," Hank said, and all the eyes in our little circle swung toward him again. He leaned nonchalantly against the counter by the coffee maker, his ankles crossed, his posture relaxed. He also ate cake and chose that moment to lick the frosting off his fork, his eyes locked with mine.

I stared at the fork as his tongue worked. I tried to swallow. I failed. Whatever Hank read on my face made him grin. He licked his lips. Then, when my eyes flicked back to his, he winked. At me.

Ripping my attention away once more, I shoved more cake in my mouth, wondering if the AC was still broken or if I'd been having one continuous hot flash since Hank's proclamation in the car.

Whenever you want me to step in and see to your needs, say the word and I will. Holy tempting offer, Batman.

"Why didn't you have someone text her?" Tina chirped, seeming honestly affronted on my behalf.

"Don't worry about it." I lifted my hand to cover my mouth, speaking around my latest oversized bite. "I wouldn't have been able to go anyhow. I needed to get home for the kids."

"Your mother couldn't have watched them? Laney's parents watched her little girl." April claimed the seat across from me, crossing her long legs and picking up a strawberry from her plate. "Isn't that what grandmas are for?"

I lowered my plate to my lap. "She'd been with them all day. She—"

"We missed you. And we don't care if you won't be working here anymore. Once you're part of this family, that's it. We take care of our own." Piper patted my shoulder, smiling down at me. "Next time, you should come."

"I—uh, thank you." I mostly managed to return her smile. "Sure."

"You don't sound sure," Hannah said, her tone drawing my attention to her. She held no plate, but her gaze held a challenge.

"It's just—" I glanced around at the group gathered. Even though I was supremely flustered, I wanted to pick my words carefully. I didn't want any of these fine people to think I would hesitate to hang out with them in the future, if it were possible. "I don't have a regular sitter. And I definitely don't like leaving my momma with the kids by herself if I can help it. She's getting older and the house is always such a mess when I get home. I usually have to stay up way too late cleaning and getting things in order for the next day, which means I get to bed too late, which means the next day is off 'cause I'm cranky when I don't get my sleep. It just makes more sense not to go out at all, you know?"

"So you . . . never go out?" Jiff traded a look with Jenny.

"No. Not really. Not without my kids."

"She speaks the truth." This pronouncement came from Sita, who had lifted her fork in the air. "Ever since I had Dominic, I rarely go out. Sunday was definitely an exception, and only because he and his daddy went camping last weekend. The only place Dominic doesn't come along is work. But he's with me one hundred percent of the time otherwise, even when I go to the bathroom."

"I haven't gone to the bathroom by myself in four years unless I'm here," Laney said dryly, quirking a sweet smile. "At this point, I just leave the door open at home, otherwise Selby bangs on it and wants to know what I'm doing, like I'm having fun without her."

"I guess that settles that." Tina stood and sauntered over to the trash, tossing her plate and fork in the bag.

"What does that settle?" Hannah asked.

Tina turned and faced us, eyeing her nails. "I'm never having children."

Laughter erupted from all the moms gathered. Once we laughed, everyone else did as well, like our humor equaled permission.

"Tina, this isn't news. You've never wanted kids." Hope rolled her eyes.

"Yeah, but now I know for sure. I can't fathom giving up all my freedom on purpose, and for what? Sorry. No offense, Charlotte."

I waved away her apology, her proclamation not bothering me in the least. My occupation wasn't for everyone.

"I don't want kids either." Serafina, the club's head chef, stood and began tidying up the remainder of the cake.

"Why not?" Laney asked. "Yours would be well fed."

"Meh." Serafina shrugged. "I like kids, but I've never felt compelled to have my own."

"That's all right. Not everyone needs to have kids." Kilby tossed her plate in the garbage and patted Tina on the shoulder. "Tina, Serafina, and Hank can babysit for the rest of us."

"Yeah, no." Tina rolled her eyes. "Unless you have a dog. Dogs are superior to humans, anyway."

"Fine. Just Aunt Serafina and Uncle Hank, then," Jiff joined in. "Ready to take kids bungee jumping for an hourly charge or give them souffle-making lessons."

"Don't forget giving them tips on salary negotiations and how to subdue an angry drunk. Hank would be great at that," someone said, and everyone laughed again.

Grinning as I listened, I let the conversation continue around me, each person taking turns remarking on what inappropriate adventures Hank and Serafina would get up to with little kids before passing them back off to their parents.

At one point, the hairs on the back of my neck prickled. Immediately, I glanced at Hank. His stare rested on me, a thoughtful frown on his features, but his eyes seemed dazed. Abruptly, he blinked, his focus returning, his stare locking with mine.

As usual, I couldn't quite read him. But one thing was for certain: he didn't look happy.

* * *

The moment Hannah shut the door behind us, she turned to me and demanded, "What's going on with you and Hank?"

Caught and once again mired in verbal bankruptcy, I could only stare at her silently.

Her stare turned teasing and squinty. "I know something's going on. It's all anyone can talk about. And it's not like he's making any effort to hide his interest. Everyone keeps asking me, so spill. What's going on?"

"I—hide—what?" My knees wobbled and I sorta collapsed into my office chair.

"Charlotte." She crossed her arms. "Don't play coy. The way he was gawking at you on Sunday? And then y'all disappear into the club. Ten minutes later, you run out and leave without a word. Then today, just now, he's licking forks, sending you sexy eyes, and you're looking at him like he invented cake. Go on. Tell me."

Gaping at her, I tried to catch my breath. I couldn't. My chest rose and fell like I'd just run a mile in bad shoes.

Her squinty stare eased, losing its edge of teasing and morphing into something different. "Charlotte?" Her voice pitched higher at the end of my name, obvious concern pulling her eyebrows together. "Are you okay?"

"I don't know." I covered my face. "I'm a mess." I felt like crying. But I wouldn't.

"Oh no, honey."

I heard her pull a chair over and sit, her hand on my shoulder a moment later. "Tell me what's going on. I promise, I'll help. No judgment. I just want to help."

Letting my hands slide down to my lap, I leaned back in my chair and looked at her. "I don't think this is something we should talk about."

"What? Why not?"

"Hank is still your boss. And I'm not sure it's appropriate. And besides that—" I sighed.

Hannah and I weren't close friends. Yes, we'd grown closer in a sense since I'd started working at The Pony and forged a bridge of trust between us. And though I needed to talk to someone, I wasn't at all sure she should be that someone.

I didn't want to talk to Sienna. She and Hank had dated at one point.

If Rae had been in town, I would've reached out to her. She was the obvious choice. I trusted Rae. But she wasn't in town and therefore wasn't an option.

What about Patty? I dismissed the idea out of hand. Between saving her mother's bar and all her classes and course work, Patty was even busier than me. Given our tight schedules, even if we arranged something right now it would be weeks before we spent time together.

Which brought me back to Hannah.

Could Hannah keep information I shared to herself? Could I trust her? And Hank being her boss made everything that much more complicated.

"How's Heather?" I asked to change the subject, my voice reedy. "Have you talked to her recently?"

Hannah's frown looked confused. "Uh, yeah. I talked to Heather on Monday. I told her that you had been asking about her and wanted to make sure she was safe. She didn't seem worried or upset by that like she might've been in the past. In fact, she's thinking about turning herself in."

"Turning herself in? You mean in Florida?"

"That's right. I should tell you first that I asked her if I could talk to you about this and she said it was okay, but she doesn't want you talking to her folks about it. She hasn't decided what to do and doesn't want them stressing out even more. But she feels like she can't move forward in any real way until she's no longer looking over her shoulder, waiting to be arrested. She also said she wants to prove to herself she can take responsibility without falling to pieces."

"Huh. I guess that makes sense." I was impressed with my cousin. Even though she must've been terrified. Heck, I was terrified for her. Clearly, she wanted to make things right and find some way to start over. "And I won't mention anything to her parents if she doesn't want me to. After you and I talked, I did just what we discussed. My aunt and uncle went back to Florida on Monday." I wondered what part Heather's parents would play in this next act of her life and how they'd react if they knew she was thinking about turning herself in.

"Good. She needs the space to make these choices for herself. I'm glad you talked them into going home."

I chuckled. "Well, I'm not sure I can take much credit for that. They were staying with my momma and driving each other bananas. After over a month living together, I think even their worry over Heather wasn't enough to keep them in town, especially since they now know Heather isn't in Green Valley."

"They didn't push you for more information?"

"They did at first, but when I explained how she had a stable job, was no longer in Tennessee, and wasn't on drugs, they eased off. I think they simply wanted to know whether she was safe." My mother had attempted to guilt me into revealing my source of information, but my aunt hadn't pushed. She'd been sad but accepting that Heather wasn't ready to talk to her yet, whereas my uncle had just been stoic. "I think the drugs scared them the most."

"I can definitely understand that. Drugs can be scary," Hannah said, giving me the sense she had wisdom in this area.

Squirming in my seat, I asked, "What did you tell her to do? Did you encourage her to turn herself in?"

Hannah crossed her legs. "I didn't. I don't tell folks what to do. She didn't ask for advice, so I didn't give her any. I listened." We stared at each other for a bit, then she added, "I'm a real good listener. And I know how to keep a secret. And if you don't want me to say anything to anyone about you and Hank, I won't."

I believed her, on all accounts. Still, my mouth remained shut.

"Charlotte." She leaned forward. "You can barely sit still. What's going on? I'm only asking because you have me worried. Did Hank—Are you saying he did something? Did he try to take advantage?"

"No. No, no. Not at all," I said adamantly.

"Are you sure?"

I caught her hands, gripped them. "If anything, he wants me to take advantage of him, and I don't—I don't think I can do that to him. I mean, I once suggested something similar to Jackson James, believe it or not, but it was so different." Oh geez, I tried not to cringe. Now that I was talking, I couldn't stop. "With Jackson, it was a joke. But even if we'd done a friends-with-benefits thing, it felt like a tidy proposition where no feelings were involved, you know? Where no one would get hurt. But —but with Hank—" I didn't finish the thought, couldn't admit out loud that feelings were already very much involved.

At least on my side they were, and probably had been for a long, long time, given how enthusiastically I'd participated in our two sexy encounters. I'd always thought I would never be able to trust him after he'd stood me up for prom all those years ago, but I was now beginning to suspect this was not the case. I trusted him.

But should I?

Could I trust myself? I'd accepted long ago that I had terrible taste in men. After Kevin, I'd assumed it would be safest to never date anyone I was attracted to. Lord knows, I'd always been attracted to Hank.

"People change, right?" I blurted, feeling obligated to ask, searching Hannah for the answer I most wanted to hear. "I'm so much different than I was as a teenager or a young adult. I'm more focused on being content. Hank has changed too, don't you think? Wouldn't you say he's trustworthy?"

"Of course he is. Why? Did he do something untrustworthy?"

"It was such a long time ago, and it's stupid. I should let it go. I don't even know why I still think about it." I bit my lip, chewed on it, fretting.

"You better start at the beginning." She squeezed my hands, facing me more completely. "Don't worry about him being my boss. I can be objective."

Torn, I slipped my fingers from hers and shook my head. "Still, I'm not sure I should."

"Listen, I've worked with Hank for a long, long time. I know his heart, though he tries to pretend he doesn't have one. I love the guy like a brother. Nothing you say is going to change that. Now, I might get irritated with him and set him straight if he's acting like an ass, but I don't want you worrying. If anything, you should know I'm biased where he's concerned, wanting the best for him. All us dancers are."

"That's lovely." I smiled, reaching out and holding her fingers again, my heart warming at the thought of Hank having so many cheerleaders.

I felt myself vacillating, wanting to talk to her. Hadn't Hannah already proven how trustworthy and level-headed she was with her handling of the situation with my cousin? Absolutely, yes. I could trust Hannah. Furthermore, the woman was wiser than her years and I could use some wisdom right about now.

"Okay. Okay, I'll tell you what happened. Honestly, I need some help with this. I don't know who to talk to and I feel like I can't trust my own judgment," I said, surrendering.

Ultimately, this is what being with Kevin had done to me, made me distrust myself.

"Aren't you friendly with Sienna Diaz?"

I tilted my head back and forth. "We're getting there. With the gossip after Kevin left Green Valley, and the kids and life in general, it's been hard to kindle friendships since I've been back in town. But I think Sienna and Hank used to date, right? I don't want to talk about him to his ex-girlfriend. And as far as I know, she's his only ex. I suppose I could call Patty Lee."

"Uh. No. He dated Patty a few years ago. Nothing serious, but he took her out a few times."

I stiffened at this news. "He did?!" I was shocked. Patty and I were pretty good friends and she had never said a word.

She nodded. "Yep. And then there was that lawyer in Knoxville for a while. I'm not surprised you didn't know about them. They both probably wanted to keep it low-key."

"What? Why?"

Hannah rolled her eyes again. "Come on, Charlotte. You're not that naïve. For the same reason men only want to date me in secret. He's Hank Weller. What 'self-respecting' woman would want to be linked to a notorious strip club owner? Or a stripper?" She'd put air quotes around self-respecting, which reminded me of Hank's bitterness toward folks in the valley.

"God. How awful." Staring at my friend, I processed this information, my heart hurting. "That doesn't sound like Patty, though. Patty isn't a snob."

Hannah's mouth tugged to the side. "I didn't say Patty was a snob, I said—and this is just my assumption, I don't know for certain—they probably kept it on the down-low since she didn't want folks to know she and Hank were dating unless they got serious. Not sure that makes her a snob so much as careful about her reputation and wanting to avoid gossip."

"I guess that makes sense." When she put it like that, I could see her point. But still, if Hank and I were together, if we were dating and in a relationship, it would never occur to me to hide it.

"His reputation isn't the best, and not just because he owns The Pony—you know that. He's never tried to clean it up or correct people's assumptions about him. It's almost like he enjoys their scorn."

I heard Hannah, but I hadn't moved past her earlier revelation. "I didn't know he actually dated people."

"What were you thinking he did? Just a bunch of hookups?" Her eyes moved over me. "If he did, would that bother you?"

My mouth opened, then shut, and I shrugged. "No. As you said, as long as folks are upfront and safe about it, and no one is getting hurt, and no one is married to someone else, and there's no cheating, I'm not going to care if he has hookups in his past. It's—I don't know. I didn't give the structure of his personal life much thought before now. It never felt like it was any of my business, so why would I think about it?"

Hannah made a scoffing noise. "Well, that makes you irregular. I don't think it's betraying a confidence to tell you that we get women customers in here all the time asking about him, especially during the hen parties. And during my shifts hosting at the Front Porch, I get twenty questions from all sorts of folks about his sex life. Their curiosity, though inappropriate, doesn't seem weird to me. You gotta admit, he's notorious in these parts."

"I guess he is." Wrinkling my nose, I thought about this. In a way, I supposed we were both notorious—me for being pitied, him for being . . . eccentric. And yet, just as I never had the time to care about being pitied, I'd never spent time or energy pondering over his reputation either, other than admiring how he marched to the beat of his own drum. I barely had time to think during any given day, why would I spend it on gossip?

"Think about what people see: filthy rich, troublemaker, Ivy League dropout. Smart and handsome, major real-estate investor in the area, philanthropist, only heir to the Weller fortune, drives a rusted old pickup, and he runs this club? He doesn't make any sense to most people. 'Course, the women who are curious rarely ask him out on a date either. They just want to speculate about what makes him tick, I suppose."

I felt her eyes on me, so I gave her mine.

She'd adopted an impish smile, saying, "Right now, you make him tick."

CHAPTER 21

CHARLOTTE

"It may be important to great thinkers to examine the world, to explain and despise it. But I think it is only important to love the world, not to despise it, not for us to hate each other, but to be able to regard the world and ourselves and all beings with love, admiration and respect."

— HERMANN HESSE, *SIDDHARTHA*

*H*annah and I should've been spending these precious hours training her on FastFinance. Instead, she stared at the wall while I stared at the file cabinet. We'd been sitting that way for at least a full minute before she broke the silence.

"Wow. That's—wow."

"I know," I muttered.

I'd told her everything. Literally, everything. It poured out of me. I told her about having a crush on Hank when I was a teenager, him not showing up to take me to prom, how I'd thought I was over the crush and unable to trust him again, but how being around him again here at the club had aroused the slumbering beast. I told her about how he'd offered me the bookkeeping job, our odd flirting exchanges, which I'd assumed were one-sided, how he'd apologized on Thursday and then been dismissive on Friday, how he kissed me and what he'd said on Sunday, and then finally concluded with the events of the day.

Her hesitation was palpable before she finally asked, "He really offered to . . . whenever you want? You just have to tell him?"

I met her gaze; it looked both disbelieving and impressed. I nodded.

Hannah's eyebrows jumped. "That might be the sexiest thing I've ever heard."

"I know!"

Her face split with a smile. "If my forever crush came to me and made the same offer, you better believe I'd be calling him every damn day and sitting on his face every single night."

I choked on nothing. Hannah sounded so sweet, so demure and soft and modest. When she cursed or made an overt sexual reference, I never expected it.

"Please, please, please tell me you're going to take him up on the offer." She looked at me imploringly, like the fate of womankind's sexual satisfaction hung in the balance.

"I can't," I moaned.

"Why not?" Her lower lip puffed out, just a bit. "If he's offering, if he wants to do this for you, why not?"

Abruptly anxious, I stood and paced to the window. "I can't use him like that. I would never use him like that. He deserves so much better, someone who will put him first. And feelings are involved. Long-buried feelings on my side."

"Then why don't you two date? Didn't he say in the car that he wanted that?"

"I can't do that either. First of all, how can I trust him? He stood me up for prom and that was devastating. It might be the scars of crushed teenage dreams, but I have to think part of me will always be waiting for him to stand me up again. And that's not fair to him."

"Charlotte, I know it made a big impression on you, but you need to let that go. Or if you can't, talk to him about—"

"You're right, I know you're right. He's changed, he's matured, he's different. I can let it go and trust him, I know I can. Except, I can't date anyone. It wouldn't be fair."

She also stood but stuck close to her chair. "What do you mean? Why wouldn't it be fair?"

"I honestly don't have time. I'm booked out until November at this point with kid obligations and events, playdates, recitals, sports, ballet, just everything. Anyone I dated would be prioritized after my children. They'd be number five in my life. How could I start a relationship with that between us?"

"But you dated Jackson."

"Yeah, and it was a disaster. Three or four dates in six months. I always cancelled last minute. One of the kids would get sick, or there would be an emergency, or my mom would cancel and I'd have no sitter. We kissed maybe five times and there was absolutely no chemistry. In retrospect, it's obvious he wasn't actually interested in me sexually at all."

"That's definitely not the case with Hank."

"True," I conceded, leaning against the windowsill. His unveiled interest had been a big boost to the old ego, but an ego-boost was the least of the reasons I was interested in him.

Hannah was right about Hank; he was a conundrum. He made no sense, and I'd always loved that about him. He was an individual, weird, surprising, and smart, ethical but on his terms. He truly thought about right and wrong and lived his life by a code that made complete logical sense. It didn't jive with what society deemed respectable, but it made sense to me.

And yeah, he was incredibly, devastatingly, irrepressibly sexy to me.

Hannah scratched the back of her neck. "Do you want my advice? Or do you want me to simply listen?"

"I could really use some advice."

"Then, I mean, why don't you try it?"

"Try dating Hank?"

"Sure. From what you said, he seems gung-ho about the idea and is super into you. What could be the harm in trying?"

I was of two minds on the subject and I voiced my concerns first. "Like I said, he'd be fifth. I'd never be able to put him first."

"But he offered to be your personal sexual servant—no slut-shaming intended, but it's true. He literally offered to make himself available to service you, no pressure, no commitments. That's an offer to put himself dead last. Fifth is a big step up from last."

Nodding, I chewed on my lip, still uncertain. My lip was now almost raw from all the chewing.

"Are you worried about what people will say?" she asked suddenly.

I frowned. "What? No. Of course not."

"Even if dating Hank hurts your reputation?"

"How much worse can my reputation get? I'm the town pity-project, as my mother loves to remind me all the time. I'm on the *bless your heart* bingo card."

"Fair enough." Frowning at me for a beat, Hannah claimed the chair I'd been in earlier and rolled it toward the desk. "I think you should take some time to think about it—at least consider dating him—and we should get started. You have to leave in a few hours, right?"

"Yes. Right. I asked my mom when I saw her in town to schedule a taxi for 7:00 PM since I didn't drive in. We should get started." Pushing away from the window, I sat in the other chair and endeavored to focus on the task at hand. "The login for the laptop is on the corkboard, but I recommend you talk to Hank about installing vault software for passwords."

When she didn't move to open the laptop, I glanced at her. Hannah's pretty eyes were focused on my face, and her expression told me she was engaging in a serious internal debate.

"What? What is it?"

Huffing, her forehead creased with a deep frown. "Let me just say this, just this last thing, then I'll let the matter drop." Hannah opened the laptop and I got the sense she didn't want to look at me as she shared her next thoughts. "From personal experience, I know firsthand that being an object of pity is a lot different than being an object of scorn. I've been both." Her attention lifted to the corkboard, her features vacant, distant, and her words monotone. "They both might be lonely, but only scorn impacts those closest to you. Your loved ones—in your case it'll be your kids, your momma—would also be on the outside looking in."

* * *

"Come in." Hank's voice sounded from the other side of the door, the benign statement cranking up the volume on my fears and doubts.

But I'd made up my mind. Ripping off the Band-Aid hadn't failed me thus far. Settling things between us once and for all, no matter how uncomfortable or scary, was the right thing to do. I couldn't have him expecting something from me I'd never be able to give.

Chin held high and shoulders squared, I opened the door to his office and braced myself for the sight of him. Hank glanced up, a frown of concentration hanging on his handsome features. He then did a quick double take, the frown immediately falling away.

"Charlotte."

"Hank."

The side of his mouth hooked up. "Is this a business or personal call?"

"A little of both."

Now both sides of his mouth hooked upward. "Please. Do come in."

Despite my nerves and the questionable wisdom of being alone with him, I forced my feet to carry me into his office and I shut the door behind me, not wanting this conversation to be overheard. I'd planned to sit in the second chair in his office while I made my case, but I couldn't get my legs to move. Instead, I stood with my back to the door, my hand on the handle, ready to bolt should he make any attempt at seduction.

"You want to sit?"

"No. I'll stand. Thank you." Unable to hold his dancing eyes, I glanced at my shoes. "I finished going over a few things with Hannah. She's a fast learner and she already used a similar program during her college courses. Teaching her FastFinance shouldn't be a problem. In fact, I'll probably have her come to the house from now on and go through things there—assuming that's okay with you."

He was silent, so I peeked at him. His stare had grown intensely scrutinizing. "You're planning to train her at your house? Instead of coming back here?"

"That's right."

Straightening in his seat, he paused a moment before standing. "Does this mean today is your last day here, on site at The Pony?"

I nodded.

A dark cloud dimmed his eyes. "Do I have a reason to apologize? Did I do something wrong?"

I took an automatic step toward him. "No. Not at all. This is my last weekend before starting work at the school, and it would be easier for me to train her at my home after the kids go to bed. My mother . . . I love her, she's so great, and I'm so grateful for her help, but she's not getting things ready, preparing for the start of the school year."

"I see." The wary cloud behind his expression didn't diminish. "Was that the business thing you wanted to tell me? You'll be working from home for your last few days?"

I nodded, glancing down to realize I was twisting my fingers in my skirt. "Yes. That was the business thing. Also that Hannah is going to do a fine job. You'll need to train her for the other part, the non-finance part. My old duties won't take her long to learn or execute. My advice is, give her more to do, not less. She's incredibly capable. Give her the chance to rise to the occasion. And then, of course, give her a raise when she does."

"So noted," he said quietly. "Thank you."

I inhaled a breath for courage, then lifted my eyes to his. He hadn't moved. In fact, he held very still, his gaze watchful and wary. A new calculating gleam had entered his stare and alarm shot through my brain.

I stiffened, rushing to speak before he could make any of his irresistible moves. "Now, listen." I held up a hand. "This next part is the personal part. No interrupting. You can't do that sexy wizardry thing you do."

"Sexy wizardry?" He cracked a grin.

I pointed at him. "I mean it. Don't start. I need to say this, and if you start, then I'll never finish."

Hank lifted an arrogant-looking eyebrow. "Oh now, angel. With me, I guarantee you'll always finish."

Squeezing my eyes shut, I shook my head. "No, no. Stop this instant. I mean it, or I'm leaving."

The sound of his chuckle—a velvety, delighted rumble—had me grabbing for the door handle behind me.

Before I could turn it, he said on a rush, "Okay, okay. Don't leave. I'll holster my magic wand until you finish. Cross my heart, wizard's honor."

Opening one eye, I glared at his barely concealed grin, but accepted his promise. Even so, I kept my hand on the doorknob as I gathered another deep breath, unable to remember the last time I'd been so nervous. I wasn't the nervous sort. This was relatively new territory for me.

Clearing my throat, I began, "I've been thinking about your offer, the offer you made in the truck. The one where you said you'd, uh, see to my needs whenever I wanted."

Hank crossed his arms and braced his feet apart, seeming to waver between expectant and amused.

"The thing is, as tempting as that is, I can't accept."

The muscle at his jaw ticked, his eyelids lowering as amusement leached from his features. "At the risk of being pushy here, why not?"

"For several reasons, not the least of which is that you deserve better. If you're truly interested in someone, then you deserve to be a priority for that person in all ways. It wouldn't be fair to you."

There was no misinterpreting his disappointment. He looked like he wanted to yell at me. Instead, he said calmly, "With you, I wouldn't feel used. I'd feel like I was being of service, helping. And Charlotte—" He paused here, gazing deeply into my eyes. "I want to be in your life. I want to see you. It would be torture knowing you're so close and I'm sitting on my hands, unable to do anything. If this is all you can offer right now, I accept it. I will be happy with that."

I couldn't help but feel indignant on his behalf. Also, flattered. Also, confused. "Why?" It was selfish of me to ask, seeing as how I'd already made up my mind about him and us, but I wanted to know. "I don't understand you. Why do you suddenly want to help me with anything? Is this about Kevin? Do you feel guilty about what happened? Please don't. Like I told you, me wanting a divorce was never about him and that woman who worked here. I've never blamed you or associated you or The Pony with his choices. I left him before he—"

"It's not about Buckley. I don't feel guilty—I've never felt guilty about that. I'm glad he left town." He stepped forward. Reaching for my hands, he pressed them between his palms, a desperation bleeding into his tone. "Getting to know you while you've been here, spending time with you, watching you interact with literally every person in your life, it's been like being carried over a waterfall I didn't know was coming, or getting hit by a car."

I winced. "Tragic and violent?"

"No." He pressed his lips together in an obvious attempt to not laugh. "No, angel. It blindsided me." Both his voice and gaze softened. "You blindsided me. Your accepting ways. How down to earth you are, how easy to be around. Your generosity, and *fuck*, your competence. You can do anything, whether it be unloading a whole damn truckload of liquor crates, reorganizing and streamlining the finances of this place in less than a week, arranging a damn car wash that makes us more money in one day than we usually make in a whole weekend, or effortlessly tricking sixteen exceptionally untrusting exotic dancers to eat out of the palm of your hand."

I felt my mouth tug with a smile. "They're lovely people. I like them."

"And they like you. They like you more than they like me."

I chuckled. "That's not true."

"It's a little true." He squinted but also grinned. "And you're funny. You make me laugh. Not many people can make me laugh. I would miss you if I didn't get to see you." Hank relinquished my hands to one of his and threaded his fingers into my hair behind my ear, his thumb moving against my jaw, his gaze cherishing. "I can't stop thinking about you. Nor do I wish to stop. I want you to have everything you want. You deserve everything you want, and you said on Sunday that you wanted me."

I opened my mouth to clarify that, yes, I wanted him; and in an alternate reality, a future with him where I could put him first and we could be that for each other. But I also wanted an end to world hunger and a self-cleaning house and for my kids to always get along. Wanting something impossible didn't mean I expected to get or have that impossible thing.

Hank pressed his thumb to my lips before I could vocalize the point. "You want to be with me, fact," he said firmly. "Don't try to deny it. But you don't think you can, right? You don't think you have the time or the energy to dedicate to building a future with anybody. And make no mistake about it, that's what I'd want if it were possible."

My brain, too busy processing his words and the feel of his thumb on my lips, couldn't decide how to react.

"You are so lovely, in every single way," he said, his eyes growing hazier the longer they stared at my mouth, his thumb brushing against my bottom lip. "You talk about fairness for me, but what about for you? What about what you deserve? What about someone making *you* their priority?"

I sensed he spoke these words mainly to himself. As much as they made my stomach flutter, I still couldn't accept my gratification at his expense without making sure he felt valued in return.

Covering his hand, I pulled it away from my face, drawing his eyes back to mine. "Thank you for clarifying. Thank you for saying those pretty things about me. I—" I gathered a deep breath, admiration and desire for this man making my chest tight and hot and achy. "I appreciate you wanting to put your own needs to the side to take care of mine, but I still can't say yes."

His frown was immediate. It looked pained rather than angry.

"Charlotte—"

"But . . ." I moved our threaded fingers out to our sides and gave him a quick kiss, saying a short prayer it wouldn't be our last.

Hank blinked, startled.

"If you meant what you said, and you're willing to give things between us a real try—building a future and all that—then I think that's what we should do." Grinning but feeling shy, I tried not to get my hopes up. "I think we should date."

CHAPTER 22

CHARLOTTE

"When I look at a person, I see a person—not a rank, not a class, not a title."

— CRISS JAMI, *KILLOSOPHY*

He blinked again, his lips parting, the shock seizing his features almost comical.

In the very next second, he dropped my hands and took a step back. "Wait a second. Are you serious?"

Without his hands in mine, my fingers twisted in my skirt again. "I am serious. I think we should give it a try."

On a short, stunned breath, he said, "Are you sure?"

"Yes. But if we do this, you have to understand what this means, that you come into it with your eyes wide open."

His feet carried him a mere inch closer, giving me the sense he was restless to close the distance between us but determined to restrain himself. "You mean you want us to date in secret."

"What?" I balked. "No."

"No?" He also balked, visibly surprised.

"No." I gave my head an adamant shake, but then stopped. "Wait, do you mean from the kids? Then, yes. I wouldn't want the kids to know that we're dating—not for a while—but we wouldn't keep it a secret from anyone else."

His confusion seemed to double. "You wouldn't care if folks around town knew?"

"No, Hank," I said softly, his uncertainty making my chest hurt and I could've strangled Patty and that lawyer woman for making him feel like he was only worthy of being dated in secret. Unthinkingly, I reached for his hand and cradled it in mine. "I would be proud to date you."

"Charlotte, no. No." Frown persisting, he leveraged my hold on his hand to pull me forward, his arms coming around me. "We can't date openly," he said, like he found the very idea appalling.

Before I could force my mouth to argue, he continued, "At least not yet. Now that I know you're willing, I'll make some changes. I'll sell the club—"

"What?!"

"And make nice with folks in town," he went on, his eyes no longer focused on me but over my shoulder, maybe on this theoretical future he'd conjured. "I'll donate money to the garden club and the church and wherever else it takes to make those people think of me as worthy of you. I'll win your momma over. Once she thinks of me as respectable, then—"

I yanked out of his arms and lifted mine to ward off his words. "Hank Weller, you will do no such thing."

His frown returned. "Yes, I will."

"No, you won't. You will not change a single hair on your head for me, is that clear?"

He reached out as though to pull me back, but I evaded him, twisting to the side. "No. Now, you listen. You are perfect just the way you are. And if the small-minded people don't like you, then who cares?"

"I care," he said flatly.

"Since when?"

"Since I wanted to get serious with a woman who has kids—kids who could be hurt by my sleazy reputation."

I gaped, startled by the severity of his words, his tone, and the look in his eyes, like he was disappointed with me. *With me!*

"Don't look at me like I'm off my rocker, you know I'm right." He set his hands on his hips. "I've spent my whole life being merely tolerated, and the last few years, ever since your ex and Carli skipped town together, being scorned and shunned. It's only been recently that folks have stopped being outright hostile. When I was younger, I didn't mind. In fact, I craved it. I wanted to be on the outside."

"And you don't anymore?" My question emerged strangled.

"If it were just me, I wouldn't mind being simply tolerated again. I don't need folks in town to like me. But I couldn't do that to you, or your kids. And that's what would happen, Charlotte. Being tolerated would be the best-case scenario. Worst case, you and Kimmy, Joshua and Sonya, and that littlest one, Frankie, you'd all be spurned, disinvited, whispered about. You must see that."

Meeting his stare, I swallowed around a lump as my mind tripped over and then halted on my ex-mother-in-law's gleeful sharing of Kevin's current whereabouts. I didn't believe for one second that Kevin had any interest in my children, but Mrs. Buckley? And Kevin's daddy? They'd dragged their feet on finalizing the custody agreement once, there was nothing stopping them from petitioning the court to modify the terms. The possibility was why I'd secured that modest beach house in the divorce, why I'd fixed it up and rented it out.

Folks in this town love to gossip and judge.

Hank was right. Of course he was right. And I was stupid, coming in here like a Pollyanna after my discussion with Hannah where she'd pointed out the exact same danger, convincing myself that everything would be fine, folks would get over it. Who would care?

Maybe people wouldn't care, but they certainly would judge.

I briefly considered and then dismissed telling Hank about Kevin's return to the area. Kevin wasn't Hank's problem, he'd never been Hank's problem, and he'd already been through enough thanks to my ex. No, I'd deal with Kevin on my own, if or when the time came.

As much as it pained me to admit it, my mother was also right. I was denser than dirt sometimes. We couldn't be together publicly. Not unless Hank's reputation underwent a serious makeover.

And yet . . .

"This is ridiculous. I can't ask you to sell the club." My eyes stung and my voice cracked on the last word. "We don't even know if things will work out between us. I don't want you to change who you are for me. I like who you are."

Hank's eyes turned soft, and he gathered my cheeks in his palms. "Angel, I like who you are, too. And I wouldn't want you to change a hair on your head either." Apparently unable to help himself, he brushed a gentle kiss across my lips, then retreated a few inches. "But this isn't me changing, not really. This would be me putting on a show. I need to play by their rules so *I* can win without you and the kids losing."

I heaved a sigh. "I understand that, I do, but like I said, we don't know if things are going to work out between us. And you selling the club, making all these changes . . . What if we don't work out? Then you've lost everything and that would not be okay with me."

"That's a—that's a fair point. It would be putting you under a lot of pressure, right from the get-go." His forehead wrinkled, his eyes moving between mine. "How about this: if you agree to see me in secret, then I won't sell the club. We'll take things slow. We'll see what happens, no pressure. But"—he stole another quick kiss, his hands smoothing down my neck, to my arms, gathering my hands in his—"if after, let's say, six months things are going well, then . . ." Hank lowered his head to my neck, placed a kiss just under my ear, and whispered, "Then I move forward with publicly rehabilitating my reputation so we can be together in the open."

I struggled to think, trying not to moan as he nipped at my skin. "I don't know, six months might not be enough time."

"How about six months and a day?" His hot breath caressed my skin as he continued trailing kisses under my jaw.

I laughed, but it caught in my throat as he sucked on my earlobe. "No, Hank," I panted, heat swirling in my abdomen. "Hank, I'm being serious. There are still some things you need to—need to—oh, please stop doing that. I can't think."

Hank removed his tongue from my ear and sighed heavily. His hands found their way to my bottom and he gave me a possessive squeeze before lifting his head.

"Fine. Talk. Tell me what I need to know."

He looked so grumpy. It was cute. But I couldn't let myself be sidetracked again.

Setting my palms on his shoulders, I forced myself to spell things out. "My priority is my children. Those four humans are my responsibility. They come first."

"Glad we're on the same page." His grumpiness morphed into a tender, accepting smile.

Now I frowned. "No. Listen to me, really listen. You were right, we can't date openly—for the kids' sakes. But even if we're dating in secret, I will cancel on you last minute. It's inevitable. Someone will be sick, or the sitter will cancel on me, or I'll be too tired to go out and I'll need to save my energy for them, for when they need me."

"Makes sense."

I wasn't finished. "I won't be able to see you for long stretches of time when things are busy. The start of the year is always hectic. Someone will get sick—it never fails—around the second or third week of September. Then it's Halloween and costumes and decorating and fall plays and pumpkins. Then we have a short lull before Thanksgiving and the holidays. The holidays are completely bonkers. I likely won't be able to see you between Thanksgiving and New Year's, and then even longer if the kids get sick again after the winter break. Six months might mean four dates, possibly even less."

"I see . . ." His eyes, sober and contemplative, drifted to some spot behind me.

My heart sank, but I soldiered on. This is what I'd come in here to do; this is what I'd decided after my discussion with Hannah.

"This is what I'm talking about," I said, and his gaze refocused on mine. I gave him a bleak smile. "I can see now you were right about us dating publicly being bad for the kids, but I'm right about this. And this is why me expecting you—or anyone—to put in the effort, to sit around and wait, to put my kids' needs above your own, to accept that you'd be fifth and they're all tied for first, that's too much to ask."

"I don't—"

"But there is no other way."

"It's not that—"

"I'm incapable of changing my priorities."

"Charlotte. I accept."

My mouth snapped shut.

Jaw set in a determined line, he said, "Thank you for spelling things out. I do accept. Consider my eyes wide open."

"Oh." Since I'd almost succeeded in convincing myself he wouldn't accept, this came as another shock.

"But I do have a question," he said, sounding hesitant.

"What? What is it?" My heart hung suspended.

Hank's eyes grew speculative in that way of his. "Is it my job? Is that the reason you want me to keep my distance from the kids?"

I rocked back on my heels. Everything out of his mouth recently were the last things I'd expected him to ask, say, or offer, which had me blurting, "I thought you didn't like kids."

"I don't." He shrugged. "But I really like Jet's kids from what I know, and your kids. Or I like the three of yours I've talked to so far. Jury is still out on the youngest since we've never been properly introduced."

Taking a step back, and thereby removing myself from the circle of his arms, I asked, "You *really like* my kids? How—how would you know if you like them?"

He scratched his chin through his beard. "I don't know them well, that's true. I sat with Joshua and Sonya at that thing a while back, at Jet's place. We talked for a while and I really enjoyed the conversation, the company. And your oldest, Kimmy, I took an immediate liking to her even though she's stubborn and mean."

My motherly hackles rose at his description of Kimmy. I felt like crossing my arms, so I did. "Is that so?"

He grinned, clearly not picking up on my maternal hostility. "Yeah, that's so. Mean and clever, a rebel. I suppose I liked her so much because she reminds me of myself at her age. It's like spending time with a younger me. Her belligerence is . . . fun."

"Fun?"

"Yeah, fun." He laughed, not looking my way, clearly lost in a memory. "Remember how earlier today she told you I'd been explaining all about my job? Well, she did the same thing to her grandma before you showed up and your mother almost had a fit." He laughed harder. "You should've seen her face. I thought she was going to faint."

My hackles reduced from a boil to a simmer and I stared at him, disbelieving my ears.

He wasn't quite finished. "But I get Kimmy, I do. I bet she picks fights with you all the time, right? The worst thing you can do is fight back or take her too seriously. I mean, that's the absolute worst thing. If she's anything like me, she needs someone to make a joke—not about her, but about something else, something unrelated—and snap her out of it. That's what Beau always used to do, for me and for his twin brother. But don't worry, I grew out of it. Mostly."

A new kind of incredulity overcame me and I asked before I could stop myself, "And Joshua? Sonya?"

"Oh, now that Joshua, he's the best. Not saying I have a favorite—I definitely don't, how could I?—but that kid is something else. Well, you were there. You saw him reading that paper, and he understands everything he reads. He spent a half hour, give or take, explaining all about the Fed and interest rates. What an interesting kid. I could've talked to him all day. And he's sweet with his sister, with Sonya." Hank paused for a moment, considering something, then went on, "But he needs to use a tissue to blow his nose, right? Why's he always using his sleeve or his finger? Something for him to work on."

What alternate reality had I stumbled upon, where Hank Weller knew my children better after just one encounter than their father did after years of living with us day in and day out? The last time I'd asked Kevin his opinion about a gift for Joshua, he'd said, "Get him, you know, whatever boys like."

Kevin didn't know Joshua at all, and he certainly never made any effort to know Kimmy or diffuse her temper.

While I struggled to process this, Hank continued conversationally, "Sonya needs to work on blowing her nose, too. Not to tell you your business, but it'd be good if Joshua set the example there. Otherwise, what a cutie—so sweet, so loving. I think her smile could melt chocolate. But she's smart, right? You can tell by her eyes. There's a lot going on there. I suspect she leans into the cutie-patootie bit to get her way." He tilted his head, apparently considering. "I'm guessing it works all the time."

Incredulous and overwhelmed, I blinked against the sudden stinging behind my eyes.

"I'd like to know them better, especially your youngest, if that's agreeable to you," he said. "No pressure, though. You're their momma and know what's best. I'll do whatever you want, and no matter what you decide, I still accept your terms." Hank hooked his thumbs in his pockets, watching me while I watched him. After a time, his stare uncertain, he scratched his chin again. "But don't expect me to like their friends. I still don't like kids. Just yours. And Jethro's."

A slightly hysterical laugh bubbled out of me while I stared at this strange creature. Knowing my kids and truly liking them for who they were, he couldn't have more effectively stolen my heart.

"How about this, then," I said, swallowing around a fair bit of emotion. "We won't tell the kids we're dating, not for a while, but you have an open invitation to come over and get to know them better whenever you'd like."

"Do you think that's wise?" He seemed honestly concerned. "What will you tell folks if they see me there? People will recognize my truck and all my other cars. Is that a chance you're willing to take?"

"If they notice or if anyone asks, I'll tell them I'm still helping you with bookkeeping for the club. I'll say I need the extra income—which is sorta true." It was the best I could come up with, the best compromise. I understood folks might gossip about me, my mother never let me forget it. On the off chance someone spied Hank's truck in my driveway and demanded to know my personal business, I figured this half truth should protect the kids from any censure.

Hank opened his mouth, maybe to protest, but before he could speak, I pressed a finger to his lips to stem his thought so I could finish mine, my momma-bear protective instincts and our long-ago shared history pushing me to say, "One last thing: don't make promises to my children you can't keep. Don't say you're going to show up if you can't or won't. Don't stand them up. If you're going to break someone's heart, break mine. Okay?"

Donning a consternated frown, he captured my hand and kissed the back of it. "I'm not breaking any hearts," he said firmly, bending and whispering just before our lips met, "least of all yours."

CHAPTER 23

HANK

"Age was respected among his people, but achievement was revered. As the elders said, if a child washed his hands he could eat with kings."

— CHINUA ACHEBE, *THINGS FALL APART*

The first week without Charlotte wasn't the hardest.
    I'd come to realize no 'hardest' day existed behind me or on the horizon. Every day and every hour would be hard. Thinking about her was hard. Trying not to think about her was hard. And when I thought about her, I was often hard.

It was all just so fucking hard.

I sucked it up, though. I made do. I met Beau for drinks at Genie's on Saturday nights—like tonight—and went through the motions. I pretended all was well. I told myself this physical separation wasn't forever.

It felt like forever.

Especially when Hannah handled Charlotte's job and learned and/or assumed almost the entirety of my duties over the course of five days. Hannah's competence made me feel obsolete in a good way, giving me the first real break and breather from The Pink Pony since I'd bought the place almost a decade ago.

And you know what? I did not miss it. I missed my staff, and I continued to fret over their well-being. But I didn't miss the work, the place, or the customers.

On the other hand, Hannah's competence also made me feel obsolete in a bad way. What was I supposed to do with all this insufferable free time?

You could go over to Charlotte's and see the kids.

I frowned, the wooden tabletop blurring in and out of focus as Beau and his brothers conversed over the ruckus of Genie's on a Saturday night. Perhaps I'd aged unnaturally fast in the last ten days since my last in-person interaction with Charlotte, but instead of appreciating the live music, I wished someone would turn the volume down. The loudness, the hubbub and frenetic energy of our surroundings made thinking difficult. I needed to think.

Charlotte had left the ball in my court. She'd told me I could come over and see her and the kids whenever I wanted, just as long as I didn't do anything to let them down. I wanted to see her and them, but I hadn't gone over due to the circular nature of my thoughts.

I didn't want to blow this chance with her, I didn't want to risk it, but I missed her and those kids so damn much. However, I'd never forgive myself if I did anything—inadvertently or otherwise—to hurt them.

Something about her warning, about breaking their hearts, had me second-guessing myself. Her words felt loaded, not quite a threat but more than a promise. Basically, *You hurt one of my kids, even unintentionally, and you can fuck right off.*

Not many people liked me and even fewer actually enjoyed my company these days. I knew my disposition over the years had morphed from belligerent and sneaky into a lot grumpy with very little sunshine. What if me simply being myself unintentionally hurt Sonya's sensitive little heart? Or what if we all got along real well but someone in town gossiped about us, spreading rumors, and those rumors hurt her children?

Now I was back to not wanting to take the risk. Our agreement would have to be enough. I'd be patient until we could rendezvous in secret. We were together officially and exclusively. Compared to what I'd been ready to settle for, that was a lot.

November 10th had been selected as our first date. Charlotte had the day off on the 11th and so would the kids, which meant she and I would be able to stay out later than usual. As she'd predicted, she had very little time or energy for me at the end of her days, though it was clear she did her best to make time. I received texts near 11:00 PM most nights, asking me about my day, telling me she missed me, or sending through a funny photo of her and the kids, snapped when the sun had still been up.

She rarely called, usually too tired. If she did, I always answered but made sure we were off the phone by midnight so she could sleep. Meanwhile, I couldn't sleep, thinking about her. I could've talked to her for hours.

I just . . . I rubbed my chest. *I miss her so damn much.* I missed getting to see her most days, her smile, her easy way, how she teased, her assessing eyes. And I wondered how the kids were doing, what Joshua was reading, what hell Kimmy was raising. I wanted more than just pictures. I wanted—

"Do you want another beer?" Beau nudged my shoulder.

I blinked at him, frowning. "Another beer?" Blinking at the pint glass in my hand, I realized it was empty. I didn't remember finishing it.

"You okay, Hank?" Roscoe asked. "You've been stewing in something meaty the whole time we've been sitting here."

Both Roscoe and Jethro eyed me speculatively, like I was acting strange, or weird, or in a worrisome way. They'd been doing this all night and it left me feeling tetchy.

"I'm fine, Roscoe. I got a lot on my mind, is all." I glowered at the empty glass in my hands and decided I would have another. Glancing up, I caught the tail end of the brothers sharing a look. Grunting to draw their collective attention, I said, "If you three are finished passing around those un-stealthy looks of concern, yes. I'll have another. Please and thank you."

"A 'please' *and* a 'thank you'? It's not even my birthday. Now I know there's something afoot." Beau put on an affected voice, no doubt an attempt to lighten my mood. He grabbed our empty glasses and scooted out of the booth. "I'll be back with another round. Don't talk about anything important until I get back." With that, he departed, leaving me with his brothers.

The live band switched songs and the scuffle of boots followed, a few *whoops* lifting over the ruckus. No doubt the bodies cluttering the space in front of the stage were arranging themselves for line dancing. The four of us sat removed from the action in the booth farthest from the crowd. It was still too loud.

Crossing my arms, I surveyed the eldest and youngest of the Winston clan. They watched me in return, saying nothing. Given the general commotion of our surroundings, Jethro and Roscoe's silence wouldn't have bothered me if it hadn't felt so heavy, their worry so obvious.

Inhaling slowly, I prepared to question the pair, but Jethro spoke before I could. "How's Hannah doing in her new role?"

I lifted a single eyebrow. He knew how Hannah was doing, since, as my silent partner in the club, I'd just emailed him the monthly update yesterday. About to remind Jethro to check his inbox if he wanted to know, a thought occurred to me. His question suddenly felt like an opportunity.

"About that." I leaned my elbows on the table. "I'm glad you mentioned Hannah. I have an idea I want to run by you."

Jethro popped a pretzel in his mouth. "What's that?"

I hesitated, an image of Charlotte's assessing eyes flashing behind mine, narrowed in displeasure. I shoved it to the side. She didn't want me to sell the club for her, fine. Fair enough. But what if I sold it—or most of it, or gave it away —for me?

"The thing is, Jet"—I lowered my voice so we couldn't be overheard—"I think

Hannah is going to be more than capable of running the club in about a month or so without any help from me."

"That's good." He munched on another pretzel.

"Right. It's good. But why am I drawing a salary if Hannah is doing everything? I should only draw a salary if I'm working there. Seems like she should be getting my salary in addition to hers."

Jet's forehead wrinkled. "That's awfully generous of you. What are you proposing?"

I held Jet's gaze, ordering my thoughts carefully.

The few times I'd brought up rehabilitating my reputation through public acts of insincerity, Charlotte had lost her temper. And that frustrated me. Why was I the only person in town who wasn't allowed to be a hypocrite? But pushing the issue when she had so little time to talk felt wrong.

Still, I needed to figure out how to convince her. I had no problem saying whatever folks wanted me to say and doing whatever folks wanted me to do if it meant polite society wouldn't tear Charlotte and her kids apart for us being together. The club was low-hanging fruit, now an easy problem to solve, thanks to Hannah.

Clearing my throat, I kept my tone light and conversational. "What if—and I haven't talked to Hannah about this, so it's pending her agreement, of course—but what if we let Hannah buy us out? Or at least buy me out?"

Jethro's hand, holding another pretzel, stalled on its way to his mouth. "You want to sell to Hannah?"

"I do. If she's interested. I'd fix the place up first, make sure everything is in good working order so she wouldn't have to worry about repairs or upkeep for a while. And I'd stay on to lend a hand if she needed, until she took full ownership of my shares. But I'd be a silent partner starting as early as next month. As far as everybody is concerned, The Pink Pony would be hers, not mine."

Roscoe and Jethro shared a quick look, the younger of the two asking, "You don't want to own The Pink Pony anymore?"

Leaning back, I rested my arm along the back of the booth. "I want my staff taken care of—they're what matter. I wouldn't sell to just anyone, which is probably why I haven't done so before now. I trust Hannah to run things right. It'd be a good salary for her, she'd make a good living from it, enough to save and invest in other ventures like I did. But that place, doing that job"—*being that person*—"I'm honestly tired of it."

"You're finally going to live the life you were born into—a Weller trust fund baby." Jethro's small smile told me the words were meant to tease, not to jab.

I smirked, about to clarify that I didn't need my parents' money to live well, when Roscoe asked, "But what about your reputation, Hank? How will you piss everyone off if you're not running the strip club?"

Reaching for one of the coasters on the table between us, I used two fingers to spin it like a top. "Well, Baby Winston, I believe it's time I—"

"I have an amber draft for Hank," Beau said, plopping four drinks on the table, "a gin and tonic for Roscoe, a *whatever is on special* for Jet, and another amber draft for me."

Beau slid into the booth while we all claimed our cups. "What'd I miss?" His attention seemed to settle meaningfully on Roscoe.

Roscoe shook his head at Beau, his eyes wide, and I glanced between the two of them, suspicion blooming anew.

"You missed me telling Jet that I want to sell my ownership shares in The Pink Pony to Hannah."

Beau reared back. "What?!"

I ignored his shocked outburst, grateful he hadn't been drinking beer. If he had, I'd be wearing beer-cologne now.

Pointing between Roscoe and Beau, I said, "Now, why don't you two tell me what's going on? Not that I mind seeing y'all, but something is up. Baby Winston is here for a reason. Spill it."

Beau sputtered, blue eyes bouncing between the three of us. "Now, hold on. You can't just drop a bomb about selling The Pony and expect me to let that go."

"We'll fill you in later, Beau," Jet cut in, then tilted his head toward his youngest brother. "Beau asked Roscoe to come. He has information for you, if you're interested. Beau seems to think you'll be interested. That's why Roscoe is here."

"Why're you here, then, Winston the Elder?" I asked, amused by Jethro telling on his brothers.

Jet lifted his drink and took a gulp, reaching for another pretzel as he set the glass down. "Two reasons. Believe it or not, y'all are more adult-like than my boys and I needed some adult time. Sienna offered to give me a night completely off from kid duty."

I smiled, but then I frowned, a pang of something unpleasant settling in my chest. When did Charlotte take a break? Who offered to give her a night off?

"The other reason is, I'm curious about something," Jet went on, a whisper of a smile behind his eyes, but he said no more.

"You're curious about something?" I asked. "Does this have to do with the information Baby Winston supposedly has?"

Jethro nodded, the side of his mouth hooking up.

Turning my attention to Roscoe, I lifted my hand. "Okay, let's hear it, then. What's this information you got that Beau thinks I want and the old man here is curious about?"

Roscoe, looking a shade uncomfortable, frowned at his drink, sipped it, and then frowned at Beau. "This feels like gossip."

Beau huffed. "It's not gossip. It's information that's over ten years old, which only you seem to remember because you remember everything, and it explains why Charlotte Mitchell has always given Hank the cold shoulder."

I sat up at the unexpected mention of Charlotte, all ears. "What's this? What's this about Charlotte?"

Something about my reaction must've been odd or amusing. Jethro grinned and muttered, "Well, that answers my question."

Ignoring him, I leaned forward and tapped the table in front of Roscoe. "What do you know about Charlotte? Is she—did something happen?"

"Not recently," Roscoe grumped, obviously still reluctant. We stared at each other and I held very still, frantically trying to figure out how to make Beau's youngest brother talk, now that he had one or two inches on me, clearly worked out, and could no longer be dangled over the edge of the back porch.

Before I could make any threats or take any action, he growled, "Fine. If you want to know why Charlotte always avoided you in town, it's on account of you standing her up."

I frowned. Blinked. Cocked my head to the side. *I stood her up?*

His words made no sense. At a loss, I asked, "Stood her up when?"

"Our junior prom."

Ransacking my memory, I glared at the tallest but littlest Winston. "No, I didn't. I would never do that. Your name is now Winston the Liar."

"Yes, you did. You asked her to her junior prom. And yes, you stood her up," Roscoe said flatly. "She went with me and the rest of her volleyball team. Her dress was red. She'd bought you a red rose for your boutonniere and I ended up wearing it 'cause it matched my tie. If you want to know more, ask her, Weller the Wanker."

"I do not recall ever doing that." I gave my head a firm, frustrated shake. "Why would I ask her to prom? I didn't even go to my own prom. And I barely remember Charlotte. When would I have asked her?"

I couldn't think. This all sounded enormously far-fetched . . . except Roscoe Winston's recall was as reliable as German trains. He never misremembered, and he never forgot.

"I'm not surprised you don't remember Charlotte." Roscoe settled his drink on a coaster. "We were only fourteen when you left for college, basically still little kids."

"I was sixteen, almost seventeen when I left," I said, mostly to myself, trying to fit together the pieces of this puzzle he'd discarded on my lap.

"I know."

I glared at Roscoe. "Of course you do, savant. What happened? Why did I ask a fourteen-year-old to junior prom?"

"She wasn't fourteen when you asked, she was sixteen. It happened over

Christmas break when you were back in town, home from college. I suppose you've heard or figured out by now that Charlotte had a crush on you back then?"

My mouth dropped open. For a moment, I couldn't breathe or think. *She WHAT?!*

Finally, I managed to sputter, "I—what? Charlotte had what?"

Movement caught my attention and I looked at Jethro. He sat across from me, his hand over his mouth and his shoulders shaking. He found me hilarious.

I kicked him under the table. "You think this is funny, asshole?"

This only made him laugh harder. "Yes. Yes, I do. It's always nice to see someone else having to pay for their youthful mistakes instead of just me."

Meanwhile, Beau hit my shoulder. "See? This explains why she doesn't—or didn't—like you for so long." My best friend sounded cheerful, as though this news was the best news ever because a mystery had been solved.

Fuck the mystery, especially when the solving of it made me out to be the villain.

"Thank you, Marty Sue Winston, for spelling it out for me," I growled, my head pounding. Try as I might, I simply could not recall the Charlotte from my youth beyond blurry snapshots of a tall, sporty girl with scraped knees. A girl who dressed for comfort rather than style, who wanted to turn everything into a debate. A young, improper miss with long, streaky, blond hair and long legs, who always chose dare instead of truth, who hung around Baby Winston, who interrupted me and Beau more than a few times, wanting in on our schemes.

But that's all I recalled: snapshots I'd never taken the time or energy to organize or save.

"Was I jerk to her?" I asked before I could stop myself, bracing.

"Eh." He shrugged, then sipped his gin and tonic. "Yeah. But you weren't any more or less of a jerk to Charlotte than you were to anyone else."

His response made the band around my chest tighter. I needed to be a more polite person, but I also needed to figure out how to stomach it. Growing up, my parents' friends would comment on my lack of manners but never comment on how my parents screamed at me or smacked me around in front of them.

It isn't *polite* to comment on abuse to an abuser, and God forbid someone be impolite.

"Come on, Hank. You've mellowed as you've gotten older." This came from Jethro. He wasn't laughing, but he still grinned. "So have I, so have we all."

"And you were a hellraiser," Roscoe said, his smile somehow both grim and fond. "You taught Beau, Duane, and me how to pick locks and pick pockets. Every card-shark move I know is one you taught me. And where'd you get all those fireworks? You seemed to have an endless supply and were always setting them off at community garden events and society tea parties."

"My mother was the head of the Green Valley Garden Society," I said, distracted by my sinking stomach.

Why would I have asked Charlotte to her junior prom? If I understood the circumstances, I'd remember more. Covering my face, I rubbed my eyes. I needed to talk to Charlotte about this. I needed to apologize. *Speaking of, why hadn't she said anything to me? Had she forgotten, too?*

"My point is, you were shipped off to boarding school during the year when you were a kid, and too busy raining down chaos over the summers and breaks to notice Charlotte or anyone else. The only person you ever had time for was Beau," Roscoe said.

I let my hands drop to my lap and regarded him warily.

Roscoe returned his glass to the coaster, seemingly careful to set it directly in the center. "When you returned for college breaks, you had no interest in a sixteen-year-old high school student or taking her to prom. That doesn't make you a jerk. I'd say it's healthy that a nineteen-year-old man didn't see a sixteen-year-old girl in that way."

"Hmm," was all I said, not wanting to interrupt his monologue, hungry for more details that might jog my memory.

"But she liked you." He shrugged, his movements looser than earlier in the evening. I noticed he'd almost finished his most recent gin and tonic. "I don't think you had any idea. During that particular Christmas break, she would ask you about what books you were reading and then force you into conversation by asking you tons of questions. Charlotte was pushy back then. I'm not talking assertive, I'm talking *pushy*. Never wanting to take no for an answer, always testing boundaries, always pushing. She's different now, but her oldest daughter is just the same."

"If I wasn't interested in Charlotte, then why I'd ask her to prom?" I wished he'd get to the point instead of editorializing the trivialist of details or telling me things I already knew.

"It was a bet," Jethro filled in. "Just tell him the rest, Roscoe. Put him out of his misery."

"Fine." Roscoe's chest rose with an expansive breath and he leaned forward, eyes on me. "The year you asked her, you weren't around as much. That summer, you only spent from July 19th until August 17th in the valley, and then you skipped coming home for Thanksgiving. But you did come home for Christmas, December 23rd through January 2nd. Those dates are the only time you and Charlotte interacted that I'm aware of, and even then, it wasn't a lot. Just a few minutes here or there as you and Beau came and went from the house."

I squinted at him and his ridiculously impressive recall while I still drew blank nothingness. "Okay . . . ?"

"But three days after Christmas, my momma was gone with Billy and Cletus overnight, leaving Beau and Duane in charge of me. Ashley was long gone to college by then. Charlotte came over. So did you. And you told us that if we could manage to score some beer from the Corner Shoppe, then you'd grant us each one wish. Her wish was that you would ask her to prom."

Staring at the tabletop, I scoured my mind, still encountering a void. "So I did?"

"Yep."

"And then?" Beau spared me from asking the next obvious question.

"That's it." Roscoe shrugged. "You said, 'Charlotte, will you go to prom?' And she said, 'Yes.' And that's it. That was the whole conversation. You and Beau left and drank all the beer, getting totally shitfaced. Billy found you both the next day—"

"Oh, shit. I remember that," Beau said, his eyes losing focus. "Damn. We got so sick."

"I remember that, too." Relieved that I finally recalled something relevant, I looked to Roscoe. "And that's it? Charlotte and I didn't make plans for the prom? I didn't bring it up again?"

"No." Roscoe, wearing a small, inscrutable smile, shook his head. "As far as I know, you didn't. Until she called me on prom night, she didn't talk to me about it either."

"Why didn't she—"

"I have a theory." Jethro leaned forward, cutting off my question. "Based on my own history of being a complete shithead, I suspect you saw your part of the bargain fulfilled. You didn't say you'd take her to prom, that wasn't her wish. Her wish was that you would *ask* her to prom. And so you did. That's my theory. It sounds like something I would've done."

Well. That certainly sounded like me, and now I hated myself.

My forehead fell to my hand. "I was such a little fucking weasel."

"Yep," all three of the Winstons said in unison.

I closed my eyes. "Again, why did she like me back then?"

The answer came from Roscoe. "You rebelled against authority. You were smart and tricky, witty and daring. You were the kid who always got away with everything."

A swell of memories, of my parents' sporadic punishments, threatened to escape the void in my mind where I'd shoved them. Even as a young child, it didn't matter what I did, I was going to be punished. I was going to be a disappointment. Never good enough. Never smart enough. Never polite enough.

Rather than deal with a no-win situation, I'd decided early on to do whatever the hell I wanted. I didn't care about hurting people, I didn't care about their feelings. If they made the mistake of putting their faith in me, of counting on me, I figured they got what they deserved, Beau Winston being the only exception to this philosophy at the time.

"To us kids, though—" Roscoe's voice yanked me out of my morose contemplations. "It seemed like you did whatever you wanted and always landed on your feet. You were a legend. We looked up to you."

"I was heartless," I said, my voice a scrape. "I was a heartless bastard and Charlotte deserved so much better."

"You didn't seem heartless to us, Hank. Not until you stood her up for prom. You seemed cool. A rebel," Roscoe said, his cadence slow and thoughtful. "And besides, Charlotte has always had a weakness for rebels."

I hadn't been a rebel. I'd been a thoughtless moron and I'd been another person to let Charlotte down. I'd been no better than Kevin. Charlotte had deserved so much better than either of our sorry asses.

Charlotte deserved a Beau.

As though to prove my point, Beau placed a hand on my shoulder and gave it a pat. "You were always good to me, Hank." His fingers squeezed, meant to be a comfort. "You're my best friend and I know you're not heartless. You're a good person."

Ashamed, I affixed a tight smile on my face, but I couldn't lift my eyes from the beer in my hand. Beau deserved better than me, too.

He'd always been the good guy, the stand-up guy, the guy who helped where and when he could, expecting nothing in return, never keeping score, doing good deeds just because. He never had to worry about harming people, inadvertently or otherwise. He was simply incapable of doing so. He'd been the only one I couldn't abide hurting or seeing hurt. And I'd loved him for as long as I could remember.

I loved him . . .

Abruptly, Sonya's voice and her words from weeks ago chose that moment to drift through my memory: *You got to love everybody because everybody needs love. And if we don't love them, who will?*

CHAPTER 24

HANK

"I can win an argument on any topic, against any opponent. People know this, and steer clear of me at parties. Often, as a sign of their great respect, they don't even invite me."

— DAVE BARRY

I needed paint and I didn't want to drive all the way to Knoxville.

Green Valley had two hardware stores, but only one of the stores sold paint. That one also sold baby chicks despite the fact that a seed and feed store existed just three blocks away. Folks who had no intention of purchasing hardware supplies often loitered at the store's entrance to gawk and coo over the birds, which meant they were ideally positioned to administer double takes and glare as I walked in.

"Pardon me. Excuse me," I mumbled as I passed. *Don't mind me, just reaping what I've been sowing.*

A man I recognized, but didn't particularly care to name or place, glowered at me. He appeared old enough to be one of my parents' friends. Based on the way his frown pinched at his eyebrows, he likely considered my existence a stain on the good Weller name.

Making a beeline for the paint aisle, I experienced a noteworthy dearth of desire to revel in the disapproval of the locals. In fact, I reckoned I deserved it.

I'd been a selfish bastard. I'd put my perverse enjoyment of townie discomfort over the well-being of good people. I deserved all the scorn and condemnation. Their condemning stares served as a painful reminder of what I desperately wanted but didn't (yet) deserve to have. Ah well.

Reap, sow.

Endeavoring to suppress the simmering, constant void that had stalked me for the last thirty-one days, I studied the paint and did not dwell upon how much I missed and worried about Charlotte. I selected a few swatches from the wall. I compared one named True Taupe to another one named Faun. These two colors looked exactly the same. This realization had me growing more irritated than I had a right to be about paint swatches.

Disgusted, I put the two cards back in their holders and crossed my arms, determined to find white. Just white. Not eggshell, not steam, not cloud, and not fucking ecru either. Just. White.

These last few weeks hadn't been easy. "Hindsight is 20/20" was a gentler phrase for the realization that one has been a total ass. I'd wanted to speak with Charlotte about Roscoe's information, understand her perspective on our shared history, but I didn't want to bring it up at the end of a long day, when she was tired, when she barely had enough energy for a quick text message exchange. We only spoke at the end of the day and all of hers were long ones. Thus, I'd said nothing and allowed color swatches to inflame my temper until my frustration reached a crescendo.

On the one hand, I didn't deserve to be part of Charlotte's or her kids' lives.

On the other hand, what the fuck was I doing? This was a waste of time. Time I could've spent with Charlotte and Kimmy and Joshua and Sonya and that other one, earning my place, earning respect by showing up, rolling up my sleeves, and doing the work, just like Charlotte had done at The Pony.

Instead, here I was, morose and stilted, grumpy about the naming conventions of white paint.

That's not why you're grumpy.

My frown tightened into a scowl. Roscoe's elucidating info dump wasn't the only source of my tension. Worry about Charlotte's lack of sleep, how much she carried and balanced, how distracted and exhausted she always sounded—especially recently—plagued me. It made me more and more restless to do something, to help, to step in and step up.

But the other worry also continued to plague me, holding me captive in a limbo of inaction. As much as I wanted to clear the air between us, ease my restlessness with action, to contribute, to lighten her burdens, I *still* worried how she and the kids would be treated, gossiped about, and shunned if someone spotted me at her house.

My desire to redeem myself and earn a place in their lives didn't negate their safety and well-being.

Granted, her idea to excuse my visits as bookkeeping business for The Pony had merit, but I didn't want to use that pretext unless my need to see her or her need to see me constituted an emergency. How many times would folks believe I needed "help with my books" before they turned the phrase into a euphemism and threw shade at Charlotte and her children? I reckoned three—four, if we were lucky. Squandering those two or three opportunities just so I could work on proving myself was entirely out of the question.

As I paced the paint aisle, I battled unsuccessfully to put a lid on my resentment.

Things would be so much easier if Charlotte would simply allow me to sell The Pony, donate an obscene amount of money to my mother's former garden club, and —I dunno—make a show of getting baptized by one of those people in the white robes, or whatever those other fellas did who needed a big, splashy, public redemption.

If I didn't find a way to visit her and the kids soon, to check on and help her without putting them at risk or misusing our one solid pretext, then I'd be left with little choice. I would take matters into my own hands, and with or without her agreement, I'd make a show of—

"Hank?"

My head whipped toward the sound of my name and I straightened, surprised to find Jackson James standing at the end of the aisle.

"Oh. Hey, Jackson."

"Looking for paint?" he asked, strolling forward, a friendly smile on his stupid face.

I squinted at him. "No. I'm looking for the US presidential Chia Pets. Isn't this the aisle?"

His smile didn't fall, but he did press his lips together like he couldn't allow himself to laugh at my sarcasm even though he found it amusing. "Nah. Just latex paint here. I think the US presidents are in aisle six." He lifted his basket toward the back of the store. "In between plastic sheeting and paint thinner."

"Thanks," I grumbled, my attention snagging on the contents of his basket. "Are you patching a wall? What happened? One of your raging parties get out of hand?" Yep. More sarcasm from me.

Everyone knew Jackson James didn't throw parties, or drink, or eat good-tasting food, or have fun. If he were a paint color, he'd be beige. If he were a food, he'd be dry, white toast. How a firecracker like Charlotte had ever dated his boring ass, I had no idea.

"No. I mean, yes. I am patching drywall, but it wasn't a party," he said, also glancing at his basket. "Rae and I were over at Charlotte's place last night for dinner, and—"

"Wait, what?" My feet carried me closer. He now had my full attention. "You were at Charlotte's last night?" She hadn't said anything in her text messages.

"Yeah. Rae's only back in town for a bit. She's got another shoot next week, but she wanted to see Charlotte. We brought her and the kids dinner. Frankie is sick, and we wanted—"

"Frankie is sick?" Alarm had me standing straighter and my focus narrowed on Jackson's tired-looking eyes. Had he stayed, or had Raquel stayed, to help Charlotte? I hoped someone had stayed. "What do you mean, he's sick? How sick? What does he have?"

A wrinkle formed between Jackson's eyebrows. "Calm down, Hank. He's fine. He's got a cold, it's fine."

Some of the tension that had dug its claws into my chest eased, and I leaned back on my heels, relieved. However, why hadn't she said anything to me about Frankie? I could've dropped off soup or supplies, or whatever she needed. "Ah. Okay. You were saying."

"Right." His eyes flickered over me, but he continued, "Anyway, Frankie was feeling better, and—"

"He's not sick anymore?"

"He's still sick."

"But he was feeling better last night?"

Jackson glared at me. "Do you want to know what happened or not?"

I lifted my hands in surrender, irritated that he hadn't gotten to the point yet. "Yeah. Fine. Go ahead."

"We were clearing the dishes and talking in the kitchen when we hear this loud crash."

Without thinking, I reached out and grabbed his arm. "Is everyone okay?"

His face scrunched, his eyes communicating that he thought I'd lost my marbles while searching for US presidential Chia Pets in the paint aisle. "It was the curtain rod, Hank. Frankie pulled the whole apparatus out of the wall and some of the drywall came down with it."

I swallowed down the spike of fear and released Jackson's arm. "But he's okay?"

"Yeah." Now he was looking at me like I'd definitely lost my marbles. "He's fine. That kid is a tank. But there's a big hole in the wall now above the patio door, and, well, I feel bad. If we hadn't been distracting Charlotte in the kitchen, then Frankie wouldn't have had a chance to make a hole in the wall." Jackson pointed to the small container of drywall mud in his basket. "I'm heading over there tomorrow to fix the hole and check on the kids."

The fuck you are.

Jealousy, like a jump-scare in a Wes Anderson movie, came out of nowhere and sucker-punched me in the stomach. Then it wrapped around my chest and throat and made everything hot and chilly at the same time.

Jackson could go over to Charlotte's house whenever he wanted. He could see her and the kids, know them, patch up holes in her wall, make her dinner on a whim.

Jackson James, the most boring sonofa—*well, now, his momma is a nice lady*. The most boring, beige asshole in town could call on my (secret) girlfriend whenever he damn well pleased because he was respectable. And I wasn't. Because I'd wanted it that way. Therefore, I couldn't do a damn thing to help her.

That's it. Fuck it. I'm getting baptized.

"I see," I said, struggling to keep the breath-stealing bitterness from my tone. "Charlotte asked you to come over and do that? To patch her hole?" Of course she would. Of course she would ask Jackson.

"No. She didn't ask, it's just—"

"Does she know you're coming over?" I crossed my arms.

"Well, no. But—"

Wait a minute. "So you just show up at her house?"

He went back to looking at me like I was strange again. "Yeah, she doesn't care. I do it all the time."

I scratched my jaw, needing to keep a new lightning strike of jealousy out of my voice. "Are you sure she doesn't care?"

My mind worked frantically. For some reason, this was the final straw. Jackson wasn't patching that hole. If anyone was patching Charlotte's holes, it would be me. No one else. I didn't care if I had to kiss JT MacIntyre's ass and get on my knees in front of the biggest townie gossip, Karen Smith. I would find a way to help Charlotte.

"Pretty sure she doesn't care." His tone sounded hesitant, clearly not knowing where I was going with my current line of questioning.

But I knew where I was going. I knew exactly where I was going, and it wasn't where Jackson was going. He wasn't invited.

Making a big show of sighing, I affixed an expression of sympathy on my features and placed my hand on his shoulder. "Jackson, of course Charlotte is going to *act* that way. But you two just broke up."

"We broke up months ago," he said flatly.

I dropped my voice to a conspiratorial whisper. "Yeah, but Kevin cheated on her, right? And then you two were dating and you left her for a movie star."

"She broke up with me well before Rae and I got together," he whispered back.

I ignored his statement, even though this information pleased me immensely, and tried a different approach. "You're going over to your ex-girlfriend's house to patch up her wall? Don't you think that puts Charlotte in a hard spot? And how do you think Raquel is gonna feel about it?"

"I don't think Rae is gonna care. She and Charlotte are great friends."

"That's exactly my point," I lied, verbally pivoting again, and let go of his shoulder. Opening my arms as though he'd just proved my argument, I said, "When does it stop? You go over there yesterday to help, and now you're going over there tomorrow to help. You're going over there all the time to help. Don't you think this puts Charlotte in an awkward position? She wants to be friends with Rae, and meanwhile, you're going over to her house all the time—uninvited—and what is Charlotte supposed to do? If she turns down your help, she looks ungrateful."

Jackson's eyes narrowed, equal parts suspicion and self-doubt freezing his features.

I pressed on, seeing that he needed one or two more shoves in the right direction. "You don't even ask, do you? Oh, wait a minute." I snapped my fingers. "I suppose I see your point, there. Asking might put Charlotte in an even more difficult position. You don't want to put her on the spot. That's good of you. But you have to see how this looks, how you've put her in a hard situation, however unintentionally."

He now looked lost, and that was good enough for me. I didn't need him to buy the bullshit I was selling, I just wanted him confused enough to ignore the price tag.

"You know what? How about this." I reached for his basket. "I'll take the stuff over to Charlotte's and patch the hole in the wall."

Jackson released the basket easily but stepped forward as I backed up. "Wait a minute—"

"I'll tell her that we ran into each other at the hardware store. You were here looking at paint and you told me about how Frankie made the hole—an amusing anecdote, right?—and I happened to be here picking up drywall supplies anyway for the club, so I might as well grab enough to fix her wall as well. No one needs to know you were planning to do it first, least of all Charlotte. We can spare her that discomfort, don't you think?"

Jackson's glare was full-on suspicious now and he grabbed for the handle of the basket, effectively stopping me. "What's your angle?"

I put on a performance of looking offended and innocent, neither of which were expressions I wore often. Or ever. "What? I can't help you out?"

He said nothing, but his unimpressed glare spoke volumes.

"Fine." I made a short grunting sound, rolling my eyes and thinking fast. "I don't like being in your debt, okay?"

This explanation made him release the basket again, but he didn't budge otherwise. "In my debt? How are you in my debt?"

"Come on. The car wash? You brought over all those police cars for my dancers to wash? It really helped us out. Me patching one little hole won't come close to paying you back, so how about this: I'll help Charlotte with her house stuff from now on. I'll take that over. If she calls you, you call me. Only then will I feel as though my debt to you has been paid." As an afterthought, I added, "And be sure to let folks know—if anyone asks—how I'm helping her out as a favor to you."

Jackson lifted his chin, inspecting me. "Taking over as Charlotte's handyman is payback for helping y'all back in August?"

I worked to wipe the threatening smile from my face and nodded. "Absolutely. I don't think you understand how helpful you were."

His disbelief and suspicion persisted, and his lips parted—perhaps to argue, possibly to question me further, maybe to sneeze. Whatever it was, I'd reached the limit on my patience.

Lowering my voice, I gritted out, "Just go with it, Jackson. Fucking hell, just follow my lead. Please." I glanced meaningfully toward the front of the store, hoping he'd take the hint. To be sure, I added, "Trust me, she wants to see me. Charlotte will thank you later."

Mouth snapping closed, the sheriff's deputy inspected me for a long, long moment. Something like dawning comprehension cleared away his confusion.

That's right, Jack. I'm her man.

I didn't care if Jackson knew the truth. He might've been a beige asshole, but no one would ever accuse him of being a gossip.

Eventually, he drawled, "All right. I suppose helping Charlotte with her place for a bit would settle our, uh, debt."

"Good. Glad to hear it." I lifted my voice and clapped a hand on his shoulder, relief soaring through me. "Now, you go home. Take tomorrow off. Spend some time with that lady of yours. I'll patch things up at Charlotte's today, no use in waiting. And—remember—if you find out she needs anything else, you let me know and I'll make sure it gets done." Hopeful we'd be overheard, I added, "Helping Charlotte with a few handyman tasks is the least I can do to pay you back."

CHAPTER 25

HANK

"By contrast, the grime of her journey, the outré inappropriateness of the state of her, it felt like armor.
I earned this dirt.
Respect. The dirt."

— LAINI TAYLOR, *DREAMS OF GODS & MONSTERS*

As I exited the hardware store with my purchases, I also texted Charlotte that I'd be coming over and—not using a single text emoji—I asked if she needed me to grab anything on my way.

That done, I stopped by my house and showered, shaved, trimmed my beard, and dug out a never-opened bottle of cologne from beneath my bathroom sink. Looking good, smelling good, and determined to make every second at her house count, I checked my phone. She hadn't responded yet. The lack of a reply didn't deter me.

For a time, and once the gossipmongers spread the word, me stopping by Charlotte's house periodically as a favor to Jackson wouldn't raise any suspicions. But this excuse wouldn't buy me forever, nor would I be able to stay for very long. We needed a new strategy, a new plan, one that allowed me to visit for a whole day instead of an hour.

On the drive over, I debated how best to convince Charlotte to let me reform and rehabilitate my reputation. By the time I pulled into her driveway, I'd practiced three or four iterations of my side of our inevitable debate. If a well-constructed argument didn't bring her to my way of thinking, then I'd have to persuade her with a different (more *hands-on*) approach, which—just keeping it real—sorta made me hope my sensible arguments were met with resistance.

Tense, I inspected myself in the rearview mirror and cut the engine, but I didn't linger for long. The thing about Charlotte's house was that it sat along a tidy street close to downtown. The driveway was short, her front yard xeriscaped with small shrubs and flowers native to Tennessee and the Smokies. But other than the low picket fence, not much hid the drive or the walkway to her front door. Anyone and everyone driving by would see my truck parked next to her SUV and they'd take note of how long I stayed.

The clock was ticking.

Gathering the patching supplies, I strolled right up to her door. Not hesitating, I ignored my suddenly clammy palms and rang the doorbell, even as wild, frantic worries flew through my mind.

What if Frankie doesn't like me?
What if I inadvertently do something to let down Charlotte or the kids?
What if folks in town don't buy me helping Jackson as a cover story?
What if Jackson—

Stomping footsteps sounded from the other side of the door. My heart in my throat, I straightened. The door swung open, revealing Kimmy Mitchell, her hand on her hip and a scowl on her face. But at soon as she saw it was me, she blinked, and her forehead cleared.

"Hey. It's you," she said.

Unable to argue with that, I nodded once. "It's me."

"What do you want?"

I lifted the bucket full of drywall supplies. "I'm here to patch a hole in your—"

A scream followed by a loud, prolonged kid-cry interrupted my train of thought and I took a small step back.

Kimmy huffed, not at all perturbed by the desperate sounds, and she stepped to the side. "You might as well come in."

"What's wrong? Is that your littlest brother?" Hesitantly, I walked inside the house, too distracted by the continuing yells and cries to take much notice of the house's interior. But I did spot what looked like a huge pile of laundry in the room beyond the entryway.

"That's Frankie. He needs a bath."

Another series of screams pierced the air and I winced. "He doesn't want a bath?"

Kimmy rolled her eyes before turning and strolling away, and lifted her voice to speak over the little one's forceful protests. "He never wants a bath."

Staring at the back of her head, I followed. "He screams every time he has to take a bath?"

"Not every time. But he's still sick, so he's a terror. Joshua! I said put your maps away. It's time to set the table."

She'd led me into the kitchen and I spotted Joshua kneeling on a chair and leaning heavily on a table, papers spread out in front of him. Despite the youngest Mitchell's persistent yells and cries, I grinned at the sight of Charlotte's older son deeply absorbed in whatever lay before him.

"Mr. Hank!"

I turned at the sound of my name spoken in little-kid voice to find Sonya in the process of standing from the floor, her eyes wide and a big, hopeful looking grin on her cutie-pie features.

"Ms. Sonya." I set down my bucket, taking note of the dolls and cars and toy dinosaurs scattered all over the floor where she'd been sitting. "How are you this fine evening?"

"Are you here to play?" She stepped over the tripping hazards and crossed to me.

I lowered myself to my haunches at her approach and stuck my hand out for a shake, but she threw her arms around my neck and gave me a squeeze. She smelled like peanut butter and honey. I grinned.

"Not necessarily," I said, giving her a hug in return. "I'm here to—"

"Hank! You came!" Joshua was on me as soon as Sonya leaned away, grabbing my hand and tugging.

Another shrill shriek sounded from my left, more protests, more cries. Distracted and worried for both Frankie and Charlotte, I allowed myself to be led to the table and turned my head toward the noise.

Joshua didn't seem to notice or care, chatting happily. "I have a map of the Roman Empire at its largest. The year was 117 AD. Do you know how far north it went?"

Kimmy appeared at the end of the table and deposited six white plates on the surface. "No, Joshua. Clear all that stuff. You can show him after dinner." To me, she asked, "Are you staying for dinner?"

"Uh . . ." I glanced in the direction of the cries, acutely aware of the three sets of eyes watching me. "Sure," I finally said. "What's for dinner?"

Kimmy's shoulders rose and fell. "I don't know. Probably frozen pizza or chicken nuggets or something. It's been *a day*."

"Not chicken nuggets!" Joshua moaned. "I'm sick of chicken nuggets."

I frowned, mentally kicking myself for not bringing dinner.

"Then don't eat." Kimmy pushed his maps to one side and began putting plates around the table. "Or eat cereal. Whatever. But get this stuff off the table so I can set it."

Grumbling, Joshua rolled up his maps.

Meanwhile, Sonya slipped her hand in mine and tugged until I glanced down at her.

"I'm going to be a corn," she said.

I lifted an eyebrow. "For dinner?"

She smiled and giggled. "No. For the feast."

"She means for the school play. She's a corn in the play," Kimmy translated, leaving the table and opening a drawer at the kitchen island.

"But her costume isn't done yet and the play is on Friday, so momma said she might have to stand in the back and wear a yellow shirt." This information came from Joshua as he set his maps on a built-in desk to one side of the kitchen.

"I don't want to stand in the back," Sonya said forcefully, her tone taking me by surprise. "I want to be a real corn cob and stand next to Aria in the front."

"You get what you get and you don't throw a fit," Kimmy recited, dumping a pile of forks and knives on the tabletop. "Joshua, go get the napkins."

"They're all dirty," he grumped. "And why do I have to help if I'm not eating?"

"Oh, you're eating," Kimmy said, and the words sounded like a threat. "And if all the cloth napkins are dirty, go get the paper towels and stop sassing back."

"I want to stand in the front next to Aria." Sonya plopped on the ground, her tone watery and insistent. "I don't want to stand in the back. I want to be a corn!"

"Well, then make your own costume!" Joshua hollered unhelpfully, throwing his hands up in the air. "Momma ain't an octopus. She can't do everything."

Sonya began to cry. Then Kimmy yelled at Joshua for making Sonya cry, and Joshua argued with Kimmy about how she wasn't the boss of him. Frankie's sobbing provided the background noise to this contentious scene while I looked on stupidly, wishing I had Dave and Marcus here.

If ever a situation called for bouncers, this was it.

The moment reminded me of the end of this one exceptionally rowdy hen party where it came out that the matron of honor had been sleeping with the bride. The groom's sister—also a bridesmaid—took a swing at them both.

I'd stepped in then. I'd walked right into the thick of it, amidst accusations and tears, threats and insults. I'd calmed everyone down. But I'd had a team. I'd had help.

There's only you now, Hank. You are the only bouncer here.

Gathering a deep breath, I closed my eyes for a brief moment as their argument increased in volume, intensity, and absurdity. I centered myself. This shouldn't be much different than breaking up a fight at The Pony, right? All I needed to do was redirect and distract. Plus, these kids weren't drunk customers, not really. They were on the same team; they were on my team.

Perhaps if I gave them each a job?

Opening my eyes, I inserted myself between Kimmy and Joshua's yelling match.

Palms out, my back to Kimmy, I crouched down to Joshua's level and placed a hand on his shoulder to get his attention.

"Can you do me a favor?" I asked, waiting for his furious eyes to meet mine. "Can you go put your maps on your desk in your room? We can look at them after dinner."

He seemed confused at first by the request, but then nodded. Sending one more incensed glare over my shoulder, he turned and gathered the rolls he'd placed on the desk in the kitchen.

"Hey!" Kimmy started past me. "You can't leave. What about the napkins?"

I caught her hand just long enough to stop her, then released it when she faced me, indignation carving angry lines between her eyebrows.

"He needs to help me set the table!"

"Okay." I nodded. "He will. But first, do you know where Sonya's costume is?"

Kimmy crossed her arms. "Why?"

"I know how to sew and can work on it while dinner cooks."

"You know how to sew?" Her look told me she found my claim suspect.

"I do," I confirmed. No longer able to stand Sonya's sad, hitching sobs, I turned and scooped her up, holding her to my chest. "If you get the costume, I'll see what I can do while I'm here."

I made a mental note to text Beau and ask him to drive my truck elsewhere so folks wouldn't see it in the driveway longer than necessary. Better yet, if he could drop off one of the Winston Brothers auto shop loaner cars, that'd be ideal.

This next part I addressed to Sonya. "You can help me with the costume. Does that sound good?"

She sniffled and nodded, wiping her nose on my shirt. "I don't want to be in the back," she croaked, her eyes pleading.

"I know. You want to be with Aria in the front." Giving my damp shirt no mind, I pushed the wet strands of hair out of her face and gave Sonya a grin. "How about this: if we don't finish before you go to bed, I'll take it home with me and finish it there."

Sonya sniffled again but her eyes brightened. A second later, she returned my smile. "Okay."

"But Joshua better help set the table," Kimmy said, bringing my attention back to her. "We split the chores and I have homework. He doesn't have any homework."

My attention flickered over her, taking in the stubborn set of her jaw, the unhappy glint in her eyes. Something other than Joshua not helping seemed to be upsetting her, and I doubted it was Frankie's loud fussing or Sonya's lack of a costume.

"What kind of homework?" I shifted Sonya's weight and stood. She wrapped her arms around my neck and pressed her cheek to my shoulder.

"It's math," Kimmy grumbled. "I hate it."

"What are you doing in math right now?" I backed up and turned my head from side to side, searching for the fridge. Finding it, I carried Sonya over and opened the door.

"Fractions," Kimmy spat, turning and grabbing the silverware. "It's the worst. I didn't do it yesterday and now I'm only getting half credit, so I don't see why I should turn it in at all."

Quickly surveying the options available, I pulled out ingredients one at a time and placed them on the kitchen island: a lidded bowl containing cooked rice, a bag of peppers, carrots, a white onion, some mushrooms, green onions, and two packages of chicken breasts. "Go get your homework, I'll help you."

Kimmy opened her mouth and it was clear as day she was about to argue.

Before she could, I lifted up the bowl of rice. "How old is this? When was it cooked?"

"Yesterday. Jackson and Rae brought it over."

"That should be fine," I mumbled. "Where are the eggs? And can you get me the soy sauce? I'll also need peanut oil. Sesame oil too, if you have it."

Her grumpy expression cleared just a little. "What are you making?"

"Stir-fry, or my version of it."

She seemed to perk up. "Are you gonna put cashews in it?"

"Can everyone have cashews?" I found the eggs and pulled them out of the fridge, hefting Sonya higher on my hip. I knew better than to put nuts on anything without checking first. Serafina almost took off my head one day when I'd made a salad with peanuts. One of our dancers at the time had a severe allergy.

"Joshua won't," Sonya whispered, turning her head the other way and melting against me. "He doesn't like nuts."

"I'll put them on the side, then," I whispered back. Then to Kimmy, I loud-whispered, "Quick. Get me the oil and soy sauce. Then go get your homework."

Sending me a side-eye, she stalked to a door and opened it wide, revealing a large pantry within. "I'm not doing my homework. It's already late and—"

"If you do your homework, I'll—I'll . . . bake you a cake," I said, bending at the waist to inspect the cabinet under the range and dipping Sonya in the process. She giggled. I grinned at the sound.

"You'll bake me a cake?" Kimmy asked, setting the oil and soy sauce on the counter.

"I will." My quick inspection of the cabinet didn't reveal a wok, so I pulled out a large cast-iron skillet and examined the knobs of the range. Finding the one I wanted for my preferred burner, I turned it to high.

"Okay. Deal. But it has to be a chocolate cake with chocolate frosting," Kimmy said, backing out of the kitchen toward the same hall where Joshua had disappeared earlier.

"Don't forget the costume!" I called after her, setting Sonya on the countertop and placing myself between her and the stovetop. "Where are the knives? And the cutting board?"

The little girl shrugged. "I don't know."

"Hmm." I turned off the range and started opening drawers, and that's when I realized it was finally quiet. Frankie had stopped screaming at some point, though I couldn't precisely pinpoint when.

I sighed. The silence felt like a gift, and I hoped it meant I'd be seeing Charlotte soon.

Opening and closing drawers, I found what I was after and set to work. When Joshua wandered out a few minutes later, patently refusing to put the napkins on the table, I put him to work washing the vegetables. Sonya put out the napkins and a bowl of cashews while I seared the chicken. But then she wanted to be held again, so I had her climb on my back, hold on using her legs and arms, and support herself.

Kimmy set her homework up at the kitchen table, which had Joshua complaining loudly and asking why she was allowed to have her stuff on the table while he was not. I tried explaining that maps were sacred and we didn't want them around food, while homework could get a little messy and still be okay. He seemed to accept this reasoning.

I brought the veggies, cutting board, and knife over so I could keep an eye on Kimmy's progress. Joshua used a butter knife to help with the mushrooms, and Sonya seemed content just as long as she was hanging on me or sitting on my lap. I let her.

Skimming over Kimmy's answers—most of which were wrong due to sloppy mistakes—I tasked Joshua with finding the costume, which Kimmy had neglected to bring out. He stomped off and I circled the ones Kimmy needed to do over with a pencil, promising her a three-layer cake if she got them all right during her next attempt. Leaving her at the table, I cooked everything in the skillet and was just finishing it off with a cracked egg when movement in my peripheral vision had me glancing toward the hall.

And there she was.

Gaping at me, looking frazzled and incredibly confused and, quite frankly, extremely dirty in a stained T-shirt and cotton shorts.

I frowned, inspecting her more carefully. Her hair had been piled on top of her head in a messy bun, her eyes were shaded by dark circles, and her usually vibrant skin looked sallow and pale. But her neck was flushed and her gaze was glassy. She'd placed one hand on the wall of the hallway, as though needing the support.

My stomach twisted, a gnashing, sudden ache I couldn't recall ever experiencing before, making it momentarily hard to breathe.

She's sick. She's really, really sick.

Biting back both my fear and the inexplicable urge to yell at her, to reprimand her for not calling me, not asking me for help, I wiped my hands on a towel. Reprimanding her in this moment would've been ridiculous and cruel for several reasons, the least of which was how she swayed on her feet. Not only was she sick, she was clearly exhausted.

Flipping off the stove, I swung Sonya off my back and set her on the ground. "Sonya, darling, please pick up your toys so your momma doesn't trip," I said, rushing over to Charlotte and her stunned, bewildered expression.

The first thing I wanted to do—dirty clothes and bewilderment be damned—was gather her in my arms and kiss the hell out of her. But her bloodless lips and the green tint to her coloring had me pulling her into a gentle hug instead.

"Are you really here?" she asked once I embraced her, her voice scratchy and weak.

"I am." I smoothed a hand down her back, her cheek burned against my neck, and I ground my jaw. Frustration an entire damn mountain on my chest.

I should've made chicken soup. I should've come over earlier. I should've ignored her demand that I hold off on selling the club. I should've spent the last few weeks cleaning up my image so I didn't have to be here under the ruse of owing a debt to Jackson 'Beige' James or asking Beau to move my truck elsewhere.

Her hands lifted and gripped my shirt, a broken sob shaking out of her. "I can't believe you're here. How are you here?"

"Shh." Reluctantly, I separated us and pressed my hand to her forehead. The ache in my stomach returned. "Angel, you're burning up." I kept my voice low so her babies wouldn't hear.

Her chin wobbled. "I'm sick."

"I can see that." I gave her a lopsided, sympathetic smile, hoping I didn't look as worried as I felt. "Have you taken anything for the fever?"

Wincing, her dazed stare moved over my shoulder. "Not yet. I need to make dinner."

"Dinner is done." I turned her around, placing my arm along her back to keep her steady. "Where is your bedroom? Does it have a bathroom?"

She didn't answer my question, but her feet shuffled down the hall, her hand braced against the wall.

Cursing under my breath, I bent, tucked an arm beneath her knees, and lifted her into my arms. "Which one is it?"

"Last one"—her head lolled against my shoulder—"at the end."

I carried her to the room and paused just inside, surveying the surroundings.

Spotting another door to the left of the tidy bed, I headed for what I hoped was the bathroom. Once there, I gently set her on the edge of a huge clawfoot bathtub and knelt in front of her.

"This is what we're going to do. I'm going to find you something for the fever and you're going to take a lukewarm bath. I'll keep checking on you, and when the fever is down, you can come out of the bath. When is the last time you ate or drank anything?"

"I don't know. I haven't slept much." A tear ran down her cheek. "I'm so sorry."

I frowned, my throat tight with emotions I couldn't name. "You have nothing to be sorry about."

She gave me a sloppy nod but said nothing else. Turning slowly, she fiddled with the faucet, again bracing a hand against the wall. I didn't move. I couldn't. Worry and fear kept me rooted in my spot at her feet.

"Did you call anyone? To help?" I thought and asked at the same time.

Charlotte faced me again, her eyes now closed, and reached for the hem of her shirt. "I—no."

That horrible twisting returned below my ribs. This time I required a few seconds to breathe through it before I could form words. "Why not? Why didn't you call your momma?"

"She's not good at this kind of stuff," she said, working to free herself from her shirt.

I helped, taking over and gently pulling it off. I then helped her stand. Not waiting for her shaking hands to do the job, I pulled her shorts and underwear down her legs, helping her step out of them. Her body was hot to the touch, her skin fevered and flushed. She looked like she'd lost weight, and I swallowed around another knot of frustration and fear.

"What about Patty? Or Sienna?" Setting her clothes to the side, I stood and grabbed her hand, guiding her into the tub. "Or Ashley Winston? She's a nurse. Or—or Jackson?"

Not even self-preservation and selfishness could stop me from asking why she hadn't called Jackson. Anyone would've been better than no one if it meant she'd have help.

"Sienna and Ashley have enough on their plates. Patty isn't in town, she's at a conference, but usually I'd call her. And Rae is leaving tomorrow . . ." Her voice trailed off as she settled into the tub, her legs curling up, her arms wrapped around her torso, her eyes still closed. She shivered.

"Momma?" Sonya's voice called tentatively from the bedroom.

I grabbed a fluffy towel from where it hung on one of the racks and placed it next to the bathtub. "Do not try to leave the bath without me here, okay? I'll be right back with juice and your medicine."

"Okay. Okay," she said, and I wrestled with a renewed, clawing worry. Charlotte never agreed to anything that quickly. She had no fight in her, no sass.

As I stepped out the bathroom and intercepted Sonya, I assigned the little girl a task. "Hey, Sonya, darling, I have a job for you."

"What is it?" She held several toys to her chest, the mini figures poking out from between her fingers.

"I want you to sit in the bathroom with your momma, okay? You can play quietly in there. Talk to her softly. Tell her a story. Come get me if she falls asleep. I'll be in the kitchen mostly, but I'll come back and check on you every few minutes."

"I'm hungry."

"I'll bring you a plate. You can eat dinner in the bathroom."

She peered up at me as I stood. "What about my corn costume?"

"Uh, I'll make it after dinner and take it home with me if it's not finished. You'll have it before Friday, I promise. Now, go sit with your momma."

I made a mental list as I strolled out of Charlotte's bedroom, leaving my little spy behind. I needed to get Charlotte her medication and get her hydrated, help Kimmy with her math, check on Joshua, figure out what was going on with Frankie—I hoped he was asleep somewhere—get the kids fed, do the dishes, make soup for Charlotte, fold the laundry I'd spotted in the family room, and patch the hole. And make a costume. And look at Joshua's maps. And get the kids to sleep. And ask Beau to move my car.

But first, I'd text Ashley Winston to come over, offering her any amount of money or favors or whatever she wanted. I'd do absolutely anything to make sure Charlotte was okay.

She needed more help than I had the expertise to provide. And I was beginning to suspect that I needed Charlotte.

CHAPTER 26

CHARLOTTE

"Nothing resembles selfishness more closely than self-respect."

— GEORGE SAND, *INDIANA*

A quiet room greeted me upon waking. Light spilled in through the open bathroom door, making the space neither bright nor dark. Uncertain how I'd made it to my bed, I blinked the clock on the nightstand into focus. It was just past three in the morning. The kids must've been asleep.

Gaze drifting, I automatically cataloged the other items on the nightstand, items I had no recollection of being present or placing there yesterday: some sort of sports drink, a bottle of acetaminophen, a prescription drug container, a thermometer, a box of tissues, and a bowl full of cough drops. I did not see my phone.

Oh. That's right. Shoot.

Frankie had grabbed it and smashed it in the bathroom during his fit yesterday. I needed to buy a new one.

Slowly pulling myself to a sitting position, I pressed a hand to my forehead to keep the room from spinning, but it didn't spin this time. It had been whirling earlier when I'd given Frankie a bath and rocked him to sleep in his bedroom. The vertigo had increased when I'd stood and—

"Hank," I whispered, my eyes flying open, automatically searching for him.

He wasn't there. I was alone. Working to sort through my indistinct memories of the evening, I wondered which of the fuzzy images had been real, which had been fantasy, and which had been both.

Reaching for the sports drink, I gingerly peeled back the covers and set my feet on the ground. I finished the contents of the bottle, wiping my mouth with the back of my hand, my mind sluggish. Hank's presence in my memory must've been a fantasy. I'd been wishing for him so hard.

Also . . . *Ashley Winston?*

My right hand sought the elbow of my left arm and I found medical tape along with a cotton ball.

Yes. Ashley had been here. I remembered her now, forcing me to drink juice, helping me out of the bath, calling me 'baby' and 'honey,' giving me something to swallow, checking my ears, and taking a swab of my throat along with a few blood samples. She helped me dress and put me in bed. Then I'd gone to sleep.

But there'd been someone else.

Maybe Ashley had brought Jackson? And I'd hallucinated Hank in his place? That seemed more likely than Hank showing up here randomly after a month of short phone calls, succinct text messages, and keeping his distance.

I tried to swallow around the discomfort in my throat. It's not that I blamed him, I absolutely did not. I hadn't expected any different. I'd warned him and myself right from the start. I'd known all along how things would go.

After our talk in his office last month, I'd hoped he could stick things out until at least our first date in November. It would've been nice to have a date with Hank, getting dressed up, seeing him laugh and give me that sexy smirk, teasing him, holding hands.

The experience of watching him fade from my life over the last few weeks had felt like an inevitable—yet still disappointing—conclusion to a lovely dream. Heart fluttering painfully, my chin wobbled. I stiffened my bottom lip.

Soon he'd stop answering my calls; soon the texts he returned would be fewer and farther between; and that would be that. It had been fun while it lasted, giving me some pleasant memories.

Anyway. No use thinking about it. I needed to check on the kids.

Standing and holding the headboard of my bed, I tested my balance. I felt better than before. A tad feverish, a scratchy throat, but my head wasn't pounding and my ears didn't ache like the dickens. Flipping off the harsh lights in the bathroom, I navigated by the moonlight instead and used the facilities. But when I caught my reflection in the mirror over the sink, I stiffened.

My hair had been washed.

Long fingers against my scalp, supporting my head with deft, gentle palms, rinsing out the suds, and placing two light kisses over each eyelid and one soft, brushing caress of a kiss against my lips.

Frowning at myself and the memory, I rubbed my forehead as I left the bathroom. Thoughts of the kids—especially Frankie—kept my feet moving while vague impressions from earlier in the night stalked me on my way to his room.

Had... Jackson given me a bath? And washed my hair? And *kissed* me?

Nooooo.

That made no sense. If Jackson had come over last night, then Rae would've been over too, and she would've been the one giving me a bath. I couldn't fathom her kissing me. But then again, she was half Italian, and they're a very touchy-feely people. I'd never noticed her hands before. Could it be that she had man hands?

I checked on Frankie. If my recall could be trusted, he seemed to be exactly where I left him the night prior, curled up in his big-boy bed. But someone must've dressed him. I'd laid him down wearing only a pull-up, not wanting to risk waking him by putting on night clothes. He now wore puppy PJs.

Must've been Ashley.

Relief coursed through me when I placed a light hand on his forehead. He was warm, like me, but not hot. Thank God. Turning, I left his room as quietly as I came in and then checked on each of the others in turn. Kimmy was sprawled out in the center of her double bed; Joshua had migrated to the floor—not unusual for him—and was twisted in his blanket; and Sonya lay pretty and peaceful beneath the covers of her princess canopy. All three of them were in their pajamas. *Huh.*

Clearing my throat of the scratchiness rather than risk a cough, I decided to grab a spoonful of honey while I was up. I did feel a whole lot better, maybe even well enough to go back to work on Monday.

On my way to the kitchen, a yellowish light from the family room snagged my notice. I altered course to flip off whichever lamp had been left on and almost screamed at the unexpected sight of a man standing inside my back patio doors, holding some sort of... *Is that a spackling tool?*

Hank?

Yes, Hank! *What the—?*

He turned over his shoulder at my strangled sound, his features changing from open and curious to a severe frown in the span of a single blink.

"What are you doing out of bed?"

Heart racing at approximately one hundred miles per hour, I pressed my palm against my chest and gawked at him, completely unprepared for... him.

"I—"

"You should be asleep." He set down the spackling tool on top of a bucket and then proceeded to wipe his hands on a towel. "Did you take your temperature? What is it? I swear to God, Charlotte—if I have to call Ashley again, I will. I will wake her up and haul her ass over here if you don't get back in that bed."

Tremendously confused, and undecided what I should do about it, I stared at him. My lungs filled with heat, a response that had nothing to do with my residual fever.

Hank was here? But—but how? And why? And when? And . . . why?

As I toiled to make sense of his presence, his glare transformed into a wary kind of concern.

Eventually, he tucked the towel into his back pocket and approached. "Charlotte, honey? You okay? Are you—do you need me?" As soon as he reached my planted position, he placed a hand—a man hand, with long fingers and a deft, gentle palm—over my forehead. "You're warm but not hot," he muttered to himself, a wrinkle forming between his eyebrows. "How's the dizziness?"

"Better," I croaked, blinking up at him. He'd been here earlier. I hadn't imagined it.

"Good. That's good. You're looking better, too. Ashley said you have double ear infections, but they're not bad and should clear up with the drops by tomorrow. It was the exhaustion and dehydration that knocked you flat." Hank drew his bottom lip into his mouth and chewed on it. Then, before I could quite comprehend his intent, he scooped me up. "I'm carrying you back to your room. We don't need a concussion on top of everything else."

My arms instinctively went around his neck and a wave of dizziness did hit me then. But again, I doubted it had anything to do with dehydration and everything to do with the fantastical man who currently held me in his arms, who I'd been indulging in fantasies about each night for the last month as I fell asleep.

He strolled through the house like he'd been here before and had familiarity with its layout, down the hallway, to my bedroom.

"You gave me the bath," I whispered as I realized the truth. "That was you."

The side of his mouth tugged and his eyes swept over my—I'm sure—owlish expression. He placed a kiss on the tip of my nose. "Technically, you gave yourself a bath. I helped you undress and washed your hair, though," he said, his tone soft, rumbly, wonderful.

Hank placed me on the bed like I was made of something more brittle than glass, more precious than a newborn and my heart seized, not knowing what to do.

"How's your throat?" He pressed the backs of his fingers to my forehead again before reaching for the thermometer on my nightstand.

"A little scratchy." I allowed him to tuck me in as I explained, "I was on my way to get honey when I saw the light on in the family room."

He nodded and lifted the thermometer to my lips. Dutifully, I parted them and he placed the instrument under my tongue.

"You seem like you're feeling a lot better?"

I nodded.

He sighed. It sounded relieved, and he covered one of my hands with his, dwarfing my fingers where they rested on my lap over the covers. "You had me scared, there. I don't know if you remember, but Sonya stayed with you in the bathroom and gave me updates."

"I do not remember that."

"Don't talk with the thermometer in your mouth," he said. "Here, let me fill in some blanks. I'll start at the beginning."

While I sat propped against my pillows, Hank proceeded to succinctly illuminate what I'd missed. How he'd run into Jackson at the hardware store in town and used the hole in my drywall as an excuse to come over, and then everything that came after: making dinner, Kimmy's homework, Joshua's maps, Sonya's costume, my bath, calling Ashley, feeding the kids, washing my hair, having Kimmy lay down Joshua while Hank worked on the costume with Sonya, laying Sonya down, doing the dishes, laundry, sending Ashley home in his car instead of hers so Hank's overnight stay wouldn't be noticed, baking a three-layer chocolate cake, and then—finally—patching the hole in the wall.

But he didn't recite the tasks as though looking for praise or some sort of reward. More like, he'd made decisions and wanted to keep me in the loop, ensure I felt comfortable with the path he'd chosen while I'd been unavailable for consultation.

"I used your sewing machine to finish the costume, but it probably needs one final try-on before Friday. I hope you don't mind, Sonya stayed up so I could make sure it fits."

The thermometer beeped. Before I could reach for it, he snatched it from my mouth and anxiously frowned at the tiny readout. His forehead cleared of worry lines.

"Just over ninety-nine. That's fantastic." Hank grabbed bottle of acetaminophen and unscrewed the child-proof cap. "You're due for the next dose. Let me go get another bottle of the electrolyte drink Ashley brought over. Be right back."

Passing me the pills, he stood, bent to give me a kiss on my right temple, and then darted out of the room.

Meanwhile, I swallowed around a ballooning lump, the reality of what he'd done —how he'd shown up, stepped in, and helped—rendering me speechless and utterly overwhelmed.

I'd been extremely attracted to Hank for a long time now, to his clever, rebellious spirit and heart-stopping smiles. I'd had a crush on him forever, which had certainly deepened due to his professional ethics and care for his business and team. During our short time working together, he'd impressed me so darn much.

I'd always considered him sexy and fascinating and desirable, but never so much as this precise moment.

Helen of Troy might've possessed a face that had launched a thousand ships, but I suspected the extent and breadth of Hank Weller's sheer competence—were it ever to be made widely known—would become the catalyst for a hundred-thousand bra and panty sets being flung at his feet.

Forget Magic Mike and greased up, rock-hard abs. Forget banter and flowers and candlelit dinners. Forget expensive gifts and grand, sweeping gestures. Forget all that.

A person in possession of self-sufficiency, attention to detail, expertise in domestic tasks—large and small—and who pitched in without being asked? Who did so with gentle kisses left on noses and temples and teasing smiles? Without complaint and expectation of constant praise and rewards and effusive gratitude?

Here I'd been for the last three or so weeks, assuming his interest in me had faded and would continue to do so. I'd believed it was only a matter of time before he simply disappeared and stopped texting me back, I'd been readying my heart for the eventuality.

And there he was, plotting to come over without triggering the gossips, taking excellent care of my kids and getting shit done, handing me pills as it was time for my next dose, and he knew when I needed another dose. He'd been tracking it.

He'd taken care of me. Of *us*.

I knew my worth. I'd promised myself after leaving Kevin that I would never accept less than what I deserved, I would never settle. At the same time, I'd never believed someone existed who would (or could) rise to and exceed my expectations.

My faced crumpled and an irrepressible sob stole past my lips. I covered my mouth with a hand to keep the rest in, but it was no use. Emotions took over like a preacher's wife at a church picnic or a three-year-old literally anywhere.

I cried, great big waves of feeling knocking me around. I didn't hear Hank come back to the room, nor did I see him. It was only when he climbed next to me on the bed and handily wrapped me in his arms, holding me tight and close, that I realized he'd returned.

"Angel, angel, don't cry." He kissed my head so sweetly and I wailed at the tenderness of it.

I didn't know how to process this, how to receive such selfless, loving actions, how to accept they were possible, given to me freely. All because he cared so much. About me.

And so I wept.

CHAPTER 27

CHARLOTTE

"I don't want learning, or dignity, or respectability. I want this music, and this dawn, and the warmth of your cheek against mine."

— RUMI, *THE ESSENTIAL RUMI*

The next time I awoke, it was to morning sunlight streaming in through the windows and to me on top of a real-life Hank-Weller-body pillow.

My sluggish brain only required a few seconds to recall why he was in my bed and how I'd bawled all over him before summarily passing out. I didn't feel embarrassed by the memory. I felt curious, slightly numb, and an erect penis through a layer of his jeans and my pajamas, pressing against the inside of my thigh.

"Are you awake?" he whispered hoarsely. "Please say you're awake."

I swallowed and closed my eyes, not willing to yield my position on top of and next to him. This was a surprise. I'd never enjoyed sleeping in the same bed with anyone. I'd never co-slept with my kids. In my youth, I couldn't sleep at camp or other situations where sharing a bed had been required. With my ex, I'd tiptoe out of the room once he was snoring and spent most of our marriage slumbering on the couch.

But this? Waking up with my leg curled over Hank's groin, my arm flung over his chest, and my ear resting over his heart? I could get used to this.

"I'm awake," I said haltingly. "But unless the kids are up, I'm not ready to move, if that's okay with you."

His hand moved on my bare back. I realized belatedly that he'd slipped it under my shirt at some point, tugging me closer until my entire torso pressed more fully against him.

"You're still sick," came his rumbly voice, giving me the sense the words were more for his benefit than for mine. "You will be sick for a while. I should keep my hands to myself until you are well . . . unless you ask me not to."

My head was still a bit cottony, my throat a little dry, but I didn't think I had a fever and my ears no longer ached. I felt almost normal. It's amazing what hydration, rest, and the presence of a sexy boyfriend can do for a person.

"I don't feel very sick," I said, my mouth curving with giddy pleasure before I could prevent it. He must've felt the movement against his chest because he chuckled.

"Oh no. Don't smile," he groaned, sounding pained. "I can't resist your smiles."

"You find my smiles irresistible?"

"You know I do. Smile at me and I'm yours to command."

Oh my goodness. I liked the sound of that. Warmth unfurled in my chest and I ducked my head.

He shifted at my silence, his hand sliding from the center of my back to my bottom, resting above the fabric of my pajamas. "Charlotte Mitchell, are you feeling shy?"

"A little," I admitted. I did feel shy. I also felt many other things, all of which were too large and unwieldy to contemplate or share at present.

Hank kissed the top of my head. "Then, you be shy. I'll stay right here, ready to be of service, just in case you start feeling bold."

My heart wanted to erupt with happiness and I let it. After spending the last month accepting that Hank was on the precipice of losing interest and walking away, it felt like being sun-warmed on the first day of spring after a long, grueling winter. I basked in him.

Wearing my shy smile, I sighed contentedly and snuggled closer. I also stretched the arm that rested over his chest to thread my fingers into the short hair at the back of his neck. And there we lay—his fingers drawing light lines and circles from my bottom to the middle of my back, my fingers playing with his hair—in the peace and quiet of a Sunday morning.

We'd missed church. That was all right. Frankie and I needed a recovery day, and obviously Kimmy, Joshua, and Sonya needed the sleep too, otherwise they'd already be up and asking for food. At some point, I'd need to message my mother. We typically met her at the church for mid-morning service after her garden club meeting and she'd likely fret if I didn't check in.

I could borrow Hank's phone; I'd texted her from Hank's phone once before and she almost lost her mind. *Hmm* . . . No matter, she'd need to accept Hank being part of our lives sooner or later.

That thought made me smile again.

It was unfathomable how much had changed in the span of twelve hours, and the incomprehensible nature of it prompted me to break the comfortable silence between us and ask, "You really tricked Jackson into making him think you were paying back a debt by patching my wall?" Remembering his concise sharing of events in the wee-early hours of the morning, this part of the tale struck me as dubious. "And he believed you?"

"I don't think he believed me—not in the end—but it doesn't matter. Just as long as those other folks overheard and believed the story, that's what matters. It might take me a full week to patch that hole." He gave me a squeeze, and I felt his mouth curve against the top of my head. My heart fluttered. I couldn't remember the last time I'd felt so relaxed and content.

But then his hand stopped its gentle glide and Hank's hold grew tighter. "Charlotte."

"Hmm?"

His chest rose and fell with a deep breath. "I missed you so much."

The words reverberated through my bones, real, and raw, and true.

I closed my eyes against the renewed threat of rising emotions but did manage to reply, "I missed you, too."

"I know you're dealing with a lot. Based on what I saw and experienced last night, I understand that you'll be dealing with a lot for the foreseeable future. You're incredibly busy." The statements sounded rehearsed, his hold squeezing me. "Furthermore, I accept that you don't want the kids to know we're together. That's obviously your call to make. However—as much as I wish I could hold my tongue, keep my distance, and wait until the right time—I think . . . I think I need you. I need to be here. I'd like to help, be part of this team, if you'd let me."

I held my breath and willed the gathering tears behind my eyes to cease and desist. God, what would it be like to have Hank's type of help every day? I loved the idea so much, it felt dangerous.

He wasn't finished. "Unless you don't want me here, then the way I see it is that the only thing keeping us apart—day in, day out—is my reputation and how folks will react to us being together. That hasn't changed."

Shifting beneath me, he sat up and rolled me back until he hovered above, our eyes meeting for the first time since he'd taken my temperature in the middle of the night. I loved his intelligent, mischievous, serious, complicated, hazel eyes.

Hank's gaze traced the lines of my face, and looking a little lost in me, he said on an exhale, "I know you said you didn't want to change one hair on my head. But I do. I've already changed. Being that person I was before, who relished shocking people, getting under their skin, who"—his hand slid down my arm and he entwined our fingers—"let folks down, who let you down, that's not me anymore."

"Let me down?" I shook my head, confused. "How did you let me down?" I stared at the contrite line of his mouth, his apologetic eyes.

His expression grew bracing and his hand squeezed mine. "Prom. Your junior year."

Caught, I smiled (sort of), shy all over again. "Oh."

"I saw Roscoe a few weeks back. He told me—reminded me—what I did. That's why you always avoided me in town," he guessed.

It wasn't a question, but I nodded anyway, successfully fighting the urge to roll my eyes at myself. "It was a long time ago."

Hank made a short, dismissive, grunting noise in the back of his throat. "It doesn't matter how long ago it happened. I am so, so sorry. I can't tell you—"

"Really, it was—"

"No, listen. I need to say this. I was a selfish, thoughtless piece of shit, and you deserved so much better than who I used to be. But I am not that person anymore." He brought our joined hands up and pressed my knuckles into the mattress next to my head, his gaze sober and serious, yet also somehow cherishing as he said, "Nor do I ever wish to be him again."

Recognizing how important it was to Hank that I hear him out, I relaxed against the bed, watching his handsome features twist with remorse and then intensify with pained sincerity.

"I want to go to the ice cream parlor and not receive dirty looks. Heck, I don't want to get any looks. I want to be invisible, just another local guy out with his girlfriend's kids, spoiling them with too much rocky road."

I laughed, then bit my lip to stem my smile.

My reflexive response seemed to cheer him, his eyes tired but also clear and focused. "I want to deserve you. I will earn my place in your life. But I can't do that, I can't be here, if it causes you or the kids problems. I would never forgive myself if any of you were hurt or slighted because of who I used to be." Bringing my hand to his chest, he pressed my palm over his heart. "I'm determined to overhaul my reputation in this town, starting with selling the club to Hannah. I spoke to her, and I'm—"

He wouldn't! "Hank—"

Holding my fingers fast, he wouldn't let me go. "No, no. It's not for you. It's for me. It's what I want."

"You're honestly telling me that you'd be selling the club if it weren't for gossipy people in this town, judging you for your job?"

"That's what I'm telling you."

Now I did roll my eyes. "I call bull-malarkey."

He grinned, his gaze heating, and lowered his lips to my neck. "Charlotte, my angel, my goddess—"

"Don't think you can seduce your way out of this conversation." Even though I was still a tad under the weather, he probably could seduce his way out of this conversation.

But I'd put up a fight. A little fight. *A very little fight.*

"It's already happening." Hank placed a nipping kiss beneath my ear and I felt it in my toes.

"What's already happening? The seduction?"

"No. Me selling the club. It's already in motion, no stopping it now." He finally released my hand only to settle his big palm over my breast, whispering a curse. "You're so fucking sexy."

Ignoring the flare of heat beneath my ribs, I asked, "And then what?" Despite my desire to argue this point, I angled my head to the side, offering him greater access. "What will you do next to reform your image? How many hoops are you planning to jump through in order to appease—Hank!" I caught his fingers just before they slipped beneath the waistband of my shorts.

My door was unlocked, one of the kids could walk in at any moment. Doing more than light kissing and touching right now wasn't an option.

"That's exactly what I mean," he said, his voice husky and irresistible. "Until my image is spotless, we'll—"

Abruptly, Hank tensed. A moment later, he lifted his head and turned it toward the bedroom door, gaze distracted. "What was that?"

"What was what?"

Sitting up fully, he swung his legs over the side of the bed. "Did you hear that?"

"Hear what?"

"I thought I heard the front—"

A knock sounded on my bedroom door, cutting him off, followed by my mother's voice saying, "Charlotte? Are you awake?"

I sat up, sucking in a sharp breath, my wide eyes swinging to Hank's frowning profile.

Before I could even think of what to do or how to answer her, the doorknob turned. The door opened. My mother stood at the entrance to my room.

"Baby, are you okay? I heard the news. What can I do? I figured—OH MY GOD!" she screeched as soon as her gaze landed on Hank, and she clutched her chest.

I lifted a staying hand. "Now, momma, calm down—"

"Charlotte Eugenia Mitchell! What is *that man* doing in this house? And in your bedroom?" She stabbed a finger in Hank's direction.

Gingerly, I set my feet on the ground and sighed. "Mother, that is none of your business. Who I have over here, and when, and how often, has nothing to do with you."

She gasped, her eyes rimmed with shock and hurt, but what could I do? I was a grown-ass woman with four kids and a lifetime of bad decisions under her belt. You'd think after twenty-eight years of watching me stumble around and resist her ideas of propriety, she would've given up on me by now.

God love her, she still wanted me to be a demure debutante.

"Well!" she said on a huff, lifting her chin. "I came over here to offer support, to see if I could be of any help—"

"Please don't fuss, I'm much better." I stood, picking up the prescription from next to the bed. "Ashley came over last night, said it was mostly dehydration, but I did have double ear infections. Sleep was what I needed most."

My mother wrinkled her nose and her forehead, visibly confused. "What? Are you sick?"

"Yes." I traded a look with Hank. He held perfectly still, only his eyes shifting between me and my mother like he didn't want to make any sudden movements. Hoping to disarm the situation as much as possible, I continued, "I know we're going to miss church. I'm sorry I didn't call. Frankie smashed my phone and—wait. You didn't know I was sick?"

"I had no idea!"

My back straightened. "Then why are you here?"

"Charlotte, no. No. I'm glad you're better, but I'm here because of Kevin and Heather!" Her voice pitched higher and I flinched.

"Kevin? Heather?" My attention narrowed on my mother's anxiety-riddled face.

"Yes, baby." Her gaze fretful as it locked with mine, she crossed to me, grabbing my hands. Her chin wobbled. "It was all for nothing. Heather turned herself in down in Florida. She's facing jail time and your aunt and uncle are coming apart, they're so worried. You never should've worked at that horrid place. I knew this would happen."

"What does Heather have to do with Kevin?"

"He's doing it, just like I feared. I saw his sister this morning at the garden club meeting after church. You know, she always liked you, but she can't talk them out of it now that the old man has his mind made up. Charlotte—" My mother's voice wavered and broke.

No. No way. She couldn't mean . . . "I don't—I don't understand."

"It's what I said would happen." My mother's whispered words, so full of despair and compassion, also held just a hint of acrimonious *I told you so.* "Kevin and his family are suing for full custody on account of you working at The Pink Pony in order to find your cousin. We never should've done it. God, baby." She lifted her hand to cup my cheek. "I never should've let you. I am so, so sorry."

* * *

Hank left.

Well, first he made pancakes and bacon for the kids. He'd introduced himself to Frankie and invited him to help flip the pancakes, but my mother wouldn't let my youngest go. Joshua happily flipped the pancakes instead while Frankie made a fuss about wanting to help. Kimmy was responsible for the bacon, and Sonya set the table. We all ate together. I couldn't tell you what was discussed or whether the pancakes were good. I couldn't bring myself to eat.

Hank and the kids did the dishes—Frankie finally getting to help—while my mother sat with me in the family room. She ranted about my cousin. I pretended to listen. I couldn't think. Hank had Sonya try on her corn cob costume one more time, showing it to everyone for comment—my momma had been reluctantly impressed by his handiwork—and he left after that.

He hadn't kissed me goodbye, not that I expected him to. We weren't telling the kids yet.

My momma decided I needed rest, so she also left . . . me with my four children. An odd combination of restless numbness shrouded my ability to process, or feel, so I took the kids to the park and let them run around like the feral children they were, keeping my eyes on Frankie. He seemed to be all better. I dreaded giving him another bath tonight, but what else was new.

I wondered tangentially who would give Frankie a bath if Kevin got custody? A nanny? A maid? Definitely a stranger.

When we arrived home, some of the stunned detachment I'd been cloaked in frayed. My throat cinched tighter with every step and my hands trembled. I balled them into fists. I closed my eyes. I tried to breathe through the rising panic and self-recrimination.

And so I prayed.

Dear Lord in heaven, why did you make me so stupid? So reckless? Why do I not see the world as others do? Why can I not see others for who they are? Why am I constantly blindsided by cruelty? Why does it always surprise me? Why am I built this way? Give me wisdom, God. Or tell me what I'm supposed to do. And please, please, please don't let that worthless, scum-bucket motherfucker steal my babies. Amen.

I loved myself. But sometimes, I didn't like myself very much. Especially the part of me that insisted on walking the train tracks, yet couldn't be bothered to look up in time to see or hear the train bearing down on me.

When the doorbell rang in the late afternoon, I yelped, nearly jumping out of my skin.

"I'll get it!" Joshua called just before I heard his little feet sprint to the foyer. I suspected he hoped it was Hank coming back and that made my heart hurt all over again.

As I approached the door, I heard him say, "Oh. Hi. Is Ben with you?"

"Not this time, pumpkin." Sienna Diaz's melodic voice carried to me as I rounded the corner. "But if it's okay with your mom, Ms. Ashley is here to take you all up to her house on the lake."

I drew even with the door, catching a glimpse of Sienna's magnetic smile before she turned over her shoulder and gestured to where Ashley Winston appeared to be removing the car seats from my SUV and putting them in her van.

A small, disbelieving laugh spilled from my lips. "What is going on?"

"Hey, beautiful." Sienna stepped into the house, her lovely brown eyes soft with sympathy, and pulled me into a hug. "Come on, let's get the kids ready to go."

I stared at her, completely bemused. "What?"

She leaned close and whispered, "Hank sent us over. He said you needed me?"

I flinched, startled by her words. But the surprise and her sudden presence shook something loose inside me, something I'd been burying and suppressing since this morning, and I nodded. Then I erupted into tears.

"Oh no. Charlotte." She embraced me again. "Honey, I'm here. I'm here. We'll figure it out. It'll all be fine, we'll figure it out. I promise."

I clung to her, and I hoped like hell she was telling the truth.

CHAPTER 28

CHARLOTTE

"It's difficult to analyze love when you're in it."

— JOHN STEINBECK, *TRAVELS WITH CHARLEY: IN SEARCH OF AMERICA*

The several minutes that followed Sienna's arrival were a blur. Ashley appeared and peeled me off Sienna. The Winston sister took my temperature and checked my ears while—presumably—Sienna packed up my kids in Ashley's car. Ashley left me tucked under a throw blanket on the couch with a glass of the electrolyte drink she'd brought by last night along with an order to 'drink all of it.'

After hugs and kisses and hurried farewells, the kids were gone, leaving Sienna and me alone in my living room.

After a beat of silence, Sienna held my hand, squeezed it, and said, "Why don't you tell me what happened?"

And then—much like I'd done with Hannah so many weeks ago at The Pony—I told her everything about Hank, our entire history and all the ways my wishes were giving me whiplash. Sienna listened with quiet grace, her features infinitely compassionate.

But this time, unlike all those weeks ago with Hannah, the story ended with my mother busting into my bedroom, clutching her pearls, and then informing me that my vile ex-husband would be suing for custody of the kids.

"I feel so stupid." I set aside the glass, the contents still untouched. "My mother warned me, but I wouldn't listen."

"You're brave."

"According to my mother, me working at The Pony didn't make any difference. Heather turned herself in down in Florida, and my aunt and uncle are tearing themselves apart with worry about her going to jail." I grimaced. "Why do stupidity and bravery often look like the same thing in retrospect?"

Her smile was sympathetic. "Let me put it this way, no matter how things worked out with your cousin, thank goodness you did work at the club. Now you and Hank have found each other."

I barely heard her, lost as I was in self-reproach. "Why am I this way, Sienna? It's like I never want to believe the truth about people. I should know better by now, right? After all those years with Kevin and the Buckleys, I should've seen this coming."

"You're not stupid. You think the best of people. Drink this." Sienna picked up the glass I'd discarded and placed it back in my grip. "It's what I love the most about you and why I think we're going to be good friends for a long, long time."

"Why? Because I'm naïve, and too trusting, and let people blindside me with their evilness?" Dutifully, I drank a gulp of the sickly-sweet liquid.

"I'm not talking about your ex-husband." Sienna gave my shoulder a tiny shove. "I'm talking about Hank. You don't seem to care how a person is perceived by others, you only care about who they are. You never gossip."

"I don't know if that's true," I mumbled, uncomfortable with her praise and hiding behind my glass. Specifically, I was thinking about Jackson James and how I'd sought out gossip about his past before agreeing to date him.

"What do you mean?" she asked, picking up her own glass of water and taking a sip. "You care about gossip? Since when?"

"I don't generally care about gossip, but I've gossiped about Jackson."

"Come on, that wasn't gossip," my friend scoffed. "That was a coordinated attack on Rae in my house last summer. We were being good friends, encouraging her to acknowledge her feelings for Jackson."

"I'm not just talking about that one time we were sitting around your kitchen table. I'm—" I huffed at myself. "Here's the thing: I've known Jackson forever, but we didn't become friends until a few months prior to dating. I didn't know folks considered him a ladies' man when he asked me out. As soon as he suggested we go on a date, I called up my old high school friends about him and asked whether they knew anyone he'd been involved with."

"Really?" The single word sounded both surprised and impressed. "Why'd you do that?"

"I didn't want to waste his time or mine if he was a stuffed shirt." I picked at a thread on my blanket. "Since we became real friends, he always seemed like a rule-following stuffed shirt to me."

Sienna chuckled. "That's funny. Jethro claimed Jackson's reputation was the opposite of a stuffed shirt."

"No, Jackson is a stuffed shirt. Yeah, he was a ladies' man at one point, but with me, he was a stuffed shirt the whole time. Remember? That was frustrating. When I asked around, everyone said he was a good-time guy, up for anything. Which had appealed to me."

"You wanted a good-time guy?" Sienna rested her arm along the back of the couch. "Nothing serious?"

"Not at all. I wanted—I hoped—we'd get serious *and* he was a good-time guy. I've never wanted to be with someone who was a rigid rule follower. I'm too loud for those kinds of people, too much. They don't appeal to me either."

"I can see that." Sienna sighed and she bent her elbow, her fingers threading into her hair as she leaned her head to the side, considering me. "Jethro is mostly a rule follower now, but I love how he breaks his own rules with me, like he can't help himself."

"Yes. That. I wanted someone who was fun and surprising, a little subversive, who thinks about things differently. Jackson seemed to be ready to settle down when we dated, and I hoped he'd bring some of that good-time guy subversiveness to the relationship." Bracing myself, I took another gulp of the electrolyte drink, wishing I had a water-chaser for the aftertaste. "That's why I agreed to date him despite only having friendship chemistry with him when we started."

"Did you think, once the two of you started to date, he'd show you his other side and loosen up?"

"Exactly." I nodded. "But he didn't. He just seemed so damn determined to be respectful all the time, and nothing I did tempted him—*I* didn't tempt him—and I hated it."

Sienna laughed. "That's right, now I remember. You broke up with him because he was a boy scout."

"I'm not saying I want someone to disrespect me. Obviously, I've had enough of that to last a lifetime. I'm saying I want someone who knows how to act disrespectful in the right situation. A little dirty, a little naughty, knowing that crossing lines of politeness can be a lot of fun."

Sienna's eyes sparkled, but she said nothing.

Thus, I felt compelled to be explicit. "Let me put it this way, I don't want someone to put me on an altar unless we're eventually having sex on it."

"Oh my God, Charlotte!" Her mouth dropped open. "That's so bad. I love it. I might steal it for a movie."

"I hope you do." I finished my drink and set the empty glass on the table, meeting Sienna's amused stare.

"You like Hank because he's respectfully disrespectful?" she asked.

"Yes, that's definitely part of the reason. But it's not just about me. Hank is respectfully disrespectful in all facets of his life." Allowing my gaze to lose focus over her shoulder, I considered this oddity in my personality and ended up speaking my thoughts, stream of consciousness. "And I guess I want my kids to know you don't have to do what's expected of you by society at all times. I've always hated how most people I know just blindly do what's expected, and I don't want that for my kids."

"What do you mean?"

I retuned my attention to Sienna. "I want them to, you know, be a rebel as long as they're doing good in the world. Stir up some trouble, make things hard for the status quo but follow a well-thought moral code that's hard or impossible to argue with or disregard. Do shocking things if you need to, but do them for the right reasons. Don't live your life guided by fear of coloring outside the lines. Folks who color outside the lines make the biggest difference. I honestly love that about Hank, how he effortlessly walks those lines. I thought that's who Kevin was when I met him, the rebel of his family."

"He wasn't?"

"Oh, he was a rebel when I met him, but instead of being respectfully disrespectful, he was just plain disrespectful with no moral code, just a selfish one." I lifted my eyes to the ceiling. "And that's even more boring—and painful, and frustrating—as being with a stuffed shirt."

"Hank does make it look effortless." Sienna, sipping her water, seemed to give me and my statements deep consideration. "And yet, sometimes things that look effortless to others, from the outside looking in, are exhausting to the person doing the thing."

I twisted my lips to the side, thinking about this. "Do you think Hank is exhausted?"

"I don't know. It certainly seemed to me like the whole thing with your ex-husband took his toll on him."

"Hank said something about this to me when I worked at the club, that folks in town treated him horribly after Kevin left town." I frowned, recalling the conversation and hating that people had been so spiteful for no reason.

"From what I've observed in Green Valley and from what Jethro has told me, it's not like people ever really approved of Hank before your ex ran off with that woman, but everyone really seemed to blame Hank—rather than Kevin—for the end of your marriage."

"I don't understand that at all." I gave my head a thoughtful shake. "Maybe it's me being stupid again, but why would people blame Hank? That is so weird to me."

Sienna sat up straighter. "You know . . . I have no idea. You're right, that is weird. I would understand a little bit of shade being thrown his way. He's an easy target as the owner of the club where they met. I was having babies during the whole bruhaha and hadn't given it much thought, just listened as Hank and Jethro discussed it a few times. I offered to stand up for him. He didn't want me to do that, so I let it go. But now that I really take a minute to consider things, the amount of vitriol he experienced in the thick of it makes no sense."

"Right? It's so weird." It felt good to discuss this with Sienna, someone who cared about Hank and his well-being. I was so grateful for her friendship. "And it's definitely why Hank wants to keep us a secret. He doesn't want me or the kids to be ostracized by folks in town by association."

"I would never let that happen, Charlotte." She reached for my hand again. "That's definitely something I can help with. I'll throw a party and make sure everyone knows I consider a slight against you a personal affront against me."

I smiled but lifted a hand to wave away her offer. "No, Sienna. You—you don't need to—"

"But I will," she said, looking stern and serious and lethal.

"And you think that'll make a difference to people? They won't avoid me if you make a show of being my friend?"

"I don't think it, I know it." She shrugged, her grin shining with all the confidence. "If we're best friends, everyone will want to be your best friend. Speaking of, Hank should take a chill pill and ask his friends for help every once in a while. You both should. I don't understand why he wouldn't let me stand up for him when your ex left."

"He probably didn't think it would be fair," I guessed. "He calls himself the fairness fairy."

"Oh brother. That does sound like him. You're probably right. But he'll have no choice this time, and neither do you."

Her pushiness made me laugh. It felt good to smile. "Fine. Thank you for your offer, I accept. Also, if you're open to it, I'd like to invite some of the dancers, too—especially those who have kids. What do you think? Can you stretch your halo to cover them as well?"

"Absolutely!" She smacked the sofa pillow next to her. "This party is going to rock. We should pin the tail on something."

I smile, but I also sighed, rubbing my forehead. "Now the hard part. Once we use the party to convince Hank that us dating in public won't tarnish my reputation or hurt the kids, I'll need to figure out what to do about the Buckleys."

Her features turned contemplative and she tapped her index finger against her bottom lip. "You were right before. It doesn't make sense how everyone turned against Hank so viciously when your ex left. There's something we don't know. I feel like if we could figure that out, we'd be able to figure out a way to protect you against any attempt by your ex's family to sue for custody."

"You really think so?"

"Yeah . . ." Her gaze lost focus. After a long moment of her staring in silence, her brown eyes sharpened on me and she said, "You know who we should ask? Cletus."

"Cletus Winston? Your brother-in-law?"

"Yes!" She reached for her phone, which she'd set on the coffee table earlier. "I bet he knows."

This statement confused me. "Why would Cletus know?"

"Cletus . . . well, Cletus . . ." Sienna seemed to be struggling to find the right words, then settled on, "Trust me. He knows things."

* * *

"I have a question for you," Sienna announced as soon as Cletus Winston stepped over the threshold to my house.

He peered around the foyer, his haphazard hair a mess of brown and gold curls offset by a few strands of red. The bulky man wore coveralls stained with grease, but his hands were clean.

"And it's not even my birthday," he mumbled. Then, to me, he said, "Does entry into this abode require that I remove my shoes?"

I shook my head. "Not unless you wish to."

"I do not. The laces are complicated." Eyes of an indetermined color swept over me. He lifted an eyebrow. "I don't suppose you have any tea?"

"I could put some on." I tossed a thumb over my shoulder in the direction of the kitchen. "Do you want black, green, or herbal?"

"Earl Grey?" He shoved his hands in the pockets of his coveralls. "I've got a taste for Earl Grey."

"I have that." I turned, motioning for them to follow. "Sienna, do you want any tea?"

"No, thank you. Cletus, Charlotte and I want to understand something and I figured you would know," she pressed.

I glanced at them, watching as she followed closely on his heels, her gaze narrowed and intent.

"Well, this is unexpected. But, uh, I'll do my best." As we arrived in the kitchen, Cletus claimed a spot on one side of the kitchen island and braced his hands against it. He cleared his throat and, looking quite somber, said, "You see, when a woman and a man love each other very much, they—"

Sienna hit him on the shoulder. "Very funny."

He flinched and rubbed his shoulder but said nothing.

She crossed her arms. "This is important. You remember how people treated Hank after Kevin Buckley left town? How, like, completely bananas they were, talking about closing down his club, calling it a menace and all that?"

I filled the electric kettle and set it to boil while Sienna spoke, returning to the kitchen island as she finished with her questions.

"I do recall something about it," he said noncommittally, his expression vacant.

I frowned. I didn't know Cletus Winston well at all, and the conversation we'd had in the foyer just now had been our longest interaction that I could recall. But whenever I did see him, he was messy. His wife was an amazing baker, and she seemed sweet but also harmless. That's how I thought of him, too. Sweet and harmless.

Why Sienna seemed to believe the sweet, generally harmless man in my kitchen could help, I had no idea. But at this point, I was willing to give anything a try.

"What I want to know is, why people in town blamed Hank Weller so much for Charlotte's divorce?" Sienna asked, titling her head toward me. "That makes no sense to me."

Cletus lifted his chin, his eyes drifting to mine. "Charlotte can't tell you why?"

"Me?" I pressed my fingers to my chest. "It doesn't make any sense to me either."

Sienna's brother-in-law frowned, it looked thoughtful, then he said, "Your ex-husband's family systematically launching a smear campaign against Hank Weller, Carli Duvall, and The Pink Pony to shift the blame to an infamous—yet, ultimately harmless—local ne'er-do-well and an exotic dancer in order to redirect public uproar and blame from their son and his disgusting behavior to literally anyone else doesn't make any sense to you?"

I gawped at him, completely flabbergasted, and stuttered, "I-I'm s-sorry. What—what did you say?"

"I said, your ex-husband's family systematically launching a—"

"Yes, I heard you. But how—why—why would you think that?" This possibility had never occurred to me.

"Because that's what happened," he said simply, as though nefarious conspiracies to destroy a person's character were hatched every day. No biggie.

"But how would they even go about doing such a thing?" I asked, stunned by the likelihood that this might be true.

His eyebrows pulled more completely together, but his mouth behind his bushy beard seemed to curve the faintest bit. "The fact that you can't conceive of how a powerful, wealthy family who does big business in 'family values' and who has a New York PR firm on retainer might run a propaganda campaign against private citizens in this little town of ours speaks to either the purity of your heart or your naïveté."

Well. There you go. Me being naïve seemed to be the answer to all my questions.

Cletus shifted his attention to Sienna. "Do you think it's a coincidence that JT MacIntyre is still the head of the Chamber of Commerce? Or that he and Flo McClure are such good friends?"

Sienna and Cletus shared a look, the meaning of which went completely over my head.

So I asked, "What does Flo McClure have to do with anything?"

Cletus's features registered disbelief for a split second as he faced me, the emotion quickly eclipsed by an expression of blandness. "Are you kidding me?"

"Flo McClure is the dispatch at the sheriff's office and a huge gossip," Sienna filled in, her smile sympathetic. "Even I know that."

"Oh. That's right!" I did know that. My mother had said so a hundred times. But Flo's status as a gossip in this town didn't put my kids to bed on time, pay the bills, or fold my laundry, thus it wasn't information I'd worked to retain.

"If anyone wanted to poison the well in Green Valley against a person, that's where to start." Sienna chewed on her thumbnail, her gaze distracted. "She's more respected than Karen Smith and, you know, nicer."

"Bingo," Cletus said, pointing to Sienna.

I peered at Cletus, working to wrap my mind around it all. "How did you know the Buckley PR firm is based out of New York?" I'd worked with them plenty of times when coordinating events in Vegas.

He stared at me, his expression still bland. "How's that tea coming along?"

My peer became a squint. That was him avoiding my question.

Luckily, Sienna chimed in, saving me from my rising hackles. "Like I told you, Cletus knows things."

Hmm.

The teapot whistled at that moment and I walked to it, removing it from the heat. As I retrieved a mug from the cupboard along with the Earl Grey tea bag, I steeped in Cletus's claims. It was terrible if true, but it certainly explained everything about Hank's treatment by the locals. The Buckleys made their money on the façade of 'family values,' no small task for a patriarch who'd been divorced more times than Henry the VIII.

"Does Hank know?" I asked, setting Cletus's tea down in front of him. "Does he know he was targeted?"

Cletus turned the handle of the mug until it pointed to his left. "I'm not Hank's confidant. That'd be Beau," he said lightly, eyes on the steam rising from the cup.

Sienna's gaze seemed to harden. "Cletus, did you ever tell Hank that the Buckleys targeted him?"

"No," he answered flatly, picking up his mug.

She set her hands on her hips. "Why not? You should've told him. Then he could've fought back."

Without taking a sip, the big man returned the mug to the counter and his gaze to his sister-in-law. "First of all, I am merely a repository of information. I'm not a gossip, nor am I everybody's savior. Second, Hank Weller is a grown man and none of my business."

"You know things about him that he might not know!" Sienna poked his bulky shoulder with her finger. "You did nothing to help him."

He caught her hand before she could poke him again. "Dearest sister, am I expected to help everyone I know something about? Then when would I work on cars and make that sausage you love so much? Besides, I don't like how he treats Jackson James." Cletus released her finger and sniffed indignantly. "Perchance if Hank learned how to be nicer to Jackson, I'd be nicer to him."

Hank isn't nice to Jackson?

Hank's story about running into Jackson at the hardware store yesterday resurfaced in my consciousness. Hank hadn't been mean to Jackson, had he? They seemed to get along fine at the car wash all those weeks ago. How would Cletus know if Hank and Jackson got along or not? But it's not like I'd seen them—

Wait.

Wait a darn minute.

A sudden suspicion had me asking, "What else do you know about Hank?"

"I know he's coming over to the shop tomorrow morning to pick up a loaner car." He shrugged, eyeing his tea. "Probably wants something folks don't associate with him. Seems he has a desire to travel around town incognito."

Hank will be at the Winston Brothers auto shop tomorrow? That was good to know. Without my phone, I had no way to reach him other than email.

"Thank you," I said, meaning it. "That's very helpful. So, what do you know about me, Cletus?"

Cletus's eyes lifted to mine, held, but he said nothing, his expression vacant again. But this time, his passiveness looked like a mask.

"Let me rephrase that." I leaned both hands on the countertop. "What do you know about me, and Kevin, and the Buckleys, and my divorce, that would help me push those people out of my life and my kids' lives forever?"

He rubbed at his beard. "Can't say that I have—"

"Cletus," Sienna cut in, her tone edged with impatience. "If you give Charlotte all the information she needs, I would be very grateful."

"Would you?" he asked, and the two stared at each other. The two stared at each other for a long, long, *long* time.

Finally, Sienna sighed, all good humor fleeing her features. "Fine. If you help

Charlotte and give her everything she wants to know about the Buckleys, I'll encourage Jethro to work on that project with you." She opened her eyes wide, her look clearly meant to convey a world of meaning. "You know, the one he keeps putting off? I will do my best to convince him."

Cletus blinked. The vacant expression fell away, and the side of his mouth twitched before slowly curving into a somewhat sinister-looking smile. "Was that so hard, Sienna? Aren't things so much nicer when we help each other? I knew you'd eventually see things my way."

She chuckled. "I love you, but you're a jerk and a bully," she said, her expression a mixture of rueful, reluctant amusement.

"I accept that." Tone unconcerned, like she'd called him tall instead of a jerk and a bully, he pointed his startlingly and suddenly intelligent gaze at me. "Now, let's see. The Buckleys."

I swallowed convulsively, nervous for some reason. "That's right."

Cletus's eyes narrowed, sharp as a blade. "Do you want to put them in jail? Or just, you know, frighten them a little?"

CHAPTER 29

HANK

"Anybody who knows anything of history knows that great social changes are impossible without the feminine ferment. Social progress can be measured exactly by the social position of the fair sex (the ugly ones included)."

— KARL MARX, *KARL MARX–FRIEDRICH ENGELS: SELECTED LETTERS, THE PERSONAL CORRESPONDENCE, 1844–1877*

Beau's older brother was getting on my last nerve. I'd expected to show up at the auto shop on Monday morning, park my truck in the back, grab the keys to a loaner, and be on my way. Nope.

As soon as I'd arrived, Cletus had come flying out of the garage to reprimand me about how and where I'd parked my truck. He made me park it again, and again. Then he'd parked it. Then he'd changed his mind and told me to park it where I'd originally parked it in the first place.

Now, for some incomprehensible reason that only made sense in Cletus Winston's head, he needed me to complete new paperwork.

"I do not understand why I need to fill out new paperwork. Just give me the keys." My feet dragged as I followed him into the garage. "You've known me since I was three. What do you think I'm going to do? And where are we going?"

"Our cloud broke," he said and kept on walking. "The paperwork is upstairs, not in the downstairs waiting area. Furthermore, I'd prefer to remain ignorant regarding your plans for my automobile. I like sleeping at night. It's not your plans I need, it's your phone number, email address, and credit card number."

"The cloud doesn't break, Cletus. You have my number and email on your phone, saved in your contacts. Besides, Beau knows my credit card number by heart." My steps stalled and I looked at Beau for support.

He presently stood next to an old Honda Civic, its hood up. He shrugged. A good-natured, unconcerned smile hanging on his features, Beau gestured that I should follow his brother up the stairs to the auto shop business office.

"Are you coming? Or have you changed your mind about the loaner car?" Cletus had turned on the bottom step, one hand on his hip, casting an impatient look at me —at *me!*—and then at the vintage digital Casio watch on his wrist. "I ain't got all day, Hank. This broken cloud business has impacted more than just you."

Grumbling, I moved to follow once more, my sour mood turning bitter. What in the name of mashed potatoes and crickets was his problem with me? We used to get along fine—never good friends, but fine acquaintances. A few years past, I'd become persona non grata. It had happened before the business with Charlotte's ex and Carli. Whatever it was, I'd have to nail him down about it.

The last person I needed as an enemy—especially seeing as how things were so precarious with the Buckleys, Charlotte, and her kids—was Cletus Winston.

Making a tsking sound, he turned and climbed the stairs. I followed, frustrated but silent. In truth, I was in a hurry. Charlotte hadn't messaged me after I left her house on Sunday. I'd texted her a few times, tried calling with no answer, and stayed up until almost 3:00 AM, hoping she'd send something. Nope. Nothing.

Inhaling deeply had grown increasingly difficult as her silence stretched. *If she doesn't want to see me again, if I'm not allowed to see or spend time with Kimmy and Sonya and Joshua—*

I gave my head a quick shake to clear it, not allowing myself to consider the possibility. If I thought about the possibility, I'd stop breathing all together. Weeks ago, she'd accused me of using wizardry to seduce her, but Charlotte and her kids had been the ones to cast a spell on me. They were magic, and I couldn't stop thinking about Sonya and her corn cob outfit. It fit, but it could be better. I wanted to add more corn silk.

And then there was Frankie. We still hadn't been properly introduced. His grandma hadn't let him go the whole time I'd been making breakfast. What if we never were?

"You'll need to fill everything out in triplicate this time," Cletus said mildly. "And the form has been lengthened. I'll need next of kin information, insurance—auto, property, and health; dental, too, if you have it—as well as a survey completed at the back so we can better meet the needs of our customers."

"I have things to do, Cletus," I seethed, but was careful to keep my voice level. "This is not the day for me to fill out forms in triplicate. And I have no interest in completing a survey." I scowled at his backside.

Was it me, or was he taking a ridiculously long time to climb these stairs? If he went any slower, he'd be going backward.

"You cannot drive off the lot with a car not in your name until we have the proper paperwork on file, Hank Weller. I don't want to be liable for an impromptu trip to Canada."

Finally, cresting the landing, he paused and withdrew a metal ring that must've held at least a hundred keys.

My eyes swelled. "Jesus, Cletus. Do you need all those keys?"

"No," he said, flicking through the metal disks slower than he'd climbed the stairs. "Most of these don't do anything."

What the hell? "Then why do you carry them?"

"They're decoys."

"Decoys? How many do you use?"

Apparently, he found the one he needed. Separating it from the others, he placed his hand on the doorknob. "Five are real, the rest are decoys. Now—oh. Look at that. It was already unlocked."

My jaw ground together so tight, I was in danger of cracking a filling. What was next? A feather quill to complete the forms in triplicate? Or would he expect me to chisel stone tablets?

He turned the knob and I didn't know whether to laugh or shout. I was close to doing both, but then the door opened and my gaze immediately connected with Charlotte's.

She looked good, her skin peachy and pink, like she'd fully recovered, and her honey-colored hair was long and loose around her shoulders. She'd even put on makeup and a nice dress—not one of her ankle-length, flowing, floral skirts, but a sweater dress that ended mid-thigh and clung to her body. I swallowed the flooding spike of lust down, down, down and grabbed the railing at my left, bracing belatedly for impact of her as she unleashed her pretty smile. Then she waved, like she was excited to see me. My heart thumped, an ache where there should be a beat, a short breath puffing from my lips.

"Charlotte," I croaked, afraid to blink.

"Hi," she said softly, shyly, but her gorgeous eyes were brash and bold and pleased and—

Cletus stepped in front of me, blocking her from view and snapping me out of my stupor.

He made a big show of looking at his watch. "Oh. Well, there you go. I just got a notification that the cloud is working again."

I blinked up at him, my brain clearing enough for me to grit out harshly, "Cletus Byron Winston, that is a Casio digital watch from the eighties, not a smartwatch. How would you get a notification about the cloud on a Casio?"

"And look at the time. Now I'm late. Sorry, Hank. I can't stand around here shooting the shit, I have things to do. But y'all are welcome to use my office if you like." He stepped around me and hustled down the steps faster than I'd ever seen him move.

He'd been fucking with me.

The whole time, the delays and opinions about where to park my truck, the threat of paperwork in triplicate. He'd been messing with me the whole damn time.

"Hank?"

I turned back to Charlotte, determined to force myself to forget about Cletus Winston's sneaky theatrics. As soon as my eyes landed on Charlotte again, I didn't have to force anything at all.

"Hey," I said, stepping into the office and shutting the door behind me, my eyes roving over her. "What are you, uh—what are you doing here?"

"I needed to talk to you." She stepped forward, but instead of meeting me, she walked to the door and locked it. Then she turned and faced me, her back pressed against the metal partition like she needed it for balance. "My phone is broken."

As much as I wanted to stomp over and pull her in my arms, I restrained myself. Barely. "Charlotte, someone could see us here. With your ex's family after your kids, why would you take the risk?"

"No, no." She waved a hand between us. "Don't worry about that. I got it covered. Kevin won't be suing for custody."

A breath held suspended in my lungs as I searched her features frantically. "What? What do you mean?"

"Cletus helped me. It's all taken care of. I have, uh, information now that will keep the Buckleys from interfering with me or the kids."

"What kind of information?"

"Part of the deal with Cletus was that I can't tell you—"

I gritted my teeth again. "That sneaky bastard."

"—but I can tell you this: Cletus sent a letter to old man Buckley this morning and it's big." Her grin became supernova, her eyes glassy with unshed tears. "I think we're free, Hank. We're free. Me and my babies will never have to worry about those terrible people again."

Her relief pulled a smile out of me and instinct had me crossing to her. She threw her arms around me and squeezed, laughing, light with her joy. I was relieved too, so fucking relieved. The fear had been a real, gnawing, living thing. I'd stayed up last night hoping she'd call, but also doing research on the Buckleys, making plans, reaching out to contacts. I'd planned to take them down on my own if need be.

However—

"This is great news and I'm so happy for you, for the kids especially. But"—I drew back, cupping her jaw and giving her a quick kiss. If I took any more than that, we'd be having sex in Cletus's office and he'd never forgive me for that—"I seriously doubt Cletus Winston offered to help without wanting anything in return. He doesn't operate that way. Everything is a trade with him."

"I know." She nodded, her sunny green gaze moving over my face, like she missed the sight of me. "Sienna gave him something in return. We're all set."

I reared back, frowning. "What's that? What did Sienna give him?"

"I don't know, something about Jethro. Doesn't matter. Sienna told me after that it was something Jethro wanted to do anyway but was letting Cletus fret over."

Hmm. "Still, we can't let Sienna and Jet do that without giving them something for their trouble. We need to—"

"No. We don't." Her hands came to my cheeks, holding me still. "We can let Jethro and Sienna be good friends to us. We can accept their help and let it be."

Despite Charlotte's words of assurance, I wasn't convinced. It wasn't how I operated. Mostly. The idea of letting them help without returning the favor didn't sit right.

"If they were anyone else, I'd buy them something. But Sienna can buy her family anything they want."

"Hank." Charlotte pressed a fast, hard kiss against my mouth. "Let it go. Accept the help, say thank you, and kiss me."

I'd still planned to argue until she'd added that last part. As soon as she said *kiss me*, the fight left, leaving just her, and me, and a locked office door.

"In that order?" I drawled, my hands on her waist now.

"In any order you like," she said, giving me a smile, her gaze dropping to my mouth. "I missed you," she said. "And I'd like some kisses before we leave this office."

"I'm yours to command," I said, lowering my mouth to hers. We both sighed as our lips met, my fingers digging into her sides. *Fuck.* I'd last touched her yesterday, but I missed this. I missed the feel of her.

Her dress might've been meant to resemble a knit sweater, but the fabric was thin. I could feel the heat of her body beneath it. Intoxicated by the hot, wet strokes of her tongue, I slid my hands lower and then groaned.

"Fuck." My fingers flexed on her bottom. "Are you—" I had to swallow. "You're not wearing any underwear," I said, my body straining with the effort to stop myself from lifting her dress and touching the bare skin of her ass, her cunt.

Or I could taste it.

She smiled against my neck and I shook, forcing myself to relax my hands. I'd been holding her so hard, I might've left marks. What had she been thinking, teasing me like this? Did she have no idea how badly I wanted her? How often I'd thought about us?

I prided myself on my self-control, but even I had my limits.

"Are you trying to make me lose my mind?" I growled, grabbing her wrists and leaning back. I'm sure I looked wild. I felt wild.

She smiled, her eyes dancing playfully, pushing me further past the point of no return.

"No," she said sweetly, twisting her hands until I released her and then smoothing her palms down the front of my shirt. "I just thought, since we don't have much opportunity to be together, we could fool around a little before—"

"Oh no. No, no." I advanced on her and she stumbled a bit as she walked backward until her legs connected with Cletus's desk. "We're not fooling around."

"We—we're not?" Charlotte caught herself on the edge of the desktop, the teasing brightness of her gaze giving way to something both fearful and hopeful.

"Nope," I said, tilting my head to get a good look at her and how fucking sexy she was, and I realized she wasn't wearing a bra either. *That's it.*

I hadn't wanted our first time to be in an office over an auto shop, but did it really matter? It didn't. Not when I planned to have her thousands of times in a thousand different places and ways. Who the fuck cared where we did it first, as long as we kept doing it?

When I reached for the hem of her dress, she caught my hands. "Hank, wait. Wait."

Needing relief, I brought her hands to the front of my pants and pressed them there. Her breath hitched and her arms relaxed, and she stroked me over my jeans, a delectable little moan caught by my lips as I captured hers with a biting kiss.

Using her palm, she pressed forward and I angled my hips, rolling them to meet her strokes. She moaned again, tearing her mouth from mine. "What—what you doing?"

Abandoning her fingers to work their magic so I could work mine, I lifted the hem of her dress to her waist and cupped her.

She shivered. "Hank. What are—"

"You know what I'm doing." I bit her jaw, the column of her throat, sliding a single finger inside her. She was ready, and so was I. I'd never been more ready in my life. "I've got a condom in my wallet. Unzip my pants and roll it on."

"Hank—"

I lifted my free hand to cover her mouth, slowly pushing her head back until the crown of it connected with the hutch above the desk. "Charlotte. Do you want me to stop?"

Her eyes widened, but she shook her head.

"Can you be quiet?"

She nodded eagerly.

"Then get the condom. Roll it on. And open your legs."

CHAPTER 30

HANK

"No woman has to be respectable to be valuable."

— MIKKI KENDALL, *HOOD FEMINISM: NOTES FROM THE WOMEN THAT A MOVEMENT FORGOT*

Her eyelashes flickered, her breath hitching, her body trembling, and her inner walls tightened around my finger. I narrowed my eyes as her body confirmed a very sexy suspicion of mine: Charlotte loved dirty talk.

Bossy, messy, domineering dirty talk.

I'd suspected as much when I'd touched her in my truck. She'd come the moment I started vocalizing my wishes. She'd asked for it. She'd loved it.

This knowledge put me in a precarious position. As already established, I was running short on self-control. I needed *inside* her, right fucking now, as long as she wanted me just the same. Thank God she wanted me to use a condom. The way heavy spikes of pleasure and pressure already tugged at the base of my spine, I wouldn't last long, not even with a condom.

My options were: I could have her roll it on me right now, keep my mouth shut, and take what we both so clearly wanted, or . . . *I'm a greedy bastard.*

"You're so wet." I watched her, eager for any reaction. "Is this for me?"

She nodded, her gaze pleading, seemingly overcome. Something inside me stretched, asserted itself, shoving and clawing to the surface. Witnessing her reaction my voice, a new wildness sank low in my stomach, swelled in my groin, urgent.

I'd have her on this desk. But first, I'd taste her on it, and then I'd tell her all the ways I wanted her.

Letting my hand slide from her lips, I observed her closely—hungrily—and said, "You want me to fuck you, don't you? You want my cock inside you, filling you up."

She exhaled another whimper, her legs widening as she rocked back, her lashes flickering again, and I almost came in my pants where she stroked me.

No, no! Not yet.

"Let me know when you've got it open and ready for me." Removing her hands, I held one captive against my thigh and slid the other around to my back pocket. Staring into her hazy eyes, I helped her pull out my wallet.

"Now spread those long legs and show me that pretty cunt," I said, giving her a nipping kiss.

Unintelligible words, more squeaks than sounds, fell from her lips. Her eyes looked lost to the moment and my words, and damn if I didn't love that look. The hand holding my wallet shook as I lowered to kneel and spread her knees wide, licking my lips as she revealed herself.

"So fucking pretty," I whispered.

The muscles in her legs flexed. "Please," she said, sounding strained and carefully quiet. "Please. Hank."

My mouth watered and I leaned forward, using my thumbs to separate her folds, wetting my lips and brushing them against the tight, swollen bundle of nerves at the very center of her. She was wet and lush, heat and soft perfection. I lapped at her slowly, groaning at the taste, dragging the flat of my tongue over her clit until her legs began to shake, her hips tilting upward subtly, searching instinctively for more.

Quiet words continued to spill out of her, praise and pleas. I smiled, undoing the button on my jeans and lowering the zipper. Refusing to give her what she needed to see stars—not yet—I kept the pressure soft, reveling in the silky texture of her and her sweet, imploring sounds.

Pulling out my cock, my eyes flicked up, crashing into hers. She'd been watching me, her foggy gaze transfixed on where I'd been working her. But she hadn't removed the condom from my wallet yet. Her hands gripped the desk uselessly, her knuckles white against the edge.

Swiping my tongue over my lips and tasting her there, I leaned back to show her where my hand was wrapped around my dick and lifted my chin toward my wallet.

"Don't make me ask again."

Her body stiffened and she beat her eyelashes at me. "Oh! God. Sorry."

Sliding my fingertips up the back of her leg, along the inside of her thighs, I parted her folds again, this time using my index and middle finger. Keeping my eyes on her progress with the packet, I traced circles around her clit with the pads of my fingers and slipped my thumb inside her body. She tensed, her attention shifting from the square package she'd just revealed to my gaze, then lower to where I grasped my cock in time with how my thumb stroked her.

Charlotte started to pant, her trembling fingers ripping open the packet. Abandoning her body and mine, I reached up and took the condom from her before she did something tragic, like inadvertently unroll it or poke a hole in it, which would likely spell the death of me.

"That's my angel," I said, kissing the inside of her thigh lightly before returning my attention to her pussy, giving her more friction from my tongue and harder strokes. I ached, painfully hard, and rolling on the condom took no time at all. The sounds she made, how her fingers slid into my hair and tugged, how she yanked me forward and pivoted her hips against my face, I had to fist myself at the base to keep from finishing before we'd even started.

A short, desperate sound ripped from her and I glanced up. Her hands abandoned my hair. She covered her mouth with both palms, her eyes closing, and I felt the first tremors of her climax against my tongue. I removed my mouth and she whined, her eyes flying open to lock with mine.

I smiled. I stood. I grabbed the edges of her dress and pulled it over her head. I lowered my mouth to her breast, tonguing it as I'd tongued her clit, and guided her head beneath the hutch of the desk. I laid her back and positioned myself at her entrance, the blood rushing between my ears reaching a crescendo as I pushed inside, filling her with one slow, long slide.

She groaned. As did I. Then I sucked in a breath and slid my hands to her knees. Bringing them up and encouraging her heels to rest on the edge, I spread her wider and moved. Knowing it would feel this good did nothing to diminish the perfection of it. The sight of her naked body spread before me, how her breasts bounced with each invading thrust, her yielding surrender—she could not be more perfect, nothing could.

Her hands remained clasped over her mouth and enthusiastic sounds slipped past her fingers despite her best efforts to muzzle them.

"I knew you'd feel this good." I'd stopped giving my words premeditated thought and I said what I wanted, not what I believed she needed to hear. It was a submersion in the moment, nothing like I'd ever experienced before. It was a confrontation, holding us accountable for every pleasure-seeking stroke, every greedy touch, every erotic thought.

"Let me look at you." Rising over her for a better look, I licked my lips as my gaze trailed over her, lowered to where we were joined. "I now know what you taste like, what it feels like to fuck you. Every time I look at you, this is what I'll be thinking about."

She moaned. It fed the hunger in me she'd awakened. I loved this. Our choices were inescapable when we spoke them out loud. The words rubbed my skin raw. I felt heated, oversensitive.

She must've felt it too. Her eyes rolled back, her body arching, more desperate noises, and those tremors, the same I'd felt against my tongue now fluttered around my dick. The knowledge of her imminent orgasm made me lose my steady pace and I thrust harder.

Charlotte's body slid an inch higher on the desk and I anchored her in place by grabbing her upper thighs. I used the convenient placement to slide my thumb back and forth over her clit. "You need it, don't you, angel? You need it so bad. You need this cock, just like I need this cunt."

She nodded frantically, her chest heaving, and she came with a stifled scream, her back lifting off the desk, her throat fully exposed. Leaning over her, I latched on to her, biting her neck, her shoulder, the need building higher until I was held in suspension, weightless, above her, with her, and I came, and it felt—she felt, this felt, we felt—so fucking *good*. Right. Perfect. Vital. Necessary.

My body bowed and I released her thighs so I could wrap her in my arms. I swore against her neck, kissing it, my lungs tight and aching with the need to breathe. I resisted, determined to stop time and be here, sharing this with her. Wanting to share every fucking part of myself with this woman, wanting her to take it and want it just as badly as I wanted and needed her.

I needed oxygen. I inhaled, the scent of her body pulled into my lungs, and I held her tight.

"Hank—you're—I can't breathe." She released a breathless laugh, her fingers twisting in and tugging at my hair.

I hesitated, but then I relaxed my arms, knowing this desire to keep her for myself—naked, beneath me, just like this—was foolish. But still . . . I wanted it.

"Holy mackerel," she said, and I heard the smile in the words.

Never wanting to miss a single one of her smiles, I lifted my head and her bright gaze hooked into mine.

"Hank Weller. Sex god."

Since I couldn't yet think, I smirked, saying nothing.

She sighed, her gaze moving over me, and the intensity of her assessment, the emotion behind it, made the hairs on the back of my neck prickle.

"You are so . . ." she began, then sighed again, leaving the thought unfinished.

"What?" I smiled, though my ears felt hot beneath her continued scrutiny. "Perfect? Irresistible?" I teased, hoping to dispel the sudden discomfort under my left rib when my mind filled in the blank she'd left open with *loveable*.

I tensed at the thought.

"Filthy," she finally said, her lips twisting with humor.

I laughed despite the swelling in my lungs, despite the nature of the word. She'd said *filthy* as though it were a compliment, the highest praise.

"I love how you talk to me when we're—you know. How do you know how to do that? Did you take lessons?" Wiggling beneath me as though to get comfortable, her stare lit with delight.

I love how you talk to me . . .

The sound of the L-word brought the room sharply into focus and I abruptly remembered where we were. The chances of Charlotte finding a comfortable position on top of Cletus Winston's desk were slim to none.

"No lessons. Actually . . ." Frowning, I gingerly pushed off her and discarded the condom in a trash can beneath the desk. I then pulled up my pants with one hand while reaching for and taking her fingers with my other hand. I helped her straighten, ensuring her forehead didn't bump against the hutch when she sat up.

When she sat up from the desk.

The desk we'd just had sex on.

Cletus's desk.

"Actually what?" she asked, grabbing my shirt and hooking her legs around my thighs, not allowing me to get too far. That's when I realized I still had my shirt on. Meanwhile, Charlotte was incredibly naked.

In Cletus Winston's office.

At the auto shop.

I scratched the back of my neck, my ears burning hotter. "Uh, what were we talking about?"

"You taking dirty-talking lessons. Fess up, who's your teacher?"

"Oh. That's right." I gave my head a shake, the weight of what we'd just done added to the pressure beneath my ribs. "No, I've never done that before. Except with you."

Her head tilted to the side and she caught my eyes again. "Never done what?"

"Dirty talk."

"Are you serious?" Her mouth dropped open. "You're so good at it. It's like you're saying everything I want to hear. It's so sexy. I think you could get me off just with your words."

I felt my lips want to curve at her statement, but it didn't last. My thoughtlessness finally caught up with me, along with recklessness and carelessness and selfishness. The ache of guilt clogged my windpipe.

"We'll have to try that sometime." I forced out the words and leaned forward to kiss her gently on the forehead—an apology—adding roughly, "You make it easy."

I lowered my eyes to some spot between us but couldn't bring anything into focus. This was the problem. She made it too easy. She made it so easy, I'd lost all self-awareness and fucked her in this office. *Is this how I treat the woman I lo—*

I winced, a reactive flicker of fear making it hard to think, and I amended the direction of my thoughts. I cared deeply about this woman. Deeply. *Deeply.* How deeply was not up for discussion.

But if I cared deeply for her, how could I let myself lose control like that? I wanted to bang my head against the wall. She deserved so much better, so much—

"Hey, hey. What's going on?" Charlotte voice, soothing but edged with concern, cut through my recriminations. Her fingers speared into my hair and she brought my forehead to hers. "What are you thinking about? Where did your mind go?"

"I can't believe I—" I had to clear my throat before I could continue. "I didn't want our first time to be in my club, and I definitely didn't want it to be in this stupid fucking office. Charlotte, I'm so sorry. I lost control. That's on me. That's—"

"Shh." She silenced the remainder of my apology with a tender kiss, embracing me and holding on tight. "No, Hank. No," she said, dipping her chin and pressing our foreheads together again. "I loved it, every second. I lost control, too. I feel so needy for you all the time. I'd do it all over again, right now, if you wanted."

A stunned laugh burst out of me.

She grinned, and her smile fractured something hidden and secret, a part of myself I wasn't ready to examine or acknowledge. Not yet. Not until she admitted it first.

I'm not saying it first.

"I don't care where we are," she said, sounding certain, confident. "Personally, I didn't need our first time to be on a bed of roses or in a fancy hotel suite. I'm more of a *let's rip each other's clothes off* kind of gal. I don't care where it happens, just as long as it's sexy as hell and we both got off. So, mission accomplished."

I laughed again, finally giving myself permission to touch her. But then, with her bare skin beneath my hands, I had to battle the urge to touch her everywhere. I fucking loved this woman.

I loved her and—*fucking hell!*—I'd loved her for a while. I'd probably loved her since the moment she put sunscreen on my face and neck, and then marched around the parking lot of The Pink Pony like the boss she was, and I'd certainly been in love with her since I watched her struggle to calm Kimmy in that alleyway, her compassion on display as she put her daughter's needs first.

That was the thing about Charlotte, she was always putting everyone else first. It was infuriating how she put herself last, how she seemed to think the best of everyone when they didn't deserve it, how she loved everyone for who they were and not what they could do for her.

So why did these faults in her character make me love her so much?

"Haaank," she said, drawing me out of my circular thoughts, her voice sweet and coaxing and stirring my blood.

"Yes?"

Whatever she wanted, I'd give it to her. I felt certain of this. She only needed to ask and it would be hers. Oddly, I didn't want or expect anything in return, and it was this realization that made the air seize in my lungs.

"You look upset." Her gaze concerned, her smile soft, Charlotte petted my beard, her nails scratching lightly against my cheeks and jaw. "Don't be upset."

"I'm not upset." I was upset, but I also wasn't. Mostly, I was freaking out.

"Then kiss me, my love, and tell me again how easy I made it for you to dirty talk."

My love.

Forcing a smile, I rasped out, "Like I said, you make it incredibly easy, Charlotte. You inspire me in so many ways."

"I inspire you," she echoed, lifting her chin, and pummeled me with a sublimely happy expression. "I love that."

Licking my lips, I stared at her. There it was again. *I* love *that*.

She said the word so easily, like she came by it naturally. But that word didn't usually come naturally to me. With Charlotte, though? It felt as natural as admiring a sunset, or listening to the ocean, or enjoying sunlight on my face.

It felt too natural.

It felt like I had no choice.

CHAPTER 31

HANK

"I fell in love with her courage, her sincerity, and her flaming self-respect. And it's these things I'd believe in, even if the whole world indulged in wild suspicions that she wasn't all she should be. I love her and it is the beginning of everything."

— F. SCOTT FITZGERALD

"Hank?"

Tipping my head back, I looked up to find Beau and Shelly frowning at me. Presumably, my presence on their doorstop at 9:30 PM on a Tuesday night confused them.

I'd only lasted thirty-six hours, just a day and a half after realizing I was totally fucked.

Thirty-six hours of lying to myself that I'd figure it out, that loving Charlotte was no biggie. A day and a half of searching for her wherever I went, of making excuses to stop by her house, of constant distraction and an inability to draw a full breath and heart palpitations. Twenty-four plus twelve hours of catching myself staring at her when she walked into a room and feeling an ache of sharp longing every time she left.

I was *pining*. PINING! I stewed, I considered, I measured, but I never fucking pined.

"Oh. Fancy running into you two here," I said, standing from their porch steps.

"We live here," Shelly said flatly, like I was an idiot.

Which I am, so . . .

"Why are you here, Hank?" Beau asked, his voice full of concern. "Did something happen?"

I glanced at Shelly and her impassive but focused attention. Beau's woman was notoriously difficult to read. This might've been her happy face. It might've been her angry face. Hell, it might've been her O face. All her expressions—as far as I'd seen—were exactly the same.

"I was, uh, hoping you had a moment to talk a matter over." I spoke haltingly, worried I might've overstepped.

I never used to worry about overstepping with Beau, but ever since Shelly and he had hooked up, she made me feel like a perpetual third wheel.

Which I am, so . . .

Beau and Shelly glanced at each other, silent communication passing between them. I braced myself. If Beau was happy, I was happy. I did my best to limit our interactions to my scheduled custody times: Wednesday morning fishing every week, Saturday night at Genie's, a camping trip here or there, an invite to dinner at the Winston homestead on occasion, a quick lunch if he had time.

I suspected Shelly didn't like me much. I suspected Shelly didn't like anybody much. Except Beau. Which was why I hadn't gotten my hopes up about—

"Absolutely," Shelly said, walking past me to the door and drawing her keys out. "You want tea?"

Only if you don't poison it. "Sure." I found a smile to put on to hide my surprise. "Tea would be great."

She didn't smile, but she did give me a single nod and opened the door wide enough for me to follow.

"Are we fishing tomorrow?" Beau asked, closing the door after us and stepping next to me.

"Yep, yep. The boat is all stocked. I'll be back here in the morning, bright and early." I glanced at Shelly's departing back as she headed to the kitchen. Once she'd exited overhearing-radius, I turned fully to Beau. "Sorry I'm interrupting, but I couldn't wait until tomorrow. I need . . ."

"What?" His eyes grew rounded, worried. "What's wrong?"

"I'm an idiot," I said starkly.

He grinned, looking at me funny. "Yeah. Everybody knows that."

"I need advice. Your advice," I whispered, ignoring his teasing.

"Okay." Beau stuffed his hands into his back pockets. "Shoot."

"Remember when you got that girl pregnant in high school?"

Beau stiffened, his lips parting, his eyes wide and startled. "Hank. Oh my God, Hank—"

"No. No, I didn't get anyone pregnant."

"Oh thank God," he breathed out, chuckling his relief, his shoulders slumping with it. "Thank. God. What a disaster that would be."

I frowned, oddly offended. "What the hell, Beau?" I hit his shoulder. "You think I'd be such a terrible father?"

He screwed his face up. "Come on. Like you want to be a dad."

Drawing myself to my full height—which was exactly one-fourth of an inch taller than Beau's six-foot-two-inches—I glared at him. "Maybe I do. Maybe I'd make a great dad. You don't know."

Beau stared at me, his eyebrows drawing together. "What are we even talking about?"

"Charlotte Mitchell."

Something flared behind his eyes, but he shut it down before I could read it, his tone cagey as he said, "What about Charlotte Mitchell?"

"She's got kids."

"And?"

"And I think—no, *I know* I'm . . ." My mouth suddenly dry, I inhaled and exhaled, then did it again, and again.

"Hank?"

"I'm in love with her," I blurted.

Beau's eyes widened to the size of pasties, but otherwise he didn't move.

"Or I'm infatuated with her competence, humor, work ethic, cleverness, face, goodness, and body—not necessarily in that order. Body and face are probably tied for first. Her smile is fucking mesmerizing, but so are her legs and breasts, and her strength. She's so strong, so damn strong. She can lift a whole damn crate, did you know that? Those are followed by goodness and humor—another tie—then competence and—"

"Whoa, whoa, whoa. Hold up. Hold your horses." Beau gave me a quick, searching stare, then paced toward the kitchen. He peeked around the corner, paced back, and then stood close, his voice a whisper as he said, "The last time we spoke about Charlotte—actually discussed her in detail, not you ogling her at the car wash, not us talking about her quitting, and not Roscoe filling us in on why she doesn't like you—you were giving me shit about her owing you a thank-you note for splitting up her marriage. You didn't want her working at your club. You didn't even want to know her."

I lifted my hands between us. "Okay, okay, let me back up a bit."

"Please do."

"I'll give you the CliffsNotes version of the last few weeks. Try to keep up." Keeping one eye on the doorway to the kitchen, I gave Beau the quick and dirty details—dates, places, names, events—that had brought me to this moment.

Unsurprisingly, he listened with patience. He also didn't have many questions until I got to the part about keeping our relationship a secret.

"Wait a minute, Charlotte wanted you to keep y'all dating on the down-low?" He looked ready to file a formal complaint.

"No. That was me. She said she'd be proud to date me, but I pointed out that it would be bad for the kids. Reluctantly, after a good deal of persuading on my part, she agreed. But that's all a moot point now since Sienna is throwing a party for us next month and making like we're all best friends."

He nodded. "Okay, gotcha. And that'll work, too. We should start calling that woman Saint Sienna. If she gave her blessing to a cow, everyone in town would line up for its milk. Go on."

I continued quickly, the sound of the tea kettle whistling spurring me to talk faster, ending my twisty tale with the events that took place in Cletus's office yesterday morning.

"I didn't know Charlotte was up there," Beau said, his eyes unfocused. "That sneaky bastard. How'd he smuggle her up to the office without any of us noticing? And how'd you get her out without me seeing you?"

"Cletus is a sneaky bastard, but he's the reason—or something he knows is the reason—Charlotte doesn't have to worry about the Buckleys anymore. He intervened yesterday, sent old man Buckley some sort of letter, and we just heard this morning that Kevin is being shipped off to the middle of Nebraska, the planned custody suit dropped. And they've agreed to stop the court-ordered visitations. Mrs. Buckley won't be terrorizing those kids twice a month anymore. It looks like she's free of them."

"Well. That's a relief. I'm happy for her."

"Be happy for Kimmy, Joshua, Sonya, and Frankie, too. That family is poison."

Beau's mouth hooked to the side. "And now you're in love with her? With Charlotte?"

"Or I'm infatuated. It's one or the other. That's why I'm here."

"I—you—what? You want me to tell you which it is?"

I tilted my head back and forth. "Eh, not really. I want to talk about that girl you got pregnant—"

His mouth flattened. "She wasn't pregnant. She thought she was pregnant, but she wasn't. It was a pregnancy scare and I offered to marry her, but she didn't—"

"Exactly!" I snapped and pointed at him. "She didn't want to marry you, but you thought you were in love with her, right? What was her name? Uh, Nancy or . . . Beth?"

"It doesn't matter," he gritted out, his eyes darting toward the kitchen again, then away. "Why are you bringing this up?"

"How did you get over her? She broke your heart, right? She rejected you.

How'd you—you know—push her out of your mind and move on?"

Beau heaved a sigh, bewildered. "Why?"

"I want to do that."

"What? I thought—did Charlotte reject you today?"

"No." I scratched the back of my neck. "I saw her this afternoon and we made out in the laundry room. Then I stayed and made dinner while she gave Frankie a bath. I think if Joshua gave him a bath, he wouldn't fuss so much, and I'm going to suggest it. But today was"—I swallowed thickly at the memory—"awesome. She's awesome. In fact, I'm certain she likes me a lot. A whole lot. She might even love me, too. You know, she probably does, but she loves lots of folks."

Beau made a face. "I don't understand. If you love her and she loves you, why do you want to know how to push her from your mind?"

"I want to be prepared."

"For what?"

"Just in case I'm wrong. Just in case I need to stop loving her and leave her and her kids alone. I don't want to—to feel like this." I waved my hand in front of my chest where the main source of pain originated. "I don't want to feel like I need to be around them all the time, like I miss them when I'm not there. Tell me, how do I—you know—move on if I need to? What did you do?"

Beau set his hands on his hips and sucked in a slow breath, and he stared at me for a long moment, his brain clearly working. I gave him time, but I did glance toward the kitchen again. Shelly and her one expression would be returning with tea any second now. Then she'd kick me out and I'd have to wait until tomorrow for Beau's advice, which meant I likely wouldn't sleep tonight, which meant I'd be in a shitty mood for fishing. I didn't want to be in a shitty mood for fishing.

Finally, he said, "I'm not sure the situation with Beth applies here."

"Why not?"

"With her, I realized she didn't make me a priority and I was better off without her, and that made it easy to stop thinking about her or having feelings for her."

My mouth turned down in a grimace. "Well. That's not going to work."

He'd turned his head slightly, inspecting me from a new angle. "Charlotte makes you a priority?"

I considered the question, but I didn't have to think it over for long. "She has. She makes me a priority, even though she's stretched super thin."

"How has she made you a priority?"

"She's honest with me, about her expectations, her limitations. She wants to make sure I feel valued, that I don't sell myself short, that my needs are met. She doesn't want me to work on rehabilitating my reputation for show if it means I'm not staying true to myself, even though it would make her life easier if I did. In all the ways it's feasible for her to make me a priority, she does."

Beau's smile was a small one, but it packed a punch. I braced myself, certain something big was coming, a brilliant nugget of advice that would help me navigate these uncharted waters and see me safely to the other side.

Instead, still smiling, he said, "What's the problem again?"

I huffed. "Stop being an asshole and help me with this."

He laughed. "I'm serious. What's the problem?"

"Fine, dummy. I'll spell it out again." I lowered my voice to a whisper and leaned close, not wanting Shelly to overhear when she walked in. "I'm in love with Charlotte. She may or may not be in love with me, which means I need to figure out: A) how to make her love me, or B) make sure she's always in love with me, or C) how to walk away when the time comes without becoming a pathetic shadow of my former self."

Irritatingly, his smile widened. "And how do you propose making sure Charlotte is always in love with you? Tell me what that looks like."

Beau hadn't whispered his question, so I scowled at him. "Keep your voice down."

"Why?"

"Shelly doesn't like me and I don't want her to—"

"Hold up. Stop right there." Beau held up his hands between us, now frowning. "Why would you say that? Why would you think Shelly doesn't like you?"

"Are you serious? Why would she? What have I ever given her?"

My best friend rolled his eyes. "You don't have to give people things in order for them to like you. You just have to be yourself and hope their kind of weird matches your kind of weird. Like us."

I sighed, glancing at the ceiling for help. "Says the guy who is universally liked by everyone because he's always giving people shit for free."

Beau laughed. "You dummy. I don't give 'shit for free.' That's not what I'm doing."

"Then what are you doing? Huh?" How our conversation had altered course so completely, I had no idea. But since we were on the subject, hashing this shit out was long overdue. "It's exhausting, watching you people give so much of yourselves away for free. Why do you do that? You and Charlotte, you're basically the same person. I see it now. You're always doing nice things for people without them asking, thinking the best of folks when they don't deserve it. Why?"

Beau's expression was the definition of fondly amused. "Oh, Hank. Haven't you figured it out yet? The receiving is in the giving."

I stared at him, nonplussed. "What the fuck is that? Did you read that in a fortune cookie? What does that even mean?"

He set his hand on my shoulder, his sky-blue eyes the picture of infinite patience. "Let me ask you this: is Charlotte a good person? Does she have a history of taking advantage of folks? Or does she try to do right by people? Is she thinking about other people's comfort as well as her own?"

I wanted to shrug off his hand. Instead, I grunted and growled, "Haven't you been listening? She's a fucking angel."

"Then there you go." He nodded, letting his hand drop.

"There I go, what?" I swore to God, if he didn't get to the point in five seconds or less, I was going to seek out Shelly in the kitchen and ask her for advice.

"Give. Her. Everything," he said, his voice suddenly firm. All amusement had evaporated from his features, leaving behind a trace of fondness but mostly just sincerity. "Give Charlotte all of you. Don't hold back. You can't hold back. You can't keep some of yourself in reserve just in case things don't work out. If you do, then they for sure won't work out. The two of you won't last. You've got to give it your all."

His words made the spot under my rib flare and I pressed my hand against the ache. "Shit," I said. That was seriously good advice. It was also scary-as-shit advice.

"Yeah. Shit." He nodded once, his features stark but also wry. "Between two people who aren't users and who love each other, you get out of a relationship what you put into it. Put everything you got into it."

"Tea is ready," Shelly called from the kitchen, and we both turned toward the doorway. The woman appeared a moment later, her eyes landing on Beau, her expression unchanging. "I also put out those cookies you like, Beau."

"Thank you," he said warmly. "We'll be there in a second."

"Okay." Shelly's hawkish stare moved to me. "How is the new AC?"

"Uh, great. Thanks."

"Good." She nodded, leaning back. "You should come over more often, Hank. It's good to see you."

Startled, but doing a good job of hiding it, I nodded and rasped out, "It's good to see you too, Shelly."

Without another word, she turned and disappeared back into the kitchen, effectively knocking my world off its axis with the short exchange.

What have I given Shelly? Nothing.

"Come on, let's go." Beau smacked me on the upper arm with the back of his hand. "And don't eat all my cookies. Two is plenty."

My movements as sluggish as my mind, I slowly followed my best friend to the kitchen, asking and wondering at the same time, "Hey, what have you gotten out of our relationship, Beau?"

"Oh, you know, some funny cat memes. Some great memories. A Rolex, a house." Beau glanced over his shoulder at me and sent me a grin, adding, "A fishing partner, a pain in my ass, and the best friend a guy could ever ask for."

CHAPTER 32

CHARLOTTE

"It is necessary to the happiness of man that he be mentally faithful to himself. Infidelity does not consist in believing, or in disbelieving, it consists in professing to believe what he does not believe."

— THOMAS PAINE, *THE AGE OF REASON*

—One Month Later—

"*D*id he text?" Beau stood next to me on the front porch of the Winston house, scratching his beard. "He hasn't texted me."

"He did text me. He said he was running late." I checked the screen of my phone again and mumbled, "He just didn't say how late."

Hank was very late. Over an hour late. This wouldn't be a huge deal except he was late for *our* party, the one Sienna and I had been meticulously planning for the last month as a way to inure us all from the scorn of gossipmongers.

We'd been slinking around for weeks, hiding our relationship, meeting up in secret. It had been fun at first, making out like teenagers in Cooper's Field, or renting a hotel room near the Parkway, but now I was just so over it. I wanted to walk down Walnut Street holding his hand without worrying Kimmy wouldn't be invited to a birthday party. I wanted to kiss him under the mistletoe during Christmas and at midnight on New Year's Eve. I wanted to go on a double date with Beau and Shelly, or Jethro and Sienna, or Jackson and Rae, to a restaurant. In public.

All the kids were inside wearing their Halloween costumes, all the Green Valley families had arrived, several of The Pony's exotic dancers had brought their kids along for the fun. The stage was set. And Hank was late.

I didn't want to fret, but I was close to fretting.

He wasn't tired of us, and he wasn't having second thoughts about us, of this I was certain. But a smoldering fear I'd been trying to ignore sparked within me.

He's changed too much, too fast. I've asked for too much. I've expected too much. I've—

"Does he use words when you text him?" Beau bumped my elbow with his, yanking me out of my cascade of doubt.

Frowning, I turned my head to inspect him. "Pardon me?"

"When you text Hank, does he respond with words?" Beau gestured to my phone.

"Uh, yes, words." What would he use other than words?

"That's great." Beau grinned his trademark sunny smile, eyes bright.

Confused, I asked, "It's great?"

"Yeah. If he responds with an actual phone call, or a text message with words, that makes you his favorite person on the planet."

I frowned, still confused. "Wait. What does that mean? He doesn't use words when he texts you?"

"Only rarely," he said, not looking upset about it. "Hank prefers to correspond via text message only, and only with text emojis."

"Text emojis?" My nose scrunched. A gust of late autumn wind lifted my hair from my shoulders and blew it around my face. I reached up and tucked several strands back into place, looking out toward the long driveway leading up to the house. "Wait, you mean those old-school faces made out of text? Like in the early days of the internet?"

"Yep. Text emojis," Beau said. "That's what he uses when we text."

"Huh." I thought about that, twisting my hair and setting it behind my back. This information struck me as totally random, but not necessarily off-putting. Also, why did I not know this? Why had Hank never said anything to me about it?

Turning back to Beau, I allowed him to see my doubt. "Really? No words?"

"If I get actual words from him, then I know it's serious. Otherwise, it's all text emojis all the time."

Okay . . .

Yeah, it was sort of immature, but so was Hank in a lot of ways. So was I. Still. How odd.

"Then I guess—" I bit my thumbnail and peered at my phone, suddenly determined. If text emojis were Hank's love language, then I would learn to speak it. "I guess I'll look some up, see if I can't communicate what I want with just those."

"Good luck." Beau set his hands on his hips. "I gave up. I send him words, he responds with his emojis. I've gotten pretty good at figuring out what he means by now."

Opening my phone's browser, I scrolled through several sites, clicking on a link that looked promising. "Let's see . . ."

Selecting one that was supposed to be a friendly version of *hi*, I copied it and pasted it into the text message screen.

Charlotte: ⊂◉⌣◉⊃"

Not ten seconds later, three dots appeared next to Hank's name.

Hank: ??
Hank: Do you need me to pick something up? I promise I'm almost there
Hank: Sorry I'm so late

I made a soft sound of frustration. "He's answering me in words."

"That's good, though." Beau gave me an encouraging nod. "He only does that with people he really likes."

My lips flattened. "No, I want to see if I can get him to use just text emojis, like he does with you."

He didn't try to hide how perplexing he found my statement. "But . . . why?"

"Because—just—just because." I turned away, unable to explain precisely why I wanted Hank to communicate with me using the same method he used with his best friend. The desire didn't make much sense.

Over the last month, I'd seen firsthand how Hank had morphed from the grumpy —albeit ethical—ne'er-do-well of bygone days into an enthusiastically responsible homebody. He played 'Tea Party' with Sonya and studied maps with Joshua. He helped Kimmy with homework and smashed trucks with Frankie. He did dishes and swept, cleaned toilets and folded laundry. He'd settled into quiet domesticity (which, with four kids, isn't very quiet at all) like a fish taking to water.

Today—him being late—had been the first and only instance where he'd demonstrated any semblance of his previous wayward ways, which was why I felt so on edge about his tardiness.

Honestly, me abruptly latching onto this new information about my boyfriend, wanting to message him using exclusively text emojis, wasn't about Hank. Or Beau. It was about me. I'd been looking for a way to prove to myself I could bend as he'd bent. I could make space for him just the same as he did for me.

I wanted to communicate with Hank on his terms, the way he preferred. As silly as it seemed, and as bizarre as it was searching through random text emoji sites for just the right one, it felt critical in the moment.

Finally, I found a page that had a huge selection, grouped by use and sentiment. I bookmarked it. Singling out the one I wanted, I clicked it to copy and then navigated back to my text messages, trying again.

Charlotte: (○ _ ○)
Hank: ?
Hank: ╮ (.❛ ᴗ ❛.) ╭

"That one means *What's going on?*" Beau said, now hovering behind me and reading over my shoulder. "But like in a *Hey there. Everything okay?* kind of way."

"I see that," I mumbled, switching back to the internet browser and copying a new series of symbols.

Charlotte: ♡˙·ᴥ·˙♡
Charlotte: (~ ͡³ ͡)~
Hank: ⬤ . ⬤
Hank: (¬‿¬)
Hank: (♥ 3♥)

I smiled, warmth coursing through me. This was fun. I loved how much he was able to convey with just symbols. Getting better at switching back and forth between the browser and the text message screen, I quickly sent a response.

Charlotte: ෆ('⬤♪⬤`ෆ)

Beau cleared his throat and I sensed him shift, moving away. "I'll just, uh, give y'all some privacy."

I only half heard him. Hank's response didn't take long.

Hank: (꭛ ᔔ ꭛)
Hank: (•)(•) furu(꭛ ͜ ꭛ ʋ)

I snort-laughed, my thumbs flying over my phone as I searched for an appropriate—or inappropriate—response and grinned like a maniac as I found exactly what I was searching for.

Charlotte: ʄつ ˘ ʖつ ˘ᴗ˘
Hank: …
Hank: ෆ=========∮(⊙_⊙)⋛

My maniacal grin morphed into a self-satisfied one and I powered off my phone, slipping it into my pocket, and turned back to Beau. "Okay, he'll be here soon."

Beau's eyebrows ticked up. "He will?"

"Yep."

"And you used all text emojis?" His mouth curved with a disbelieving smile.

"Yep."

He beamed at me. "Wow, Charlotte. I'm impressed."

I shrugged like it was no big deal while making a mental note to add that *me want your dick* text emoji to my shortcuts.

Feeling Beau's eyes on me, I glanced at him again. He was still looking at me, but his expression had grown abstract, like he wanted to say something but wasn't sure how to start.

"What's up, Beau? You look like you got something to say."

Beau's gaze sharpened in a way that reminded me of his older brother Cletus, startling in its sudden shift from affable to piercing.

I swallowed around an abrupt flaring of nerves.

"After today, after y'all go public and these folks' hands are tied due to Sienna's clout, I reckon many of them are going to issue warnings to Hank." Beau hooked his thumbs in his pants pockets, his friendly tone laced with something sharp. "You know, things like 'Don't hurt Charlotte,' or 'Keep that woman's heart safe.' Stuff like that."

Trying for self-deprecating, I lifted my hands away from my legs and shrugged. "Well, I *am* on the *bless your heart* bingo card."

"That's cute." His smile spread, his eyes narrowed.

I gulped.

"Charlotte."

"Yes?" I squeaked.

"Don't hurt Hank."

I shook my head, a denial on the tip of my tongue.

Beau lifted his hand. "No. I don't want reassurances. Those are just words. I mean it. Don't hurt him. Don't. I will not be happy if you do."

I nodded, intending to say nothing. But then feelings disguised as words simply rushed out. "I will not be happy if I do either, Beau. I don't think I could ever be happy again if I hurt Hank."

Holding Beau's steady stare, I watched as the sharp edge yielded to introspection, then finally warmth. "Good," he said, his grin now entirely sincere. "I'm happy to hear it."

* * *

A petting zoo.

That's why Hank had been late. He'd bought—or borrowed? Or rented?—a whole damn petting zoo for the party. Everyone was wowed, me included. All worries about Hank's tardiness were forgotten.

After his grand entrance, the event had been a huge success. When folks spotted Hank kissing me on the cheek and holding my hand under Sienna's approving and watchful eye, no one dared to bat an eyelash. In fact, we as a couple were invited by JT MacIntyre to sit at his table for the Chamber of Commerce's annual fundraiser. The invite was akin to being dubbed a Diamond of the First Water back in the olden days, except—you know—without the feathers and ball gowns, or queen.

The only person who kept sending us side-eyes had been Cletus Winston.

I was so grateful for all he'd done to help me get the Buckleys to back off. How Cletus had discovered and obtained proof that both Kevin and his father had been hiring prostitutes, I had no idea. Nor did I want to know. But I was glad Cletus had the documents, and the photographs, and the video recordings.

Though he'd never confronted us about the morning we'd utilized his office to—ahem—sort things out, I suspected Cletus guessed that Hank and I had employed the room for more than just talking. Cletus's suspicion delighted Hank to no end. I couldn't feel regret for what happened, but whenever I expressed fleeting guilt about misusing Cletus's workspace, Hank would only laugh and say something like, "Serves him right, sneaky bastard."

The workers Hank had brought along for the zoo had set the whole thing up in an hour, unloading every farm animal under the sun. There was even a pony. Kimmy had been beside herself.

When we got home from the party, she couldn't stop talking about it and—to my horror—even asked Hank if he would buy one for her.

His eyes cut to me, a dangerous-looking—i.e., a *malleable*—expression sliding over his features. "Well, now, let's see—"

"No!" I cut in, covering his mouth with my hand and glaring at Kimmy. "You do not ask Hank or anyone else for a pony."

Kimmy looked pained. "But—but he's got the money!"

I felt Hank's mouth curve into a smile beneath my fingers while I fumed. "Kimberly Dawn Mitchell, that was incredibly rude. Mr. Weller is a friend to our family and asking him for expensive gifts is no way to be a friend. How would you like it if people asked you for expensive gifts all the time? Would you want to be their friend? Or would you feel like they were using you for your bank account?"

My daughter glared at me, but I could see I'd made my point. Her neck flushed hot with embarrassment. Biting her bottom lip, her gaze flickered to Hank's.

With a warning look in his direction, which he'd returned with nothing but wide-eyed innocence, I let my hand fall away.

"I'm sorry, Hank," Kimmy said, and I relaxed at the truly contrite tone she employed. But then she continued, "I—I like you a lot and not just 'cause you're rich."

Now I clapped a hand over my mouth, and my eyes closed. I needed a moment.

Good Lord in heaven, help me with this child.

"Thank you, Kimmy," came Hank's easy response. "I like you a lot too, and not just 'cause you're right-handed."

Peeking one eye open, I looked at Hank.

He lowered to his haunches in front of my daughter, his smile immense in the face of her confused frown. "When you like someone—or express like for someone—for something they didn't necessarily choose or value, it doesn't make them feel good about themselves. You can't help that you were born right-handed. I could probably help being rich, but it's not something I'm proud of. It's not something I particularly like about myself, definitely not compared to the other things I work on and value."

"What do you work on?" she asked, sounding honestly curious.

"Recently? Being patient." He tilted his head back and forth, considering the question. "My jokes. Being open. Fishing. Giving without expecting anything in return."

Oh my heart.

"Your jokes are funny, and you are good at fishing. I like that about you, too," she said softly, tentatively, the words a peace offering.

I blinked against the stinging behind my eyes. Goodness, I was turning into a watering pot, the moments between my wobbly chins growing shorter and shorter. It seemed like every time Hank and the kids were together, they ultimately did something wonderful that tenderized my poor heart.

"Thank you," he said graciously. "And I like how clever you are, how smart. And how good you are at telling stories."

Kimmy pressed her lips together and I recognized it as the face she made when she didn't want to smile but was in serious danger of doing so.

"I'm hungry!" Joshua's wail sounded from the kitchen. A moment later, he appeared, leading Frankie by the hand, a pathetic look on his face while Frankie clutched at his stomach mournfully.

"What's for dinner?" Joshua asked.

"We just ate at the party." I frowned at my pitiful babies. "That was—"

"Hours ago," Hank said, giving me an amused smile. "It's not too late, we could order something?"

"Fine. Fine." I pulled out my phone. "All y'all go get ready for bed. Hank and I will order something, but you're not eating until you're in your PJs."

"Yay!" The kids scattered.

Hank called after my sons' departing backs, "Y'all need baths! Joshua, help your brother."

"Okay!" came Joshua's reply, and I could just make out him say to Frankie, "You want to play battleship and sink some boats?"

Hank turned to me. He looked exhausted but happy. I imagined I looked just the same.

I winked at him. "You did good today, Mr. Weller."

"Thank you, Ms. Mitchell." His eyes twinkled at me. I knew if we'd been alone, he'd pull me in for a breath-stealing kiss. But we weren't alone, so he didn't. "Sorry I was late."

"No. Don't worry about it. Everything worked out perfectly." I woke up my phone and navigated to the food ordering app. "I think your petting zoo made every kid in Green Valley fall head over heels for you. What do you like on your pizza?"

He didn't respond.

I glanced at Hank just to find him looking at me with the most curious expression —dazed, caught, like I'd asked him to tell me his political affiliation rather than what he wanted on his pizza.

"Hank?"

"Pizza?" he croaked. "You want to share a pizza? With me?"

My spine straightened at the mystery of his shift in demeanor. "Yes. Pizza."

He cleared his throat. "I like everything. I'll—uh—share whatever y'all want." His voice was still a little scratchy.

"Are you okay?" I inspected him. "You're not getting sick, are you?"

"No, no. I'm not sick." He cleared his throat again and glanced around, presumably searching for any nearby kids. He then stepped close and kissed my temple before leaning back. "It's just . . . I haven't had pizza in a long time."

"Do you not like pizza?" I navigated back to the search screen. "We could have burgers instead. Or—"

"Pizza," he said firmly, something in his tone drawing my attention. Hank wore an odd smile, and his eyes were a bit glassy. "I can't think of anything I'd love more than to share a pizza with all of you."

I folded my arms over my abruptly fluttering heart. Why it had chosen this moment to flutter, I had no idea.

Trying to lighten the inexplicably serious mood, I teased, "Really? Nothing you'd love more? You can't think of a single thing you want more than pizza?"

It didn't work. His gaze grew more intent, his chest rising and falling with bracing breaths.

I held very still. Something was happening, or about to happen, or had happened. I felt it, and so I braced myself.

"Charlotte," he said, staring at me.

"Yes?"

"I love you."

I blinked, my lips parting as the words rushed through me. But they didn't rock my world, though. I'd figured as much already.

I mean, we hadn't discussed our feelings much since that morning I'd been sick and he'd taken care of me, both of us seemingly taking for granted that we were in this for the long haul. He loved me, and I loved him, and we both loved the kids, and we were figuring things out.

At least that's what I'd assumed.

"Charlotte." He said my name in that way of his, making it sound like a pained plea. "Please. Say something."

"Hank, I—" I shook my head, wondering what the big deal was. "If I'd known ordering pizza would make you love me, I would've ordered it a month ago."

A laugh erupted out of him, but his eyes narrowed. He reached for me. "You are hilarious."

"And you love that about me," I said, grinning, wanting to kiss his face off.

"I do," he said, and that's when I detected the reluctant vulnerability in him, the steadying shade to his eyes.

My heart fluttered again, twisting for this absolutely stunning soul, who I loved so much, and who . . . *Wait a darn minute.*

I gasped. "You think you love me and I don't love you!"

His mouth flattened. "Well, I'm the only one who's said it, Charlotte. What am I supposed to think?"

"I'm—I'm insulted!" I pushed out of his hold, dropped my voice to a harsh whisper, and jutted out my chin. "How dare you think I don't love you. I love you, you stubborn, lovely man. I've loved you this whole time. How could I not? The way you obviously love my children, the way you're always here—right here—for me when I need you, your sexy-wizardry smirks, your intelligence, your heart, your patience, the orgasms—THE ORGASMS! Hank, you make it unbearable for me to do anything else but love you. I have no choice!"

By the time I'd finished my whispered rant, a massive grin had absorbed his whole face. Hank's eyes shone brightly and caressed my face lovingly.

"I love you," he said again, this time without any trace of his earlier reservations. "And for the record, you also make it unbearable for me to do anything else but love you."

"Good." I nodded firmly. "Because I love you."

He reached for me again, pulling me close, his gaze on my lips. "And I love you."

I angled my chin, ready to receive his kiss, when a loud, "Moooooooooooom!" detonated from someplace behind Hank.

We jumped apart and twisted around, searching. Sonya appeared a moment later, rubbing her eye and looking sleepy. "Can someone lay me down?" she asked around a yawn.

"Don't you want pizza?" Hank asked, scooping her up. "We're just about to order it."

Sonya cupped his face with her little hand. "I'm tired. Can I have it for breakfast?"

I opened my mouth to respond, but before I could, Hank turned and walked Sonya toward the back hallway, saying, "Of course. I'll save you some. What book are we reading tonight?"

"*A Wrinkle in Time*," she said, her head falling to rest on his shoulder. "Will you do the voices?"

I clutched my heart, my eyes stinging once again, my emotions rooting me in place as I watched and listened to them go.

"I always do the voices," he said. A moment later, I heard him ask, "Hey, did you brush your teeth?"

Staring at the spot where they'd disappeared together, I waited until the urge to cry passed.

One day, I hoped Hank would carry Sonya off to bed, or teach Kimmy a lesson about friendship, or read the newspaper with Joshua, or toss Frankie in the air to make him laugh, and it wouldn't pull tears out of me. But for now and for the foreseeable future, I rejoiced in the wonder.

I basked in the feeling of falling more deeply in love with this man every time he was simply himself.

EPILOGUE

HANK

"Every individual has a place to fill in the world and is important in some respect, whether he chooses to be so or not."

— NATHANIEL HAWTHORNE

—Many Years Later—

"Have you seen Tommy?" Pasting on my best impression of innocent ignorance, I shrugged and asked a question instead of lying. "Did you check the boys' hotel room?"

Kimmy leaned her hip against the doorframe, her body half-in, half-out of the suite and mostly hidden by the door. "Momma said he was probably with you. We haven't seen him and he's the only one who doesn't have on his suit."

"How do you know he doesn't have his suit on if you haven't seen him? I'm sure it'll be fine." *It better be fine.* "I didn't see you for breakfast. Why don't you come in and eat?"

"I skipped breakfast. What's all this?" She abandoned her post by the door and marched into the room. The bathrobe she wore, which was tied at the front, swished around her ankles. Hands on her hips, Kimmy's blue eyes swept over the long table. "You ordered pizza?"

Over the years, I'd split many pizzas with my kids. I'd split so many pizzas, you'd think by now I would be tired of pizza.

I wasn't. Most of my happiest memories involved pizza.

"Yeah." I grinned. "Hungry?"

Kimmy's expression flattened. "Dad, the reception is in three hours. You know they're feeding us. You paid for it."

"But . . ." I swept my arms toward the table, hoping to entice her. "Pizza."

Charlotte and I served pizza at our wedding reception. The day I'd officially adopted Kimmy, Joshua, Sonya, and Frankie, we'd had a big pizza party. When Charlotte came home from the hospital with Tommy—our youngest—Kimmy had made homemade pizza for everyone.

We ate pizza the day after Christmas every year, after every big game or school play, every graduation, every time we moved someone into a dorm room, and every time we moved someone out of a dorm room.

And when Sonya had introduced us to Alessandro last year, the fella she was about to marry today, we'd met them at a pizza restaurant.

Kimmy—a grown-ass woman with a few Ivy League degrees under her belt, a string of broken hearts in her wake—wrinkled her nose at me like she used to do when she was eight. "Why are you always ordering pizza? Whenever we do anything, you're ordering pizza."

I stood straighter, smoothing a hand down my suit front.

I liked pizza. I liked that I knew precisely what each of my kids wanted on their pizza and what they'd pick off it when I insisted we all share.

Kimmy wanted spicy sausage, pepperoni, and bacon; Joshua liked the simplicity of tomato and basil; Sonya preferred mushrooms, onions, and olives; Frankie ate everything, he didn't care as long as it was food; and Tommy had a taste for feta cheese, tomato, and spinach.

But I wasn't going to tell her *that*.

So I said, "Because it's delicious. And it's a family tradition. And I said so."

Kimmy's eyes narrowed. I narrowed mine right back until we were both squinty-smiling at each other.

Our wonderful moment was interrupted by Frankie barreling through the door and shouting, "We got it!" His arms raised in the air in a victory pose.

Kimmy turned and faced her brothers as they bolted into the room, but then stopped short upon seeing their sister.

"Got what?" she asked.

I made a slicing motion across my neck and bared my teeth at the boys.

Both Frankie and Joshua rocked back on their heels once they realized their error, attention darting between me and Kimmy.

"Uh . . ." Joshua shoved his hands in his pockets, his shifty green eyes a travesty to con artists and fibbers everywhere. "We . . . got . . . drinks."

I closed my eyes, my forehead falling to my hand. They weren't holding any drinks. What a pitiful cover story. Had they not learned anything from their father? How had I failed them so spectacularly?

"Yes. Drinks. For pizza. For going with the pizza."

I peeked at my boys through my fingers.

Frankie, towering over us all at six-foot-five-inches, lifted his giant hand toward the table. "Obviously."

Our oldest daughter's pointed index finger moved between her brothers. "What's going on here?"

"Nothing," the three of us chorused in unison.

My hand dropped back to my thigh. *Damn.* Real smooth. *Not suspicious at all.*

Crossing her arms, Kimmy faced me. "*Dad?*"

"Daughter."

Her mouth twitched, but she didn't smile. "Does this have anything to do with your missing child?"

"Tommy isn't missing," Joshua volunteered, earning him four eyeballs of ire from me and Frankie.

"Come on! Just tell me what's happening." Kimmy heaved a dramatic sigh. "All of you are supposed to be in your suits and over at the church in an hour. Nanna and Alessandro's momma are whipping each other into a frenzy because no one has seen Tommy, and momma is trying to get her hair done but spent the morning calming them down instead."

A pang of guilt made me grimace. I didn't know that. When Charlotte left earlier to get her hair done, it didn't occur to me that she'd be plagued by the wedding witches.

My sons looked to me for direction, their mouths clamped shut, waiting to follow my lead. I wavered.

On the one hand, I'd kept Sonya out of the loop for obvious reasons—she didn't need her baby brother ruining her big day. Kimmy and Charlotte had been kept out of it. The less people who had to cover for Tommy the better.

On the other hand, Kimmy didn't mind lying. This wasn't a reason to tell her, per se, but it did mean we could trust her not to spill the coffee beans before the ceremony, which was more than I could say for my youngest.

"Fine," I sighed, pushing a hand through my hair and then scratching my salt and pepper beard—still more pepper than salt. "Here's what happened. Tommy woke up late, which— whatever, we're on vacation. But then he put on his suit first thing. When he came out here for breakfast, he wasn't watching himself and spilled coffee all over the front."

Kimmy grimaced, and then she grinned, and then she laughed, her expressions a whole damn journey. "All over the white suit? Really?"

"Yes," I confirmed. "All over his white, custom-made, Italian suit."

Joshua also chuckled. "You should've seen his face. He was strutting around, acting like we all did at fifteen, thinking he was hot shit and sweet potato pie."

"And then he picked up a coffee cup as a prop." Frankie, also laughing 'cause he'd been there with me and Joshua when it happened, mimed Tommy picking up the cup, his pinky out. Then he mimed Tommy setting the full cup down too hard and the contents splashing everywhere, Tommy freaking out, knocking the cup over, and spilling it down the front of his pure white—not eggshell, not steam, not cloud, and not fucking ecru either—suit.

All three of my kids were in stitches after Frankie had finished his hilarious pantomime. Despite the stress of the situation, I chuckled, too, and shook my head at their antics. They always made me laugh.

"But we found a new suit," Joshua said, wiping at his eyes. "It's not white, but it fits."

"It fits?" Kimmy, also wiping her eyes, looked to me.

I shrugged again. "Don't look at me. I've been ordering pizza. I'm not the one who found the suit."

"He tried it on and it fits. It's black, so he'll match the rest of us." Frankie pulled the credit card I'd loaned them from his breast pocket and held it out to me. "We bought a white suit shirt and tie from the shop downstairs, too. And an undershirt. He's all set."

"Alessandro's mom is going to be pissed." Kimmy rubbed her hands together, a mischievous smile on her pretty face. "So will Nanna."

"Kimmy," I warned. "Don't be mean to Alessandro's momma. She's stressed. It's a big day for her, her only son getting married."

"But it's not her wedding," Joshua grumbled. "It's Sonya and Alessandro's wedding, and she just took over and then made you and momma pay for it. Sonya doesn't care what color our suits are."

"I know, I know." I lifted my hands to pacify them, playing my part as arbitrator. Even though I'd taken a fair amount of glee in telling Mrs. Calbrini that I used to run a strip club, and that's how Charlotte and I had gotten together—*and then I watched all the blood drain from her face*—I'd learned enough about adulting over the years to know keeping the peace was important. These people were Sonya's in-laws, or would be soon, and making their lives difficult would just make Sonya's life unbearable.

Sonya was precious to me, to all of us, and Alessandro was a decent fella. No one would ever be good enough for any of my kids, but he'd come pretty darn close.

"Where is he?" I directed my question to Joshua while accepting the credit card Frankie held out. "Still sulking?"

"He really loved that white suit," Joshua said, his tone not quite managing to sound sympathetic.

Kimmy snorted inelegantly and marched toward the door. "I'll go tell Nanna I found him and he'll be ready in an hour."

"What will you tell her about the suit?" Frankie asked, moseying over to the table and lifting the lid on one of the pizza boxes.

"I'm not telling her anything." She opened the door, pausing and looking over her shoulder to add, "They'll find out when he walks down the aisle with the rest of the groomsmen. It was a ridiculous idea, having him in all white as a junior groomsman. That boy is accident-prone."

I took a step toward her. "Wait. Will you be back to share pizza?"

Kimmy's gaze shifted to mine and seemed to soften. "Of course, Dad. I'll be back when I have my dress on. I hope someone brought an apron for me."

"'Course we brought you an apron. We wouldn't want your yellow ball gown to get dirty." Frankie winked at his sister, tugging at the cuff of his suit. Thank God it wasn't Frankie's suit that got damaged, we'd never find a replacement big enough.

"It's flaxen lemon, and it's not a ball gown," Kimmy grumbled. "It's a mantua."

With that proclamation, she shut the door, leaving us.

"What's a mantua?" Frankie picked up a whole pizza box and carried it to a clear spot. Placing it on the table in front of him, he sat, opened the lid, and dug in. This was not unusual. He'd stopped sharing pizzas and started eating his own extra-large years ago, as soon as he'd started playing ball in high school.

Joshua's gaze turned introspective and he drifted closer to the table. "If memory serves, it's a gown in the French style. You know Marie Antoinette?"

"Yeah," Frankie answered around his bite of pizza, which was basically half of a whole slice.

"The dresses she wore—you know, with the draping of the skirt and such—that's a mantua."

"Oh. Like Belle in *Beauty and the Beast*," Frankie said, finishing the first slice with his second bite.

"You two keep a low profile? Or did you see anyone downstairs?" I grabbed a plate and opened a random box, finding Kimmy's favorite inside.

"We saw Uncle Beau and one of his brothers. Aunt Shelly wasn't around, though." Joshua waited until I'd finished serving myself before shuffling through the boxes to find his preferred toppings.

"That's okay, they're staying the week and going fishing with us tomorrow." I claimed the seat across from Frankie. "Plenty of time to catch up."

Beau and Shelly had been lifesavers for Charlotte and me. They'd basically been a second set of parents for our entire brood, frequently came along with us on vacations, and were Tommy's godparents.

That's right, Tommy—unlike his old man—had been baptized.

"Anyone else see you? I don't want word getting back to your nanna about the suit."

"Let's see." Joshua scratched his short, dark beard. He'd done a good job of trimming it, must've been using the clippers and straight razor I'd sent him for his birthday. "We saw Jackson and Rae, but only in passing. Ms. Melanie and her husband, cousin Heather and Brian, the Hills."

"You saw Heather?" I asked, the slice of pizza halted halfway to my mouth. "I didn't know she and Brian were coming."

Charlotte's cousin Heather, who I reckoned I should credit for bringing us together in a roundabout way, had served her two years in a Florida jail and then went on to graduate from college with a bachelor's and master's in psychology. Last I'd talked to her, she was working as a drug counselor at a facility in south Florida. Her husband seemed to be a nice enough guy but a bit too straight-laced for my taste. Some sort of accountant or actuary or something.

"They were in the gift shop buying shampoo. She said hers exploded on the plane." Frankie made a face as he chewed. "Same thing happened to me last year when they flew us out for the Rose Bowl. I'll never pack shampoo next to my underwear again."

Joshua leaned an elbow on the table and turned to his brother. "All you gotta do is put the bottles in a plastic bag. It's the pressure change that does it."

Frankie opened his mouth, but whatever he was about to say was cut off by the suite door flying open. We all turned in unison and I stood on instinct.

Charlotte, looking like an absolute knockout in a bathrobe similar to Kimmy's, dispatched a stormy look in our direction. "I passed Kimmy in the hall. She told me what happened with Tommy's suit." Walking further into the room, she crossed her arms. "Why didn't y'all tell me?"

Kimmy! That's the last time I tell her the truth.

Before I could answer, Joshua piped in, "Momma, I'm sorry, but you're terrible at keeping secrets. If Nanna and Mrs. Calbrini found out before the ceremony, they'd run around here, acting like the sky was falling. Now they'll find out at the ceremony when it's too late to do anything about it. It's a solid plan."

The love of my life made a scoffing sound. "I keep secrets."

Frankie and Joshua glanced at each other and then laughed.

"You can't lie, Momma." Frankie tore into another slice of pizza, shaking his head. "You're the worst liar."

Her head moved back an inch on her neck and her assessing green gaze swung to me. "I try not to lie, but I do keep secrets. What about when you were kids, when Hank and I were dating? I kept that secret from all of you until we were sure you were ready to hear it. See?"

"Come on." Joshua wiped his hands on a napkin. "We all knew you were never 'just friends.' We knew you were together. Y'all thought you were so sneaky, keeping it from us kids, but we knew."

"I—I—what?" Charlotte's arms dropped, her mouth hanging open.

"All that kissing in closets, you should've just saved yourself the trouble and told us from the get-go. And when you sat us down and wanted to know what we thought about y'all being together? Remember that? We knew the whole time." Joshua sighed.

"You did?" I asked.

"Of course we did." Frankie, who'd been only four when we'd sat them down, smirked at his momma. "Kimmy used to tell us to be quiet about it and let y'all tell us in your own time. She didn't want to rush you."

"Kimmy did that?" Charlotte's eyes landed on me, her gaze probing.

I shrugged for the third time in less than a half hour, finding these versions of events just as surprising as she seemed to.

"Your problem is you trust too easy, Momma. You take folks at face value. You shouldn't do that," Joshua said pragmatically, and I fought an eye roll. He did the exact same thing. Not to the same extent as his mother, but he trusted more than was wise. One day, someone would break that trusting heart of his. I just hoped it wouldn't turn him bitter.

"Well." Charlotte's arms dropped. "I'm—you all—you should have told me. I'm hurt and—and upset." Charlotte's voice broke, making the fine hairs on the back of my neck raise.

Before I could cross to her, she darted into the bedroom, apparently taking my heart with her based on the intensity of the ache in my chest. *Damn it.*

Grimacing, I glared at the boys. "You two need to be nicer to your momma. She does so much for you and picking on her ain't how you get to heaven."

Looking abashed, my sons shared a look and ducked their heads. I turned toward the bedroom, but then turned back suddenly, needing to say one more thing.

"Your momma is trusting, but she's not the problem here. The problem isn't the people who trust, the problem is the people who are untrustworthy. It shouldn't be on your mother to change something about herself that's good and pure-hearted. The world needs to change, not her."

Joshua swallowed thickly and nodded once. "Sorry."

Frankie said nothing, just gave me a contrite head nod, so Joshua smacked the back of his head.

"Oh. Yeah. Sorry, Dad." Frankie rubbed his neck. "We'll apologize later."

"You better." I backed up toward the bedroom, giving them my serious-business face. "Dance with her at the wedding, that'll make it up."

"Okay," they said, munching on their pizza with less enthusiasm.

Rounding the corner for the hall, I sighed and mentally prepared an apology. I knew after this many years married to the woman and her tender heart, she'd expect an apology from me. Obviously, I didn't like seeing Charlotte upset and I never wanted to see her hurt. Her tears were like little drops of acid raining on my brain, making me feel desolate.

That said, after I'd promise her the moon and then deliver it, she'd settle down, work through her disappointment, and we usually ended up having make-up sex.

So . . .

"Charlotte?" I knocked on the door lightly. "Can I come in?"

"Yes," she said, her voice sounding tight.

I frowned, prepared to offer her another moon, and gathered a deep breath.

I then opened the door. "Angel, I'm so sorry . . ."

I blinked, and that's all I could do because my wife did not look upset. She looked sexy as fuck and I hastily shut the door behind me, my eyes moving over the burgundy bra and panty set, the matching thigh-highs, and the spiked heels encasing her feet.

"Hank," she said, using her temptress voice.

I responded with the only word in my brain. "Wife."

Her slow smile had me locking the door behind me.

Not knowing where to look, I looked everywhere. "I'm here to apologize."

"What for?"

"Whatever you need me to apologize for, just as long as it increases my chances of getting laid in the next"—I glanced at my watch—"forty-five minutes."

She laughed, venturing closer but not close enough. "And I can't keep secrets? I had y'all fooled. That'll teach them to underestimate their mother. I still got it going on. Ha!"

"So you're . . . not upset? About Tommy and his suit?"

"No." She made it to where I stood and gripped my tie. She then walked backward until her legs connected with the console table along the wall. "Putting a fifteen-year-old in an all-white suit was a terrible idea."

"But you're not mad we kept it from you? What happened?"

Mesmerized, as usual, I didn't notice she'd unbuckled my pants until they were already undone. She reached inside, stroking me through my boxer briefs, sending my heart racing and white-hot heat straight to the base of my spine.

Jesus. I loved my wife.

I sucked in a breath and grabbed her waist, holding on for balance, loving the feel of her bare skin.

Charlotte's shoulders lifted, her palm hot friction against my cock, making me wild. "I don't like being told I'm bad at something—like keeping secrets." She nipped at my bottom lip, her voice barely a whisper. "But I trust that you had a good reason for not telling me."

Staring down at my beautiful wife, who'd just spent several hours having her makeup and hair done, I fought the desire to mess it all up. She looked gorgeous like this, but she looked unbelievably stunning when she was hot and flushed, her lipstick smeared, hair tumbling over her shoulders and breasts in chaotic disarray.

"Where can I touch you?" Stepping between her legs, I encouraged her to sit back on the table and spread her legs so I could hook my thumb into the lace covering her. "Can I kiss you?"

She shook her head, smiling, looking like the meanest tease. "Not on my lips."

Pushing two fingers inside and pumping roughly—just the way she liked—I watched with satisfaction as her eyes drifted shut and her lips parted with a silent gasp.

Bending forward and caging her in, I placed a gentle kiss on her neck, then whispered in her ear, "Can I fuck you, angel? Would you like that?"

Her exhale was shaky and her hand faltered where she stroked me, but I felt her head nod just before she said, "Yes."

My hand stilled. "Yes, what?"

"Yes, please, Hank!" she whimpered.

I grinned.

Good enough for me.

* * *

By some miracle of modern makeup and hairspray science, Charlotte looked perfectly put together when we emerged from the bedroom forty-three minutes later. In fact, we both did.

Relaxed and in an exceptionally good mood, I almost forget to be nervous until Charlotte reminded me we'd be swinging by Sonya's hotel room for a few pictures before we escorted her to the church. My heart tripped, rising then falling, and suddenly I couldn't inhale deeply enough. This was it.

In less than an hour, I'd be expected to walk her down the aisle and leave her in the care of someone else.

Nope. Don't like that.

Numbly, I entered Sonya's room behind Charlotte, tangentially aware of the women's squeals and sighs of delight.

"Momma, you've already seen me in this dress when we picked it out," Sonya said, giving her mother a patient look.

"I know, I know." Charlotte wiped at her eyes, her tone watery. "Goodness, I can't cry. I'll mess up my makeup," she said, but then her face crumpled.

Still in a bit of a haze, I automatically withdrew my handkerchief and passed it to my wife, lifting my chin toward the bathroom. I didn't trust my voice.

Though I didn't have any makeup on to mess up, and though my eyes were currently dry, I somehow knew and accepted that the moment I opened my mouth, I was going to cry.

Sonya and I watched Charlotte walk to the bathroom, then my daughter turned back to me, a gentle smile on her mouth and behind her eyes.

"How're you doing, Mr. Hank? You hanging in there?"

Even though she introduced me as her father, and when the kids were together she referred to me as *Dad*, when it was just the two of us, she still called me Mr. Hank.

I nodded, struggling to make my mouth curve. I finally forced it into some semblance of a smile.

"How do I look?" she asked, stepping back and glancing down at her dress.

Bracing, I allowed myself to take a look at her, this woman before me who I used to scoop up and carry around the house, who used to ride piggyback while I made dinner, who always asked me to do character voices for every book we read, who I'd fallen in love with from the very first moment I laid eyes on her.

Because I had. With Sonya, and Joshua, and Kimmy, and Frankie, it had been love at first sight. And with Tommy, too—*the little shit*. The very moment he'd emerged from Charlotte's womb, kicking and screaming and throwing a fuss, I'd loved him just the same.

"So?" Sonya prompted, lifting her arms slightly away from her sides. "What do you think?"

I cleared my throat and managed to force out, "You look lovely, Sonya."

She beamed at me and reached out her hand. I took it and tucked it in the crook of my elbow, covered it with my other hand, and wondered how I was supposed to let her go when the time came. It seemed impossible, unfathomable, incomprehensible.

I'd never let her go, I'd never let any of them go. They were mine, and I was keeping them. *And I belong to them, whether they like it or not.*

Surprising me out of my stubbornly determined thoughts, Sonya rested her temple on my shoulder. "Thank you, Mr. Hank," she whispered. "Thank you so much."

Holding perfectly still, I asked, "For what?" my voice sandpaper.

"For walking me down the aisle today," she said, squeezing my arm. "For being my dad."

The End

Scan me to receive new book updates and news from Penny!

Scan me if you'd like a signed copy of this or any Penny Reid book!

AUTHOR'S NOTE

The kids
Like all the adults I write, the kids in this book are based on real people, their dialogue directly lifted from conversations I've heard and transcribed both in preparation for this book and just because. (Yes, I do transcribe real-life conversations that I find enchanting, especially when my own kids are speaking. I'd like to hold on to those memories.)

Parts of Joshua are based on my son, who also liked to read *The Economist* at age seven (he started at six before he could actually read, studying the charts and graphs). He still reads it (at fifteen), but now he's made efforts to diversify his news sources. Similarly, he's acquired an appreciation for cartoons as he's grown older, though he eschewed them as a young child.

Like Joshua, my son always had difficulty finding other people his age who wanted to play the games he played or shared his interests—ancient civilizations, etymology / the history of language, the philosophy of governance, physics (especially the subatomic realm)—and my worries about him "fitting in" and "finding his people" still persist today (I guess Charlotte in this one regard is based on me).

Regarding The Pink Pony, strip clubs, laws, ordinances, lap dances, and so forth
Creative license was taken with what activities were and were not allowed at The Pink Pony based on local and state laws in Tennessee.

While living in Tampa, I personally knew a number of exotic dancers—many were college/post-grad students. I was always fascinated by their stories and experiences. Reality had to be altered in fictional-Tennessee for the purposes of this book so I could tell some of these stories and perspectives. Thus, I made it different because I wanted to create the ideal strip club, if such a thing were to exist. A place where the owner focused on keeping everything safe and fun rather than the other end of the spectrum, i.e., dangerous and exploitative.

Green Valley exists in a fictional county somewhere between Blount and Monroe counties in Tennessee. The laws and ordinances controlling strip clubs, nudity, and the serving of alcohol are not the same as Blount and Monroe because I say so.

I am fully aware that the "City of Knoxville passed a licensing ordinance in May 2005 that prohibited total nudity and touching by patrons, prohibited alcohol on the premises, limited the businesses' hours of operations, and required the businesses and their employees to obtain licenses." [The Free Speech Center, MTSU, July 2021] See also the Adult Oriented Establishment Act of 1998 [https://law.justia.com/codes/tennessee/2014/title-7/local/chapter-51/part-11]

This means counties in Tennessee mandate that dancers must be several feet from patrons at all times (no lap dances) and no alcohol can be served on the premises (no need for a bartender).

These types of laws and ordinances have been upheld in Tennessee time and time again despite "adult business owners" and entertainers suing, claiming the ordinances/laws violate free speech, etc.

SIDE NOTE

I put *adult business owners* in quotes above because I personally feel like the term "adult business owners" should refer to individuals who own home remodeling stores, appliance stores, and retirement portfolio / financial advisers—not strip club owners. If I tell my children that my husband and I are having an 'adult conversation,' it's typically because we're discussing how to pay for a new water heater, not how to dance mostly naked and maximize tips while serving alcohol . . . but that's just us. To each their own.

END SIDE NOTE

One term I came across often while researching this book was "secondary effects" relating to strip clubs and other adult/sex businesses. Secondary effects basically means negative impact to a geographic area—e.g., increase in crime, decrease in property value—due to proximity to any particular business. Pawn shops, strip clubs, adult bookstores, even dollar stores have all been accused of being businesses that generate secondary effects and are therefore subject to stricter zoning laws (not everywhere in the USA, but during my research, the number of incidences/mentions felt like more than an outlier).

In summary, yes. I know Tennessee law prohibits many of the activities that occurred in this book. But I am a writer of fiction and I spent my twenties in Tampa, Florida, where the strip club laws are *SIGNIFICANTLY* less stringent. One might even make the argument that Tampa has "better" strip clubs than Vegas. (Define "better" for yourself . . . if you know what I mean.) I'm the writer, this is my world, I get to decide.

Moving on.

A note about Hank

I can and do write flawed romance heroes and heroines. My protagonists have been known to be violent, liars, selfish, ignorant, sneaky, stubborn, cowardly, reckless, feckless, and so forth—just like real people. I don't write ideal people; I don't know how because I find them boring to both write and read. That said, like all real people, my characters also live in their own little bubble of day-to-day concerns and worries. They make mistakes, can't concern themselves with every evil occurring in the world (sorry, but that's impossible; none of us are Wonder Woman, none of us are Superman), but—I hope—my characters are always doing their best to not cause harm within their bubble.

The only exception to this is Cletus Winston, and if you've read his books then you know what I mean. But I digress.

This is all to say, in order to write a strip club owner, I had to write someone who owned the club for reasons other than the enjoyment of holding power over desperate women/men/people and exploiting them. Based on my (admittedly limited) interactions with strip club owners, all of whom were male, it always felt like they wanted to own the club so they could be in proximity to women who couldn't refuse their whims, and that made me feel sick. Again, this is my limited experience and not meant to be a sweeping statement. Obviously, not all club owners are of this ilk. #NotAllStripClubOwners

Hank obviously isn't.

If I'd written Hank to be like my perception of the club owners I've met and interviewed, he wouldn't be a flawed character, Hank would be an irredeemable character. A villain. People in Green Valley see Hank as a villain because they assume he must exploit the women who work for him.

In order for Hank to be a "hero," I felt that the core motivation for his character had to be creating a home for the desperate because he had once been desperate. He created a place for people who society had abandoned or never cared about in the first place, making it safe and profitable, teaching them how to create and hold firm boundaries for those who would exploit them, so they didn't have to be desperate, so they could make money and take control of their own futures.

A clear flaw (to me) in Hank is that he starts the book with an "eat or be eaten" mentality. As I mentioned above, he teaches his dancers to exploit rather than be exploited. This is not ideal (or good), but Hank doesn't care about being good, he only cares about being fair (at the start of the book). Like Hank or hate Hank, I understand his logic. I may not agree with it, but I understand it. He's someone who takes perverse delight in leveling the playing field through rebellious acts because he understands that being good and being fair are often opposed to each other, and he values fairness above all else.

Which was why I felt he was the perfect partner for Charlotte.

Charlotte

Charlotte is based on a number of real people. There exist plenty of individuals in this world who have made a poor choice when choosing a spouse, marrying in a haze of infatuation and being too immature to understand the difference between passion, excitement, lust, and enduring love. It's an honest mistake, and I believe we should be compassionate toward individuals who find themselves in this situation rather than revile or judge them. I'm guessing that Charlotte drove you a little crazy at times, but as long as she felt realistic—like a real person, making real choices and real mistakes—then I consider my job done.

Like these real people I know, Charlotte is so concerned with being good *now*, being a better person, more responsible, and less selfish than the teenage version who ended up making poor decisions, that she often treats herself unfairly, ending up with the short end of the stick. She's not a pushover, she stands up for herself, but she (like all of us) has no control over the decisions of others.

Thanks for reading my weirdo stories. Until next time!
    <3 Penny

ABOUT THE AUTHOR

Penny Reid is the *New York Times*, *Wall Street Journal*, and *USA Today* bestselling author of the Winston Brothers and Knitting in the City series. She used to spend her days writing federal grant proposals as a biomedical researcher, but now she writes kissing books. Penny is an obsessive knitter and manages the #OwnVoices-focused mentorship incubator / publishing imprint, Smartypants Romance. She lives in Seattle Washington with her husband, three kids, and dog named Hazel.

Come find me -
Mailing List: http://pennyreid.ninja/newsletter/
Goodreads: http://www.goodreads.com/ReidRomance
Facebook: www.facebook.com/pennyreidwriter
Instagram: www.instagram.com/reidromance
Twitter: www.twitter.com/reidromance
TikTok: https://www.tiktok.com/@authorpennyreid
Patreon: https://www.patreon.com/smartypantsromance
Email: pennreid@gmail.com …hey, you! Email me ;-)

OTHER BOOKS BY PENNY REID

Knitting in the City Series
(Interconnected Standalones, Adult Contemporary Romantic Comedy)
Neanderthal Seeks Human: A Smart Romance (#1)
Neanderthal Marries Human: A Smarter Romance (#1.5)
Friends without Benefits: An Unrequited Romance (#2)
Love Hacked: A Reluctant Romance (#3)
Beauty and the Mustache: A Philosophical Romance (#4)
Ninja at First Sight (#4.75)
Happily Ever Ninja: A Married Romance (#5)
Dating-ish: A Humanoid Romance (#6)
Marriage of Inconvenience: (#7)
Neanderthal Seeks Extra Yarns (#8)
Knitting in the City Coloring Book (#9)

Winston Brothers Series
(Interconnected Standalones, Adult Contemporary Romantic Comedy, spinoff of Beauty and the Mustache)
Beauty and the Mustache (#0.5)
Truth or Beard (#1)
Grin and Beard It (#2)
Beard Science (#3)
Beard in Mind (#4)
Beard In Hiding (#4.5)
Dr. Strange Beard (#5)
Beard with Me (#6)
Beard Necessities (#7)
Winston Brothers Paper Doll Book (#8)

Hypothesis Series

(New Adult Romantic Comedy Trilogies)

Elements of Chemistry: ATTRACTION, HEAT, and CAPTURE (#1)

Laws of Physics: MOTION, SPACE, and TIME (#2)

Irish Players (Rugby) Series – by L.H. Cosway and Penny Reid

(Interconnected Standalones, Adult Contemporary Sports Romance)

The Hooker and the Hermit (#1)

The Pixie and the Player (#2)

The Cad and the Co-ed (#3)

The Varlet and the Voyeur (#4)

Dear Professor Series

(New Adult Romantic Comedy)

Kissing Tolstoy (#1)

Kissing Galileo (#2)

Ideal Man Series

(Interconnected Standalones, Adult Contemporary Romance Series of Jane Austen Reimaginings)

Pride and Dad Jokes (#1, coming 2023)

Man Buns and Sensibility (#2, TBD)

Sense and Manscaping (#3, TBD)

Persuasion and Man Hands (#4, TBD)

Mantuary Abbey (#5, TBD)

Mancave Park (#6, TBD)

Emmanuel (#7, TBD)

Handcrafted Mysteries Series

(A Romantic Cozy Mystery Series, spinoff of *The Winston Brothers Series*)

Engagement and Espionage (#1)

Marriage and Murder (#2)

Home and Heist (TBD)

Baby and Ballistics (TBD)

Pie Crimes and Misdemeanors (TBD)

Good Folks Series

(Interconnected Standalones, Adult Contemporary Romantic Comedy, spinoff of *The Winston Brothers Series*)

Totally Folked (#1)

Folk Around and Find Out (#2)

All Folked Up (#3, TBD)

Three Kings Series

(Interconnected Standalones, Holiday-themed Adult Contemporary Romantic Comedies)

Homecoming King (#1)

Drama King (#2, coming Christmas 2022)

Prom King (#3, coming Christmas 2023)

Standalones

Ten Trends to Seduce Your Best Friend

Printed in the USA
CPSIA information can be obtained
at www.ICGtesting.com
CBHW032233301024
16686CB00007B/229